# BEYOND THE ORBIT

## AUSTRALIAN SCIENCE FICTION TO 1935

## ALSO EDITED BY JAMES DOIG

*Australian Hauntings*
*Australian Gothic*
*Ghost Stories and Mysteries*

# BEYOND THE ORBIT

## AUSTRALIAN SCIENCE FICTION TO 1935

## EDITED BY JAMES DOIG

**WILDSIDE PRESS**

Published by Wildside Press LLC.
wildsidepress.com

# CONTENTS

# INTRODUCTION

## JAMES DOIG

The history of early Australian science fiction has been well chronicled by literary historians, critics and bibliographers like Graeme Stone, Van Ikin, Sean McMullen, Janeen Webb and others. In searching for a synthesis of colonial Australian science fiction, they generally identify three genres into which most Australian science fiction of the period can be placed: lost civilisation novels, which include Lemurian novels and utopian novels; historical fantasies, which re-imagined Australia's colonial past, particularly the history of Australian exploration; and future invasion or future political novels, which dramatized fears of racial invasion or social chaos resulting from political upheaval or natural disasters like plague. Together, these genres expressed the fears and anxieties of the colonial experience: the unsettling alienness and vastness of the physical landscape, the precariousness of political, cultural and historical identity in a new land, and a sharp paranoia, real or imagined, of the hostile and unsympathetic forces they saw surrounding them. Of course, these genres did not emerge fully formed from the Australian experience; they had a long history behind them and proliferated in the wake of commercially successful novels by British authors such as H. Rider Haggard, Edward Bulwer-Lytton, William le Queux, Sir George Chesney and others. These books provided exemplars for Australian authors—and they were available in Australia in colonial editions and serialised in Australian journals and newspapers—who saw an opportunity to profit from what were popular genres, but also the possibilities inherent in these genres for social and political exposition. So, the interests of early Australian science fiction novelists were firmly terrestrial; very few featured other worlds or extrapolated technological advancements in the way that Jules Verne or H.G. Wells did.

In the short form, early Australian science fiction is more heterogeneous. There were more outlets for the short form and more short stories were published, so we would expect a wider range of themes and subject matter, and indeed this is the case. The stories collected here indicate something of the richness and variety of science fiction written by Australian authors up until the mid-1930s. We see some of the themes mentioned above, for example the lost civilisation story (Phil Collas's "The Inner Domain") and the future invasion story (Ernest Favenc's "What the Rats Brought"), but they offer something new and original, while other stories are built on the consequences of technological discoveries or advancements, for example Ernest Favenc's "The Land of the Unseen," H.B. Marriott Watson's "The Instrument," and Beatrice Grimshaw's "Lost Wings."

Many of the authors represented here were popular writers who wrote in various genres for the popular fiction magazines of the day. H.B. Marriott Watson was a prolific author of adventure novels and stories who occasionally crossed over into detective fiction and historical romances. Beatrice Grimshaw wrote adventure fiction set in the South Pacific where she lived and travelled for many years. Ernest Favenc and Erle Cox were journalists who successfully crossed over into fiction for important Australian literary journals like the *The Lone Hand* and *The Bulletin*. Robert Coutts Armour and J.M. Walsh both left Australia for London as young men to pursue their literary ambitions, and became prolific writers of popular fiction. Armour wrote dozens of stories for the Harmworth magazines, including much science fiction and fantasy. Max Afford is best known for his Australian radio serials, but he did write a number of detective novels and stories, which were published by mainstream British publishers. None of these authors wrote exclusively or even predominantly science fiction, in fact most of them wrote only a handful of stories that could be considered science fiction. Of course, a key date is April 1926, the publication date of the first issue of *Amazing Stories*, and the subsequent rapid development of exclusive markets for science fiction. Writers like Desmond Hall, Phil Collas and Alan Connell, while not prolific, wrote for the pulps. The latter two would have published more if the 'tyranny of distance' did not cut short promising writing careers.

1935 does not mark any particular watershed or event in Australian science fiction publishing, though it was a year in which three of the stories reprinted here were originally published: Phil Collas's "The Inner Domain" and Alan Connell's "The Reign of the Reptiles" and "Dream's End." The watershed year was the outbreak of the Second World War, which prompted the introduction in November 1939 of a licencing system covering all items imported into Australia. The licencing system effectively banned all non-essential imports including cheap American pulp magazines. The upshot was that from the 1940s and 1950s a home-grown publishing industry developed built around popular fiction—westerns, hard-boiled crime, and science fiction. However, although more science fiction was written by Australian authors during those decades than before, the quality was poor as the Australian pulp publishers of the 1940s and '50s demanded stories written to order in quick time. Of the authors represented here, only Alan Connell wrote for the burgeoning Australian pulp industry, and that was only an unsold novel of a Lemurian civilisation in South America, *Serpent Land*, which was published as a trilogy in digest format by Currawong in 1945.

This anthology also hopes to fill a gap. Early Australian science fiction has been quite poorly served by anthologists and very little of it has been brought back into print since first publication. Van Ikin's *Australian Science Fiction* (1982) is an exception, though his selection of early Australian science fiction is almost all extracts from novels. The important bibliographer of Australian science fiction, Graeme Stone brought back into print examples of early novels and stories, but they were self-published and are now difficult to find. Partly this gap can be explained because science fiction stories generally do not age well and there is little to be gained from resurrecting them except as literary curiosities. However, I believe there is enough quality writing and originality in these stories to justify the present volume.

Another reason why this is a neglected area of Australian literary history is because the stories themselves have become difficult to source, even in this age of mass digitisation. Many are locked away in scarce magazines and short story collections that I have been able to access at the National Library of Australia and from collectors like Graham Stone and Mike Ashley.

Another reason I have for publishing a volume such as this is to present new biographical information about some of the authors represented. While quite a few of them, like Erle Cox, Ernest Favenc, and Beatrice Grimshaw are well known and have been the subject of biographies or entries in the *Australian Dictionary of Biography*, others like Phil Collas and Alan Connell are quite obscure and I've been able to find new biographical information from sources like military service files.

## ACKNOWLEDGEMENTS

I would like to acknowledge Graham Stone, who suggested numerous stories for inclusion in this anthology in correspondence prior to his death in 2013, and Mike Ashley, who provided the texts of the two Robert Coutts Armour stories. I am also grateful to John Betancourt for his help in bringing the anthology into print.

# WHAT THE RATS BROUGHT

## ERNEST FAVENC
## (1845-1908)

*Phil May's Illustrated Annual,*
No. 15, Winter 1904-05

It was during the prolonged drought of 1919, just about Christmas time, that the steamer *Niagara* fell in with an apparently abandoned barquentine about fifty miles from Sydney.

It was calm, fine weather; so, failing to get any response to their hail, the chief officer boarded her.

He returned with the report that she was perfectly seaworthy and in good order, but no one could be found on the ship, living or dead.

The captain went on board, and, being so close to port; he was thinking of putting some hands on her to bring her into Port Jackson, when a perusal of the barquentine's log-book in the captain's cabin made him hesitate.

From the entries it appeared that the crew had sickened and died of some kind of malignant fever, the only survivors being three men—a passenger, one sailor and the cook.

The last entry, which was nearly three weeks old, stated that these three had provisioned a boat and intended leaving the vessel in order to make for Australia, as the only chance of saving their lives, as they felt sure that the vessel was infested with plague.

The value of the barquentine and cargo being considerable, and the weather settled, the captain determined to take her into port.

He put three volunteers on board to steer her, took her in tow, and brought her into Port Jackson, and anchored off the Quarantine Ground.

On reporting the matter to the medical officer, he was ordered to remain at anchor until it was decided what course to take.

The season was very hot and unhealthy, and when the story spread it occasioned a slight scare amongst the citizens.

Both vessels were quarantined, and the barquentine thoroughly examined.

When it was found from the log that the deserted craft had sailed from an Indian port where the plague that had so long devastated Southern Asia was then raging furiously, the consternation grew into a panic.

It was determined to take the vessel to sea and burn her, for nothing less would pacify the public.

The claim of the owners and the salvage claim for compensation were rated, and the *Niagara* towed the derelict out to sea, set fire to her, and then returned to undergo a term of quarantine.

Nothing further occurred, and in due course the *Niagara* was released, and the people forgot the fright they had entertained.

The drought reigned unbroken, and the heat continued to range higher than ever.

Then, when the winter had passed, and the dry spring betokened the coming of another summer of drought and heat, a mortal sickness made its appearance in some of the low-lying suburbs of Sydney.

When it had grown to an alarming extent, grim stories got to be bruited about, and a tale that one of the sailors of the *Niagara* had told was repeated.

He was on watch the night before the vessel was to be destroyed, the two ships lying anchored pretty close together.

It was about two o'clock when his attention was drawn to a peculiar noise on board the ship.

He listened intently, and recognised the squealing of rats, and a low pattering noise as though all the rats on the ship were gathering together.

And so they were.

By the light of the moon his quick eyes detected something moving on the cable.

The rats were leaving the ship.

Down the cable they went in what seemed to be an endless procession, into the water, and straight ashore they swam.

They passed under the bow of the *Niagara*, and the sailor declared it seemed nearly half an hour before the last straggler swam past.

He lost sight of them in the shadow of the shore, but he heard the curious subdued murmur they made for some time.

The sailor little thought, as he watched this strange exodus from the doomed ship, that he had witnessed an invasion of Australia portending greater disaster than the entrance of a hostile fleet through the Heads.

The horror of the tale was augmented by the fact that the suburbs afflicted were now haunted by numberless rats.

People began to fly from the neighbourhood, and soon some of the most populous districts were empty and deserted.

This spread the evil, and before long was universal in the city, and the authorities and their medical advisers at their wits' end to cope with and check the scourge.

The following account is from the diary of one who passed unscathed through the affliction. Strange to say, none of the crew of the *Niagara* were attacked, nor was the boat with the three survivors ever heard of.

* * * *

The weather is still unchanged.

It seems as though a cloud would never appear in the sky again.

Day after day the thermometer rises during the afternoon to 115 degrees in the shade, with unvarying regularity.

No wind comes, save puffs of hot air, which penetrate everywhere.

The Harbour is lifeless, and the water seems stagnant and rotting.

And now dead bodies are floating in what were once the clear sparkling waters of Port Jackson.

Most of these are the corpses of unfortunates, stricken with plague-madness, who, in their delirium, plunge into the water, which has a fatal fascination for them.

They float untouched, for it is reported, and I believe with truth, that the very sharks have deserted these tainted shores.

The sanitary cordon once drawn around the city has long since been abandoned, for the plague now rages throughout the whole continent.

The very birds of the air seem to carry the infection far and wide.

All steamers have stopped running, for they dare not leave port, in case of being disabled at sea by their crews sickening and dying.

All the ports of the world are closed against Australian vessels.

Ghastly stories are told of ships floating around our coasts, drifting hither and thither, manned only by the dead.

Our sole communication with the outer world is by cable, and that even is uncertain, for some of the land operators have been found dead at the instruments.

* * * *

The dead are now beginning to lie about the streets, for the fatigue-parties are over-worked, and the cremation furnaces are not yet available.

Yesterday I was in George Street, and saw three bodies lying in the Post Office colonnade. Dogs were sniffing at them; and the horrible rats that now infest every place ran boldly about.

There is no traffic but the death-carts, and the silence of the once noisy street is awful.

The only places open for business are the bars; for many hold that alcohol is a safeguard against the plague, and drink to excess, only to die of heat-apoplexy.

People who meet look curiously at each other, to see if either bear the plague blotch on their face.

Religious mania is common.

The Salvation Army parade the streets praying and singing.

The other day I saw, when kneeling in a circle, that two of them never rose again. They remained kneeling, smitten to death by the plague.

The "captain" raised a cry or "Hallelujah! More souls for Jesus!" and then the whole crew, in their gaudy equipments, went marching down the echoing street, the big drum banging its loudest.

As the noise of their hysterical concert faded round a corner, a death-cart rumbled up, and the two victims were unceremoniously pitched into it, one of the men remarking, "They're fresh 'uns this time, better luck!"

Such was the requiem passed on departed spirits by those whose occupation had long since made them callous to suffering and death.

All the medical profession stuck nobly to their posts, though death was busy amongst their ranks; and volunteers amongst the nurses, male and female, were never wanting as places had to be filled.

But what could medical science do against a disease that recognised no conventional rules, and raged in the open country as it did in the crowded towns?

Experts from Europe and America came over and sacrificed their lives, and still no check could be found.

All agreed that the only chance was in an atmospheric disturbance that would break up the drought and dispel the stagnant atmosphere that brooded like a funeral pall over the continent.

But the meteorologists could give no hope.

All they could say was that a cycle of rainless years had set in, and that at some former time Australia had passed through the same experience.

A strange comet, too, of unprecedented size, had made its appearance in the Southern Hemisphere, and astronomers were at a loss to account for the visitor.

So the fiery portent flamed in the midnight sky, further adding to the terrors of the superstitious.

It was during one night, walking late through the stricken city, I met with the following adventure.

My work at the hospitals had been hard, but I felt no fatigue. The despair brooding over everyone had shadowed me with its influence.

Think what it was to be shut up in a pest-city without a chance of escape, either by sea or by land!

I wandered through the streets, Campbell's lines running in my head, "And ships were drifting with the dead to shores where all was dumb."

Suddenly a door opened, and a young woman staggered out, and reel-ing, almost fell against me.

I supported her, and she seemed to somewhat recover from the frightful horror that had apparently seized her.

She stared at me, then said, "Oh! I can stand it no longer. The rats came first, and now hideous things have come through the window, and are watching his breath go out. Are you a doctor?"

"I am not a doctor," I answered; "but I'm one of those who attend to the dying. It is all we can do."

"Will you come with me? My husband is dying, and I dare not go back alone, and I dare not leave him to die alone. He has raved of fearful things."

The street lamps were unlighted, but by the glare of the threatening comet that lit up the heavens I could see her face, and the mortal terror in it.

I was just reassuring her when someone approaching stopped close to us.

"Ha, ha!" laughed the stranger, who was frenzied with drink; "another soul going to be damned. Let me see him. I'll cheer him on his way," and he waved a bottle of whiskey.

I turned to remonstrate with the fellow, when I saw a change come over his face that transformed it from a frenzy of intoxication into comparative sobriety.

"Your name, woman; your husband's name?" he gasped.

As if compelled to answer, she replied, "Sandover. Herbert Sandover."

"Can I come too?" said the man, addressing me in an altered tone. "I know Herbert, knew him of old; but his wife doesn't remember me."

"Keep quiet, and don't disturb the dying," I said; and giving my arm to the woman, went into the house.

We ascended the stairs and entered a bedroom; the rats scampered, squeaking, before us.

On the bed lay a man, plague-stricken, and raving in delirium.

No wonder.

On the rail at the head of the bed and on the rail at the foot sat two huge bats.

Not the harmless Australian variety that lives in the twilight limestone caves; nor the fruit-eating flying-fox; but a larger kind still, the hideous flesh-feeding vampire of New Guinea and Borneo.

For since Australia became a pest-house the flying carnivora of the Archipelago had invaded the continent.

There sat these demon-like creatures, with their vulpine heads and huge leathery wings, with which they were slowly fanning the air.

And the dying man lay and raved at them.

Disturbed by our entrance, the obscene things flapped slowly out of the open window, and the sick man turned to us with a hideous laugh, which was echoed by the strange man who had joined us.

"Herbert Sandover," he said, "you know me, Bill Kempton, the man you robbed and ruined. I'm just in time to see you die. I came to Australia after you to twist your thievish neck, but the Plague has done it. Grin, man, grin—it's pleasant to meet an old friend."

I tried to stop him, but vainly; and from the look on the dying man's face I could see that it was a case of recognition in reality.

The woman had sunk upon her knees with her head in her hands.

Kempton still continued his mad taunting. Taking a tumbler from the table he poured some whiskey into it, and drank it.

"This is the stuff to keep the plague away," he shouted; "but you, Sandover, never drank. Oh no! too clever for that. Spoil your nerve for cheating. But I'll live, you cur, and see you tumbled into the death-cart."

So he raved at the dying man, and one of the great vampires came back and perched on the window-sill.

Raising himself in bed by a last effort, Sandover fixed his eyes on the thing, and screamed that it should not come for him before his time.

As if incensed by his gestures, the vampire suddenly sprang fiercely at him, uttering a snarl of rage.

Fixing its talons in him and burying its teeth in his neck, it commenced worrying the poor wretch and buffeting him with its wings.

Calling to Kempton, I rushed forward to try and beat it off, but its mate suddenly appeared. Quite powerless to aid, I picked up the woman, who had fainted, and carried her out of the room.

Kempton, now quite mad, continued fighting the vampires, but at last, torn and bleeding, he followed us into the street.

I was endeavouring to restore the woman, and he only stopped to assure me that the devils were eating Sandover, and then reeled off.

When the woman came to her senses I left her by her own request, to wait till the Death-Cart came round.

I called there the next morning, but never saw her again.

Amidst such sights and scenes as these the summer passed on, burning and relentless.

The cattle and sheep were dying in hundreds and thousands, and it looked as though Australia would soon be a lifeless waste, and ever to remain so.

\* \* \* \*

One morning it was pasted up that news had come from Eucla that the barometer there gave notice of an atmospheric disturbance approaching from the south-west.

That was all, and no more could be elicited.

The line-men at the next station started to ascertain the cause of the silence; and after a few days they wired to say that they had found the men on the station all dead.

But the self-registering instruments had continued their work, and the storm was expected daily from Cape Leuwin.

The days preceding our deliverance from the pest were some of the worst experienced; as though the approaching storm drove before it all the foul-brooding vapours that had so long oppressed us, and they had assembled to make a last stand on the East coast.

One morning I felt a change, a cool change in the air.

Going into the street, I saw, to my surprise, many people there, gathered together in groups, and gazing upwards at a strange sight.

The vampires were leaving the city.

Ceaseless columns of them were flying eastward, and men watched them with relieved faces, as though a dream of maddening horror was passing away.

Then came a sound such as must we been heard in the quaint old city of legendary lore when the pied piper sounded his magic flute.

The pest rats were flying.

Forth they came unheeding the people who stood about; and Eastward they commenced their march.

All that day it continued, and some reported that they plunged into the sea and disappeared.

At any rate, they vanished utterly, and with them other loathsome vermin that had been fattening on the dead and the living dead.

Everyone seemed to see new life ahead.

Men spoke cheerily to each other of adopting means of clearing and cleansing the city, but that work was taken out of their hands.

That night the cyclonic storm that had raged across the continent burst upon us. All the long-dormant forces of the air seemed to have met in conflict.

For three days its fury was appalling. The violent rain and constant thunder and lightning added to the tumult.

No one stirred out during those three days of tempest and destruction.

Nature in her own mighty way had set to work to purge the country of the plague.

It was while this storm was at its fiercest that the Post Office tower and the Town Hall tower were shattered and hurled in ruins to the ground. No one, so far as I know, witnessed the catastrophe.

The morning of the fourth day broke calm, dear and beautiful.

At midnight the tempest had lulled; and when daylight came, the sun rose in a sky lightly flecked with roseate morning clouds.

Accompanied by a friend, I started out to see the ruined city, and those who were left alive in it.

The streets still ran with flood-water, but the higher levels had pretty well drained off; and once they were gained, our progress was easy.

Martin Place was choked with the ruins of the tower, and many other buildings that had succumbed; while not a single verandah was left standing in any street. We went to the Harbour.

The tide was receding, carrying with it the turbid waters that rushed into it from all points, carrying with it, too, wreckage and human bodies.

A strong current was setting seaward through the heads, and bore out to the Pacific all the decaying remnants of the past visitation.

The deserted ships in the Harbour had been torn from their moorings and either sunk or blown ashore.

Wreck and desolation were visible everywhere, but the air was pure, cool, and grateful; and our hearts rose in spite of the difficulties that lay before us, for the looming horror of the plague had been lifted.

\* \* \* \*

Of what followed, your histories tell you.

How the overwhelming disaster knit the states together in a closer federation than legislators ever had forged.

How from that hour sprung forth a new, purged, and purified Australian race.

All this is the record of the Australian nation; mine are but some reminiscences of a time of horror unparalleled, which no man anticipated would have visited the Southern Continent.

# THE LAND OF THE UNSEEN

## ERNEST FAVENC
### (1845-1908)

*Phil May's Illustrated Annual,*
No. 14, Winter 1902-03

When I first knew George Redman he was an ordinary pleasure seek-ing man of the world, with an independent income, which afforded him the means and opportunity to indulge in occasional fads.

Photography was one of them for a time, but of course it was neglected when the novelty had worn off, and something else, 'biking' probably, took its place.

For a week or two he dropped out of his usual haunts, and he was often seen in familiar intercourse with an aged man, who was reported to be either an anarchist or a lunatic.

Lunatic or not, he was a man with a striking face and wonderful eyes. The eyes of a visionary or an enthusiast, but certainly not of one deficient of reason.

Gradually Redman withdrew himself more and more from his old friends, and not having seen him for some time, I ventured to call at his rooms one night.

He was at home, and did not seem quite pleased at my coming. How-ever, as we had always been close friends, I did not take any notice of it, and accepted his half-hearted invitation to stay.

His old friend was there, and was introduced to me as Mr. Whitleaf. For a time our conversation turned on subjects to which the old man paid little or no attention, but kept me under a steady fire from his eyes, which made me feel most uncomfortable.

His gaze did not seem so much concentrated on me as on something near me, giving me the uncanny feeling that he was looking at something that I could not see. I was relieved when he changed his gaze, and spoke a few words to Redman in a tongue strange to me.

Whatever he said, Redman seemed greatly relieved, and his manner towards me altered at once, he became quite cordial, and like his old self.

"Did I tell you I am going in for photography again?" he asked.

"No; you know I have not seen much of you lately."

"Well, it is a new phase of photography that I am studying,—or rather, what I hope will prove a new phase."

"Some further advance on the X-rays business?"

"Quite the opposite. The X-rays have developed a wondrous future, but what I hope to arrive at is something far different and far higher."

I noticed that Redman was beginning to get excited, and the old man interposed.

"I will tell your friend," he said, in a clear and singularly fascinating voice, "what is the goal we aim at.

"Listen! I have known for long that the air around us is full of invisible and impalpable beings. Beings I must call them, for want of a better word, but what they are cannot be explained by that word, for they are not—and yet they are.

"They exist—but yet have no existence; they are terrible in their power—and yet they have no power, for they, too, are swayed by an overmastering will. We are their slaves and their masters.

"In this room they are mustering in force, even as we sit here; I cannot see them, but I feel their presence, and know by sure tokens that those that have accompanied you into this room are not inimical to us, therefore I told Redman that we might speak before you.

"Listen again! You may search the universe with the most powerful telescope that the genius of man has invented; you can track down to the uttermost bounds of infinity almost, the last wandering sun; and the plate of the camera when exposed will give others, and still others, in illimitable spheres beyond those the human eyes can see.

"Why is this? Why should the wonderful power of the camera be able to do what the trained eyes of men cannot? Why can it see through the living flesh and record on its surface the bone it sees beneath?

"Because it has power beyond our feeble strength, because it can search out the stars hidden in immeasurable distance, and make them visible to us. And it, too, when we have found the right method to use it, will seize these unseen forms that surround us and reveal them in actual shape.

"They are around us now in countless numbers, but we move through them unknowingly and unwittingly; and yet they, too, are fraught with all the powers of good and evil that sway the human heart.

"That is the work we are engaged in now, and if we succeed, we bridge, at one step, the gulf between the known and the unknown, the seen and the unseen, that has existed since matter was formed from chaos."

In his excitement the old man had arisen from his chair, and with burning eyes and eager hands emphasised his speech, as though he actually saw the formless beings he spoke of hovering in the seemingly empty air.

"It is true, Cameron," said Redman, after a pause.

"I have been studying the matter closely, and am now assured of the existence of these invisible companions crowding the space that surrounds us. Why am I assured? Because we have attained a partial success. Dimly and indistinctly; constant experiments with the camera have given us some results.

"I will show you them tomorrow. Why should it not be? The bones of the body are no longer hidden from view. The stars shining in the immensity of space, so distant that a telescope fails to find them, reveal themselves on the plate.

"So will these invisible beings in time, and I tell you I dread the day of our triumph."

"Why so?"

"Why so? The Gorgon's head that turned the rash onlooker into stone will be as nothing to what the man is doomed to witness who first solves the dread secret.

"Do not suppose these forms will be human; they will be the embodiment of the good and evil passions of those that have passed before; what awful shape they will take I cannot guess—something so fearful that the first glance may blast the eyesight of the man who looks. But, on the, other hand, they may be beneficent and blessed."

"But surely you are not reviving the old jugglery of ghost photographs?"

"Pshaw! We are searchers for the hidden secret, honest and straightforward, not shuffling charlatans, gulling a foolish public. But come to-morrow and see what we have done. Don't talk of this outside."

I rose and took my leave, for it was nearly midnight, and as I walked the almost deserted streets I seemed to be haunted and followed by a ghostly company of phantoms. Horrible, because I could not guess their shape; awful on account of their impalpability.

They thronged around me, and shed their unholy influences on my sleepless pillow for the remainder of the night. I had taken the first rash step into the forbidden, and was suffering the penalty.

The next morning I went to Redman, according to my promise. He took me to his gallery, which had been enlarged and improved since I saw it last, and in it we found old Whitleaf working amongst some chemicals.

"I promised to show you how far we had got," said Redman, opening a locked drawer. "Look at this."

It was a large photograph of the interior of an empty room that he had put into my hand, but at first I could see no more than that. He smiled slightly at my openly-shown disappointment, and, taking it from me, placed it on a frame, and bade me look through a splendid magnifying glass fixed above.

Then I saw.

I saw, and I did not see. The room stood out in bold perspective. It was empty, and it was not empty.

Shadows obscured the light from the windows where no shadows should have been. There were eyes, of that I am certain; such eyes—eyes that could kill with a glance if one only saw them plainly and clearly.

The room was full of beings without shape, without form, but stamping their invisible presence by a way that was felt and not seen.

As I looked, entranced, I prayed that I should not see them, for the mere thought of the possibility brought cold terror to my heart and the limpness of death to my limbs.

"Look not on what is forbidden," was the mandate I seemed to hear, as by an effort I turned away, shuddering, and caught my friend's arm.

"Oh, they are here!" I gasped,—"the awful ones. Seek no further. Man must not see their shape."

"They are there," repeated the deep voice of Whitleaf. "Ay, and they are here."

I covered my eyes with my hands and tried to forget, while every nerve and fibre shrank with dumb terror.

"Look again," said Redman.

I could not refuse, though my whole being revolted at the ordeal. I looked.

He had changed the photograph, and now I gazed on the sea, calm, motionless, and lifeless. And as I looked there gradually grew on me a monstrous horror.

It was not in sea or sky, but it was there. A momentary resemblance of evil—evil made palpable, such evil as man could not conceive, could not execute.

The maniac homicide would have recoiled, shuddering, from the mere suggestion of it, and died, shrieking with terror at its presence.

And the awful thing was still not there in form and substance, only in its dreadful influence.

I withdrew my eyes and sat down on a chair.

"Can such things be about us?" I asked.

"Do you not know that they are?"

"But why seek to make them visible when the vision would bring madness?"

"There may be more beyond—there is more beyond," said Redman. "Look at this." He changed the picture.

I hesitated.

"Nay, it will restore your courage."

Once more I gazed through the glass. It was a bedroom, and on the bed lay a corpse composed for burial.

Slowly there stole over me a wonderful feeling of peace, of everlasting happiness.

I strained my gaze to find out what caused it; it seemed to me that if I once succeeded in seeing that benign presence I should sorrow no more, but joy eternal would be mine. All my former fear and horror vanished.

"They are gods in good and evil," I said as I looked up. "Will you ever rest till you see them?" I went on, forgetting all I had said before.

"Never!" said both men together.

I became now as infatuated with their prospects of success as my friends were, though I could do little to help them, and circumstances called me away for six months.

When I returned I hastened to see Redman, having learned from his letters that a discovery was shortly expected. I found Redman and Whitleaf waiting together, and learned that I had just arrived in time to witness the success or failure of a trial they were then making.

The plate was even then exposed in the gallery. Both men, I could see, were in a condition of strongly suppressed excitement, and when at last the time expired Whitleaf proceeded to the gallery alone, under some pre-arranged agreement.

Redman paced up and down, repeatedly looking at his watch.

"He must have seen by this time," he said at last, and as he spoke a cry thrilled through the house and pierced our ears—a cry for help, a cry of terror and horror, indescribable overpowering horror, so great that you felt your heart stand still, paralysed and aghast.

We rushed to the gallery.

Whitleaf lay on the floor, with stony eyes and bloodstained mouth. He was dead—dead, with wide-open eyes that spoke still in silent testimony of the death he had died—killed by the shock of seeing what man should never see.

With a shuddering hand Redman closed the eyes that had seen more than mortality is allowed. There was black blood on his lips and white beard, and seemingly it had welled from his mouth.

The plate had fallen from his failing grasp, and lay on the floor, broken, pulverised, and ground to powder—by whom?

Redman said little; he seemed stunned and bewildered at the terrible power that had shown itself.

There was a medical examination into the cause of Whitleaf's death, and the doctor certified it was caused by sudden stoppage of the heart's action.

I had a chance to go away again, and gladly accepted it. I was cured for a time of any desire to pry into such fearful mysteries as Redman's pursuit seemed to lead to.

As for him, blank disappointment had fallen on him. I know what his thoughts were: what use was it to make absolute this fresh discovery of science when the success of the experiment meant the death of the investigator?

And yet I could see he had an irresistible longing to look on the sight that had blasted Whitleaf's eyes for ever. I urged him to seek travel and change.

I did not see him again for more than six months, and then his mood had greatly altered for the better.

The gloomy effect of the catastrophe of Whitleaf's death had disappeared in a great measure, if not entirely; and, above all, he had fallen in love with a young girl who, both in mind and body, seemed in every way fitted for him, and worthy of the utmost affection.

Yet this fair young girl, who was devoted to my friend, was the means of plunging him back into the blackness of madness.

One day I met him with his fiancée and her mother, going to lunch at his rooms, and he invited me to accompany them. During the meal his prospective mother-in-law asked him if he continued his photographic pursuits.

He answered "No," and the old lady, prompted by the devil, proposed that he should take a likeness of her daughter, and to my surprise Redman consented.

The gallery had been locked up since the fatal day of Whitleaf's death, and Redman led the way there, and unlocked it. Dust lay thick everywhere, and the place was close and unpleasant, and I, for one, felt the evil impression of it.

Redman placed Miss Torrance in position, got his apparatus ready, and took her likeness in two or three different attitudes, then leaving the plates in the dark room to develop at another time, we left the room, I, glad indeed to get away from the place.

Next morning I went to call upon Redman, and to my surprise and grief found him sitting on a lounge, haggard, wild-eyed, desperate, and half-mad. He looked like a man after a long drinking bout, on the eve of delirium.

"Good Heavens, Redman! what's the matter?" I asked.

He turned his awful eyes on to me, and spoke—"I have seen them, and live."

With the words came back to me the old thrill of cold horror, and I looked at him without answering.

He spoke again with an effort—"I developed those portraits I took of Miss Torrance, and there was one," here his voice dropped, "that must have been on one of the plates that Whitleaf and I prepared. *They* were there!"

He stopped, and leaned back with the beads of perspiration standing on his forehead.

Presently he arose, and asked me to come with him to the gallery, "Not to see that," he added; "it is utterly destroyed."

We entered the gallery, and he brought me the negatives. I held them up to the light, and looked at them. They were all happily caught, one in particular in which she was seated leaning back with a smile on her face. So might a young mother have smiled at a child at her knee.

He selected that one.

"It was almost in the same position as this," he said; "and when I looked on it but for an instant, I saw the horror there. Seated in her lap it seemed to be—that awful thing of loathsome evil! And she smiling down on it. It was but an instant I saw it, and then it was snatched from my hand, and ground into powder there. He pointed to a place where some fragments lay.

"Snatched from your hand?" I repeated in amaze.

"Yes; I know no more. When I came to myself I was on the floor of this place, with the moon shining through the glass overhead. Fancy, in one moment all my happiness cast to the winds.

"Can I marry that girl knowing that she sat there smiling and innocent, and in her lap a being of hell, a vile monster that could slay humanity with its basilisk glance if it were permitted?

"Oh! the raging torment I passed that night in—for that one glance has cut me off from my fellows for ever. Would that I had died like my poor friend!"

"What was it like?"

"Like? How describe what human language is not capable of describing? How describe what is so far removed from humanity, so utterly beyond and apart from it that no words of mine can make you apprehend it? One thing only I saw, that there were eyes in the monster—eyes that were darts of death.

"Ask me nothing more. This marriage once broken off, I shall leave this."

The marriage was broken off. Redman's strange, sudden, and unaccountable change of manner led to not unjust suspicions of insanity, and Miss Torrance never knew the frightful secret.

He, poor fellow, wandered through the world a haunted man.

I met him a year afterwards. He was worn down with grief, and I doubt not his brain was disordered.

Morbidly his imagination dwelt continuously on the unseen horrors by which mankind are surrounded, and unconsciously walking amongst.

He shuddered at the mention of photography, and kept himself almost entirely shut up.

At last a change took place. It seemed as though he had mustered up a despairing courage to meet and fight his unseen foes.

He resumed his photography, and avowed to me his intention of following his discovery to the bitter end—giving his life to it.

There was a large public gathering shortly coming on, and he told me that he would try his next experiments there. He asked me to call on him the day after the function had taken place.

It was in the morning that I went, and found the servants relieved to see me.

Redman was locked in his photographic gallery, and about half an hour before they had heard a loud fall in there, but no cry; and since then all their knockings and callings had received no attention.

Suspecting the worst, I hurried to the gallery door, and at once forced it open. Redman was, as I expected to find him, dead on the ground.

He had been writing at the table, when a heavy iron rod, one of the supports of the glass skylights, had fallen, with no apparent cause, on his head, killing him instantly.

The photograph was in minute splinters and powder on the floor; but the writing on the table was addressed to me, and I immediately took possession of it. It ran as follows:

"I took the photograph on the prepared plate, and developed it this morning. So strung were my nerves from the constant contemplation of this subject that I contemplated the negative without more than a momentary spasm of terror.

"Would you believe it, that the large crowd was scarce to be seen; blotted out and hidden by the unseen creatures, now made visible. I had not more than time to take in the details, when it was again snatched from my hand and crushed to atoms. This I anticipated.

"I had noticed the plate well in that brief glance I caught, and saw what I had seen before, that the eyes I told you of were directed against me from all quarters, and I gather from that that these beings are only secure in their invisibility, and fear their discovery.

"Are they the source of all evil, restrained and limited in their action by the occasional presence among them of a Supreme Power, omnipotent and beneficent? It may be so, and they shrink from being observed.

"Would it end in their leaving for another planet world if they should become visible like men?

"I have seen them and live; and lest anything should happen to me, I will leave you, Rupert Cameron, directions to prepare the plate, so that my secret will not be lost.

"In the first place, you…"

* * * *

Here the bar had descended, and a splash of blood on the white paper was all that was left.

The terrible and fatal secret had not descended to me.

# THE INSTRUMENT

## H.B. MARRIOTT WATSON
## (1863-1921)

*Chapman's Wares*
(Mills & Boon, 1915)

I have decided that I ought to put on record all that I know concerning the death of Edward Haviland, and of the events that led up to it. This I shall do without comment or any attempt at explanation which I know myself incapable of giving, and with only just such facts and circumstances as I was able to observe and note at the time.

Haviland, who has left a name of sound importance in scientific research, was a distinguished mathematician, and it was for his services in mathematics that he was made a Fellow of the Royal Society. Naturally he looked out upon the world through a mathematician's eyes. He approached all science with a mathematical bias. He lived, I always believed, as much among figures as among warm human things, detached from life by his main absorbing interest. When he was withdrawn into his study he passed as it were out of reckoning, he became merely the sign and symbol amid which he lived and laboured.

His natural disposition was kind and sympathetic. For his friends he had always a welcome which was by his type of mind rendered rather aloofly spiritual. He was full of charity, and his purse was at any man's disposal for a generous object. He had been left in good circumstances by his father, a wealthy banker, and he had no need to rub shoulders with the sordid sides of life. At the age of forty he astonished all his friends and acquaintances by falling in love and getting engaged.

There is no other way of putting it than simply that way, yet I will confess that the phrase seems to apply to him only in remote and occult and ghostly way. The girl—a Miss Westermain—was some thirty years of age, and was an admirer of his work, or, at least, of his reputation. She was a plain, wholesome woman of rather liberal views, which were neatly held under the restraint of a modern conventional manner. There was something attractive about her, though she had no claim to beauty, and, I think, it was mainly a quiet womanliness.

I had met her once or twice when Haviland's engagement was announced, and I had liked her. I saw a little more of her after their engagement, and my liking increased. Though, in common with many who knew him, I doubted Haviland's qualifications as a husband, I felt that if anyone was a proper mate for him it was Marion Westermain. His engagement did not interfere with Haviland's arrangement of his life. He told me shyly that Miss Westermain did not wish it to, and she herself broached the subject to me in the same sense.

It was in Haviland's rooms she spoke to me; Haviland was showing Lady Cope, her aunt, over his laboratory, which must have been an inordinate sacrifice for him, and I fancy Miss Westermain had engineered the opportunity to get me alone.

"I'm afraid Edward's friends are fearing that I shall hamper his career," she said after preliminary approaches. "But I want you to get rid of that idea. I am anxious to help him, not to hinder him."

I told her frankly that if she could humanise him more all his friends would rejoice.

She seemed surprised, and I thought she was a little displeased, for she said, after a pause, and with some coldness:

"I should be the very last to desire him to give up his work."

"He is not likely to do that," I told her. "If you can hold him back from making too great demands on himself it will be a service to him."

I think she liked it better put in that way.

"I shall hope to look after him, and to serve him in all ways," she said warmly.

"I am sure of that," I said; and I was.

I was right in supposing that nothing could derail Haviland from his appointed course, not even marriage. For several years previously he had been at work on a certain field which had engrossed him more than ever. It concerned organic life, and its relations to mathematics. He had been drawn to it by his astronomical studies, finding the highest mathematics the touchstone of stellar and cosmical problems.

"You remember the old theory," he had said to me once as he lay back in his arm-chair and looked at the ceiling in abstraction. "The ancients founded their explanations of the universe on various elements. One was Fire, another was Water. A third was Numbers." He paused, speaking in his curiously phantom level voice. "Perhaps there's something to be said for the idea. Numbers! Have you ever considered the mysticism of figures in relation to the problems they solve? We think we endow them with life and significance, but it may be these are inherent in them. They puzzle and baffle us, even when we use them. They are our masters. After all, what control have we of them? They are arbitrary, supreme. We have to deal with them from suppositions, with suggestions, with postulates and hypotheses. When you get back to the essence of things how can there exist quantities less than none, and what is an infinite power? If I could get on the track of that—"

He mused, and continued shifting his position so that the firelight flickered on his deep brow and delicate nostrils.

"The longer I live, Ellery," he went on, "the deeper grows my conviction that we are only at the beginning of accomplishment as far as mathematics are concerned, that we have hardly yet touched the fringe of a vast unexplored subject." He was silent for a moment, and then added: "I hope to do something. I hope to learn something. I am moving now in provinces of which I had no idea once."

When I rose to go a little later he did not hear me, I think; he was gazing abstractedly at the fire. I spoke to him again, and he started.

"That you, Ellery?" he said. "I thought I saw... Did you ever feel that you had got near to a solution of the universe—to the key? I mean did you ever think it was just that little way off which you could compass presently—in a little, in a flash, perhaps, but almost certainly?"

"No," said I bluntly, looking on him curiously.

"I have," he said dreamily. "There are combinations. With the simple element of figures one can accomplish so much. But how much more? You know what the physiologists have brought us down to—a simple cell. All things are correlations of simple cells, but they can get no further. How far so ever they go they don't get beyond that. Now the elements of mathematics.... Numbers are as simple as cells, and as wonderful in combination and complex structures as any organic products. Who is going to set a limit or a term to the power of figures?"

These speculations, as you may conceive, were too deep for me, and I could not follow him. But you will see why I was justified in my statement to Miss Westermain that it would be well if she could humanise Haviland.

After the engagement I doubted often. What sort of reaping would ensue from that fallow heart? Haviland was at best a shadowy friend. What sort of husband would he be?

That conversation of ours was recalled to me by Miss Westermain herself. I had not seen Haviland for some weeks, having been away from town, and when I met her by accident in the park she let me know in her straightforward way what troubled her.

"I have been thinking over what you said," she said, after a little change of formalities. "Perhaps you are right about Mr Haviland's overwork. I don't think he is very well. He looks run down. I wish you could persuade him to take a change. Do try, Mr Ellery!"

That pitiful appeal sent me, as a matter of fact, to Haviland's house that very evening. He had a rambling place in an old-fashioned square, and had built out a huge laboratory over the yard. I must confess that I was agreeably disappointed by his appearance and bearing. He was in high spirits, and, for him, very human. He greeted me with warmth asked after my travels, and said no word of himself or his work. Finally, he suggested that we should dine at the club to which we both belonged.

"The fact is, my dear fellow," he said, when we were comfortably settled in the cab, "I've been keeping my nose to the grindstone, and I want a change."

I took the opportunity to carry out my promise to Miss Westermain at this opening, and he listened agreeably.

"Yes," he assented, "I think you're right. I've only one or two small points to settle, and then I shall be free."

At dinner he was quite human, talked of a current play, discussed politics with detachment but a broad intelligence, and brought up the affairs of several friends we had in common.

It was not until after dinner that he alluded to his work.

"You can congratulate me, if you will, Ellery," he began, and a fine smile lit up his delicate features. "I've practically got what I've been working for these five years, the interpretation of the cosmos in terms of numbers."

I suppose my face was blank, for he went on quickly:

"I can hardly expect you to credit me, for I can hardly believe it myself. Of course, I don't mean to say that I have solved the riddle of the universe. That would be an absurd claim. All I can say is that I have discovered and set up a definite relationship between the Cosmic Force and Numbers."

"My dear fellow!" I gasped.

"There can be no doubt so far," he proceeded with a certain feverish eagerness, plucking at the cigar with his fingers. "I have established the relationship, but I don't quite understand it myself yet." He laughed a rather frightened deprecatory laugh. "It's only the beginning, of course. I shall hand it on to other workers presently. It is not one man's work; it is a thousand men's—ten thousand—" He waved his hand. "There is no end to the vistas this discovery opens up. But I have done my share and shall do. Ah, Ellery, if life were only infinite!"

His chin sank dejectedly upon his breast, and he stared sadly into vacancy out of eyes that saw nothing. I began to feel some alarm. Was it possible that his long and sedulous devotion to science had ended in turning Haviland's brain? I broke the silence which had grown awkward to me.

"I give you my best congratulations, but I don't profess to understand."

He looked up suddenly, recovered in sanity and cheerfulness.

"You shall see it, Ellery, although it is not complete. There is a little more to do to it. But you have always been so sympathetic that I should like you—only you, to see it."

"To see what?" I cried, with sharp emphasis in my fears for his reason.

"The machine," he said dreamily. "I worked it into a machine. It was complex; it was a web of intricacy, but it seemed better, wiser, more permanent."

"A machine?" I repeated, marvelling.

Haviland rose suddenly.

"Yes, an instrument! We will go back now," he said with an air of authority. "I will show it to you. But you must consider it incomplete. Come!"

We drove back to the house, Haviland once more elated, and myself in a tangle of vague alarms and doubts.

The house, cheerfully lighted, seemed to forbid any fears as morbid, and the laboratory into which Haviland led me was a bright, comfortable room very workmanlike and well-fitted. Innumerable signs and evidences of the man's work lay about on floor and table, chemicals, batteries, a gas engine, retorts, charts, and electric appliances of all kinds.

Haviland proceeded to the farthest corner and pulled back a curtain which screened a part of the laboratory.

"It is run partly by electric motor and partly by a device of my own in connection with polarisation," he said in a low voice, and then lifted a silk wrapping which enshrouded a tall object some six feet in height, in front of him.

I got the impression then, and it remained with me, of a huge brazen altar, sparkling with innumerable tiny discs of brass and silver and copper. It was built in a nest of domes and was circuited by a ravel of golden wires. It looked alive, a delicate sensitive thing shivering in nerves of its constituent metals. Its tendrils quivered, its discs shone.

Haviland was speaking in a voice which was keyed very low, almost hushed:

"The manipulation is made with that board and these switches. I use the silver domes as detachers in the various degrees and spheres. The antimony zones isolate. The gold cam controls the periodicity of the negative."

"But, my dear fellow, I don't understand!" I gasped.

A gentle smile crept over his face.

"How can you expect to when it has taken me five years, and I am only just beginning?" he asked.

I was amazed; I was astounded. Was Haviland mad? Yet this astonishing and supremely beautiful thing could hardly be the work of a madman. It glittered at me in the electric light as if it were watching, as if it pondered and considered. Its mesh of wires was like a golden texture, an intricate pattern. There was something unearthly in its perfection. One copper strand lay inert, detached, as the one thing dead in that cage of live beings. Haviland touched it with fingers as sensitive as the wires among which they played.

"I haven't made this connection yet," he said. "But I shall make it tonight. I finished the calculation this afternoon. It has taken me months. There is nothing now between me and the Cosmic Force! Here is the interpreter, the key, the window, the door into the unknown and the unknowable. If only we had a thousand years to use it!"

He replaced the silk covering and turned away, sadness once more investing him; and together we returned to the house. I was dazed, and I did not know what to think. In Haviland as I watched him I could see nothing now even of the fanatic; he was just a tired man, resting his head on his hand in a reverie. Presently he came out of his dream.

"I'm sorry, old chap," he said. "I was thinking. You'll have some whisky, won't you?"

He rang for the glasses, and until the man brought them chatted on indifferent matters. When the door was shut upon the servant he leant over to me:

"I'd like you to see it at work," he whispered. "You must come when I've got it quite finished—after tonight."

His eyes trailed to the door wistfully. I drank my whisky hastily.

"Look here, Haviland, I should go to bed and get a rest if I were you," I told him. "You're played out. It's only fair to Miss Westermain."

"Yes, yes, you're right! I'll go to bed after the—as soon as I've finished—tonight," he said absently.

I could do no more. I saw where his thoughts were, and I said goodbye, and left him. I went away still debating in my mind the ugly question of his sanity.

Two days afterwards I received a letter from Haviland. It was quite short and written in a scrawling hand which I did not recognise.

DEAR ELLERY (he wrote),
   You were the first to see my cosmic instrument. I want you to be the first to try it. Can you come tomorrow evening at eight o'clock?
   Yours sincerely,
                                    EDWARD HAVILAND.

I accepted by wire, and had to put off an engagement to do so. Somehow Haviland claimed me. I did not understand the degeneration of the handwriting. It opened an appalling vista of possibilities. In the afternoon I ran across Lady Cope at a concert, and I enquired after her niece.

"She is very well, thank you," said the comfortable lady. "She didn't come with me, because she was busy packing."

"Packing?" I repeated interrogatively.

"Yes. She's going abroad for a week or two to join friends in Bordighera.

She leaves by tonight's train."

When I had parted with her I wondered why I had not said something about the marriage. What I could not ask Miss Westermain might very properly be put to her aunt. That marriage somehow had got on my nerves. I liked the girl, and I was a little afraid for her.

I was at Haviland's house punctually, having snatched a brief meal on my way, and the first sight of him gave me instant relief. He was bright and smiling, and beamed with cordiality. His right hand was bound up with a handkerchief, and, he informed me, had received a slight injury—an explanation of an obvious kind which rendered my forebodings rather ridiculous. It appeared that Haviland had expected me to dine, and was crestfallen when I told him that I had already had my dinner. He was as simple as a child in such matters.

"Anyway," he said, his face clearing, "come and see me eat. I have had nothing yet today."

This did not look so well, but he showed no signs of fatigue, eating sparely but quickly, and talking all the time. He spoke of Miss Westermain apropos of my meeting with Lady Cope, and he suddenly stopped eating and stared before him with a frown.

"I'm sorry," he said slowly. "I'm afraid I forgot. Do you mind handing me that batch of letters yonder, Ellery?"

I did so, noticing that they were almost without exception unopened. They might have been the fruit of the post for several days. He searched among the envelopes and found what he wanted.

"I'm sorry," he said in tones of distress. "I don't think I can have read it properly. Marion wrote asking me to see her this afternoon." He frowned. "I forgot," he said in a low voice.

"Lady Cope said she goes by the night boat tonight," I said.

"Yes. I'm sorry." He dwelled on his regret musingly for a few minutes, and then said deprecatingly: "You see, I've been taken up by this thing."

At that mention all remembrance of his default slipped from him as it were by magic, and he turned to me with his eyes shining.

"Ellery, I've been experimenting. It's marvellous. It's astounding. Man, it goes beyond all human conception!"

"Tell me what it is like," I said, myself excited by his fervour.

"The opening I have made have been entirely experimental," he said, controlling his musical voice to a monotonous level. "You see, I am only feeling my way—the instrument is greater than I knew. I don't understand it all yet. That is why I must be careful." He glanced at his hand.

"Is that how you came by your injury?" I asked. "The instrument—the electricity?"

"No," he shook his head. "Not the instrument, or the mere materials.

It was through the essential, the beyond. I don't know what happened. The long side of the marl was rushing past."

"What?" I cried in fear.

"The slide." He looked up out of his dream. "Oh, I forgot! I haven't told you that. I began quietly with the lowest commensuration to test it all. The sensation was extraordinary. Ellery, whenever I have put it in operation I have had that long slide of marl and the sensation of falling. It comes first with a mist, a wreathing giddy mist, and then all opens out. I see the unplumbed space and the moving cosmic dust. Then the slide comes. I have felt somehow as if I were in some relationship with the Cosmic Force at those moments. What does it mean?"

He sank into silence. As to what it meant alas, I thought I knew now. These were the manifestations of sheer insanity, of a monomaniac. Research had wrecked that intricate and delicate brain.

"I suppose those repeated chords come from something incidental. I don't suppose they matter," Haviland was proceeding. "Do you know I was absurd enough to remember the phrase—I believe you told me of it—the music of the spheres. Only it wasn't that. It was—"

"Look here, Haviland," I broke in. "Do you mind telling me something? Did you sleep last night?"

"Sleep!" He seemed to switch off as it were. "No, I don't think I did. I forget. I think I was in the laboratory."

"Haviland, I'm going to tell you something," I said, rising. I was a bigger man than he, and I felt the strength and force of mere physical humanity in my blood and muscles. "You're ill, you've been overworking; and you're going to see a doctor now."

"Yes, yes!" He waved his hand, speaking pleasantly. "I expect you're right. But I'm going to take a long rest. As soon as I've shown you this I'll turn in and we'll go tomorrow to—what was that place we spent a day in somewhen? But I must explain just a little before we go into the laboratory. I laughed when you said the other day that you couldn't understand. Of course you couldn't! Why, it's taken me years to come to the gates and knock on them. But I'm going to put your feet on the way."

After a long pause he went on:

"You know enough, Ellery, to understand that all sciences are interchangeable—that all forms of force are related, co-ordinated, and pass into one another. Sound, heat, electricity—all are modes of motion. All mathematicians know that there are planes and planes of combinations still unravelled. If a man lives to a century he has unbounded horizons—of the science still pressing for solution. It is only possible under a scheme which will reduce to a system."

I had heard a ring a few moments earlier, and now the man-servant opened the door of the dining-room.

"Miss Westermain sir" he said flatly, and without emphasis.

Haviland stared bewildered. I looked at the clock. In an hour or two Miss Westermain was due at Charing Cross, according to Lady Cope.

She came into the room with a little rush.

"Edward!" and then she saw me. "Oh, Mr Ellery!" She showed no sense of confusion to be discovered there at that time of night. "Edward, I did not hear from you, and I am going tonight. I called on my way to the station. I sent my boxes in advance. I couldn't bear to leave without seeing you. You didn't come. I was afraid you were ill!"

"I am afraid I forgot," stammered Haviland. But he had pretty manners when he returned among human things. He took her to a chair. "The fact is, dear, I have been up to my eyes in work," he said, "and it passed from my mind. I will never forgive myself. But my stupidity has brought you here. It is charming."

I could see the pain in his face, and, perhaps, foolishly I jumped into the gap.

"Haviland has just completed an important discovery," I said. "I'm afraid he has been dead to the world."

She glanced from me to him with a dawning sense of admiration.

"Edward, you are working too hard!" she cried. "Mr Ellery promised."

"Yes, yes," he said eagerly. "He and I are going to take a holiday tomorrow, like you, Marion. Where was it, Ellery?" He didn't wait for all answer, but continued, "Ellery is right. I have just finished something which is very interesting, very"—he hesitated as if for a word which would soothe her—"very epoch-making. I asked him to come and see it. Now you are here, dear, it is doubly delightful. My best friend and my future wife." He turned to me, quite recovered and gay. "Ellery, this will increase the interest of the investigation."

"What is it, Edward?" she asked. "I only called in on my way to Charing Cross."

"Oh, it won't take long!" he said gleefully. "I'm so glad you came. You and Ellery will be the first people to bridge the gulf."

"Bridge the gulf!" she echoed.

He laughed.

"I will tell you later. Ellery understands. But as you have so little time, let us get to work. Marion, this is a crucial moment in the history of the world—of life. My dear, I am glad you came."

I knew she understood no more than I did, but we both followed him. He passed out of the dining-room, along the wide corridor to the study at the back, and into the laboratory which was built beyond it. It was a large room, and of a handsome design; but when we entered was in gloom save for one corner, in which stood the instrument. Haviland pointed to chairs beside the table over which the electric light swung under its green shade, and he himself went to the silk-covered instrument. Miss Westermain took a seat on the opposite side of the table from Haviland and myself. Haviland withdrew the silk, and the instrument shivered and glittered at me. It seemed alive.

I saw Miss Westermain look at it, and put her hand before her eyes.

"I will try the lower grades first," said Haviland in a low voice.

His figure came between me and the instrument, and I heard a tiny buzzing as of an electric current fizzing in a telephone. It grew in volume and suddenly a curtain of heavy smoke, as it were, clouded my eyes, smoke lit with flashes. Then there was a vast field of blue mist, no, of blue space, and a drumming was in my ears. I was conscious of acute distress, even of terror, of palpable terror. Haviland's voice issued out of nothingness to me.

"I wish I knew what that was. It opens always that way. Is it the primal whirl?"

The room came back to me. Miss Westermain's eyes were covered with her hands. Haviland was shaking as he leant against the table.

"I went out that way from the first," he said. "But it is only the beginning."

"It—Oh, it's horrible!" gasped Miss Westermain.

Haviland did not hear.

"I will try another combination," he went on in his low voice.

He moved to the instrument again. It blinked and flashed at me in the brilliant light. Miss Westermain put out her hand, as if to restrain him, and her cloak fell open disclosing a flash of pink silk about her neck.

I did not see Haviland touch anything, but his fingers wavered before my eyes; then he appeared to throw up an arm as if to ward off something. After that came the blue mist, not the blue space, and a sense of fear. It passed into elation. Then there was a sense of motion, of motion infinite in its effect. I was falling into a gulf of blue, a great wide empty boundless chasm of space. There, again, I was spindrift in space, a tangle of broken senses, of half-lights, of new feelings. I was fulfilled with a great power as of knowledge—things were breaking in on me And then something went by swift, infinitely swift—a slide, a country of marl extending forever—a vivid flash of pink in the slide.

I was aware of a cry, but I could not tell if it was I who had cried. It died in a faint moaning, like echoes in eddies—and then I saw Haviland. One arm dropped helplessly, and his face was ghastly white.

"What is it?" he gasped. "Did you see it? What did you see?"

"I saw a slide," I said tremulously; "and a world of marl. Something went down it infinitely swift, with pink."

"I saw it too!" he cried. "Nothing else?" he asked fiercely. "Nothing else?"

"Nothing else," I replied; "only the pink."

We looked across the table together. Miss Westermain was not there. We stared at each other, and Haviland's lower lip was sucked in pitifully.

"The pink!" he said like a whimpering child.

"Nonsense, man!" I said, but my voice was weak and lacked conviction. "Let us call her. She has been frightened."

"She wore pink," he whispered.

"Nonsense man!" I said. "Your infernal machine has scared her. Let us look for her."

"I can't move," he said in the same voice, and then I saw. His right leg was broken below the knee, and the left hand was cracked across the knuckles. It hung helpless.

"My God!" I said, and got to my feet and staggered down the darkened laboratory.

Once back in the house I recovered some of my wits. Miss Westermain must have gone that way in her flight. I called the servant, who told me that no one had gone out by the front door. We made a search together, but found no trace of Miss Westermain in the house.

"She must have gone by the yard door," I said to the man. He had gathered from me that his master's experiments had frightened his guest.

I went back to the laboratory, having forgotten Haviland's condition, which did not say much for my complete recovery. He sat where I had left him, and apparently he expected no news from me, for he said merely:

"It was the slide. You saw the pink, Ellery?"

For him it was a certainty. What was? My God, I could not believe or credit it? Was I mad?

"She has escaped by the yard," I said almost angrily.

He shook his head.

"It was the pink, Ellery. I have played with things I don't know."

"Look, man," said I. "Bear up. I'm going to send for a doctor for you at once; and meanwhile you must drink a whisky. Wait!"

He pointed with his uninjured arm at a bottle of pure alcohol, and I managed to mix some for him to drink. Under the fire in his blood he stirred anew.

"Ellery," he said, "I know what happened; but I can undo it. I can reverse the movement. That will bring things back. Yes, yes, help me to the keyboard. Quick!"

He leant forward eagerly, but I shook my head.

"Haviland, for God's sake, don't monkey with that again, and let loose forces of which you have no knowledge. Wait, and I will come back in a moment as soon as I have seen your man."

I hastened from the laboratory and encountered the servant in the hall, gave him instructions to fetch a surgeon at once, and when he had gone was returning to Haviland when I heard a noise in a room on the right. At once I thought of Miss Westermain, and entering, swept on the light. It was empty.

I went to the window and threw it open. Outside was a still cloudless night. And now something happened which chilled me to the bone. The night, as I say, was absolutely still; not a breath stirred on a frosty October night. But along the hall came the sound of a fierce rushing wind, whistling and howling. And then it died away, and a low moaning ensued, and that too died away.

With a nameless dread at my heart I burst out of the room, rushed down the hall, and into the laboratory.

Haviland, despite his broken leg, had dragged himself from his chair and was standing with his uninjured arm on the instrument. He was supporting himself entirely by the accursed thing, his face was violently contorted.

"Ellery, Ellery!" he moaned. And then: "She came back. I reversed it. She came back. Oh, my God! If you had seen! Has, she—has it gone? Has it gone?"

Suddenly he made some movement on the discs, and with a lurch fell forward almost noiselessly to the floor; the accursed instrument fell over too, and shivered in pieces about him, so that he lay in a pool of broken glass and metal. When I reached him he was dead.

I have put everything down as I recorded it at the time, and I offer no explanation. If you ask if I have any theory, I must reply, "No."

Miss Westermain was never heard of again. The boat-train for Calais by which she was to have travelled met with disaster in the early morning, and two carriages were completely burnt. It was always assumed that Miss Westermain was one of the unhappy victims.

The doctor who arrived shortly after Haviland's death certified it as due to failure of the heart from the shock of the accident which had befallen him in carrying out an experiment. I have never broken silence as to the fell story till now, but I have never ceased to wonder.

# LOST WINGS

## BEATRICE GRIMSHAW
## (1870-1953)

*The Valley of Never-Come-Back and Other Stories*
Hurst & Blackett, 1923

You know the smell of the rubber matting in the saloon companion, and the narrow doorway opposite as you come in, blazing light at you, and the knees and shoe-tips of the other passengers, where they sit reading, humped on the lounges. You know it all how that steamer world comes back in a rush to you, who have been long away from it, and how you realize that you have, after all, come home. The elbowing feel of your bunk, and the round glare beside tight-compressed alley-ways, with mirrors in strange places the old sense of laziness and leisure, wedded to a feeling of achievement, of important things being effortlessly done—how right it seems, how glad you are of it all.

Yet as the steamer shears her way to the high seas, and the great steel mountain, deck-terraced, funnel-crested, that lately rose so strong and still at the quay side, becomes a mere light, hollow toy in the hands of the Pacific—as the green of reef-water shades to Prussian blue of uncounted deeps—as you are off at last beyond doubt, off and away, something from that fast-receding shore begins to tug at your mind.

You think you have left or forgotten some matter ashore—a piece of luggage, a commission, a farewell. You cannot think what it may be, because you really finished with everything before you left. Yes, everything! It can only be fancy.

But it pulls and pulls.

The strong sea-wind gets up and slaps you on the breast like an old, rough mate of yours who meets you gladly again. You press down your hat and lean to the steamer's roll while you seek a place for your deck chair. On the weather side, the large green island has become a little blue one; the palms prick up like pin- points. Oh! it's far and far away now, and the wide seas lie before; and why do you feel—still, still—the pull of that tiny land—

you who have done with it all…

David found me before long; he had been in our cabin putting away his gear. David and I are mining experts. We had been wanted in Naula; we had done what was wanted and were going away. He put his chair beside me and sat smoking, never saying a word, while the liner bucked and rolled through the big seas. There were other passengers on deck; a drummer or two, bound for Fiji, a brace of missionaries, one little woman, in a dull blue dress, who seemed to be travelling alone. Not many were 'under hatches,' in spite of the roll. Island folks are well seasoned to the ways of the unpeaceful Pacific.

I looked at all these and wished them dead, except the little blue woman; she seemed harmless, and she was not very young. If she had been eighteen, tall, waisted like a palm tree, and bosomed as an island ship is bosomed when she spreads her curving royals to the wind—if she had had eyes like dark lagoons with the stars in them and a mouth like a fallen hibiscus flower, I should have fled from the salty, windy deck and gone to bury myself in the beetle-haunted dusk of the hole they called a smoking-room, where never woman comes to worry us, on the blessed island boats. Because then she would have reminded me…

But she was five-and-thirty or so, palish, slight, with hair that seemed to have been golden and was now only light in colour; with large grey-blue eyes that scanned the horizon curiously, almost as a sailor scans it… I found myself thinking that she must have been much at sea to catch that look. I saw, when she walked, that she leaned to the motion of the steamer with the unconscious ease of one who has lived long on ships.

I was not curious about her, you must understand; she occupied my eyes, but not my mind. I said to myself, lazily—"Some captain's widow who used to travel with him" (it was odd that I should have thought so, was it not, seeing that she wore no mourning?), and settled down to my smoke. My pipe went out a good deal and I lit it several times; you know how it is sometimes. And the steamer reeled up the sides of the waves, and "scended," which is not descending, but going crabwise down the valleys of them. And I thought and thought and thought, and kept re-lighting my pipe, and David didn't say a thing. You could not help loving David; he is forty-something, a big man very well made, with a certain likeable baldness, and a good Roman nose, and three strips of fur on his face, one big one above his well-shut mouth, and two, not so much smaller, over his good, very bright, very kind grey eyes. He stretches a leg out in front of him and looks at you a bit sidewise, and then takes to his pipe again, and you know he is damned sorry for you and won't bother.

It is a pity there are not more Davids. You women ought all of you to have one David each. A few of you have; you will recognize my description and feel so glad you have got a real David who is made of kindness from the little likeable bald spot on his crown to the long, sensible feet in his good boots. Some woman, who hasn't taken this David I speak of from me, his mate, has lost more than she knows by it.

At last the lunch bell rang and I got up to go and plaster my hair back with two brushes—because, no matter what has happened to you, twenty-six is twenty-six, and one doesn't see all the passengers in the first half-hour. And David—his other name is Shaw—took his pipe out of his mouth, looked at the bowl of it, and said, to the pipe apparently:

"She isn't worth it; nobody is, old man; buck up."

"Who told you I want bucking up? How do you want me to buck any more than I'm doing? What way are people expected to buck, and how does anyone know when they've bucked enough?" I asked.

He did not seem to hear me. He knocked the pipe on the edge of his deck chair, looked into the empty bowl, and then went on:

"Because, you see, black's black, even when it's cream, and you can't make an island girl the mother of your children—not to speak of the mistress of Kirwyn, when you get it."

"Who's a denigin' of it, Sairey?" I said.

He went on again—David has a way of answering what you think, while ignoring what you merely say.

"I've seen a lot of island girls—quarter, half, eighth and all the rest of it. I never saw one to match Ailala."

Now that was like David; another man would have run her down; but he knew that praise of her beauty was like oil on a burn, to my sore mind; and, being a man, he admired her himself—though not as I had—to my bitter cost.

"I don't think there is another girl like her this side of Tahiti. An old Greek coin, it is, when she looks away, side face, with that curling hair that rushes back, and the ribbon she ties in it. Beautiful figure, too—but that's more common…You have pluck, you know, because of course…"

"I guessed that," I said, rather hastily. I was not coxcomb enough to say right out what we both knew.

We were standing now, leaning, east, west, east, west, to the steamer's ceaseless roll.

"Some absentees from lunch, I bet," commented David. "Come on and have a peck."

"Of course," I answered loudly. "I'm dashed hungry." But the food, when I got it, wasn't good; it had no taste—been in cold storage too long; that is the way with steamer food. I am an excellent sailor; nevertheless my plate went away piled up. David didn't seem to see. He insisted on my coming to play bridge afterwards with himself and a couple of the drummers. We played for more money than I've ever seen David give in to. I won a good bit. He seemed better pleased than if he had won himself, and the day went on, bit by bit, and hour by hour. And there was dinner, and then night, when one could not talk, or smoke, or play cards, or eat, or, least of all, sleep. One could only lie in hell, and think.

For Ailala had other lovers, and if she had not secured me, Gerald Kirwyn, mining expert and next heir to a very good old property, there were plenty of lesser fry. And I knew, as clearly as if I had seen and heard the thing which had not happened yet, that she would accept one of them.

About that time, I think if I had been a millionaire, and not afraid of being put down a lunatic (which most millionaires are), I should have bargained with the captain to put back to Naula town. But no one ever does do such things, even when he can. So the *Avatele* rolled her way along, unchecked, towards far Fiji, and I kept on frying in hell, and thinking of Ailala, with her Greek-coin face, married to this or that good match. For Ailala, though she was said to be "coloured," was a girl carefully brought up by the elderly white couple who had adopted her; there was no question of light island loves with my beauty of Naula town, and if I, held by the thought of Kirwyn and Kirwyn's county folk, had been madly scrupulous, so were not others.

It was a short run to Fiji, but I don't care to say what bores the passengers were—all except my old David and, oddly, the little woman in the dull blue dress. It turned out that we were bound for the same place, an uninhabited island lying far from steamer tracks, and reached by schooner or cutter from Suva. I don't know which was the more astonished, Mrs. Pirani or Shaw and I, when we discovered that Remora was our common objective.

"But what can you want there?" we all three said at once. I won't pretend that the words were identical; still, that was the general trend of the cry we all set up. Mrs. Pirani—the captain had introduced us to her by that name, but she was obviously English—got hold of the conversation first; I suppose we allowed her.

"What can anybody want with Remora but myself?" she demanded a little imperiously. She had pretty hair, when you looked at it, loose and yet satiny; and I could imagine that those blue, pale eyes of hers had once been lovely, before tears washed out their light. You could not look at her twice and doubt that she was one of those who wear the 'sorrow's crown of sorrow.'

Because of this, I suppose, she knew that things had been going ill with me, and was specially kind to me in a hundred little womanly ways that you could scarcely notice. She remembered, just after she had spoken, and said to me, more gently:

"But I suppose you are going to do some business there; I hope you'll find it interesting."

"Not so very," answered Shaw. "We've only got to poke about a bit, and go home."

I may say that we were representing a company that wanted to sell Remora to the Fulcrum people for copra making. They wanted to be sure no minerals of value were included in the deal. Years ago, before our company acquired the place with a dozen others, there had been rumours of something valuable hidden away there, but if there was, no one had ever found it, had ever, even, put a name to what it was. It was just the silly kind of yarn that means nothing at all; however, since Shaw and I were bound to go to Naula anyhow, they thought we might as well come on a bit further.

"May one ask what you want with it, Mrs. Pirani?" I suggested, in my turn. I was perhaps a bit curious—not very—I was too sick of life just then to feel anything strongly. But I thought one might as well know.

Mrs. Pirani's eyes took on a strange, shadowy expression as of one who looks upon

*'Old unhappy, far-off things'*

before she answered:

"I'm trying to find my husband."

Shaw and I felt embarrassed. They had told us on the ship that "the little widow was a shingle short," and, though we had not believed it, her reply seemed to suggest, at least, a curious attitude of mind. For she had been widowed twenty years—so it was said—and there had never been any particular doubt about her husband's death, except the small uncertainty that, for a time, attends the death of anyone who meets his end by drowning. Pirani had been drowned; and if he hadn't been, it was plain he would have given some sign of it in all the years that had run since the beginning of the century, and here was his widow "trying to find him."

"Oh!" she said, immediately sensing our doubts, "I don't mean that I think he may not be dead. I'm obliged to suppose that he is—dead. But there are things in connection with his—death—that want clearing up, and I am going to spend the rest of my life till I die in trying to clear them."

"But Remora—" I suggested.

"It was in Remora," she said in a kind of hushed tone, "that we spent our married life; we were married on the ship and landed there on our wedding day. All my happiness is there."

"He died on Remora?"

"I don't know." She would say no more.

\* \* \* \*

Two weeks later, Shaw, Mrs. Pirani and I stood on the beach of Remora Island watching the little auxiliary schooner that had brought us from Fiji go plunking and smelling away. A pile of bags and cases lay on the beach; half a dozen Fijian boys, brought on from Suva, lounged nonchalantly staring about them and combing their upright hair till it stood more stiffly than ever. The sun was beginning to set above a wide, lonesome lagoon enclosed in the circle of the island; man-o'-war and bo'sun birds, planing and crying, showed dark against the orange of the west. There were palms and palms, inside and outside the atoll, fringing it so that it looked, as one has said, like a great green wreath flung down upon the water. No native huts were visible, no brown canoe furrowed the flawless jade of the inner lagoon or rode the wild, white horses that tossed their manes upon the seaward beach. It was a Robinson Crusoe island, void of human life.

"I think," said little Lucy Pirani, furling her sun-umbrella, "that the shortest way to the house is along the inside beach; it will probably be overgrown."

"House?" we said together.

"Yes, I have been here once or twice since the old days. Theo built well, our little place was standing when last I—you can see it now"—as we ploughed side by side through the deep sand. "That whitish block. The roof probably wants mending, but our boys can do it in an hour to-morrow morning, and I don't think it will rain."

We found the house, built of sawn coral blocks from the reef, fairly weathertight, and our camping gear furnished its two rooms well enough. The boys ran up a shelter for themselves. At a table made out of packing-cases, Shaw, the woman and I supped together that evening. It was almost cold when the night wind rose and went howling down the lagoon. The stars, seen through the doorless doorway, looked wondrous bright, as if the wind had brushed them clear. There was no moon, but you could see quite plainly the peelings of white foam blown along the water, and the grey-ivory terrace of the long, untenanted beach. It had the look of a place alive and exulting in itself, which you only find in very remote and lonesome spots, and which makes you feel, when you do find it, as if you were a bubble, a fragment of dust, a nothing... The lands that you have made and railwayed and roaded and builded on have no voices left to tell you of such things. But the wilderness speaks the truth.

For all that I was thinking thus, I was thinking of Ailala just the same. I never stopped thinking of her, underneath the other things. You know.

Lucy Pirani knew. She looked up by and by from the tea she was drinking out of an enamelled iron cup, and said in that extraordinarily sweet voice of hers:

"Did you understand that we've really been going towards Naula all the way from Fiji, Mr. Kirwyn?"

I had understood. South Sea travel is like that. We had gone to Fiji, eight hundred miles off, to get to a place not two hundred miles away from our starting point. But then Naula hadn't anything except whale-boats and the calling steamer from south.

Yes, I had known I was veering back towards Ailala all this time. It had kept me consoled, though really it meant little.

I put down my own cup and sat looking out into the star-filled night. Shaw plugged away at the hard bacon on his plate. Mrs. Pirani, sitting upright on the box that served her for a chair, with her hands folded on her lap, looked at us both and then remarked conversationally:

"When we lived on Remora, my husband flew to Naula twice."

"The devil he did!" exclaimed Shaw, startled out of all composure.

You must remember that this was nineteen-twenty and that Teodoro Pirani had been dead, or lost, for twenty years. And in the days of the Boer War, who talked of flying?

"I'm not mad," stated Lucy Pirani, coolly. "I thought it was time you knew, that's all. What do you think we came here for in nineteen-hundred, except to have that great big, safe, shallow lagoon to practise over and the privacy of the place to keep things quiet? My husband," she spoke now with an uplifted head, and eyes relit, of a sudden, with all the fires of youth, "my husband was a greater genius than Lilienthal, or the Wrights, or Bleriot, or any of them all. You couldn't rank any of the flight people with him. You could rank Marconi if you liked—Marconi was his countryman, and he was like Theo, he discovered something that no one else had ever thought of. Those aeroplanes—those Zeppelins"—she almost spat the words out—"what are they? Do they give you your dream?"

Now here she touched on something that all the world knows, but that nobody dares to say. I will say it, for once, out loud as Lucy Pirani did:

*'We are disappointed with flight.'*

It isn't what we dreamed of, when we were little and longed to fly when the human race was little and played about with the swan pinions and wax wings, and nobly broke its legs and heads with them. A big motor car of the air was not the toy we cried for, it is all we have got; but what we really wanted though none of us dare say so—was to *fly*.

We wanted to put on wings or something—well, wings then; why be ashamed?—and just flop and flap about ourselves. We wanted to be like the angels in the Bible pictures, the fairies in the prize books. We thought we'd love to go flapping a yard or two above the ground, quietly, like big moths, down country lanes full of flowers; to dip and soar among the tree tops.

No, don't tell me that the flight to-day is that. It isn't, any more than motor-boating is swimming. It's a magnificent thing, a heart-shaking, glorious thing, a new faculty added to human nature, a new kingdom given to mankind—anything you like. But it's not *flying*.

Tell me, Flight-Lieutenant, home from the war and fresh still from amazing feats dared in mid-heaven—would you not, just as you are, like to try the real, personal flying that not one of the Air Service has ever known? Would you not like to go as a bird goes, moved by your own muscles, swimming in the air?

Mrs. Pirani said these things and many others to us as we sat on the packing-cases by the doorway of the ruinous old house on the island, looking out on the stars and hearing the thunder of the wind. She made our hearts within us ache with the longing for flight, real flight, such as the world knows not yet, but such as it will know one day. And then she told us that she, she herself, had tried it.

"I wish I never had," she said, longingly. "It is like being given one sip of a magic drink and then seeing the cup broken before your eyes, while you have to go on all your life without another drop. You are never content when you have flown, really flown. Theo would have died if he could not have put on his wings every day."

"Wings?"

"Yes. Real wings, what people want, what they want for themselves, you know. Aeroplanes and airships all right, of course traffic, journeys, and that sort of thing. But we want to fly."

I realized it. Who has not? Who hasn't dreamed of the actual flight that people naturally long for? The slow, perfect movement, the hovering and dipping, the smell of road dust close under your toes as you skim along ...

"I will show you something," said Lucy Pirani.

She took a worn morocco case out of her pocket and opened it. It showed a photograph of a man with wings on, just starting in flight across this very lagoon of Remora.

I don't know what I said in my astonishment. I have an idea I swore. Mrs. Pirani said nothing; she kept on holding up the case, while Shaw and I in the lamp-light looked at the photograph and looked.

The late Teodoro Pirani wore a swimming suit of some striped material, cut short above his fine muscular thighs. His head was bare. His arms could not be seen; they were enclosed from shoulder to finger-tip in large, flexible bat wings, which seemed to extend a good way beyond the hands. The bat pattern was perfect. There was the central rib, the long slanting phalanges, the translucent tough membrane in between, and Pirani, upheld by these contrivances which, beautiful as they were, could not have carried a tenth of his weight by any known law of mechanics had just cleared off from the roof of the house and begun to fly steadily and surely over the lagoon. You could not see his face, silhouetted against the sky, but the rest was clear.

"Good God!" was all that David Shaw found to say.

"I took it myself," said Lucy Pirani, still holding it up. "Do you see the tail? That was an essential part; Theo used to say that the angels in books couldn't have flown a yard without stopping, because they had none."

We noticed now that Pirani had a tail fastened to his feet a curious skinny, fishlike contrivance with a big spread.

"He steered partly with that and partly with the wings themselves," she said. "You could do it the third or fourth time you tried. At first you would tumble into the lagoon and wade ashore, just slipping your feet out of the tail-pockets first. But then you got the way of it, and it was Heaven—oh, Heaven. Anything that fulfils a basic need of human nature is Heaven—cold water, sleep… And you know how you long and dream for this; it's so clearly one of our needs, though one doesn't know why. Flying, flying! Oh, when I think that I'll never fly again!"

"But, Mrs. Pirani," cut in David's homely bass, "if this thing really did happen, why can't it happen again? Seems as if Pirani had got ahead of everyone; well, he wasn't a god, you know, and other men may find what he did. Was it a special material?"

"Piranite," she answered instantly. "No one ever dreamed of it before. No one ever will again."

"Oh, I don't know. What was it like?"

"It had practically no weight at all, and immense strength. It was strong in two different ways, if you understand just as you prepared it. It could be stiff, with a little spring in it for the phalanges, you know, or else it could be flexible and tough, for the webs. And as for weight I could carry both wings in my hand and scarcely know they were there."

"The woman's mad, of course," I thought to myself, looking at her face, all lighted up with the enthusiasm which had never failed her (one could swear) at any mention of Pirani or his work. "Mind unhinged by trouble. Case of monomania. She—" and then I jolted up, mentally, against the photograph. Fake? No. It was old and yellow, and they didn't know how to fake twenty years ago. But if the photograph was right, then she was speaking the truth.

David, leaning forward with his arms laid across his knees, went on asking her things. His eyes looked bright.

"How were they worked?" he asked.

"There was no engine," answered Lucy Pirani, proudly. "They worked of themselves."

"Oh, but that is—"

"I'd give my life—gladly," said the little woman, "if I'd had the education to understand. But you know I'm not a bit clever, and there was only the governess on the station at home. These new flappers, with their knowledge of machines and so on… But I never was like that. I hated technical things; girls did twenty-five years ago. And then I married Theo, and he was a real

Latin—they never want their women to know things, only to be pretty and nice. So I just picked up words—like a parrot. I've tried to learn since, but I can't. I haven't the head. And most people think me mad. You would too, if you hadn't come to the island with me. About the wings, I only know that Theo had more knowledge of atomic energy than anyone in the world, but I don't know what it is. He used to kiss me, and laugh, and draw himself up he looked so handsome when he did it and say, 'Little Bird, thy husband is half a century older than the world; he has harnessed the steed that no one else can see.' And then he would look at his sheets and rods of Piranite and the electric battery"

"Battery? What for?" David snapped the question out like a shot. It was clear that he was enormously interested.

"I don't know, I don't know! I'd give my life if I—He kept it in that little concrete room there, and did something to the stuff with it. It was an awfully big battery and he told me never to touch it."

"What effect did it have on the Piranite?"

"It made it expand and contract, and keep on doing it for hours and hours and hours—I don't know how long. Theo could shut off the expanding and contracting when he liked, and plane, like these flight men with their engines." She spat the word "engine" out as if she would have scrapped every engine in the world, had she had the chance. "So you see, the thing did its own flapping, and you guided by your muscles. It was just like Heaven."

"Of course," said Shaw, half to me, half to himself, "we've always known that wings of sufficient power and size would carry a man, but we haven't the proper pectoral muscles, and our bones aren't hollow, so we couldn't work anything big enough. It is not impossible, given this Piranite stuff; I can even see, in a woolly sort of way, how the atomic energy could be used as she says. Mrs. Pirani, if all this is correct, your husband must have been a very great man."

"Of course," she said, scornfully. Then, with a brusque yet kindly changing of the subject—"It's time to go to bed; there are plenty of to-morrows."

Next morning, David, the conscientious, hauled me off to make a general survey of the island, and see if any geological formation promised the valuable things that had been hinted at in connection with Remora. Our survey was short. We came to the conclusion—which no one is ever likely to dispute—that Remora was a coral atoll pure and simple, that it had no guano, no phosphates, no soil to speak of, and of course no minerals. I wondered what the starting point of the rumour could have been; but David, poking about idly in the sand with his stick, remarked that he had no particular doubts.

"It has been this Pirani business," he said. "Some report of a 'valuable discovery' has drifted away on one of the island boats and been generally misconstrued. We're on a wild-goose chase, Gerry my boy, and we may as well acknowledge it. We have just got to put in our time fishing and yarning till the boat comes back."

I did not mind; the deadly apathy that follows on a nervous strain had got fast hold of me, and I wanted nothing better than to lie half asleep under the palms by the lagoon, watching the daylight wax and wane, and hearing the sea-birds scream above the reef, feeling little and thinking not at all. I did not believe I should ever want to work again—ever wish to go back to the world of rushing, train-catching, office-inhabiting folk. I spent that day in a grove of cool iron woods, couching on their dry, fallen needles, and listening in a half dream to the sighing of the wind through the green-haired boughs above. Pacific people plant these trees on graves. I think I understand why.

I don't know what David was about, except that he was talking a good deal to Lucy Pirani, and walking here and there about the atoll with her. She came to me at one o'clock, followed by a Fijian bearing food.

"You can lunch out here where it is quiet," she said, and went away again. About four o'clock she came back. I was pretending to read then, but I don't fancy she was taken in. She drew out some knitting work, and, clicking away at it so that she did not see my face, she said, quite simply:

"Tell me if you like. I've lost, too."

"Oh, there's nothing to tell," I answered her, scraping up the dry fir needles with my hand. "I suppose you know, anyhow. Ailala Pearson, that adopted daughter of the Pearsons—you know the old scandal of Naula; how her mother was a white girl and married a Naula chief, and died a few months after, when Ailala was born. You'd never know Ailala wasn't white Spanish or something, she's a face like an old Greek coin but the black is there, and it will out. No white man in his senses—"

"A face like an old Greek coin," said Lucy Pirani, slowly, an odd sleep-walking look in her eyes. She did not seem to have heard anything else I said. "A face—have you her picture?"

You will guess I had, I took it out and handed it to Mrs. Pirani. She had a big shade hat on; I could not see her expression as she held the picture up and looked at it. She kept it quite a long while and never said a word. By and by she handed it back to me, got up and went away, still without speaking. I didn't mind her much. I liked the little woman, but I was almost sure her troubles had shaken her mind in some degree.

The light sank down among the ironwoods and palms; the bo'sun birds began to hurry, screaming, homeward. The sand grew chill beneath my hands. It seemed that it was time to rise and go back to the concrete hut by the beach, so I went.

Mrs. Pirani was helping the boys to cook dinner. I found David alone, tidying up things in his trunk.

"What have you been doing all day?" I asked him. I did not care to know but one must talk, if one is to go on living.

"Looking for Teodoro Pirani, deceased, or his remains."

"What! you really shouldn't let that little lunatic—kind as she—"

"She isn't a lunatic, my boy, though I will allow she is somewhat taken up with one idea. It's a curious story; want to hear it?"

I did not, but I said yes.

"Well, said David, snapping the lock of his cabin trunk and sitting down on it for want of a chair, "it seems that Pirani brought up his apparatus from Melbourne here, in nineteen-hundred, and brought her too; they'd been married on the trip and they spent their honeymoon learning to fly about the lagoon. Jolly good place for it; couldn't well break yourself up at a moderate height and Pirani's flying allowed you to go on just like the birds do, skim along the ground or water, perch on a tree if you liked. They stayed some months, I forget how many, and Pirani used to go off for flights now and then, and at last he took to flying too far and too long, and could hardly get home. He went to Naula more than once and it nearly broke him up. You see Pirani's flying wasn't like the aeroplane sort where your engine buzzes you along at a hundred miles an hour—"

"I say, do you really believe all this?"

"My boy, I do," was David's answer, given gravely, with those sensible, kind eyes of his looking out very straight from under their furry brows.

"Well, go on! Pirani flew too far, and what happened?"

"What you'd expect. He never came back, and the Piranite wings were lost with him, and Mrs. Pirani was a widow, but she always thinks there's just an off chance she mayn't be after all."

"Why on earth?"

"Partly because she won't let herself think anything else, and partly because she never heard of his being seen after he arrived on Naula Island the last time—nobody saw him leave. There appears to me to be a mystery somewhere or other—or I might say the smell of one, as it were—but I can't locate it exactly."

"Why was she on Naula?"

"She's been visiting Naula and every island within three or four hundred miles of Remora for the last twenty years. She thinks she has a clue now."

"Clue to what?" I asked. I did not want to know. If I had guessed—had dreamed—how vitally important all this was to me—But I did not.

"She's worked it out that Teodoro Pirani didn't leave Naula the last time he flew there. So he was not lost at sea, as one would have supposed."

"Oh?"

"No, she came here to have a last hunt, she says, for any bit of the Piranite that may have been carried out into the lagoon and swept up again she says it was indestructible, practically—but I don't think she found it. However, she has found something, I don't know what, but it seems to have worried her more than a bit. She came in a while ago looking like death, and those eyes of hers—pretty eyes they are; wonder she's never—Well, she looked like a person who's seeing ghosts, and not nice ghosts at that. Do you know what's the matter?"

"Yes," I said. "I know what's the matter with you. You're falling in love with her."

David is good natured, but you may take him too far. I'd have remembered that if I had been less miserable.

"I suppose," he said, "that's your notion of a joke. It's not mine," and he walked off.

It was odd how the notion of flying—wing-flying, such as Teodoro Pirani discovered—took hold of me in dreams that night. I suppose it was the sight of the photograph, and perhaps the memories with which Remora Island must have been filled. Memories do float about places where things have happened; we all know that. At all events I spent the night skimming and dipping, soaring, sailing slowly over the green mirror-glass of the lagoon, not as our flying men of to-day go, but as Pirani and Lucy Pirani, and they alone of all the human race had flown in Remora twenty years ago.

Don't tell me you do not want to do it yourself. I know you do, I know you want to know if you ever will. Read on and see.

Ailala's face, of course, was with me in my dreams; the lovely Greek-coin profile and the backrushing, deeply waved dark hair, held in by the gold fillet she loved to clasp across that little classic head. Ailala was flying too; she looked as if Nature had built her for that purpose and no other. Always Ailala had had the look of a winged victory about her of something lightly poised and passing. Now I knew what the look had meant. I cannot tell you how exquisitely she flew. The grace of a dancer, of a skater, of a sailing, snow-winged gull, blended as flower-perfumes blend in a perfect bouquet, was hers; and I could even see the ruffling of her thin white dress against the wind she made, and the opening of her blossom-red mouth as she panted with her own speed. It was amazingly vivid. When I woke, I found the image of Ailala herself almost obscured by the aching hunger that had awaked in me, through that vision, for wing-flight over the green-glass, still lagoon. I knew how Lucy Pirani, who had tasted of the wonder, must have been feeling all these years.

"There's something a bit uncanny about this place," I said to myself. I went back to the grove of ironwoods to laze and dream the morning hours away; what else was there to do? And, as before, at one o'clock Lucy Pirani came to join me, and a boy with her bringing food. She seldom seemed to eat herself; I do not know what she lived on.

I found her changed. She looked like one who has heard disturbing news. But she did not speak herself at first, only asked me, simply, if I was feeling less troubled about Ailala.

"You have been so plucky about it," she said. "Most men would have married a girl like that and never thought of the trouble that was bound to follow. I've never known a mixed race marriage that didn't cause—By the way, were you long enough in Naula to meet Itari, the chief that her mother married?"

"I saw him," I answered. "He lives on another island and has nothing to do with the girl. He gave her up to those Pearson people as soon as she was born—you know her mother died then. I gathered that he didn't care about her. He isn't like her, except for the little touch of dark colour she has, and that's so little, anyhow, that it hardly tells."

Mrs. Pirani had a palm-leaf fan in her hand; she waved it to and fro for a minute, and then, still fanning, asked me:

"Did it ever strike you that Itari was a murderer?"

It struck me, anyhow, that the little lady had a habit of springing surprises on you. I don't know that I took her seriously.

"Why, I don't know," I answered, lazily. Then a sudden recollection of Itari's face—dark, hatchety, tight-lipped, fiery-eyed—sprang into my mind and I amended: "Come to think of it, he did rather."

"He was," said Mrs. Pirani. She fanned and fanned away. Her eyes had the hard, sparkling look that only blue eyes take on in anger. I should not have liked to meet her with a dagger in her hand and that look upon her face.

"Listen," said Lucy Pirani, suddenly laying down her fan and leaning over to touch my sleeve. "Listen; I'll tell you, and it will do you good to get out of your own troubles for a while. Besides, this concerns you."

"Me? How could it?"

She did not hear me. She was 'off' as I put it. By this time I had come to regard her as a charming, amiable sort of Ancient Mariner, who felt bound to tell her many-times-told tale whenever she met a fitting listener. When one has an idea that a story has been told, perhaps often by the very person who is relating it to you, it is sure to lose value in your eyes. Still, I listened, lazily, held by the heavy apathy of the mood that had been my constant companion ever since I said good-bye to Ailala under the wind-blown flame-trees of Naula shore.

"You think," said Lucy Pirani, "that you are very miserable, don't you? When something hits us, we're all the same. We say like the man in the Bible: 'Is there any sorrow like unto my sorrow?' And we don't think there is."

She fanned herself in silence for a moment, looking out over the long-lined, level green of the lagoon, and seeing—I have no doubt—those days of twenty years ago when she and Teodoro Pirani, her glorious young lover, wheeled and hovered like the birds over those still waters. And it seemed to me, oddly, a kind of allegory of human life. Don't we all fly gloriously for a little while and walk dully through the rest of our days?

"If you had had Ailala," said Mrs. Pirani, "and lost her by death think of it."

"I don't want to," was all I found to say.

"If you lost her by death, and by worse than death as well, how would it have been?"

"Damnable," I said. It seemed to me I knew what she meant. "I'd have killed the other," I added.

"Men do kill for a woman they love," she said. "Itari did."

"Whom did he kill?"

"My husband." It was almost a cry. She held the fan tight in both hands.

"For—for—you?" I said dully. I did not understand.

Lucy Pirani snapped the fan-stick in two, flung it down and rose to her feet. Her dull blue dress fluttered as she ran through the ironwood trees—away, away…

It occurred to me that she must really be mad. I went in search of David, who had been somewhat cold to me since my ill-advised remarks about falling in love. He was busy—David was always busy in the main room of the cottage, sorting out on the top of a packing-case the mineral specimens we had gathered up at Naula. They were not of much account—some iron ore, a handful of black sand with a few, too few, sparks of gold in it, lumps of mica schist, half a dozen miscellaneous chippings from here and there. I asked him plainly if Mrs. Pirani was in her senses or not, and if she was, what she could be driving at about Naula, and chiefs, and murders and me.

David, too kind to bear malice, looked at me with his usual pleasant smile as he answered:

"She thinks that her husband was murdered on Naula, because of some woman."

"Herself?"

"Not herself. It seems to have hit her hard. She evidently got on to the idea the other day, after talking to you—I don't know what you said—"

"Nothing at all; I was talking about my own affairs."

"Well, that's her idea, and she is half mad over it. She thinks he flew to Naula to visit this woman and was killed in consequence, and—"

"But what proof has she, after all these years?"

"I don't know. But she seems to think she has some. She—she—"

*"What have you got there?"*

It was Lucy Pirani's voice, but strange and breathless, a voice damped down by some strong emotion as you damp piano strings with the pedal. She had come in unnoticed, on her small light feet, and was leaning over David Shaw's big shoulder.

He got up at once and offered her his seat.

"What have you got there?" she repeated, without taking any notice of his words. Her arm, in its dull blue sleeve, was stretched out, pointing to a fragment of micaceous stuff, of a pretty opaline colour, that lay among the specimens.

"That?" said David, picking it up. "Don't know, but it doesn't appear valuable. I only brought it away because I couldn't identify the stuff."

"When you hold it up, what colour is it?" asked Mrs. Pirani, in the same odd, damped voice.

David picked up the specimen—it was like coloured talc, rather—and held it in the light. It showed, as the light from the doorway fell through it, a peculiarly beautiful dull blue colour.

"Why it's just like your dress," I was going to say when Mrs. Pirani, without ceremony, snatched the thing out of David's hand.

"Where did you get it?" she asked, and her voice was now a scream. "Did you get it on Ranarana?"

"Ranarana? Yes, that was the place."

"Where Itari lives?"

"Think so. What's the matter?"

Mrs. Pirani, holding the fragment to her heart as if it were a child, made answer:

"It's Piranite."

"Piranite?"

"Yes. Don't you see? It has practically no weight—bend it—" It bent like rubber. "The colour—I always dressed in that colour because I loved it so." She kissed the glowing piece of talc-like mineral. "That'll give the clue to someone wiser than I am," she said, cuddling and crooning over the prize, "and Theo will live again in his fame, as he ought to have lived. And it will do more than that, it will hang Itari some of these days." Her eyes shone brighter than the Piranite as she spoke. "He killed Theo and broke up the wings, but they'll fly with him to death and hell yet."

Her face was very white, and though she spoke with a kind of fierce joy I saw no joy in it.

"Why did he kill him?" I asked, all amazed. For indeed I did not see.

"Oh, you young fool!" she cried, turning on me, "don't you see? It was because he wanted the girl that Theo—Theo—loved—"

"She didn't know he killed your husband when she married him?"
"No."

"Why did she marry a native, anyhow?" I asked, still puzzled.

"Because," answered Mrs. Pirani, very low, "she was in despair…"

I opened my lips again, and as if maddened by my question she snatched at my breast-pocket and pulled out the morocco case that held my picture of Ailala. From her own pocket she took a small miniature case—not the folder that held the photograph of Pirani flying—opened it, and held it beside the picture she had taken from my case."

"Look," she said.

And I looked, and saw two faces—one of a man in the dawn of life, young, splendid, with a profile like an old Greek coin, and short, richly curling hair. He was dark, as Italians are dark. The other was Ailala—line for line, tint for tint, the same.

While I was staring, Mrs. Pirani wrapped the piece of Piranite in a soft lawn handkerchief and slipped it in her pocket.

"Stay till you are wanted," she said. "You've got to hang one man, and make another famous, and marry another. You're worth more than any diamond ever found on the Rand."

"Marry another?" I said, and then it burst on me. Ailala, daughter of Italian and English parents, might—should—be the mother of my children and the mistress of my home, no black shadow forbidding. I gave a cry.

"So you understand, do you?" said Lucy Pirani, her hand pressed over her treasure. "Someone always has to pay. I've paid for you."

David looked at her as I had never seen him look at a woman.

As I went out to the sandy beach and the sun, bent on looking for any sign of our returning boat—though indeed she was not due for days—I heard a word that was not meant for me.

"You're young enough to begin life again," he said, and his hand felt for hers.

"I'll begin it again," she said, " where there is neither marrying nor giving in marriage."

She did, a few months after. I am stupid, but I had guessed from the first she would not long survive the blow that had taken from her dearest memories. David has gone on an Antarctic expedition. Ailala and I and two men whose names you do not yet know (but you and the world will know them soon) are on Remora Island; the hut is a laboratory now, and we're getting on well with Piranite. Ailala has a madness in her for flight—bird flight.

She lives only for the day when the first pair of wings will be completed, and the first of us—she swears it shall be herself—will float out over the green-glass lagoon. All things considered, I do not wonder.

# THE SOCIAL CODE

## ERLE COX
## (1873-1950)

*The Lone Hand,*
January 1909

"I envy you, Gray; you don't know how much!" said Tarrant, head of the Commonwealth Astronomical Department. "Think of your chance! Youth, in the first place, and then, the bridge we have built for you.

"You're 32 now, with perhaps 35 priceless years in front, and to-night you start. Oh, yes, I envy you".

Warren Gray, the international officer in charge of the Mount Kosciusko Stellascope, walked smartly over the snow to the great circular building that crowned the summit.

To-night, for the first time, he was to take sole charge of that wonder of the age.

Chosen for the task from more than a thousand candidates by an international committee, his task was to carry on, to the best of his powers, the work of formulating practicable means of communication between the earth and Mars that the great Barstow's invention had made possible, and to give the results of his investigations to the world.

The work was one of tremendous difficulty, on account of the almost entire absence of a basis to work on and the great dissimilarity of the conditions or life existing on the two planets.

Gray nodded good-evening to the two assistants in the ante-room, and passed straight on to the instrument chamber. This was a vast domed apartment, 150ft from wall to wall unbroken by a single pillar; but the great size was dwarfed by the tube of a giant telescope, some 20ft. in diameter, that was reared to the open roof, its muzzle being almost lost in a maze of guys and stays that held it in position. Radiating from the main column ran a series of stands, each bearing its appointed instrument, many of them under glass, all glittering like an array of jewellers' treasures under the steady glow of the electric light.

Gray wandered amongst them with keenly observant eyes—here adjusting a screw with delicate touch, there noting carefully the reading of some beautiful piece of mechanism with anxious precision. Satisfied at last, he walked to the frame and unveiled a circular reflector, 15ft. across, that was set in it, then took his place in an easy chair some 10ft. away, and busied himself with the array of delicate machinery on a table beside him. All around were telephone-receivers, speaking tubes, and buttons. He frowned over the readings of a thermometer, and called down a tube that the temperature of the observation chamber was three-tenths of a degree too high. Even that variation affected the adjustment of the instruments that were built for absolute accuracy at 60 deg. C. His face cleared only when the mercury receded the offending fractions and became stationary.

At last his critical survey was complete. Gray leaned back in his chair, and, taking up a telephone receiver, gave a few brief orders. Each was followed by a movement through the room as the great telescope slowly picked up its appointed spot in the heavens. A small voice from the receiver told him that his orders were carried out.

Then he switched off all the lights in the room, except a carefully shaded one at his elbow, and as the velvety darkness settled down, the reflector glowed with a soft light. Gradually the light became brighter, and vast distorted images began to flit across the polished surface—images that became clearer every moment, until they showed a weird and fleeting landscape, as from a great height in a balloon.

Seas—and lands, cities and rivers, sped past in the field of view in bewildering succession. Gray still held the receiver and as he caught sight of a familiar mark his orders altered the movement of the stellascope.

At last a great city spun into view, and was held in answer to a swift call. Reaching his hand in the dark his fingers worked swiftly on screws and buttons. The towered and domed buildings seemed to rush upwards to meet him. In the midst of all was one of tremendous proportions and Gray worked it swiftly into the centre of the reflector.

Nearer and nearer it came. First the reflector held it all, then only the central dome, then only a window-like aperture in the roof, until at last the whole interior was exposed and then Warren saw in the mirror a view of a portion of a room almost the exact counter-part of the one he occupied, except for strange and subtle differences of detail of workmanship and architecture.

Practically the instruments were the same, and he knew he was in contact with what was officially known as the No 10 Martian Observatory, at that time some one hundred and twenty millions of miles away from the earth. A glance showed him that the chair in front of the reflector was empty, and Gray turned impatiently to a chronometer on the table. It wanted three minutes to the half hour.

"My friend is nothing if not punctual," he murmured to himself, and settled to wait with an occasional glance at the large hand on the clock. Precisely as it touched the point of the half hour there was a movement on the reflector, and a man clad in a long, dark robe stepped into view and faced him. He was below the average terrestrial height, and would pass for perhaps 60 on this planet.

His long hair was quite white, and under his high, round forehead were two dark, deep-set eyes, as brilliant as an eagle's. The face was hairless, and showed a straight, firm mouth, under his thin, hooked nose. It was a stern face, almost cruel, but one that told of great intellectual force. Gray had become familiar with the man's appearance during his probationary period under Tarrant.

To-night, however, he regarded him with keener interest. He arose from his chair as the Martian stopped and held out both arms towards him in salutation. Warren repeated the action with a nod and a smile, and then each took his seat.

The far-off observer seemed quite unaffected by the absence of Tarrant, and gravely commenced to carry out a chemical experiment for the edification of Gray, who watched every movement with close attention. It was by means of such demonstrations that much of the common knowledge of the two planets was made manifest.

Warren followed the progress of the work, judging from experience and results the chemicals used, and subsequently he repeated the work under the eyes of the Martian, to show that the formula was known on earth and understood. Sometimes they would come to a deadlock, as some operation foreign to one or the other was uncomprehended, and then would follow an earnest search for the missing link in the chain. It often happened that weeks were spent over some trifling detail, until the solution of the trouble was found.

They usually worked for about five hours, and succeeding nights were much like the first, the only breaks being due to meteorological troubles on the earth that prevented free observation, and this time was utilised by Gray to write up his notes and reports, and to compare them with those of other stations.

Six months passed, and left Warren Gray still as far as ever from the faintest clue to the work he had promised himself to undertake. The Martian observer absolutely ignored all overtures towards elucidation of their social code. Gray had prepared an elaborate series of enlarged photographs of scenes from our every-day work and occupations, and exhibited them to his far-off vis-a-vis.

Some were examined with curious care, but others in which women figured always had the one result. The Martian immediately covered his face with the flowing sleeve of his robe—a decided hint that the subject was distasteful, and would not be investigated—and on such occasions Gray swore vividly at the reflector. He instructed Mars in the use of photography, in the hope that the result would give him a clue. It took three months' hard work, and when the Martian observer proved he had mastered the art he quietly but firmly dropped it.

About this time, too, Gray had another annoyance to contend with, for the observer in No 10 Martian station on several occasions went to sleep at his post. At first Warren was able to rouse him when he nodded by flashing a magnesium lamp, the sudden glare recalling him to his senses, but at other times the man slept for two or three hours, leaving the terrestrial observer in a state of helpless anger.

Then came a wonderful night. Gray had started early, and after an hour's work the old observer nodded and finally sank to sleep. Warren shook his fist at the unconscious figure, and started to write quietly by the shaded lamp. For an hour he worked, when a movement on the reflector brought him to his feet with a start. For the first time on record there was a second figure imaged in the Martian observatory. Gray held his breath with astonishment. It was a woman!

She was leaning over the man in the chair. She was veiled as was usual, from head to foot—not even her hands were uncovered, but Gray knew from her attitude that she was intently watching the sleeper. Apparently she had not yet noticed the reflector. As he watched her she straightened herself, and as she did so her figure seemed to start with astonishment under the robes. He could see every movement with perfect distinctness, even the quick heaving of her breast.

Gray held out his arm in salute, but the figure remained motionless. He cursed his inability to make her understand. He caught up a rug from his chair, and, throwing it over his head, he suddenly tossed it back, as though unveiling. He saw his meaning was understood from the start she gave. For a moment she bent over the sleeper again, and then turned her back and made as though to leave. Gray threw out his arms in entreaty. Suddenly, almost as she was lost to view, the woman paused, turned, and walked slowly back again.

Watching her, Gray commenced in his excitement to speak aloud : "Ye gods! What a chance. Daughters of Eve! She hesitates. They're the same all over the universe! I win! I win! She'll do it!"

The figure had paused behind the sleeping man and bent again, alert intentness in her every attitude. She appeared to be listening to his breathing. As though satisfied, she stood erect. Gray saw the hands moving under the veil. Then, while he scarcely drew breath from anxiety, she paused a moment. Then suddenly two slender white hands parted the shimmering fabric from head to foot, and Warren gave a gasp of mingled pleasure and amazement. He was looking straight into the woman's eyes.

From that moment onwards Gray knew he was a changed man. In a second his office and his training were forgotten. Science and the work he was living for, which had hitherto occupied the sole place in his thoughts, fell into a distant background, and in their place was the image of a woman. He could always remember her as he saw her then shadowed in the great mirror.

Her pale oval face was framed in the soft folds of the parted veil. Its wonderful, its appealing beauty, and changing expressions of timid curiosity and surprise moulded themselves on his memory. He never knew how long they stood watching each other. He knew that she feared something, for her glance went uneasily now and again to the sleeper, and he realised that she was listening as though for some unseen danger.

Once when he involuntarily held his arms towards her she placed her finger on her lips as though to warn him to silence, not realising the vast gulf that parted them. But across the gulf the man bowed his heart in mute worship of the being whose voice he could never hear, and who could never be more than an intangible shadow in his life. Minute after minute went by.

He was wondering vaguely what fascination kept her there, until slowly she held her arms towards him and then let the veil drop forward till it hid her completely, and turned with halting footsteps and disappeared.

It was long before Gray roused himself from the stupor that held him, and sank into his chair with his mind in a whirling hurricane of self-questioning. His first rational action was to work swiftly at an elaborate calculation, and when he finally solved the problem he sat staring first at the figures and then at the reflection of the Martian station in the mirror.

Hitherto he had looked on the constantly varying space that separated the two planets as merely a scientific fact on which comment was unnecessary. Now, for the first time, he realised its meaning. Between himself and that woman who had so suddenly flashed into his life lay the awful distance of one hundred and twenty three million miles of space!

The whole idea was monstrous. He was mad, he told himself. What was the woman to him? He would never see her again. Hours passed, but still he sat there gazing straight before him, with unseeing eyes, one moment feeling the intoxication of passionate love and the next all the despair of its absolute hopelessness. At last he roused himself, and seeing the Martian still sleeping, he left his post.

Next night he waited anxiously for signs of weariness in the old observer, but quite a month passed before he fell from grace and dozed again: but even then, although Gray waited eagerly, watching tor a sign of her coming, his hopes were unrewarded, and so they remained for three months and then she came once more.

With beating heart he saw her advancing through the gloom. This time she went straight to the sleeper, and, after bending over him and satisfying herself that he was unconscious, she threw back her veil and faced him.

To his famished eyes she appeared more beautiful than ever. Her expression was alert, and she moved quickly as with a fixed purpose.

She held a scroll in her hands, which she unrolled and held towards him. Gray saw at a glance that it was a rough but accurate chart of the solar system, on which the earth and Mars were deeply ringed with red.

She indicated first Mars, and then touched her breast, and then the earth and pointed to him as though to verify her ideas. Gray nodded in affirmation, and she let the chart fall to her feet.

She smiled at him with infinite sadness, realising the gulf that separated them. Then, to his great wonder, she held out her arms to him and slowly sank to her knees. There was no need of spoken word to read her meaning. There is just one language that is formed neither of sounds nor written characters, but is most eloquent to those who have learned it, and that language passed between this man and this woman through countless miles of infinite space.

It was the commencement of the strangest wooing the worlds have ever known. For over an hour that night she stayed with him, but he understood by her restless anxiety that there was risk in the meeting, and, though he feared her departure, he began to fear still more for her in staying. At last she went, lingering as though loath to leave him, but he knew she would come again.

For three days after, a storm that forbade work howled round the summit of Mount Kosciusko, and Gray raged with increasing impatience. The storm passed, and Gray was early at his post. The familiar old observer came as usual. They started their work, but in ten minutes the Martian was in the deepest slumber. In ten more the impatient man saw the girl beside him.

This time there was no hesitation. She immediately commenced to shake the sleeper vigorously, but without rousing him. Then, being apparently quite satisfied, she stood before him unveiled and smiling. After their first mute greeting she took a metal vessel, and, pointing to the sleeping observer, raised it to her lips as though drinking. Next she rested her face in her hands and closed her eyes in imitation of sleep.

Then she looked up laughing merrily, and shook the Martian again. Gray knew that she had drugged the watcher to clear the way for their meeting, and signalled his appreciation.

That night was the first of many. The man was too deeply in love to stop to ask himself where it would end. He was living only in the present. With a speed far beyond his hopes a thorough understanding was established, but the understanding was one that Gray considered would not interest the inhabitants of the earth.

They formed hundreds of ways of recording their impressions. Every night a splendid spray of flowers was laid before the girl as an offering, and she never failed to express her delight with them. She learned to kiss the tips of her dainty fingers to her terrestrial lover, and taught him many quaint devices that gave them both infinite amusement. They even quarrelled once, because he was late at the tryst and had kept her waiting.

For an hour or more she declined to move the veil from her face, in spite of his entreaties. Then he turned his back in anger, and when he looked again she was standing with tearful eyes, an exquisite picture of penitence, and did not smile until she read full forgiveness in his face.

In Melbourne, Tarrant, head of the Astronomical Department, reading Gray's reports, observed uneasily the frequency of interruption through neglect at No. 10 Martian station.

It was not so in his time, and he was worried. Not that there was any falling off in Gray's work; it was always keen and brilliant, but latterly it had become woefully brief, but one day, when Gray wrote asking him to purchase and forward a diamond ring costing over a month's pay and enclosing a cheque for the money. Tarrant did as he was asked, but packed his bags for a visit to Mount Kosciusko.

"Some infernal woman," he said to himself. "I must investigate. We can't afford to spoil so good a man."

Gray's greeting, though warm, did not deceive his old friend. There was something being kept back, a reticence that could only be due to one cause. Over dinner that evening Tarrant boldly taxed his chum with the heinous crime of being in love. He did it not unkindly, but firmly as between father and son. Gray squirmed and floundered hopelessly, and finally confessed to his amazed hearer the truth of the matter. Warming up to the subject, he raved as only a lover can to a sympathetic friend.

"It's no use, Tarrant," he concluded. "It would kill me if I lost her. I'm only living now to watch for her coming. She's my life, and all there is in it. Don't laugh, old man; it must sound mad to you, but it's all in all to me."

Tarrant listened with increasing gravity. Never did a man feel less like laughing. Ahead he saw inevitable tragedy. "What is the end to be?" was all he said.

"I haven't dared to think of the end. I simply dare not," was the answer he got. He would have asked to be present at a meeting between the two, but he knew that Warren would never consent, and therefore his anxiety made him decide to prolong indefinitely a visit he had only intended to last for a few hours.

Something warned him that the end was not far off, and that Gray would want him then.

The end was nearer than even Tarrant dreamed. That very evening he sat up before the fire long after Gray had left to take up his post at the observatory. He was nearly dozing. The hour was after midnight, when suddenly a furious ring at the telephone brought him to his feet.

He snatched the receiver to his ear. "What? What, Gray? Yes! Yes! Right! I'm coming!" Without waiting for hat or cloak he ran from the house to the observatory. There was something in the agonised cry from the far end of the wire that told of disaster.

Gray met him at the door of the instrument-room, wild-eyed and with his face deathly pale. He seized Tarrant's arm without a word and hurried him to the reflector. There a strange scene met his gaze. Crouched on the floor was the cowering figure of a veiled woman, and over her stood, storming with furious gestures, the old Martian observer. His face was twisting with rage. With impassioned violence he was evidently addressing a dozen or more men grouped round him, pointing first at the shivering woman and then at the mirror.

When he saw Gray he shook his fist savagely, and looked as though spitting venom in his fury. To the two watchers, helpless as they were to interfere, it seemed like a vile dream. Though they knew they were confronted with a terrible crisis, the very silence of it all appalled them.

When he ceased his harangue a man much older than all present stepped forward, and, after first speaking a few words to the old Martian, he looked down on the girl at his feet. He held out one hand over her.

They saw his lips moving, and as he spoke she rose slowly and stood before him with bowed head. The others closed round her, as though preparing to move her away, but as they did so she broke from amongst them, and swiftly tore her veil aside and faced the reflector, and for a brief moment stood gazing at Gray in mute farewell. Then, with a rush, the men closed on her and dragged her from view.

When they were gone Tarrant heard the story, told in a voice alternating between rage and despair. They had met as usual. The old Martian was apparently soundly asleep.

Gray was trying to make the girl understand the significance of the ring he had procured, when suddenly he observed that the man was only feigning sleep, and was observing their every action. Gray had tried, but in vain, to warn her of the danger, when suddenly the man had sprung to his feet and flung her to the floor, and the others had rushed in.

Tarrant persuaded Gray to return to his quarters. Nothing could be done, and they could only await events, but there was no sleep for either that night. Tarrant had a terrible foreboding that he dared not mention to his friend.

With keen anxiety they awaited the night, and when the time came they found the No. 10 Martian station empty. Gray refused to leave the observatory, and Tarrant stayed out of sympathy. The night dragged on until in the small hours of the morning a telephone bell broke the aching silence. Gray mechanically picked tip the receiver. It was the Singapore station speaking.

It reported an unusual excitement in the city in which the No. 10 station was situated. He repeated this message to Tarrant, who grew pale when he heard it.

"Gray, you had better go," he said.

Tarrant was thinking of the one time previously he had seen an unveiled woman in Mars.

"I must know," said Gray. "The doubt would be worse than the truth. Turn the instrument on to the great square."

Tarrant obeyed, and then almost wished he had refused to humour his friend. Each one of the Martian cities had this feature in common—an enormous square in its midst, and in the centre of it a cone shaped mound of dark stone. When it swung into the field of the reflector both the watchers saw that it was occupied by countless thousands of men, and the cone, usually sombre and forbidding, was wreathed and festooned with masses of vivid scarlet flowers.

Tarrant knew his surmise was correct, and the memory of a similar awful scene came back to him. At all costs Gray must be spared the end.

"Gray, you must go."

"No. Tarrant, I'll see her once more if it kills me. I must stop."

Even as he spoke the head of a procession appeared, and the crowd fell back to right and left to give it room. Straight for the cone it came, and parted on each side. Tarrant saw the girl's figure separate from the rest, and again he urged Gray to leave, but the other remained staring into the reflector, rigid and motionless.

Then she stood alone on the summit, and as she threw back her veil the thronging thousands fell prostrate.

Gray made no sound or movement, but an involuntary cry of wonder came from Tarrant. On the supremely beautiful face there was no sign of fear. Her gaze turned upwards as though seeking something above her, and her eyes were so full of pride.

So she raised her arms as though in signal. Then came a blazing blue flash, but Tarrant had shut out the scene with his hands. When he turned again he saw that Gray was sitting smiling vacantly, and when he realised what had happened he was glad, for he knew that it was not good for a man to see what they had seen and live to remember it.

# BEYOND THE ORBIT

## ROBERT COUTTS ARMOUR

### (1874-1945)

*Red Magazine*, 117,
15 February 1914

The first tidings of the disaster that obliterated Mars came from the observatory on Ben Nevis, a mountain of Scotland and the highest point in the British Isles; for, by singular good fortune, one of the assistants happened to be observing the planet at the moment when a sudden outrush of steam or smoke proclaimed its dissolution. A few seconds apparently sufficed for its disintegration; a blur of luminous vapour took the place of the clearly defined disc in the telescopic field, and slowly this became thinner and dispersed.

Later, the news was confirmed by reports from observers all over the world, and speculation was rife as to the cause of such a gigantic catastrophe. The dark star, beloved of fiction writers, was dragged into the discussion and dismissed; for, argued the pundits, collision with such a body would have involved an instantaneous conflagration, whereas all eye-witnesses concurred that the planet seemed rather to fall apart, driven by the force of internal convulsion. But all the experts agreed that climatic changes, due to a readjustment of the solar system, would certainly come to pass very quickly, and the gloomier hinted darkly at a melting of the polar ice-caps, inundations, and finally a torrid and tropical heat, caused by a nearer approach to the sun. One or two anticipated that some portion of the fragments of the lost world might come within the sphere of the earth's attraction, but no man foresaw the rain of terror that began some three months after the disaster.

A sunset of most extraordinary brilliance heralded in Europe twenty hours of horror for the whole world. The sky was filled with dancing motes of gold, quivering on a ground of incandescent scarlet. The afterglow was prolonged till near midnight, when the smaller fragments of the dead world began to arrive, travelling with such velocity that they ignited through friction on entering our atmosphere, and sped earthward blazing.

At first these meteors were so small as to be consumed before they could come to ground, but quickly the missiles increased in size, and Mars, the planet of war, justified its name at the last by subjecting the earth to a terrible and almost overwhelming bombardment.

The sky was filled with a stream of light; a mighty cataract of white-hot material swept shrieking through the air. Cities and forests blazed and flared, rivers boiled, and the air was thick with clouds of steam and the smoke of universal conflagration.

Those who could took refuge underground, in mines, in railway tunnels. In London, alone, thousands were saved in this way, though many were suffocated, and more were trampled to death in the dreadful struggles which took place at every opening to subterranean shelters. Later, it was estimated that over two-thirds of the world's inhabitants perished through fire and frenzy, whilst at least a quarter of the remainder died by the famine and pestilence which followed. The number would have been even greater had it not been for the fact that the downfall seemed to concentrate about the Poles, and diminish towards the Equator. Some tracts of the tropics escaped with comparatively little damage, whilst, by a curious chance, an island of the Outer Hebrides, inhabited by five fisher families who had formed a sect of their own and renounced all dealings with an unregenerate outer world, was untouched by the shower. It is said that, not unnaturally, they attributed their escape to peculiar sanctity, were mightily uplifted by spiritual pride at being singled out as the inheritors of a new, cleansed earth, and correspondingly depressed to find themselves not the sole survivors.

However, the miserable remnant of the once populous British Isles had no time to reprove this monstrous egotism, being busied with the urgent business of reconstruction. A provisional Government, gotten hastily together, decreed what amounted to a general confiscation, or State Socialism—that is, they pooled all available resources and supplies, and set the people to procuring food and building houses from the wreck of their old homes. All over the earth the same conditions prevailed, and gradually, as communication was re-established, a fusion of nationalities began, made necessary by absolute need and dependence. Whether this hitherto ideal state of affairs will continue, or whether, having weathered the storm, mankind will gradually re-erect its old-time barriers, I do not know. So far, at least, there are no signs of any such absurdity; perhaps the lesson has been salutary.

Physical as well as political changes were brought about by the cataclysm; mountainous fragments were scattered over the surface of the earth, altering the course or rivers, and impeding the navigable straits of shallow seas. For instance, a huge mass of earth and rock, corresponding to our Jurassic formation in a marked degree, nearly fifty miles in length and almost as broad, blotted out Cardiff and blocked the Bristol Channel with a barrier over a thousand feet in height; whilst the shock of its impact destroyed Bristol, Taunton, Bath, many villages, and people uncounted who had taken refuge underground within a wide radius, burying the blazing towns under detritus.

Paris, as rebuilt, now stands on several hilly islands, surrounded by a shallow lake which is fed by the Seine, whose waters, barred by a series of miniature mountain chains, have been diverted by a canal into the Eure, and thence back to its original bed.

Considering, therefore, that devastation on this or an even greater scale had been wrought, not at two only, but at many places, that an appalling crisis had to be met and overcome, it is not wonderful that half a score years passed before anything in the nature of an organised investigation of the Martian relics became possible. Even now a vast field for research work exists in the material collected, and every day brings to light new evidences of a civilisation totally unlike, but far transcending our own in some respects. Our engineers are filled with wonder and admiration by fragments of Cyclopean machines whose use they can hardly guess at, and it is universally admitted that this lost people possessed scientific knowledge undreamt of by the most daring of our theorists.

But to the average man all this is of little interest, compared with the discovery of the amazing and almost incredible fact that Mars had received a human visitor, and that its annihilation was brought about by his agency.

Henry Wark, a young and enthusiastic civil engineer, conducting excavations at a spot near the ruins of Chichester, delving in the conical hill dumped on the flat ground towards the sea, came upon a tangle of machinery constructed from a metal which resembles a combination of steel and aluminium, having the tensile and ductile properties of the one and the lightness of the other, in better preservation than any hitherto discovered. When the earth and the remnants of a large engine-shed had been cleared away, he found that the thing was a pump—or, rather, a series of pumps—though what force actuated it he was entirely unable to comprehend. But in the midst of the mechanism, securely bound to an upright stanchion by many coils of Martian wire rope, was a large cylinder of wrought steel, originally made to contain oxygen at high pressure by a London maker. That was the "Biddle cylinder"—an astounding find, you will admit—and it contained the manuscript narrative of James Biddle, the greatest voyager ever known.

Who he was, nobody now can tell. An incidental reference shows that he was at one time a student in the Kensington Science Schools; another, that he inherited a large sum of money which made possible the construction of the apparatus which conveyed him to Mars. It may seem altogether impossible that an unknown man should have been instrumental in wrecking one planet and almost depopulating another; but if you accept the possibility of a human being making such a voyage through the depths of space, you are driven to believe his story, however it may upset your notion of the fitness of things.

Part of the earlier pages of the manuscript, and some portions of sheets towards the end, have been destroyed by a missile which had driven clean through the toughened steel, whilst other parts are absolute gibberish, apparently written whilst the author was suffering from mental derangement. I scout the suggestion which has been made that these passages are an attempt to render the Martian language into English phonetics, for no system is apparent.

The first pages being missing, which may or may not have contained a description of the vehicle that transported him through the many millions of miles separating Mars from Terra, we begin with the first decipherable entry:

"…and, having set going a second supply of oxygen, rewound the chronometers. Temperature had fallen to—10°, owing to failure of battery. Put on a spare and took another dos—"

The suggestion is that Biddle passed the greater part of his time in a drug-induced sleep. How his vessel was steered, what power impelled it, whether he had discovered some means of neutralising the earth's gravity pull and utilising that of the world, to which he was bound, all remain tantalising mysteries. The next entry—"Land in five hours. Detail plainly visible. Making for nucleus of 'canals.' Temperature beginning to rise"—implies that he had full powers of direction and control over his craft. Indeed, he must have, for otherwise the violence of impact would have destroyed him. Evidently he landed without great trouble, for further down the same page, beyond the charred, gap of the paper, we read:

"…jar, but—no consequence. Have tested air. Thinner than terrestrial; proportion of nitrogen higher' but breathable. Shall take small oxygen tube as precaution. Set about opening door. Terrestrial time (which I shall adhere to for the moment), 10.27 a.m."

Strange trait in a man who had gotten where never man had gone before—he must needs drag his equator with him! By the same reckoning, it was 11.1 when:

"I, James Biddle, set foot on the planet Mars. The atmosphere is curiously exhilarating. I felt impelled to run and leap; but, remembering that the bulk of the planet being much less than that of our earth, the gravity pull is correspondingly diminished, I refrained, lest I should land myself in difficulties. The landscape is strangely unlike anything earthly, being made up of fantastic rocks, coloured prismatically. There is no vegetation of any kind near me, but some two miles away is a thick belt of palm-like trees of a reddish-purple colour. I have taken a big oxygen cylinder, instead of the small one, as I find I can carry it easily. Set the flag-staff in position, and fastened on the Jack. Cheered."

Again one pauses, gasping at the colossal impertinence of James, flaunting his national colours across the solar system, taking possession calmly of a world peopled by beings who—But wait.

"As I anticipated from my bird's-eye view, the rows of palmate trees bordered a broad canal. I saw no signs of animal life. On drawing near, I noted that these trees have no leaves, but are covered with hair-like fronds, having clusters of waxy-looking, greenish-grey fruit hanging at intervals along each stem. They recall the aspect of certain mosses, or even the mould one sees upon preserves—greatly magnified, of course."

Here Biddle betrays the limitations of his training. A botanist would have been able to suggest some clearer analogy, though perhaps he might have been startled by what follows.

"For the first time it occurred to me that I was hungry. I approached the nearest of the trees, which were planted at regular intervals, perhaps twenty yards from the canal, or river, which gleamed milky white beyond, and stretched my hand to the nearest cluster of fruit. The whole tree seemed to shiver, the long, hanging fronds drew up swiftly far beyond my reach, and the trunk bristled out close-set thorns sharp as needles. I experimented with several others, always with the same result. My near approach was a signal for the tree to set itself on the defensive. They seem to have developed a sense equivalent to that of the terrestrial 'sensitive plant.' But why?"

This was only the first of many questions which presented themselves, and not always could he find an answer. And it was fortunate that he had an abnormally cautious position, for:

"The canal is an amazing work, banked with a greenish-white metallic substance, arranged in a series of half a dozen steps of a foot high. Possibly the bed is of the same material, but that the swift-flowing stream of milky liquid prevents my seeing. As I drew near, I was conscious of a nervous tension, such as one sometimes experiences in the presence of a high-powered dynamo, and, taking from my pocket the electrometer which I use for testing accumulators, observed that its needle had swung to the full limit. By induction! The stream is highly charged with electricity, the steps bordering it a simple but efficient death-trap. Is it a means of defence? And against what? I begin to feel uneasy."

The first few words of the next paragraph are written with a shaky hand. Little wonder!

"Safe for the moment. Impelled by hunger I returned to my vessel. The strong sunlight made a dancing heat-haze on the orange-red sand, very trying to the eyes, so that I kept them directed on the track I had made, and did not look up till I was within two or three hundred yards of the machine. My first glance showed that the flag was missing, though the staff still stood, and I halted in something like panic. From the nearest clump of rocks a scarlet band streamed across the sand to the machine, which was half obliterated by a heaving mass of the same colour. The band was alive, and composed of an infinite number of creatures, swift moving and almost indescribable, though they somewhat resembled spiders; they appeared to pour from the crannies of the rock, and the ridges against the skyline heaved tumultuously with uncountable hordes; whilst I paused they seemed to notice me for the first time, the heap about my machine dissolved into several columns, and poured towards me. The foremost were within a few yards before the stupor induced by the spectacle left me. Turning, I ran for the canal in ten-yard bounds; aided as I was by my earthly muscles and the diminished gravity pull, they were not far behind when I reached the bank. The stream was nearly fifty feet in width, and in cold blood, I should not, even in Mars, have attempted such a leap with the probability of electrocution if I fell short, but I was convinced that the creatures swarming after me were utterly malignant. Swinging the oxygen cylinder, which I could scarcely have lifted on earth, I sent it whirling clear across the barrier, and with the courage of desperation leapt after it. I landed with one foot perilously close to the uppermost band of the metallic bank, took a huge stride, and fell gasping.

"On the further shore the scarlet things poured to the margin; the front ranks appeared to halt, but those behind, urged by the weight of their fellows, swept on and over them, on to the steps. Then the whole mass of millions leapt and heaved as the current flashed through it, and lay still. A horrible, pungent smell like burning leather rose; thousands of the creatures toppled twitching into the stream and were borne away. Beyond the tree-line I can see great, seething patches of scarlet, acres in extent, retreating to their fastnesses, warned by the fate of these others, which lie shrivelled and dead. I begin to comprehend the function of this wonderful work of defence. The beings who made it must be marvellous engineers, for it extends as far as the eye can see into the distance on either hand. I am hungry and sleepy. I am going to rest for a little."

So far the narrative is written in indelible pencil; hereafter it is written with an intensely black ink, till near the end.

"I do not know how long I slept, but I was awakened by something passing gently over my face. Sat up, and confronted the most extraordinary of beings, the Martian, in whose dwelling I write. I am scantily acquainted with the inhabitants of terrestrial seas, but my instant impression was that he was a crustacean. An enormous head covered with bony or shell-like plates, two large protuberant eyes set on short stalks, mobile as a chameleon's, regarding me with an inscrutable expression, that yet conveyed the idea of almost superhuman intelligence, a very small aperture fringed with short bristles—his mouth—with a long feeler, prehensile and sensitive, projecting from either side; by way of arms he had a pair of three-jointed limbs, ending in delicate compound claws, instruments which I have since discovered are at least as capable as the human hand. The body, of jointed segments, like a lobster's, was comparatively small, and supported on four squat, bony, or shell-like legs, finishing with spatulate, plated feet. He was some five feet high, and from the head to conical tail about the same length.

"For a minute we gazed at each other mutely. Then he made a low, modulated, whistling sound, pointed a feeler to the opposite canal bank, and looked at me interrogatively. It was evident that he recognised my status as an intelligent being, so the first portion of the programme I had prepared for such a meeting—a series of geometrical diagrams with their demonstrations—was unnecessary. I proceeded to introduce myself by producing a small pocket atlas containing several astronomical maps, laid my pencil-point first on the sun, pointing at the same time to the blazing orb above us, next on the earth, and drew a line thence to the planet Mars. He followed each movement with comprehension, and, taking the book gently from my hands, turned the pages with some show of curiosity, till he arrived at one exhibiting the globe, and stopping, placed a claw tip upon it. I was identified.

"Next he interrogated me as to the means by which I had accomplished my journey, and, having made a slight diagram of my apparatus in my note-book, I showed it to him, and pointed in the direction where it lay. He shook his ponderous head clumsily, and waved it claw towards the scarlet masses still visible through the shimmer. Evidently he had no desire to adventure in that direction. Next, I pointed to my mouth, and rubbed my stomach in sign of hunger, whereon he approached the nearest tree, which did not move a frond, plucked a cluster of the fruit, and presented it to me. Can it be possible that these vegetables possess intelligence? The fruit is very palatable, somewhat like passion-fruit in flavour."

Here comes another gap in the manuscript; evidently a description of some kind of vehicle by which the Martian conveyed him through a country indicated by the surviving line— "—borate system of irrigation. They grow only in the vicinity of water. We passed swiftly, at—" —is destroyed, also a note of the Martian architecture, concluding with the words, "—gives to each doorway a strange suggestion of a sea-cave, overhung with sea-weed. We halted before one of these, alighted, and our car glided to a smaller door which opened to receive it, and disappeared. Beckoning me to follow, my host thrust aside the hanging curtain, and, to the infinite relief of my eyes, I found myself in a lofty hall, flooded with cool, green light.

"The floor is covered with smooth slabs of stone decorated with curious fish shapes, and I believe these to be fossils. The whole interior seems to carry out the submarine suggestion which I have already noted. Is it not a feasible theory that these Martians are the descendants of marine animals which, rising to supremacy in the course of ages of evolution, became amphibious, finally deserted the waters, and, having established themselves on land, constructed and decorated their homes according to the dictates of ancestral memory?

"Everything seems to point to such a descent. The food which is now being placed before me is contained in vessels which have a likeness to some terrestrial shells, though they are made of a glassy substance. My host has reappeared with a large metal box. I have seen nothing made of wood or anything resembling it, so far. The food is strange, but palatable, though I have no idea what it is.

"Later.—I have become confused about time. The chronometer I carry has stopped, and will not be persuaded to go. I think it has become magnetized through proximity to the electrified canal. Yesterday, after I had eaten my first Martian meal, my host took from a box a number of thick metallic plates fronted with crystal, and set one in a frame fixed in the wall. He made some adjustment, the crystal surface became luminous, and a coloured picture appeared, representing a huge building of many storeys surrounded by mountains of ice. Snow was falling, several little figures of Martians swaddled in wrappings appeared on one of the platforms of the building, and from the mouth of a tremendous culvert below it gushed a cataract of the milky water which fills the canals and the lake I have seen. The picture was infinitely superior to any kinematograph I have ever seen; how, it was produced is to me incomprehensible.

"I signified as much, but the Martian only shook his head, and substituted another plate, the interior of the great house, as he explained by signs. Gigantic machinery in frantic movement, with more little figures crawling about it, the milky water pouring from numberless nozzles through a kind of luminous screen which sparkled and flashed intermittently; then a view from far off—a canal brimming with a raging torrent in the foreground, the power-house perched in the middle distance.

"I understood then the genesis of this marvellous people's system of irrigation; far away amidst polar snows stood these stations which in some way converted or melted the ice. I do not know why the water is milky; perhaps the luminous screen has something to do with the electrification, but again I am ignorant. Perhaps later I will learn more.

"The next picture showed the beginning of the arid tract, the forking of the canal and a sort of guardhouse by some variety of sluice. Along one bank moved acres of the scarlet things. I pointed to them, and looked at the Martian, who nodded and tapped the box, as if to tell me that I should see presently.

"Picture after picture, I followed the course of that canal through interminable, groves to a great lake like the one we had passed,[1] from which ran a number of small channels fertilising widespread fields. Then my good Martian, remembering my interest, displayed the scarlet creature, taken at close range, a fearsome thing of hooked spines, a globular body, and perhaps a dozen legs. While I looked it seemed to grow larger, subdivided, and lo! there were two, the new-born increasing rapidly in size till, as the picture faded, it was near as big as its parent. This multiplication by division accounts for the swarms that evidently exist, but I should have thought that people of such transcendant scientific ability as the Martians would have found a way of dealing with them. With this plate the exhibition concluded, and my host makes signs that I am to accompany him."

The succeeding passage notes the beginning of that insomnia which finally wrecked Biddle's mind:

"Midnight.—In spite of resolution, I cannot close my eyes. I am afraid. This is a strange and terrible world. When we left the hall where I had been shown the pictures we found the little car awaiting us, and slid away over the polished road at a good speed, encountering many other similar vehicles whose occupants stared at me. Several of them followed close behind to see me better, and kept up a whistling conversation with my conductor. One came right alongside, and, keeping pace with us twisted his antennae about those of my patron. Neither made a sound, but judging by the other's eyes they communicated in this strange manner. When we came to the outskirts of the town, which consisted of houses all resembling the pattern I have described, with little variation, our following left us. We passed several Martians on foot, moving slowly and heavily, who stood aside as we passed, lifting one claw—a salute which my companion acknowledged in like fashion.

"We were near the borders of the lake I have mentioned when the incident occurred which has so disquieted me. From a long, low building of the universal greenish-white metal, whose windows were guarded by grilles, came a strange being, almost human in shape, with disproportionately long legs, short, sturdy arms, a small head almost like a man's save for the want of a nose or any external ears—and a tail. It bounded forth from the half-opened doorway, hopping like a kangaroo, with clumsy leaps, and as it passed athwart our course I saw that, quite unmistakably, the creature was a mammal. After it waddled a Martian, armed with a long boat-hook affair barbarously barbed, who as he caught sight of us whistled something. Instantly my companion turned the car, and, heading the creature off, drove it back on the keeper, or whatever he was. The hook thrust out, caught the frantic leaping thing through the flesh of its shoulder; shrieking horribly, the unfortunate was dragged within, the door shut with a clang, and we

---

1      Doubtless alluded to in the part of the MS destroyed.

proceeded.

"I felt shockingly upset with the callous brutality of the business, for the kangaroo thing, with all its limitations, was nearer akin than the utterly alien crustacean who regarded my shudders of disgust with a mild curiosity. I had pulled myself together, however, long before we reached our destination, which proved to be an edifice larger and loftier than any I had yet seen, the first and most important building of another hamlet or town much more populous than that we had left.

"To a chorus of whistled comments I was led through a crowd of crustacea to a large hall, green lit, hung with trails of artificial seaweed, to a dais set in front of a great rock studded with glittering stones, whereon squatted three Martians, to whom all seemed to pay respect. I am quite confirmed in the theory I have mentioned—namely, that these folk had a marine origin. Nothing could have been more pregnant with the suggestion than that weird interior; almost, I imagined myself in the depths of the sea.

"Leaving me alone on the dais—which was fashioned from a red coralline substance—my conductor hoisted himself painfully and-clumsily to a level with the triumvirate, and joined his antennae to theirs, and, after an interval returned to me, and patted the pocket where I carried the small atlas. This I produced, together with a book of photographs of some of our mechanical masterpieces, a locomotive, a steamship, an aeroplane in flight, and so forth, which I handed to him.

"A long pause ensued whilst these were being scrutinized; the throng circled about me, silent save when two bodies clashed together with a noise like colliding crockery. I noted that the parties to these collisions invariably saluted ceremoniously with uplifted claws. At last the inspection was at an end, and my Martian led me to a small apartment where, after some confusion of ideas, I understood that he desired me to disrobe. Conceiving the request to be prompted by a very natural scientific curiosity I complied, turning about as he directed me before an aperture in a screen, which I believe to be an apparatus for the making of pictures such as I have referred to. Also, it occurs to me as I write that they may have wished to know if I had any caudal appendage.

"After this I was taken back to the dais, my guardian made his report, and, after a silent discussion between the three, I was dismissed. When we emerged it was growing dark, but this did not embarrass my companion, who guided the car confidently as before. I believe he can see in the dark; but luckily for me his house was lighted when we returned, with a dim glow proceeding from the crags which depend from the ceiling. I had some more food, and was taken to a small room—quite bare—and given some close-woven mats for bedding. The temperature remains high—nearly seventy I should guess—unfortunately, all my instruments are in the ship. I wonder if

I shall be able to regain her? I wish I could sleep.

"*About an Hour Later.* —I am going out. Nothing is stirring. There is not a sound save the distant rushing of water in the main canal. My window gives on a paved path leading to the street.

"*About Two Hours Later.* —I do not know what to think. I proceeded in the direction we went in the car till I came to the long, low house near the lakeside, and prowled about it. A high wall encircles its rear, but this I easily surmounted, and found a paved courtyard with a shed, or, rather, a row of hutches. And in each hut was chained one of the kangaroo creatures, sound asleep. They did not wake when I flashed my little electric torch. In another place were many young ones huddled together on bedding like the tan used in riding-schools. One of them awoke, and began to cry out for all the world like a human infant, and I stole away quietly. I looked for some trace of a slaughter-house, but there was none. I must be careful what I eat. They looked strangely human, in spite of their short, soft fur. I am sleepy at last, thank Heaven!"

From this on, a vague horror of his surroundings took shape, and grew ever stronger in Biddle's mind. He seems to have decided on the flimsiest evidence that these "kangaroo creatures" were in a way akin to humanity, and their woes impressed him accordingly. It is, of course, possible that they were mammalians who had gone under in the struggle for supremacy with the crustacean types; but one notes the man's passion for finding earthly analogies to everything Martian.

"I awoke much refreshed. My host heard me stirring, and conducted me to his living room, where food was already set out. I forgot to mention that the Martians have nothing resembling a chair, though metal tablets sliding from the wall serve as tables. He ate with me, picking his food from the platter with his claws. When I produced the pocket knife, fork, and spoon which I had hitherto forgotten, he watched my proceedings with great interest, for I do not think the Martians possess such implements: I am filled with a sort of nervous irritability whenever I look at his immobile mask. His inscrutable eyes, ever on me, engender fear. I drew a diagram of my vessel, and pointed in its direction, intimating a desire to visit it. If I only had it nearby I should feel more at ease. He waved his claws as if to deter me, but, seeing me determined, assented. We proceeded in the car to the spot where I crossed the canal, and all being apparently quiet, with no sign of the scarlet creatures, I leapt across in spite of his whistles of protest, and proceeded on the trail I had already twice traversed; but hardly had I come in sight of the vessel when I had to beat a hasty retreat before a tremendous outrush of the infernal beasts. They pursued me quite to the brink of the canal, and millions perished once again.

"As I sat exhausted by my efforts, the Martian laid his antennae on my temples. I cannot easily explain how it was, but with the contact I understood that these creatures were deadly but necessary. I presume his mind communicated with mine, but my limitations forbade full understanding. I could not comprehend how these abominations were essential; perhaps bacteriologists, who affirm that certain varieties of germs are needful to human well-being, might explain. The things certainly looked like bacteria on the gigantic scale.

"I returned disconsolate. Later I was taken on a great journey—nearly forty miles, I should reckon—to an immense machine house, but though I have an excellent mechanical engineering knowledge, most of what I saw was beyond me. But I have discovered their source of power—nothing less than the internal heat of their planet, tapped in some mysterious manner, and conducted by enormous shafts to receivers or converters. I was given a glimpse of the interior of one of these shafts through a transparent, non-heat conducting shield; it was white-hot. I noticed that one of the omnipresent canals ran dangerously close to this artificial volcano, and it occurred to me that a cataclysmic explosion might easily be brought about by turning the one into the other. Incredible as it may appear, I do not think they have knowledge of the properties of steam.

"Several times during this voyage of instruction my Martian laid his antennae on my head, but I only partially understood. I gather that the whole life of the planet depends upon its water supply, and that the whole energies of the people are bent to this end. Something very important connected with this is to take place to-morrow. Returned. Very tired. I cannot sleep. Surely I can find some means of recovering my vessel—."

The manuscript tails off into incoherence with meaningless scrawling, the efforts of a man suffering from agraphia, and returns with an effort to legibility in the repetition "I cannot sleep."

The next day brought a crisis. What Biddle witnessed unquestionably unhinged his already overstrained mind. His account begins "Very tired." Then a blank line, then half a page covered with a species of hieroglyphic, a conventional drawing of the kangaroo-like being which excited his pity, repeated again and again; as his brain clears—one can follow the process in the script—the page becomes intelligible again.

"Were brought to the lake's edge, howling lamentably, and driven into the cage-covered boat which drove straight to the shore of the island in the middle. The door was opened and they were thrust out upon the rocks. One hopped to the top of the cage, but was pushed off again, and the boat returned—. Wish I had never seen such a sight! And all the Martians whistled. I cannot stand it any longer! I will—"

There he broke down again. Something very terrible must have overtaken those miserable kangaroo folks. One surmises some frightful sacrifice. It has been objected that the Martians were a race of high mental power, and therefore would not perpetrate such atrocities; but human history furnishes too many instances of culture hand in hand with fiendish cruelty to make any such comforting theory tenable.

The remaining pages of the journal are chiefly scribble, interspersed with sentences which only deepen the painful certainty of Biddle's insanity. "Columbus crossed the Atlantic. I've gone one better. Arise, Sir James--" And just before the final legible passage: "hero of Syracuse discovered steam; James Biddle thanks Hiero." And now to the finish:

"One of the lot of things they knew nothing about. The bullet raked him. From stem to stern, and he dropped with a crash. The rest bolted, but I nailed six more, and then the magazine was empty. I filled it again, but they had all gone. I am about to set to work. It will be quite easy, for the metal cuts like cheese, and there is a full head of water. I reckon the first burst will let the lakes loose into the other shafts. What a gorgeous surprise for the beastly crabs! This goes inside the oxygen cylinder I brought from Mother Earth. Perhaps it'll be a homing bird, but—"

The remaining sheets of the book are destroyed, but I do not think they contained anything. And the above are, I fancy, almost the last written words of James Biddle, the most remarkable voyager, and, considering that he destroyed one world and brought unparalleled devastation to another, the greatest conquering hero of the universe.

# TAKE IT AS RED

## ROBERT COUTTS ARMOUR
## (1874-1945)

*Red Magazine*, 213,
15 February 1918

All the facts in this story are fully authenticated by the researches of those most eminent astronomers and biologists, Messrs. Ball, Lankester, Flammarion, Huggins, Huxley, and many others, but here and there, liberties have been taken, as, for instance, with the Martian colour scheme. Owing to differences of vibration, the colours referred to as red, blue, etc., are only approximate to these terrestrial divisions of the spectrum.

For this and a few other obvious instances, in which, for the sake of clarity, he has departed from the strict letter of scientific truth, the author begs the reader's indulgence.

All the ruddy hills of Mars were aglow with the dawn light creeping down towards the great plains, through which leapt or meandered many water-courses branching out of the broad main canals that foamed for thousands of miles across the world from the high, remote polar ice caps, which never melted, till they were lost in the arid sands of the equator.

These irrigated fields could not have existed otherwise, since rain only fell sparsely at intervals of many years; it was, in fact, the system of terrestrial Egypt on an immensely larger scale, with not one, but many, artificial Niles, the product of tremendous, long-sustained labour and marvellous engineering skill. For miles on either side of these canals the country glowed with herbage and foliage of varying reds, ranging from deep crimson through every tint of scarlet and vermilion to the especially vivid orange-red of a low-growing sort of grain which dominated the landscape. The many trees were mostly of a deep vermilion, and, since it was early autumn, they bore heavy loads of violet or emerald-green fruits.

There were buildings here and there, at points where the smaller canals branched from the larger, strange-looking erections that conformed to no canon of architecture as it is understood on Earth, though they vaguely resembled the fantastic pilings of coral caverns beneath tropic seas. They were built of irregular blocks of cinnabar, lapis-lazuli, onyx, and other brightly hued materials, laid together with an eye to contrast, and when the broadening sunbeams touched them they blazed out in an utterly indescribable, lurid efflorescence.

At the same moment, an apparatus placed on the top of each house, and actuated by the rays, began to acclaim the day in deep, loud, majestic organ chords.

* * * *

The fine-meshed wire window screen of a house perched above the tumbling waters roaring down one of the half-mile wide, secondary canals opened, and Nhoj, who was the son of Samoht, who was the son of Yrneh, came out upon the irregular ledge which served as a balcony, the short antennae projecting above his eyes twisting and twirling like inquisitive tapeworms as he drew in long, satisfying draughts of the sweet morning air.

Deep breathing and high thinking are synonymous in Mars, and Nhoj was a type of its ruling race. Don't run away with the notion that he resembled you or I. Oh, no! Not by a long chalk. Evolution had run on different lines from the earthly in the red planet, and its dominant inhabitants were of a demi-semi-crustacean order. Away back, near the beginning of things, a gigantic species of hermit crab, inhabiting the primal Martian seas, had contrived to gain the ascendency over all competitors. Gradually it had become brainy, and shed such of its original crabbed characteristics as were useless in the widened sphere it attained, until it resembled its great ancestor no more than a man resembles, say, a ring-tailed lemur.

Gone were the superfluous legs, the huge pincers were modified to something resembling hands of wondrous dexterity, the unyielding shell had become flexible, with some loss of toughness, and the bony eyes on stalks had retreated under the brows of a head set upon a practicable neck.

But, curiously enough, the soft, shell-less tail, which is the weak point in a hermit's anatomy, had persisted in an elongated form. About this appendage clung a wealth of traditional etiquette. It was usually covered with a flexible metallic glove, which was wholly or partly withdrawn according to the degree of intimacy, when greeting a friend. Newly-wedded couples wreathed their tails in flowers, whilst a white tail-glove was a sign of mourning for a near relative or dear friend. They also served as an index of the owner's mental condition. When he was depressed, his tail drooped in a melancholy, falling curve; when jovial, he wore it tightly curled; but when it stood stiffly erect all who were not in a fighting mood gave the bearer a wide berth, for that showed he was feeling pugnacious. To pull another's tail was the deadliest possible insult, only to be expunged by the puller's pale-green life blood.

But, since Nhoj felt at peace with all the world, his tail was arranged in a neat volute as, poising but an instant on the parapet, he plunged headlong into the milky waters thirty feet below, and flashed to and fro with an effortless ease that might have called for admiration had it not been a common heritage of all the race of Sgubgib.

The water was chilly, so Nhoj did not remain in it very long, but, climbing up the terraced canal bank, entered his house by a door of the same close-meshed metallic webbing as his chamber window, and, halting in a sort of hall, lifted up his voice in a squealing howl. At once half a dozen little creatures, furry two-legged things, rather like a cross between a man and a kangaroo, bounded to his side, and commenced to rub him down with large towels. They twittered among themselves in queer, thin voices, very much resembling the noise made by rubbing a squeegee on a pane of glass.

These were Sgodrednu, the helots of the Martian world, creatures of an entirely different species from their masters, with intelligence enough to carry out their lords' orders, though quite unable to initiate anything. They were, in general, kindly treated, and when they became too old to work were painlessly extinguished, though sometimes they were allowed to linger to their extreme age. On the feast day of Yadnus, or Mid-summer's Day, one was solemnly sacrificed and afterwards sacramentally eaten in the great temple of the sun at Tohmad, near the equator, a spot so warm that near half the deputies who came from the more temperate zones annually succumbed to prickly heat.

On mid-winter's day every Sgodrednu throughout the world, without regard to age, was ceremonially and severely flogged, that their united entreaties might stimulate the return of spring. This flogging served to keep them in good order for the remainder of the year, and only rarely were they guilty of disobedience.

Nhoj's slaves were deeply attached to him, for he was an indulgent master, and the whips he used for the annual thrashing were made of fibre, not of wire, such as less kindly Martians employed. They fussed over him till he shone, and finally arrayed him in the light summer robe of green, delicately embroidered with a diaper of wavy lines, amidst which conventionalised fish slid in and out. Then he devoured a light breakfast of little cakes, resembling terrestrial biscuits, but very rich in proteids, and, putting on an emerald-green conical hat of straw, went forth to his morning duties.

They were easy, but very important. The whole life of the Martians centred upon the water supply. If it was stinted, the whole community suffered; if it failed, the whole community, would have perished, for, apart from the necessity of irrigation, every Sgubgib must have at least three baths in a day, and drink several gallons of water. Deprived of moisture for twenty-four hours, their skins cracked and peeled off, their bones became too brittle to support their weight, and they died miserably, so you may guess that they took no risks. All their engineering skill, their talent for organisation, were spent upon this all-absorbing problem of supply and distribution.

The most onerous duties were, of course, those of the devoted Sgubgib, who controlled the huge melting plants at the Poles, but apart from these were many other important officials, who looked after reservoirs, sluices, the canal banks, and so forth. Nhoj was a sort of district supervisor. He was responsible for the good condition of all the water-works in a tract of country one hundred and forty miles long and about fifty wide, with a command of a hundred Sgubgib and near a thousand Sgodrednu to assist him. As he was an efficient and conscientious officer, he was in the habit of flitting about his district, arriving unexpectedly at out of the way places, a practice which kept his subordinates up to the scratch.

This day he proposed to visit a place called Yltsaeb Eloh, situated in a strip of hilly country at the edge of his territory, a desolate and undesirable spot rightly detested by the whole staff. He had not received the usual weekly report from the engineer in charge there, and he feared some catastrophe had overtaken the station. If not, there would be a very hot half hour for Ymmot, and a bad mark against his name in the service records. Nhoj's tail stiffened with anticipatory wrath as he mounted the retoocs which his servants held ready, and sped away amidst a farewell chorus of squeaks.

The retoocs was a strange little vessel, somewhat resembling a shoe. For sole, it had a series of laminated plates made of a metal nearly impervious to gravity, which by an ingenious device could be closed or opened, so that the vehicle rose a few inches or a thousand feet from the ground. A series of fan-like propellers, set at the sides, urged the thing along at any speed up to some twenty miles per hour, while the passenger, seated in comfort, could observe the condition of the banks of the canal above which he travelled.

At least that was what Nhoj did as he swept along, the breeze of his passing pleasantly tempering the growing heat. Here and there he paused before a reddish fungoid growth that crept over the stone parapet, and made a note of its position. Several times he stopped at sub-sluices and conferred with the engineer in charge. At the last of these halts he stayed to share the keeper's midday meal.

"Something is certainly amiss at Yltsaeb Eloh," said the young fellow. "As a general rule they only allow a full head to come down during the hours of sunlight, but all this day it has been running at maximum. I have had to pond all I could."

"Quite right," replied Nhoj, waving his tail in approval. "I have noted your efficiency for some time past, and you will shortly be transferred to another position, with permission to sing for one half-hour nightly."

The junior gave thanks in the conventional squealing wheeze conveying delight; permission to sing was one of the greatest rewards open to anyone in the service, and certainly the most coveted, for the exercise was forbidden to the great majority of Sgubgib. There was reason for this; as indeed for everything else in the Martian code. The Sgubgib singing voice was of a truly terrible, raucous quality, very distressing to everyone, and so appalling to the Sgodrednu that the little creatures had been known to run mad and bite their masters under the influence of a love-song. About two centuries before, therefore, singing aloud had been forbidden under pain of extermination. A little later, a great organiser, one Sekysllib, to extend the list of rewards, which bulk much larger than penalties in the body of Martian law, hit upon the happy idea of permitting the discordant delight to a select few, under restrictions.

The recipient of honour had to perform in a sound-proof chamber in the company of not less than three of his peers, who saw to it that he did not exceed his time limit; a very limited number, heads of departments and so forth, were permitted to perform in public to their hearts' content, provided that they were not within earshot of any inhabited building, but as these were nearly all persons of great age and sedentary habits, the privilege was seldom exercised. Absurd as the system may appear to Englishmen accustomed to associate honours with success in money-making, it pleased the Yetenorab, as they were called, and they wore the symbolic bunch of bristles with as much pride as though it had been a coronet.

So now you can appreciate the young Sgubgib's pride and the solicitude with which he helped his superior into the retoocs.

"You will be cautious," he wheezed. "The Regnits are very thick just now."

"I shall be all right," replied Nhoj easily, shook tails heartily, and flew off at full speed.

Presently he entered a deep cut, several miles in length, and when he emerged from it the character of the country had changed for the worse. Here was no pleasant expanse of refreshing red and orange to soothe the eye, but only barren stretches of harsh, greenish sand and black rock outcrop, with here and there a small herd of fruit-trees all laboriously moving towards the ridge which he had traversed, each in charge of one or two Sgadrednu.

Nhoj grunted uneasily. He was not, of course, astonished at a sight which would have flabbergasted a terrestrial, because nearly all the vegetation of Mars is more or less mobile. As a general rule, cultivated plants and trees were quite content to stay in any place where there was a sufficiency of water, and usually remained in the same spot for years. But they could, when moved to it, withdraw their roots, and, by alternately shooting them forth and drawing them in, caterpillar fashion, travel considerable distances at a pace seldom exceeding a couple of miles an hour, though one species of flowering bush bred for its speed could cover short distances at the pace of a greyhound, and was often raced by sport-loving Sgubgib.

However, the sight of these hurrying fruit trees, notoriously lazy vegetables, which hardly ever troubled to travel more than a few score yards during their whole existence, was sufficiently curious to attract Nhojas full attention. He turned towards the nearest group and interrogated the Sgodrednu, who were obviously very much perturbed. He got little satisfaction. The creatures prostrated themselves, making deprecatory noises, but as they had been trained solely to agriculture, their limited vocabulary wouldn't allow them to explain what troubled them or their charges. They squeaked and squealed and stuttered so that Nhoj could only vaguely comprehend. Something bad had scared the trees. They had begun to stampede during the night. So soon as daylight made it safe to emerge from their shelters, the Sgodrednu had followed, and tried to persuade the herd to return, quite vainly; then, since nothing short of chopping it to pieces could induce a tree to halt when it was decided to move, they had followed. They prayed that the high, high one would pardon them, because they were not to blame.

Nhoj wheezed soothingly to them, waved his tail graciously above their bowed top-knots, and went on his way, vastly puzzled. Several kinds of dangerous creatures inhabited Mars. The equatorial belts were infested by the Tsaebyggulb, a monstrous, nightmarish thing, scaly, decapod, with sharp, poisonous-toothed jaws on each tentacle, which lived in crannies of the rocks and preyed on the equally abominable though less formidable giant land-crab. Both of these menaced the traveller in those regions who was foolish enough to come near the surface, but such accidents seldom happened, and the creatures hardly ever approached the well-guarded settlements on the desert borders.

Then there were the Regnits, which came abroad only in the darkness, compelling Sgubgib and Sgodrednu alike to remain within the shelter of wire-gauze screened houses on pain of an evil death. This terror of the night was a species of hornet, large as an earthly partridge, with a sting to match its size. Emerging from underground nests when the afterglow had died, huge swarms droned their way to the fields and groves, where they spent the hours till sunrise hunting insect pests and the abundant feathered rats to be found there. Incidentally, they fertilised all vegetable life, and this prevented Martian science from attempting their extermination. They were a necessary evil. Without them vegetation would have disappeared, as exhaustive experiments had proved, so, though not loved, they were tolerated.

But none of these things could account for the panic of the trees, since they did not menace vegetables. Nhoj racked his brains in vain for a solution, but nothing occurred to him which would explain the signs of wholesale devastation that grew more frequent with every mile.

A tumbled tangle of trees heaped at the head, of a small valley caught his eye, and skimming towards it, he found that all were dead and already decaying beneath the fervent sun. A little to one side lay the body of a Sgedrednu, horribly swollen, with one or two strange yellow spikes deeply imbedded in it. Beside him was the sharp billhook tree-herds carried to protect themselves against rats and other vermin. It was covered with clots of yellow, viscous fluid. He examined the trees. Each had a similar spike thrust far into its trunk.

If it had been possible for a son of Sgubgib to feel fear, Nhoj would have been terrified, but the tough fibre that had carried the race to supremacy in an age-long struggle against the most appalling odds was proof to such weakness. Anger, not terror, was the emotion that filled him as, with bristling tail, he turned once more in the direction of Yltsaeb Ebb, where he might find some explanation of the mystery

Presently he surmounted a low hill and came within sight of the station, but not the trim, well-ordered place that he had known. The sluice-house still stood, but of all the scores of trees that had shaded it from the noonday glare, not one remained standing. They lay in clumps and rows, some trailing their withering boughs in the swirling waters of the canal, others heaped higgledy-piggledy upon the bridge that crossed it, as if death had overtaken them as they fled. There was worse to follow. Hovering over the fallen, he saw that the wire doors of the house had been burst open, while on the first balcony above lay four Sgodrednu and Ymmot, the engineer in charge. Circling the place, he found the remainder of the station staff, all conclusively dead and all pierced with so many yellow spikes that they looked like hedgehogs.

Nhoj wheezed an enormous, grunting call. There was no answer. Nothing stirred within sight. He stopped the retoocs and alighted; then, drawing from its case the triuqs, a small, cylindrical weapon projecting a spray of virulent poison, which every Sgubgib of rank carried to enforce his authority, if necessary, he entered the house. He was greatly perturbed.

Ymmot had been similarly armed, and had attempted to protect himself, for his weapon lay beside him, empty. What in Mars could be the foe that was able to withstand an arm so deadly?

With the full knowledge that he might never come out alive, Nhoj stole across the wide hall, and peered into the rooms that opened off it.

There was nothing there. Then, somewhere in the house, there was a faint stir, as though someone had moved a heavy weight incautiously. He listened. The sound was not repeated, but he felt certain that a living being of some sort was not far off, and, making up his mind with characteristic speed, lifted his awful voice in a love song, calculating that if any Sgubgib yet lived, he would answer the call, while a Sgodrednu would be driven from cover by the terrible fur-raising discord.

> *"Thou art blue, O love, thou art blue!*
> *And thine eyes are a purplish hue.*
> *Link thy tail with mine, O queen divine,*
> *And we'll sit in the sun and coo!*
> *Oo-oo!*
> *Oo-oo! Oo-oo! Oo-oo!"²*

As the echoes of this blasting cacophony died away the sound was repeated, then, in a higher key yet none the less shocking, came the second verse in reply:

> *"I am green, O my love, I am green!*
> *But I'll bl-oom for thy sweet sake, I ween,*
> *Tail with tail gently twining,*
> *We'll give o'er repining,*
> *And sit in the sun and scream!*
> *Scree-ee!*
> *Scree-ee!*
> *Scree-ee!*
> *Scree-eam!"*

"Great Nus!" ejaculated Nhoj. "It's an elamef!"

And an elamef, or female Sgubgib, it truly was. A door that he had previously overlooked, because it was of the same hue as the walls, opened, and, the lady came slowly forth from what had been the unfortunate Ymmot's singing-room, her triangular mouth quivering with emotion, her large, lustrous, staring, purple-red eyes ashine with unshed tears.

"At last!" she said in a squeal muffled by deep emotion. "I had given up hope of life when your sweet voice penetrated even that sound-proof door."

"My sweet voice!" repeated Nhoj mechanically, too dazed by her pale beauty to be astonished at the words. "Who are you? What has done this damage? How long havee you been here?"

"My name is Ammenna, the only daughter of Sttuoe Enabsirb, the Keeper of the Archives. I was journeying to Nwotgib when my retoocs broke down. I descended here, and then—then 'They' came. Ymmot thrust me in here, and that is all."

---

2     This, of course, is but a rough rendering of the original, for the Martian intonation is capable of imparting a wealth of meaning to words which in raw, black type lack all the colour and fire that squeals and bellows alone can convey.

"But what were 'They'?" he asked.

"Yellow, horrible things darting yellow thorns. They were like bundles of slimy weed. They rolled and then expanded. Ymmot's trinqs was of no use against them. Ow!"

The shell-like skin about her mouth wrinkled and cracked as the sob burst from her. Tiny beads of blue blood appeared. Nhoj started.

"How long is it since you have had water?" he demanded.

"Many hours," she growled in a weak tremolo. "Nearly a day ago. I was preparing for death when I heard your voice."

Nhoj wasted not a moment in vain words, but gathered her in his arms gently, lest he should crack her brittle frame in twain, and, shuffling to the canal, walked in.

"Ooh!" breathed Ammenna; and began to drink and drink and drink, not through her triangular mouth only but through every pore of her parched hide, expanding each moment till she was near double the size of the emaciated elamef who had staggered to meet her deliverer five minutes before.

Nhoj drank also, gazing on her admiringly the while. He forgot all about the flight of time, the lengthening shadows, the new terror that had come into his world, so drank and gazed, gazed and drank, till soul and body were full as they had never been before; while she, sweet creature, played the like, returning his ardent glances with interest.

Perchance they might have lingered there, up to their necks-joints in whirling water, till the Regnits came out to play, had not a faint noise, and the plop of something light dropping beside them, roused their common-sense afresh. Nhoj tore his eyes away, and saw one of those abominable thorns which had settled Ymmot drift past him down-stream. Turning, he beheld the further bank of the canal heaving with queer, tumultuous shapes, which tossed a profusion of thin, flexible arms against the sky, whilst others rolled towards the bridge.

Plop! Plop! Plop!

Abruptly the couple were wide awake to the horrid reality. "They" had returned, and were launching their deadly missiles at extreme range, inaccurately, though still too near to be comfortable. It was time to be going, for that particular patch of water was no longer healthy.

"Your retoocs!" she wheezed. "If we can reach it---"

"We can't," he growled in a breaking falsetto. "They are close to it. We should be perforated before we could reach it. We must swim for our lives, and trust to luck. Quick! Down!"

They dived together even as a shower of darted thorns whizzed towards them from the raiders on the near bank. When they rose they were out of reach of the missiles, but certain swiftly rolling bundles on either shore warned them that they were not yet out of danger, though, fortunately, the creatures could not move and throw their horrid thorns at the same time. Aided by the swift current, they held their own, and presently, as the banks rose at a cutting, began to gain on their pursuers, who, shortly seeing that their efforts were useless, discharged a last volley and gave up the chase.

But the couple dared not relax their effort. The stream behind them was full of the floating death-darts, and the sun was at the horizon. In a little it would be dark, and the gentle Regnits abroad, while many weary miles still lay between them and the refuge of the next station. Side by side they swam on and on, slower, slower, and ever more slowly as Ammenna, weakened in the beginning by her long abstention from liquid comfort, grew exhausted. Her tail, which had so far remained resolutely curled, began to relax; soon it drifted flaccidly behind her, the panting of her lungs grew louder, and, at last, with a dismal squeal, she ceased swimming.

"I can go no further!" she gasped. " Save yourself, Nhoj, son of Samoht, and leave me here to drown."

"Nonsense!" he bellowed in his singing voice. "We will live or die together!" And so saying, wrapped his tail tightly around her neck and swam on, though he knew well that, thus burdened, he could no longer hope to reach safety.

The sun set, the twilight flushed for a little with the afterglow, then deepened to darkness. Suddenly Nhoj paused. He had just remembered something that he might have recollected earlier had his mind not been filled with thoughts of his sweet burden. In this very reach of the canal he had noticed, and noted for repair, on his way up, the beginnings of a hole in the bank caused by a species of mobile red fungus. Behind the outer casing of stone the earth was soft and easily moved; perhaps he could dig a burrow large enough to shelter Ammenna through the dark hours. For himself--well, another memory occurred to him, of something heard in childhood and almost forgotten till now, something that offered a possible chance of salvation, which he would shortly have the opportunity of testing. With a glance at the last lingering bars of red in the darkling sky, he swept in towards the bank.

Fortune was kind. Almost at once be found the spot he sought, and gently disengaging Ammenna, who had sunk into a drowsy stupor, carried her ashore, and furiously began to excavate with his strong hinder claws, his auricles a-quiver for the humming that would herald the coming of the Regnits. The earth flew, the burrow grew. Soon it was deep enough to hold the couple. Nhoi stooped to lift Ammenna.

Brrrrerrrooo! Rrr! Ooom!

Faint at first, but swiftly growing in volume, came the sound of a myriad wings working at high velocity. Somewhere amongst the grass a rat howled a warning to its fellows. The Regnits were coming like an army with trumpets, a thousand thousand strong.

Animenna roused as Nhoj raised her; her great luminous eyes, dewy with tenderness, shone on him.

"This is the end!" she squealed softly. "At least we shall be together."

"You will be saved!" he bawled stoutly. Then, since the respite was short, thrust her firmly into the bottom of the burrow and followed himself, filling the breach with his broad feet and sturdy legs—so tightly that, although air could percolate through the interstices, no Regnits might hope to crawl through this living barrier.

"But I will not have it!" shrilled Ammenna, "You shall not sacrifice yourself for me, an elamef you have never seen before to-day."

"Is the height and depth of love to be reckoned by time?" grunted he gently. "Though this be my last hour, yet I reckon it the most precious by far of all my life. Even the bites of the Regnits will be sweet because they are taken for your sweet sake."

"Horror! Horror! Ragas dna sgnot!" roared Ammenna at the top of her voice, bursting into tears. "I will not survive you!"

"Hush!" he commanded. "The Regnits will certainly hear you, and if you weep like this the flood may cause the bank to cave in, and all my labour will be lost. Listen! They may not find us, yet even if they do I may survive. My father was a Thrice-Bitten. Do you know what that means?"

"No," she gurgled.

"Here and there among the race of Sgubgib are found persons who can withstand the poison of the Regnits' bite or sting. If they have the courage to allow themselves to be bitten three several times, they are immune thereafter, and I have heard it said, though I do not know if it is true, their children for a generation or two are immune also. Perhaps I may be bitten and live. If it is so, may I hope that you will share my life hereafter?"

"Yes!" she whispered; and thereafter lay silent, thinking the long, long thoughts natural to an elamef who has found her mate and may very shortly lose him.

Outside, the hum of leathery wings had risen to a booming roar which rolled like thunder far out into the dreary wastes that lay beyond the cultivated areas. Every night of their lives the two Sgubgib had heard that awful music, always from the shelter of well-guarded houses, but it was with very different feelings that they listened now to the throbbing cadence that rose and fell in volume as the swarms drew near or retreated.

Ammenna's whole mind dwelt upon her lover, though his was mainly centred on his undefended latter ends. He wondered if hereditary immunity would suffice, if the stings would be very painful—

"Those yellow horrors!" said Ammenna suddenly, "I wonder if there is any cure for them, or if our happy land is going to be decimated, as it was when the Rechtans swarmed out of the waters in the old tines when Mars had seas. I have often heard my father talk of it. They were only exterminated after a terrible contest."

"These creatures will prove less formidable," hissed Nhoj consolingly, "I observed that they avoided the water. At all events, our science will be equal to the occasion. I suspect the abominations have risen from the deep caverns that open in the Eulb Hills. It will be easy to bottle them up after blasting those that have ascended with liquid fire dropped from a squad of retoocs. If we can only—EEEow!"

Without any warning, a red-hot pain had thrust itself through a joint of one spatulate foot.

"A Regnits!" he chortled horribly. "I am stung!"

She shuddered syrpthetically.

"Does it hurt?" She murmured, musically for once.

"A—a little," he admitted. "Arrrh! There's another! And another! That is three!"

"And you are not dead!" sobbed Ammenna joyously. "You are safe now, for does not the poet sing:

> *" 'Who feels the Regnits' deadly thrust.*
> *Feels nothing more, becauSe he's bust! '*
> *And poets always tell the truth. "*

So, for the remainder of that long night, Nhoj patiently endured the shafts and arrows of outrageous insects, till at the first glimpse of dawn the mighty booming rose once more in awful crescendo and died away as the swarms winged towards their underground desert home.

Then at last Nhoj uncoiled himself and his betrothed, and sliding into the cool stream soothed the smart of his aching feet ere, side by side, they swam away towards safety and happiness.

* * * *

Seven moons had waxed, waned, and gone where the old moons go. The peril of the yellow abominations was over and past, for, thanks to the timely warning that Nhoj had brought, they had been overpowered and bottled up very much as he had suggested. His services had been recognised by a truly superb and unique honour. Both he and his beauteous wife were, by a special order of the planet's Supreme Council, permitted to sing as and when they listed! Lest accidents should occur, however, it was provided that all Sgodrednu should be fitted with ear muffs, which they must close at the first note, on pain of extermination.

Thus it came about that Nhoj, returning from a tour of the larger district that had been placed under his control, greeted Ammenna, standing in the portico of their stately mansion, with a fearless and bubbly howling yell.

She did not reply. Instead, she held a paw over her triangular mouth warningly and whispered:

"Hush, Devoleb! I have something to show you."

And wreathing her tail tightly about his, she led him into a lofty, well-ventilated room, in the centre of which stood that typical Martian substitute for mankind's cradle, an incubator.

Reverently Nhoj raised the lid and peeped. Within lay some three-score beautiful pea-green eggs!

A minute he gazed at them with all the awe of a new-made father, then turned to Ammenna:

"Ours!" he yelped brokenly. "All ours!" And took her to his bosom.

# AFTER 1 MILLION YEARS

## J.M. WALSH
## (1897-1952)

*Wonder Stories,*
October 1931

I am the last man, the last man of all earth's teeming millions to be left alive on this once populous planet. I have seen this world, woefully, incredibly aged, bleak and desolate, writhing in its death throes—yet I have escaped to tell this tale.

So much I write, then turn to look out my window on the busy, crowded street below. I hear the hum of traffic and I see the movements of people, many thousands of them. I know that I am somewhere in the centre of a city of eight million souls. Not one of them realizes the doom ahead. If they did, it would not matter. They will all be dead and gone long before it comes to pass. Seeing that, realizing this, my story seems well-night incredible, even to myself, who went through it all.

I can hardly expect it to be believed. At times I can hardly credit it myself. But for two things I should end by fancying that I had dreamed it all, that I had been a victim of some particularly vivid nightmare. But no dream, no nightmare could possibly linger with its details so sharply etched in my mind. And, as I say, there are two things left me from that time, two proofs, if one can call them, that my experience was not altogether the product of a disordered mind. Why such as adventure should have come to me of all men I cannot say. It came—that is all—and I must record it as best I can.

My name? It is John Harling, my status that of a real estate broker, surely a prosaic profession. That much no doubt is proof for the credibility of my tale; my clan is unimaginative; we cannot invent such tales. But let that rest.

My story opens out-of-doors on a summer day in the third decade of this, the twentieth century. I was, to put it plainly, hiking, dressed in the conventional costume for such a pastime, my rucksack on my back, a staff in my hand. I was making for the crest of one of those deserted paths of leafy Surrey hills. A way not yet invaded by the ubiquitous London motorist.

The crest of the rise lay before me. I had nearly reached it. In my mind there was forming already the pleasant picture of a halt, a drink and a bite beneath the shade of the trees before I proceeded on my way. There was nothing then to tell me that a million years would pass before I drank or ate again. Unless that seeming hint of thunder in the air had anything to do with it.

Abruptly I saw a flash. Lightening, I thought, out of a clear sky at that; and I wondered why I had heard no peal. Then on the heels of the flash some branches crashed with a rending sound, as though some heavy object had torn its way through them. A lucky escape for me. The lightning might easily have struck me rather than that tree towards which I stared. Then I rubbed my eyes. What I saw was so different from what I expected.

It might have been the original fiery chariot from Heaven. Such was my first confused thought, for even at a glance I could see that it was no vehicle such as I was familiar with. It seemed much like an airplane minus the wings. Yet there was a subtle difference. The body was slightly stream-lined, but nose and tail were blunt, with a cluster of sinister-looking tubes fore and aft. From these a thin golden vapour rose in thin, lazy wisps.

The machine itself—I could hardly think of it as anything else—was of an odd kind of metal, weird and strange. It was the green of an emerald, so that I might have taken it at first to be some species of crystal did not everything in me cry out that it was metal. I learnt later that such it was. The length of the machine was studded with bosses, seemingly of quartz. Port-holes, windows, perhaps doors. Their exact function did not appear at the moment.

I stood and stared, even then not quite convinced that my senses had not played me some strange trick. Then gingerly I reached forward my staff. The machine seemed real enough. It was solid to the touch. More daringly, I tried it with my hand. It was warm to the feel, yet not unpleasantly so.

A door opened in the machine. A section of the side slowly slid away into the hull, and I waited, wondering what was to be revealed. I think I was more curious than frightened, and the one idea in my mind was that this un-doubtedly was a visitant from some other planet. To me, first of all men, was to be given the privilege—or the horror, which I knew not—of meeting the strangers. As the door slid gently open, speculation after speculation raced furiously through my mind. I tried to picture a hundred different and alien forms of life, any one of which it might be my lot to view.

I was wrong.

One person only stood framed in the opening, a being in human form. More staggering still, it was a girl. Call her that, though at a glance she looked more mature. A Junoesque figure, clad in something that looked odd-ly like chain-mail. It was golden and it seemed to glow—a little. The head was bare, though I saw she held some sort of a helmet in one gloved hand.

I am no weakling; I am built, if anything on a large size, without unnecessary flesh. But this girl was every inch as tall as I, though naturally better proportioned.

While one could count ten we stood and stared at each other. I take it that she was quite as surprised at my appearance as I was at hers, each of us fumbling for words adequate to the situation.

Then she spoke. It was a soft musical voice in its way, though it held an odd hint of power that I did not like. Had she spoken in some language utterly unintelligible, I don't think I would have been at all surprised; the fact that she was using English of a sort—queer, distorted, and to my ears archaic—was more astounding. Yet it was not hard to follow. One could sense the drift of what she was saying.

Actually she was asking me what year this was. I told her. 1935. She frowned a little.

"I have made an error, an error in calculation," she said, "but a few years out in a million is not so much after all."

A million? I gasped. Then: "Who are you? What do you mean? Where do you come from?" I asked with a rush.

She smiled a little, as one of superior wisdom to a child.

"I am Leela Zenken," she said simply, "and I have not come from anywhere—in space. But in time I have come from an age a million years ahead of this."

"In that thing?" I said, taking a step forward.

She nodded. We were becoming more intelligible to each other now, our pronunciations seeming less odd. "Yes. A time traveler. That is it. But is not this London?" She stared about her at the green trees.

I shook my head. "You are perhaps twenty miles from the nearest part of Greater London," I told her. "It doesn't extend as far as this—yet. Perhaps in fifty years—"

She did not wait for me to finish, but darted inside the machine, was gone in a second, and returned.

"That is it," she said breathlessly. "An error. Fifty years out in time. And thirty feet in space. In my day the land, this point, is that much higher. But you, what are you, what do you do?"

I told her briefly. Though at first she did not understand the function of a real estate broker, she did at last. She did not seem so pleased.

"I has hoped for perhaps a scientist;" she was watching my face as she spoke. Some passing shadow must have given her a wrong idea of what was in my mind. "I mean," she added hastily, "I wanted one who would not discredit what he cannot understand."

It was all Greek to me. That some object lay behind her words I did not doubt, but at the moment what it was was not apparent.

"What exactly," I said, "do you want and what precisely is it you hoped to do?"

Her answer was evasive enough in one sense. "I had hoped to reach the year 1985," she said. "My reasons—" she waved them aside, unuttered, perhaps because they were no concern of mine. "It is a strange world to me, a strange time, a strange people. But we seem to understand one another. If this had been 1985 no doubt you would have helped me."

One idea after another chased through my mind. After all, even though it was not 1985, why should I not help her? I was young, unattached, no relatives, no one but myself to worry about…and this was adventure, of the sort one might never come across again.

"Why shouldn't I help you now?" I said, greatly daring.

She looked me up and down. "You are of the wrong age," she said deliberately. "I go fifty years ahead."

"But the people of fifty years' time should not be so radically different from what they are today," I protested.

"That is true. I might after all…" She looked back again into the interior of the machine, thought a moment, then, "Come," she said.

I had little or no idea just what was in her mind, but I obeyed her invitation and stepped inside. No sooner was I in than she touched a lever and the door slid closed. She touched another lever and there came a roar of sound from outside.

## A MISCALCULATION

"What are you doing?" I asked bluntly.

"Raising the machine," she said calmly. "I miscalculated before. It has taught me a lesson. In the years the land has risen. If we went back to my own day we might arrive to find ourselves thirty feet under the earth. In fifty years' time, who knows but that we might come to rest inside a building, with disastrous consequences."

"Then we are not yet traveling in time?"

"No, only rising. It is better to do the traveling in free air."

"I see." I bent over the bank of keys and dials in front of her, and tried to make something of their arrangement. But I could not. The theory of time traveling I had read of vaguely. The idea of time like a river. One could travel with the current, drift from source to mouth. Mechanically one could quicken one's speed on that river, beat the drift of the current, as it were. The faster one moved the further behind would be left the particular patch of water surrounding the boat when one started. Conversely, the boat could travel against the current.

That much, admitting the analogy between the flow of time and the flow of a river was clear enough. The mechanical means necessary to achieve this result were a trifle more complicated. Her explanation of it all was necessarily brief. Some of it I grasped, and some I did not. In many respects the science of her age was couched in terms unintelligible to me.

She cut her explanation short. "Are you ready? Then please sit down." She pointed to one chair, and seated herself in the other. "We will start our flight through time. Not long, only fifty years."

She leaned forward, and set a pointer on one of the dials, then pressed a button immediately beneath it. The machine seemed to behave crazily. I had the impression of walls whirling and dissolving and I fancied I heard a stifled cry from the girl. Then…nothingness.

I came to myself abruptly, with a growing sense of strangeness, a feeling that all was not as it should be. The girl herself had slid to the floor; her head was resting against the back of the chair, and her eyes were closed. From the look of her I knew she was unconscious, but whether she had fainted or it was the result of the time traveling I could not say. The bank of keys ahead of her looked oddly twisted; the glass stuff of some of the dials had broken, and everything looked crushed and crumpled as though it had impacted heavily against something.

But the machinery's injuries could wait. I turned to the girl, wondering how I could revive her, but she saved me the trouble. Her eyes opened, flickered, closed again, then with an effort of will, opened once more and remained open.

She sprang to her feet with a little cry the moment she got command of herself, glanced at the dials, then rushed to one of the porthole-like objects and stared through it. She remained there some time. What she saw I do not know, but when she turned back to me it was with an expression of consternation on her face.

"I have failed," she said. "But the fault is not altogether mine. First my original miscalculation, then the jolt the machinery received when I landed in your era, both together may have caused it."

"Tell me," I said, with a queer sense of tightness about my heart, "just what has happened."

She looked at me squarely in the eyes, and—I liked this—though she felt the fault was hers, she did not flinch before my gaze.

"It is this," she said a trifle unsteadily, "I am back in my own age, you with me, a million years ahead of yours. The machinery did not function as it should have. The moment I pressed the lever we were shot with an extreme time velocity back to the point from which I started."

"Well," I said, for one age seemed quite as good as another now I had taken to time-travelling, "I don't see that it matters much—as far as I am concerned."

"But you don't understand," she said quickly, with an edge of consternation in her voice. "Unless I can manage to repair the machinery, which I doubt, you are marooned in time, a million years ahead of your day. That in itself might not matter so much to you or to me, were it not that the very days of this earth, which is the home of us both, are numbered. Is that not sufficiently appalling for you?

It was. I sat down heavily, and stared at her unbelievingly. For a moment I did not know what to think. The prospect was too stupendous for me to take it all in. She left me to my thoughts.

In a little while I saw that she was opening the door that led outside the machine, and she beckoned me to come with her.

"But first," she said, "you must put this on." It was a suit similar to the one she was wearing, designed, I learned, to protect the wearer against any extremes of cold that might be met.

Something of my numbed state I had no doubt put down to shock at her announcement had given me. Now I began to realize that the air was cold, almost like the blast of a refrigerating chamber. Perhaps the Earth was passing through another ice-age. That may have been what she had meant.

Or perhaps the planet had tilted again, as it had already done more than once in its history, and the poles had shifted. I did not know. I could only wait and see for myself what had happened. At least she made no move to enlighten me then, but instead seemed all impatience to be about whatever business she had in mind.

We stepped out of the machine. I had expected to find myself in the open air, but instead, looking up, I saw we were in a vast building made of some transparent substance like glass. The air in it was keen, almost icy, and I looked in vain for signs of life. We two seemed the only human beings alive.

The girl did not speak, but merely motioned me to follow her. We passed down through the huge building to one part that had been partitioned off into rooms. Since they, too, were made of the same glass-like substance as the rest of the building, it looked as though the divisions had been made more for the convenience of work than for the sake of privacy. Despite the warmth given out by the electrically heated suits we were wearing, the girl shivered a little.

"It's colder than it was," she said in a low voice. "The power must be giving out, the heaters running down. I pray nothing has happened. I have been away so long…"

"Why? What does it all mean?" I asked.

"Presently," she returned. "It is a long tale. I cannot tell it all to you now. First I must learn what has happened."

We came to a room. The floor was bare, but the walls were covered with a profusion of dials, keys, and plates not unlike those of television screens. She studied the apparatus carefully for some seconds, then made some adjustments with switches and levers. One of the television screens glowed to life. I became aware that I was looking at a vast building, similar in some respects to that we were in. She made other adjustments, localized the view, so to speak, so that we were looking at one particular section of the building, vastly magnified. It was full of people, men and women dressed after the fashion of the girl by my side. They were sprawling about in all manner of attitudes, but everyone of them was dead, frozen stiff. The cold of space had crept in and killed them where they lay.

An hour or more we spent there while the girl searched one screen after another, the television eye roaming from one point of our globe to another, and always with the same result. No where on the whole round of the Earth was there life! It was a dead world.

At last with a little moan she turned away, then dropping abruptly to a crouching position on the floor buried her head in her hands, and began to sob. Woman to the last. After a million years, the sex had altered but little.

I caught her by the arm, and raised her, a little roughly, I am afraid, but I felt she needed to be shaken out of her bog of despair.

"Tell me," I said, "what has happened. I am still very much in the dark. I think it is time I should know."

She faced me with burning eyes. "It is all my fault," she declared vehemently. "I have been the last hope of my race and I have failed...lamentably."

"But how? All may not yet be lost. Perhaps I can be of some help. Not much, I'm afraid, but the telling of your story may throw a new light on something hitherto obscure. Who knows?"

"I doubt it," she said, almost sullenly—angry with herself— "but it is right that you should know. I have brought you here. It is for you to judge me."

## A TALE OF DOOM

With that she started her tale, making it under circumstances, necessarily brief. Some I understood of what she said, and some I did not. Remember, in many ways the science of her age was a million years ahead of ours, and again they had forgotten many things we know.

A tales of a world suddenly face with the prospect of dissolution. The Solar System swimming into some uncharted reach of space encountered a stretch of unknown substance, a gaseous entity, a hole in space—no one seemed able to say with any degree of certainty just what it was—that possessed the singular power of intercepting the heat-giving, life-giving rays of the sun.

"Then," I interrupted, "it is not a case of a dying sun? The sun still lives?"

She nodded. "Look," she said. She pressed a button. One of the television screens came to life. I found I was looking at the sky, not materially changed from that which I had known. The sun was climbing towards the zenith, no smaller, no larger than I remembered it, but it was a sickly red in hue. I could look at it without hurt to the eyes. I might have been regarding it through heavily smoked glasses.

"Go on," I said. I was beginning to understand a little.

She went on. This unknown element, a substance with the power of shutting off the heat of the sun in the same way that a lead shield will cut off the emanations of radium, augured death for the earth. Time was short. From the day the fantastic properties of this unknown element had first been discovered, scarcely two years were left before the curtain would be drawn completely between the sun and its family of planets.

The scientists of the earth were mobilized. Some suggested one thing. Some suggested another. None were of any practical help. In the millions of years that had passed since my day secrets had been discovered and lost again, inventions made and destroyed. The story of human history was the story of good things used not always wisely. There had been conflicts between nations, between the inhabitable planets even; civilizations had risen and had perished; a graph of human progress would have shown a series of alternating peaks and depressions. Old records that might have been of use had been lost or destroyed in one or other of the many conflicts when the red lust of destruction had been let loose.

It narrowed down to this in the end. To save humanity some means of replacing the sun's heat must be found. The desperate need spurred men on to further efforts, the while the glass-roofed cities were built in the hope of staving off the final calamity for years if all else failed. Old records, such as remained, were feverishly searched. Mention was made in them from time to time of the discovery of a principle of atomic energy, light- and heat-giving. If such a thing could be rediscovered the world would be saved, for it was felt that the blotting out of the sun's power was only temporary, that in the course of time the Solar System would have passed out of the area of malefic influence.

Feverish work, almost to no purpose.

Leela Zenken had her own ideas. Her mind ran on the possibilities of time traveling. If she could construct a machine that would take her back through the myriad years she might be able to make contact with one or the other of those men of the past who claimed to have discovered the principle of atomic energy. For a time she was laughed at.

Time-traveling was a theory then as now. The mechanical difficulties seemed insuperable. But she worked away, making this experiment and that, failing always, yet always seeming just within measurable reach of success. And at last it came. She discovered the vibratory rate necessary to make traveling through time a feasible proposition.

Yet even then much remained to be done. She must search backward through time, a long and wearying process, for the data on which she had to work was meager. Some of the alleged discoverers of the power she sought must have been chartatans, since there was no record of their discoveries ever having been put to practical use, an unthinkable thing they had done what they claimed. In this she overlooked one solitary possibility.

Her search began. She left her world almost in despair. So many things had failed that they had little faith in this last hope. She came back through time, pursuing her inquiries. The people of other ages treated her badly. She met with incredulity, contempt, derision, everything but belief and help. In some eras she was even regarded as a mad-woman. Once, during one of the Interplanetary wars she was treated as an invader, and barely escaped without injury. The machine itself was slightly damaged before she could get it to start.

At length she came across one item of information that looked explicit. A scientist in the year 1985 had made the discovery she sought. His word had been doubted; he had been jeered at, and when at last he had succeeded in convincing the world, his experiments were regarded as too dangerous to be allowed to continue. In a fit of pique, anger, or because of broken hopes—call it what you will—he destroyed his apparatus, everything that would throw any light on what he had done, and ended by destroying himself and his laboratory. That, it seemed, was what actually happened, though popular account had it that an experiment had gone wrong.

1985. The year of the great discovery. To Leela, it appeared, that if she could reach the man while he was in his first flush of enthusiasm, before he found his invention and its possibilities ignored, she might get the formula from him, might even persuade him to return with her.

But the damage to her machinery had thrown her calculations out of gear. She landed in my year, as I have described. She could not face the prospect of traveling alone again, and the need for company was what actually decided her to take me with her.

Several points, made by no means clear to her, presented themselves to me.

"All isn't lost yet," I tried to console her. "Perhaps if you can repair the machine you can travel back again, find the man and set your return for a date here before the others have perished."

She shook her head. "One factor I have overlooked," she pointed out.

"The past is immutable. I cannot go back and change the order of things. They have happened in a certain way. I cannot make them happen in any other. The future, yes, that I can influence. Events yet to come are still in a state of flux. The future can be moulded, but the past, no. To make it clearer, there is no record that I ever reached that scientist of the year 1985; there is no record that I succeeded in my mission and returned in time to save my people. Therefore, it is hopeless to try. I should have realized it before."

"But you have taken me out of the past," I protested. "Is that upsetting the order of events?"

Again she shook her head. "No," she said. "Somewhere it has been recorded—you will find that—that you made this time trip, that you and I met. If you had lived your life without our having met, I could not have gone back and brought incidents into that life that had never occurred. You understand?"

"Dimly," I said. "I fancy I see what you're driving at. But tell me why you should have come back to your own era and found you were too late? I should have imagined that you have been able to have returned to the exact date you left."

"Let me explain. This is how it presents itself to me. When I travel in time the process is to all intents and purposes instantaneous. I do not expend time, so to speak, in the way that I expend power. I do not live that time. I merely pass through it. But when I reach any desired era and stop traveling time begins again for me. I spent fifteen minutes stationary in your year, talking to you. That is fifteen minutes out of your life-period and mine. You have fifteen minutes less to live.

"My searchings through the centuries cost me the matter of a year, in accumulated time, outside of the influence of the time machine. That year also has gone out of my life. It is part of the allowance of my existence that I have expended. For instance, now I can see that I could not possibly have returned here to the exact date on which I left. The amount of time I spent in other centuries when I was not actually time-traveling amounted to a year. That year must be subtracted from the sum of my existence. Therefore I arrive back to find that a year here has elapsed in my absence."

### NEARING THE END

"Then," I said, "if I were to remain here a year, and then could return, I would find it 1936, not 1935?"

"That is it exactly," she agreed, then looked at me with wide-eyed horror.

"But," she said slowly, "the machine is broken."

"You may be able to repair it. There is no harm trying."

She thought with knitted brows during one long, pregnant minute.

"Why not?" she said at length. "There is nothing to stop your returning in that case, even if I cannot go."

"You may be able to come with me," I suggested. "There is no reason why you should not. Even what you have told me does not debar you. Your life span is such and such. You must live the full period allotted to you, either here or in some other era."

There may have been a flaw in my reasoning. Perhaps so. Perhaps not. At any rate she seemed convinced. No doubt she wished to be convinced. Also I was a man and she was a woman, not altogether repugnant to each other, and whatever else had changed, a million years had wrought but little alteration in the fundamentals of human nature.

At least she set to work with an almost feverish haste. But for my suggestion I really believe she would have done as the others, let in the cold of space and die by her own act, reasoning it was far better to pass out in a few moments of exquisite agony than linger day by day, each day seeing the thread that bound one to life grow frailer and thinner until at last it snapped.

But I—I flatter myself—gave her something to live for. Nothing much. Scarcely a worthy object, no doubt. But there it was, the human heart being what it is.

I could not help her. She would not let me, preferring to work feverishly and alone. I occupied my time in various ways. I could not go outside the building in which we were housed. To do so would have been to court the frozen death. I had my camera with me and I had a supply of films, and I would dearly have liked to have taken many photos. But I compromised. Some of the television screens were still functioning; their power had not yet been drained; and by their aid I secured some photos worth preserving. Whether they would be credited I could not say. At least, as records, they were worthwhile to me alone.

Daily the red disk of the sun grew more dim, and daily the cold increased. The glass surface of the building now was frosted over so that it was opaque. We began to feel the chill bite of it in our bones. The power that warmed the building was running out. Yet I was heartened by Leela's announcement that a few days more would see the repairs completed. I could have wished that she would let me help her, but every time I broached the subject she refused my offer, saying that it was work that only one could do, that it was intricate and that with my lack of knowledge of the subject I would be more of a hindrance than a help.

However, I found much to occupy me. The building itself was a storehouse of strange appliances. I had wondered quite a lot since I had arrived why the power that warmed the building should have lasted so long after the power seemed to have run out in the buildings—one might almost call them cities—that had once been inhabited. The answer was very simple, it seemed.

The building was small compared with those others we had seen on the screens; the amount required to warm it was not great, and since it was something in the nature of stored solar energy it could be kept unused for quite a while. Leela, as a matter of fact, had started the motors immediately after our arrival, and only run them at half-capacity since. Knowing there was no way of replenishing the supply once it was exhausted, she had been careful about that.

One discovery I made while her work held her to the machine. In one of the compartments of the furthest end of the building—one that we seldom went to, since the cold there was more intense—I discovered a series of apparatus not unlike the switchboard of a telephone system; and exploring further I found head-phones. One day in an idle hour I put on a head-set, and snapped one switch after another, simply to see what would happen. Great was my surprise to hear a voice in my ear.

I nearly dropped the phones in my excitement, then recovered my equanimity as I realized that I was listening to something in the nature of a mechanical reproduction, a phonographic record, or whatever corresponded to it in this age.

My idle working of the switches had released one that set the machine in operation. I listened to the end—a short record it was—and then switched back. Sure enough the voice, metallic and measured, began all over again. I had paper and pencil in my pocket and for reasons of my own I took a transcript in short-hand of what the voice was saying. That finished, I looked round the switchboard to see if there was anything that would show me where the voice was coming from.

There was much that I did not understand, but I was able to puzzle out enough to realize that the record I had heard was being transmitted from the building we had first seen in the television screen. Probably it had been so adjusted that anyone attempting to call the place would immediately set the machine in motion.

I went back to Leela in a thoughtful mood. The moment I reached her I could see by her face that success had come at last. She had repaired the machine. We could start as soon as she liked. The news decided me to say nothing about my own experience. Yet on one point I must satisfy myself before I allowed her to take the decision.

"Leela," I said, "are you prepared to come back with me to my own age, to stay with me there always, and never know a life apart from me?"

She looked at me oddly, I thought. "Why," she said, "do you ask that?"

"Because," I answered steadily, "I would not care to think that you were doing this simply to save me from being marooned here in time. In the while we have been together I have grown to think of you as someone I would not care to have pass out of my life again. You have brought something into it that it had never known before—love!"

"And you, too," she said softly, "have brought it to me. If I were not going back with you, I would not care what became of me. I have failed in what I tried to do; I have lost all my own world held up for me, and had you not come to make up that loss for me, I…"

She did not finish, but said abruptly, "Let us go before I begin to say foolish things."

We went. I think in one way she was reluctant to go, for she shed an odd tear before she put her hand to the key-bank, and moved the lever that would bring us back to this year of grace.

We arrived on the very spot where we had taken off. I made a careful calculation before we ventured out, found that we had spent two months and three days away, and satisfied of that we opened the door and stepped out into the fall sunshine of a living world.

"What will we do with the machine?" I said, as we turned and stared at it. "It will be a bit difficult to explain away, won't it?"

"This," she said, answering my first question, ignoring the other.

I saw then that she held a length of cord in her hand, and that the other end of it disappeared into the machine itself. Even then I did not realize what it was she intended doing. Abruptly she jerked the cord. It was twitched out of her hand. The machine itself rocked crazily, seemed to dissolve, and before my astonished eyes vanished utterly.

I took a step forward and caught her by the arm.

"What have you done?" I cried.

"Sent it back to my own time," she said. "It is better thus. Without it I will not be tempted…"

To do what she would not say.

That is three years ago. We have been very happy since. No cloud has marred the serenity of our lives, yet sometimes I fancy Leela's thoughts go back—or forward, if you will—to the days that are yet to come. It has taken me all that time to summon up courage to tell her of that last experience of mine in, for want of a better term, I call the telephone room of the building that was her experimental laboratory. To my surprise she took it better than I had hoped.

"They did not think you would return," I told her. "They believed you had failed and were lost in time. But they prepared in case you did come back. There is the chance that they were not dead, that many of them are but in a state of suspended animation. There was a new discovery made while you were away, a drug somewhat similar to that we call avertin. It could suspend animation completely over a short period, but whether its effects would be lasting over years was problematical.

"Some of the population were willing to try at any rate, and were given the drug. From first to last it was all a pure gamble, you see. A few of your scientists believed that the solar system would pass out of the region of this strange gas—call it that—in a century or so, but they admitted they might be wrong. The majority were almost certain the Earth was doomed. They hoped that if it was not, that if this was but a passing phase the warmth of the rejuvenated sun would bring life back to those who were in a state of suspended animation. They gambled on everything, on the potency of the drug, its ability to protect against the inevitable cold, gambled on their hopes that the sun would once again shine out as before.

"Nowhere was there any degree of certainty, for they were dealing with exceptional circumstances, and had nothing on which to base their calculations, other than the hopes they had in mind."

"No, I do not blame you," she repeated at the end. "You did what you thought was for the best. Had you told me then, when my mind was in turmoil, I might have taken a course that I would have regretted afterwards. No, I do not regret I am here with you…"

But what else she said does not matter.

Nevertheless the fact remains that Leela has the knowledge and the means to build another time machine, and, if she will, to send us traveling again. We have discussed the matter between us without reaching any definite conclusion. Were we to go forward again, a century or so ahead of her day, we might find the world awakened once more. On the other hand we might not. It would be more than heart-breaking to find at least a world locked in a slumber that had become eternal. While we do not know for certain we can sustain our minds with the hope of possibilities…

Yet I do not know. Some day we may decide to build another machine, take the risk of black disappointment, and solve at last the enigma that perplexes us both.

# THE GLAND MEN OF THE ISLAND

## MAX AFFORD

### (1906-1954)

*Wonder Stories*,
January 1931

### CHAPTER I

To many who read my account of our amazing adventure on the island of the Gland Men, it will serve as just another illustration of how devious is the path of science. It will illustrate also how, from the darkness that girds it round, terrible possibilities loom black and menacing, terrifying those daring enough to wander from the beaten track.

Another, and I fear greater, section of my readers may harbour no such sentiments, labelling the whole as a tissue of preposterous lies, but to those who condemn me, I say this. Take the facts—meagre, garbled—as they appeared in the newspapers and attempt to account for them in any other way. There is only one answer. It is impossible.

The intimate details were far too terrifying and astounding to permit of the facts being published verbatim, and it was mainly due to the newspaper's reticence that something bordering on a world-wide panic was averted.

Doctor Bruce Clovelly, DD., F.R.C.S., will, of course, need no introduction, for his recent surgical triumphs in glanding have made his name almost a by-word, and it is with Guy Follansbee that we must concern ourselves. Follansbee, as I knew him in my days as laboratory assistant to the doctor—one of those singularly fortunate individuals who know exactly what they want and how to get it without offending a single soul—inclined to be cynical, yet straight as the proverbial string. He had inherited from his father an insatiable desire for adventure and an income that ran into I forget how many figures. Being a man of somewhat simple philosophy, he used the latter to appease the former.

It had taken our combined arguments, practised often and over long periods, to make the doctor even consider such a thing as recreation and I had experienced the hardest task of my life in getting him from his chambers in Gower Street, to which he clung like Diogenes to his wooden cavern. Even after his actual transplanting on to his opulent friend's yacht, the Silver Lady, he took his enforced holiday like a small boy takes his medicine, but as the illimitable miles of sparkling water grew between our vessel and his stuffy chambers, he turned about to enjoy himself.

We were midway between the Solomons and Santa Cruz Islands when the queer affair began. The morning had been oppressively calm and Follansbee, the doctor and myself had taken the electric launch to examine the rock fauna that flourished so prolifically hereabouts. It was characteristic of the doctor that he could, when required, produce inexhaustible stores of unexpected knowledge on the most out-of-the-way subjects; and though I had never before heard him mention marine growths, here he was expounding in his most didactic manner to his slightly amused companion.

Having little taste in such matters, I was reclining upon the collapsible canvas chair, smoking a cigarette, and occasionally dipping my hand into the water, in order to convince myself that it would not emerge dyed blue. Whether, rocked by the gentle motion of the boat, I fell into a semi-doze or whether the change swept down so quickly that its coming was unnoticed, I cannot say. But I remember that I suddenly jumped to my feet and called my companions' attention to the unpleasant condition of the weather.

In the east, the sun, flattened to a disc of unhealthy brown, was gradually giving way to a dense bank of cloud that rushed down with the rapidity of a drop curtain. The water had lost its turquoise hue and undulated in a long oily swell that was strangely suggestive of hidden power underneath. Everywhere a heavy, pall-like silence hung over the face of Nature, fraught with an indescribable sensation of impending danger. Now and again there sounded, very faint and far-off, a curious humming sob, as of some gigantic beast in an agony of torture.

"Without the slightest intention of being a first-class Jonah," it was Follansbee's first remark as he boarded the launch. "I should say that we were in for something extra in the way of dirty weather."

Doctor Clovelly shrugged his shoulders. "I should have expected something like this to happen," he said irritably. "We should have never left the yacht. What are our chances worth if it catches us in the open sea?"

The explorer snapped finger and thumb. "Just that," he said grimly. "The only thing possible is to cut for the nearest island. With the weather like this the storm may be on us in five minutes, but on the other hand it may hang off for hours." He swung the wheel as he spoke and the launch cut through the swell with a curious sucking motion. "But the Lord help us," it was Follansbee speaking again, "if it brings typhoon in its wake."

I leaned over the side and glanced at the approaching island. Through the haze, I discerned the woods that flanked the shining stretch of silver sand, unsullied by mark or impression, the thick vegetation that grew, tangled and luxurious, down to the water's edge. Here was a tumble-down native hut, raising its battered head above the mass of tropic greenery, there a sturdy giant palm, the trunk hidden from view by the enveloping folds of some flaming parasite. As we neared the beach, I saw that the land sloped sharply into rolling hillocks, cut and serried by deep gullies whose black, forbidding extremities were lost beneath the shadow of the higher mountains.

I turned to our host. "Does it possess a name?" I queried.

He shook his head. "Probably one of the numerous islands that stud the Polynesia like stars in the Milky Way. They are here today and gone tomorrow, thrust up by some volcanic eruption, sucked under the sea by a tidal wave or some similar undersea disturbance."

"I sincerely hope that it remains stable during our occupation," I remarked. Then the launch grounded on the shore and I jumped out to aid Follansbee to beach it high and dry. This done, we took our first close look at the island, our enforced landing place.

As we stood on the clean fringe of sand, the hush of the elements was even more apparent. Not a leaf moved in the thick humid heat, not a bird flew or animal moved. It seemed as though all Nature was waiting breathlessly for the opening of the cataclysm. But for the low rumble of the breakers, we might have trod another planet, some long-dead world; and the thick sand, deadening our footsteps, gave us a peculiar disembodied sensation that was unpleasant in the extreme. It was Follansbee who broke the silence. "No good cooling our heels on this beach," he said. "Under the circumstances, I think it would be worth our while to do a little exploring. That track through the trees seems to suggest unlimited possibilities." He broke off and pointed to where a worn track wound its way through the undergrowth.

"At least," remarked the doctor, as we made our way toward it, "we cannot claim to be true Crusoes. Someone has used this path pretty frequently—and not so long ago, if we are to judge by its appearance."

"Animals—?" I suggested.

"Much too narrow," interjected Follansbee. "Then again, the beasts have no object in coming here; there is no water to drink, nothing to eat and from my experience of animals, they generally shun the seabeach." He glanced at the dry rotted grass. "No, my sonny, that track was made by one thing only—a number of men walking in single file."

I looked blankly at the waste of matted undergrowth and stunted trees, "But where on earth did they go?" I asked.

"That," was the reply, "is what we are going to find out."

In single file we followed the circuitous path for over a mile, Follansbee leading, his grey eyes gleaming, the doctor next and I bringing up the rear. Through virgin greenery that walled us on either side, so thick that one seemed to be treading some matted corridor we went on; beneath wild and tangled growth through which the sickly light scarcely penetrated, over young lush leafage that overlay and half disguised the dank rottenness of the older vegetation, through which loathsome creeping things scuttled as we approached, things hideous and detestable to look upon.

The last portion of our journey was terrible. Here a fair-sized stream had become bogged by matted reeds and the spread of water was rapidly turning the surrounding country into a poisonous swamp. Clouds of insects hung over the black evil-smelling pools, some huge as wasps, with bodies of every conceivable hue and blend, some whose sting was death, others bred in the fever areas, carrying with them their dread legacy. The sibilant hum was discernable quite a distance away, and it sounded eerily out of place in that region of silence and decay.

Suddenly, with the abruptness that was almost startling, the forest ended and we saw ahead of us a flat plain. We were just about to step out on to the wide clearing, when Follansbee, who was leading, uttered a cry of amazement, stiffened and stood stock still. He was staring at some scene below him on the plain, and as we approached, he turned and finger on lip, pointed. Stepping quietly, we drew alongside him and I choked down the gasp that rose in my throat.

We were looking on a wide barren area of land, in the centre of which was a cluster of iron buildings. That they were tenanted was obvious by the thin trail of smoke that curled its way from the chimneys. One edifice, slightly isolated from the rest, was surrounded by a high wooden stockade, pierced at intervals by loopholes.

## THE CREATURES OF THE ISLAND

As we watched, thunderstruck by our discovery, from one side of the stockade came a troupe of figures. There seemed no doubt that they were men, but such men as I have never before set eyes upon. They were of enormous stature, most of them being over eight feet in height. They moved with a peculiar lumbering gait, that was vaguely suggestive of something that I could not place. Their arms, swinging at their sides seemed absurdly out of proportion to their bodies, and the great hands clasped tightly upon an object that, at the distance looked like an axe.

Each wore a kind of khaki shirt and breeches, with leather leggings that reached from instep to knee. A sun helmet took the place of a hat and as one turned away from us, I noticed a peculiar irregular blotch upon the back of the shirt. At first, I took this to be some personal damage, but a further glance showed me that each wore a similar adornment. At the distance, however, it was impossible to distinguish the outline. "By Gad," exclaimed Follansbee, as he unslung his glasses. "We seem to have stumbled on a modern Brobdingnag. Thank Heaven for that storm."

The doctor was already examining the monsters, so after a scrutiny, the explorer passed his glasses to me. I adjusted the powerful lens to my sight, and the approaching creatures leapt into my field of vision.

If, at a distance, these creatures looked unprepossessing, they seemed doubly so at close quarters. The lens picked out every detail with horrifying clearness, the broad, hunched shoulders, the long muscular arms, covered with coarse black hair, the slouching movement, caused, I now perceived, by the ridiculously short bandy legs. As one stopped to converse with his neighbour, he turned and the ragged blotch on his shirt took definite shape. I started again, thinking that my eyes were playing me tricks. The shape was that of a five-clawed dragon, reared in the act of striking. It was either stamped or sewn on in black cloth.

But it was the features that drew the eye and held it in sheer horror, so hideously repulsive were they. The tiny head, with its wide slobbering mouth, the wicked red eyes and the flat coarse nostrils inspired one with a thrill of disgust and loathing. The low receding forehead and the forward position of the ears showed that, were they humans, they were of a very low scale of civilization.

"My God!" I heard Clovelly gasp. "Are they man or beast?"

I opened my mouth to answer, when from behind there came a rustle of disturbed undergrowth. I swung around, but there was nothing to account for the sound, when, acting on some unknown impulse, I glanced up into the tangle of branches above. A cry of horror burst from my lips, for there above us, silent and motionless as the surrounding forest, crouched four of those hideous creatures that we had been watching. How long they had sat there, their blood-shot eyes contemplating our movements, will never be known, for as I sighted them, they became galvanized into life. With guttural screams they sprang upon us, and I was just about to run for my life, when one gathered me beneath his arm like a bundle of hay, and, with a curious wabbling stride, made for the walled-in building.

## CHAPTER II
## A PLACE OF TERROR

In an incredibly short space of time, we had reached the high partition. Here the creatures paused and shouting something in the guttural tongue, pointed to the gate, then to his companions in the rear. In my awkward position, I was unable to glimpse the one to whom he spoke, but it was obviously the guardian of the portal, for even as I screwed my neck to breaking point, the obstacle swung back, and we passed through.

I judged, by the stamp of the feet behind, that my colleagues were likewise captives, and by the sounds of struggle, that they were not submitting so tamely as I. Perhaps I was unfortunate in possessing a particularly irascible gaoler, for my puny efforts at escape had resulted in nothing more than a cuff across the face that nearly took my head off. Maybe it was just a gentle reminder that he would stand for no nonsense, but it served to quiet me beyond further resistance.

We traversed a slight dip and breasting the slope, came to the main residence. It was much more pretentious than the outbuildings, with neatly laid paths and flowerbeds, though the blooms could not be called healthy. Across the roof were looped slender wires, standing clear against the coppery sky, terminating in twin aerial poles. It strengthened my conviction that we had reached the headquarters of this amazing island.

Four wooden steps led us into a wide hallway, carpeted with rush mats, that strewed the floor at regular intervals. A number of doors, dimly discernible in the uncertain light, opened off this passage, whose extremity was lost in the prevailing gloom.

It was here that my guard at last set me down and turning, signed to his companions to do likewise. I smoothed my rumpled apparel into something approaching order and turning, beheld Follansbee, as imperturbable as ever, in the act of lighting a cigarette. Clovelly, seemed still stunned with amazement and he looked at me with eyes that hinted a thousand questions.

Before he had time to utter a word, one of the creatures wheeled around and disappeared into one of the rooms. As he opened the door, I became aware of a peculiar odor—sweet, sickly—that emanated from behind it. For just a second it eluded me, then as it grew stronger, I recognized it immediately—chloroform.

I glanced at Clovelly, and smiled wryly. He was sniffing the air like a thoroughbred, his professional instincts aroused. I noticed the slender white fingers quiver like the antennae of some giant insect, itching for the scalpel or the forceps.

Seeing my interest, he opened his mouth to speak, but what he meant to say will never be known. Suddenly, tearing jaggedly across the stillness, there came a horrifying shriek of some poor soul in mortal agony. Higher and higher it rose, in shrill cadence, then at the highest note it ceased abruptly, to die away in a gurgling mumble, then silence—thick—enveloping—sinister—

I am not easily frightened, but an icy horror gripped my heart. Clovelly was white to the lips and even Follansbee was shaken out of his customary equanimity. Our huge guardians seemed absolutely unmoved by the horrid experience, not an emotion was discernable upon their animal countenances, they were as devoid of expression as a rubber doll.

At that moment the door re-opened and our guide appeared. Taking advantage of the diversion, I crossed to the half-open door and essayed to peep inside. I was almost there when one of the creatures sprang forward and with an angry grunt, grasped my arm and with such force that I cried out. Our huge guide turned quickly and looking questioningly at his subordinate (as I took the other to be) fired a volley of unintelligible jargon at him. Suddenly the creature released me as though I had become red-hot and a look of something akin to deference crossed the bestial face. But I hardly noticed this, for my head was buzzing with a new discovery. The opening and shutting of the door had afforded me a momentary glimpse beyond—a fleeting vision of a modern operating theatre, the tables, instruments and assistants showing spotlessly clean in the bright artificial light.

One of the creatures crossed to a portion of the wall opposite the door and pressing on it, moved his hands in a curious circular manner.

The reason for this was plainly obvious the next moment, for there came the sound of a metallic click and a section of the wall swung back to reveal a door, set flush in the woodwork. With more haste than ceremony, we were thrust through this door, it clicked behind us—and for the first time since our capture, we were left alone.

But we had no desire to converse. We were struck silent by the extraordinary appearance of the singular apartment in which we found ourselves. I can close my eyes now, and recall every feature of that bizarre apartment as though it were yesterday, so indelibly are the details engraved on my mind.

It was circular in shape and lined with books from floor to ceiling, the reds and golds of the bindings reflecting the light from the mosaic-shaded lamp that hung in the center of the room. Beneath this was a huge bowl of roses, the colours shading from one extreme to the other. Some there were so dark as to appear almost black, to vivid scarlet and flaming yellow, to others so delicately tinted as to truly rival the shy blush of the maiden. They filled the room with a heavy, exotic perfume and as I gazed, one of the flowers, fullblown in that superheated atmosphere, burst slowly and the creamy petals drifted slowly—one by one—lightly as thistledown—onto the rich red carpet on the floor.

Behind this great bouquet was a square block of perfectly grained black marble, flanked on either side by fantastically wrought incense burners. Poised on the marble base was a five-clawed dragon, in the act of striking, carved from solid ivory with the meticulous care that characterizes the oriental artist. So cleverly was it wrought that the object seemed to possess a personality that was both fascinating, yet repellent. It was wickedly beautiful in its own way, and it recalled to me similar emotions when I had first handled a Renaissance stiletto.

Directly opposite the carving, the books ended abruptly, to recommence at an interval of about three feet wide. Across the aperture was hung a heavy plush curtain, crimson with golden edging, and worked with poppies and roses. It fell in heavy folds that hung motionless in the still air, exuding an influence of the obscene and the unmentionable.

I turned and something caused me to rub my eyes. Of the door we had entered, there was no sign. Save for the curtained aperture, the book- lined walls continued in an unbroken line around the room. Hardly able to believe the evidence of my own eyes, I walked up and ran my fingers over them. My hand encountered bindings—red—gold—that winked mockingly in the vari-coloured radiance.

The choice of books in themselves was remarkable. The titles covered a wide range from the transcendental and metaphysical and all manner of works on the processes and oddities of the human thought seemed to be assembled there. They ranged from the days of black magic to psycho- therapeutics of the modern analytical school.

There were volumes by Zaasman and Jung, together with other foreign scientists on the morbid phenomena of the brain.

Interested in spite of myself, I took down one book in German, a tongue with which I am fairly conversant, but after a hurried glance returned it hastily to its position.

It was a study of Dementia Praecox and its plates of naked German lunatics almost turned my stomach, quite unused as I was to the German scientific treatment of the more repellent disorders of life.

At the end of the highest row were a number of volumes touching on the influence of suggestion on the human mind. They ranged from the early investigations of Bertrand and of James Braid to the more recent studies of auto-suggestion by Coue and other modern French writers in this line of thought.

"By Jove, Follansbee," the doctor's softly spoken remark brought me round like a shot. "You wanted adventure, you craved something different—well, you've got it, with a vengeance."

## A NARROW ESCAPE

The big explorer shrugged his shoulders. "There are more things in Heaven and Earth, my dear Horatio—," he quoted. "We seem to have stumbled fairly into the latest six shilling sensationalism." He glanced at the watch on his wrist, "By the Lord Harry, it's almost ten o'clock. I could tackle the proverbial leg of an iron pot, I'm that peckish. I sincerely hope someone puts in an appearance shortly," he broke off and glanced round the room. "Who owns this musical comedy apartment, anyway?"

The doctor paced the room, his hands locked behind his back. "Do you know," he said, as he drew abreast of us, "I rather fancy that we are on the eve of a momentous discovery. Taking the curious events in their sequence, we have the finding of the Islands, the well-worn path through the woods of an apparently uninhabited island and our discovery of the giant creatures that eventually captured us. Add to that the fact that there is installed here something in the form of an operating theatre—so much is plain by the use of chloroform—and we are left to arrive at only one conclusion."

"Why," I broke in, "behind that door from whence the ether fumes emanated, is an operating theatre, up-to-date and modern in every respect. Though I caught just a glimpse as the door opened, I recognized the New-ington naphtha flares, and they have yet to be installed in the Prince's Hos-pital. Evidently, whoever uses the room insists on every known appliance."

Clovelly nodded absently. "Exactly. It bears out my theory that before we leave this island, we are going to learn that science, in the hands of the unscrupulous, can do quite so much harm as it can do good." He turned to me. "You, Huxley, with your medical knowledge, can you not glimpse at what is taking place here?"

I shook my head and coloured slightly. "I can perceive nothing more than is apparent to all of us. In some manner, the ruler or owner of this island has possessed himself of some secret formula for the making of supermen. This he does by some delicate operation, for the elaborately equipped oper-ating room and the modern Blood Filter are both necessary in the course of the metamorphosis."

"And have you no idea of how this transformation is effected?"

"Not the slightest, but I know enough to be aware that he has a tre-mendous power for good or ill. Just how he intends to use it is a matter for conjecture."

The doctor turned to Follansbee, but that gentleman was gazing intently at the curtained-off aperture. He closed his eyes tight and shook his head. "Either I'm going clean blind batty or my eyes have developed the shakes, but I'm certain that I saw that curtain move. I was just standing here when— look, there now, do you see it?" he broke off abruptly and pointed a finger at the gently moving cloth.

We stared as if fascinated at the slowly writhing folds, as it twisted and coiled itself into thick pleats, to belly out like a sail in the sea breeze and then resolve into tiny undulations that rippled across the crimson sur-face. But the culmination came when from behind it there arose a peculiar coughing grunt, followed by a gasp of someone or something struggling for breath.

"What fresh deviltry is this?" muttered the explorer uneasily. He raised his voice. "Anyone there?" he called.

There was no answer, but I for one was hardly surprised. It was not enough for Follansbee, though. He squared his broad shoulders and clenched his fists. "I say," he called again, "is anyone there behind that curtain?"

But the silence of the weird circular chamber was unbroken. The curtains were motionless now. Another rose bloom, a flower almost dead black, fell to pieces. Almost mechanically, I counted the falling petals—one—two—three.

The big watcher paused just one second, then with chin jutting ominously, he strode toward the aperture. I could not but admire the stark courage of the man, facing unarmed a danger, increased a thousandfold because of its indefinable quality. Though my heart beat suspiciously fast, I stepped up beside him and we were almost to the curtain when an unlooked-for contingency occurred.

"I would advise you, gentlemen, to leave things that do not concern you, untouched. The consequences of spying are sometimes painful in the extreme."

THE voice was suave and modulated, but it possessed the quality of a revolver shot, it could not have startled us more. We whirled as if stung and gazed with wide eyes at the author.

He was standing a little in rear of Dr. Clovelly, and his manner of entry was a matter for conjecture. Certainly none of us had heard him, but as he was standing where I presumed the secret entrance to be situated, I judged that he had achieved egress in like manner.

It needed only a second's scrutiny to place the man as an Oriental, but he was clothed in a neat fitting grey suit and shod with smart, square-toed patent shoes. His skin was smooth and butter-yellow and a pair of large tortoise-shell glasses bridged his nose, the huge pebbles making the eyes absurdly out of proportion with the rest of the countenance. He wore his hair long and brushed back off a high intellectual forehead. He spoke with just a slightest trace of accent, a metallic enunciation of the consonant "r"—a trait which characterises even the most educated of Chinamen.

"I trust, gentlemen, that you will excuse the somewhat rough handling. Strangers are not welcome on the island of Ho Ming, especially white strangers."

As the insolent voice ceased, a thin ironical smile curved the thin lips, revealing two rows of yellow teeth. But there was no humour in the narrow-lidded, purple-black eyes, for in their inky depths there lurked the cruel passionless look of one who had gazed too long on agony and suffering to feel the sorrow and pity of it all. They reminded me of the loathsome orbs of a hooded cobra.

Follansbee was first to recover from his surprise. "If we are not asking too much," he asked quietly, "may I enquire just where we are and what relation you bear to all this." He waved his hand around the bizarre apartment.

With all the slow dignity of his race, the Chinaman raised his hand. "I will explain in my own time," he said blandly. "It is I who give orders now and you will obey—" He smiled at the angry Follansbee. "No? Then steps will be taken to make you obey. We of Hankow have many methods of curing obstinancy."

Dr. Clovelly started forward. "We are British subjects," he cried. "If you harm us in any manner, the government will blow your island to Glory and you will end your career with a rope around your neck."

The Chinaman bowed and spread his hands. "If it eases you to entertain such delusions, Dr. Clovelly, by all means do so. But you have evidently forgotten the necessity of communicating your unfortunate position to your Government."

"How do you know my name?"

"I know many things, for I am the chosen ruler of the People of the Ming Dragon. You have arrived at a most opportune moment—" the Oriental broke off abruptly. "Gentleman, I have a proposition to put before you."

He walked over to the black marble dais and seated himself thereon. For a moment he sat thus, seeming deep in thought, then he raised his eyes and glanced at each of us in turn.

"Now," he began, "I want you to hold no delusions as to your position on this island. You are my prisoners, for me to do with you as I whim. But you are all men who have achieved some fame in your respective professions and I have no desire to rob the world of your talents. So—I offer this truce."

He turned in his seat and directed a long slender finger at the doctor. "I know you, Clovelly, as one of the greatest of living authorities on the gland-grafting treatment. Your studies with Steinach in Vienna, when you unearthed the Cod Bone method proved to me that you had the business of glanding and rejuvenation at your fingertips. Mr. James Huxley, your assistant, needs no introduction to me, nor does your friend, Mr. Follansbee.

"You have, no doubt, been rightfully bewildered over the strange creatures that inhabit this place, hesitating to categorise them as either man or beast. Let me set your mind at rest, and inform you that they are neither and yet both. That is to say, they possess the characteristics both animal and human, because they are of a scale of civilization that is intermediate. They eat, walk, talk and work, possess the strength of ten men, live to an almost prodigious age, and lastly, possess a certain immunity from sickness and disease. They are my Gland Men and are the latest triumph of modern science."

The monotonous tones ceased and the speaker, taking from his pocket an inlaid case, extracted a cigarette. I blinked my eyes and breathed hard, thoroughly convinced that I was mad or dreaming. The coloured shade stained the floor with its dancing hues, the rose-scented air seemed charged with the dominant personality of the owner. The scratch of a match recalled me and I saw the smoke curl through the nostrils of the Oriental, as he lay back and surveyed us with his narrow oblique eyes lowered to mere slits.

## CHAPTER III
## A GIGANTIC SCHEME

"Now, gentlemen, behind this is a story of patience and attention to detail that can only be achieved by one in search of an ideal. Up on the slopes of the White Headed Mountain, on the Western border of Tibet, there stands a Lamasery known as the 'Brothers of the Golden Khan.' It is the holy of holies, this desolate edifice, for in its sacred precincts there dwells the Most Illustrious Deity, the Grand Lama Dalai. He is a beautiful youth, with skin as soft as a maiden and limbs muscular and symmetrical. Though he has attained the distinguished age of two hundred years, he has the appearance of an unsullied youth, a fit spectacle for the thousands of devout Chinamen who yearly visited the shrine, leaving it richer by gifts and money.

"Now, my father entered that Lamasery as a youth, not because of any religious urgings, but because he regarded the permanent youth of their Deity to be nothing more than a gigantic hoax to attract money and notoriety to their shrine. He knew that the priests must possess some miraculous secret of preserving eternal youth and he meant to obtain that formula, cost what it may. That the task was no sinecure was obvious, but he had the patience and perseverance that only one of the East can inherit.

"For forty long years, my father lived with the priests, and he was just on the point of achieving his life's desire, when he was betrayed by a treacherous servant. He was caught and after a year of endless torture eventually made his escape. He fled to Hankow, where I was studying surgery and delivered into my hands the sacred tomes containing the great secret formula. Further information I could not receive, for amongst other things, the Lama priests had torn my father's tongue from his mouth, thus making him dumb forever.

"Then followed a reign of terror for us. My father and I flew from place to place, but nowhere could we escape the watchful eye of the vengeful priests, who, by that time, had discovered the missing volumes. At length, I evolved a plan by which we would be free from further persecution. I personally sought an interview with the Great Emperor Dragon, the great Shem Sing, and laid my plans before him. He was delighted with the idea, and not only gave orders that I should be protected, but also agreed to finance the scheme in view.

"One of the chapters in the book dealt extensively with that branch of anatomy known as the Endocrine Glands. As you gentlemen are aware, this is but a newly discovered phase of surgery, but to the Holy Brothers, it had been old knowledge. There is nothing in this earth so strange and fantastic as the history of those obscure bodily organs that mean more than life to us.

"Amongst other things, the two most frequently mentioned were the thyroid, that shield-like gland astride our Adam's apple and the pituitary, hanging from the base of our brain by a hollow stem. The pituitary controls our growth, but the thyroid controls everything that makes our life worthwhile.

"Children with deficient thyroids—from atrophy, removal or injury—become things horrible to look upon, gibbering idiotic dwarfs—heavy featured and twisted in body. Cretins they are called, for they never metamorphose into normal adults. Hence the importance of the obscure organ.

"But the Brethren experimented on aquatic larvae. They caught a tadpole and removed its thyroid. It never became a frog, but remained a tadpole for the remainder of its existence. On the other hand, they gorged a tadpole with thyroxin, and almost immediately it changed to a frog. I say changed, gentlemen, not grew—because the tadpole did not grow. The frog, fully developed, remained only as large as a tadpole. Thyroxin feeding produces two results, it hastens metamorphosis, but retards growth.

"With this information, my father and myself started out upon our momentous scheme. We obtained the thyroid from an ape and transferred it to that of a three-months-old baby. Almost immediately the child began to exhibit simian characteristics—then the body began to alter shape. But the child grew no larger than the day the gland was transferred and it was to overcome this difficulty that we set ourselves.

"Now the growth, or pituitary gland is not a vital organ, but a normal gland is essential to normal life. An operation on the pituitary is enormously difficult—for one thing, it is only as big as the tip of the little finger and it is so near the centre of the head that it is next to impossible to localize. But we finally overcame this difficulty and all was ready for the final experiment.

"THIS was the scheme in mind. If a grafted thyroid could transform a child to an ape, would it not be possible to transplant the glands of an anthropoid to that of a growing human? An operation on the pituitary would overcome the difference in growth and the finished product would possess the strength and power of an anthropoid and the intelligence and appearance of a human being.

"Such was the scheme that occurred to me. Luckily I was possessed of twelve sisters, and each, in turn gave their lives for science. Still we were unsuccessful, the creatures of our experiments being things hideous and fearful to look upon, that were killed as soon as tested. Then our faithful servants professed themselves willing to give their lives. Three there were and by a strange freak of Fate, it was the last attempt that was successful. We achieved a huge beast, such as you see here today, and it was this creature that we took to the Emperor as proof of our good faith. Then we outlined to him our momentous scheme.

"What a great thing it would be for our decadent empire could we but manufacture an army of these Gland Men. They would be immune from hurts and outlive the strongest of soldiers. Again, they would seek for nothing in return, fighting but to appease their brutal instincts. With an army such as these, we could wipe the entire White Race from the world and restore China to her rightful position as Mistress of the World. The magnificence of the scheme fairly dazzled me, such prodigious possibilities did it possess.

"Here you see the great scheme in embryo. Thanks to the magnificent generosity of the Emperor, we have unlimited facilities for the great scheme in progress."

Once more he paused, and the hard black eyes, alight with the fire of fanaticism, gleamed and sparkled like wet anthracite coal. He leaned forward and waved a thin yellow hand in our direction.

"White men," he said, "Here is an undoubted truth. In a decade this colony will be a serious menace to your white civilization—and in fifty years we will sweep you off the earth. China will return to her rightful position, and the world will bow down to the despised Chinaman."

"Really," Follansbee's coolness was superb, "And if we whites are considered such a nonentity, why expound to such a length to us?"

The light died out of the Oriental's countenance and the eyes narrowed perceptibly. He inhaled deeply on his cigarette and as the smoke curled through the flat nostrils, the pungent odour hung in wisps on the heavily scented air.

"My Gland Men," he murmured, so softly that the purring voice was scarcely heard, "lack but two things. One—the method of human speech, and the other—of paramount importance—is their sexlessness. It is upon you gentlemen that I rely for the rectification of those surgical errors."

Dr. Clovelly took a step forward. "And if we refuse?"

The Oriental shrugged his shoulders. "I have just attended to two operations this morning," he replied meaningly, "and in the advent of your refusal, I will attend three more tomorrow morning."

"Do you mean that you operate here?"

"Certainly. Why not? We have every facility of modern science, and a laboratory that is the last word in the up-to-date."

"But—but—" babbled Dr. Clovelly, amazedly, "Your supplies—and chemicals." Ho Ming gave an upward gesture of his hands.

"Wireless," he explained. "A call to our base will bring a ship load of supplies within a few days. That is what has cut that path through the undergrowth."

"But your—er—patients do not recover immediately. You must have a hospital, or something of the kind?"

"If you consent to my proposition, Dr. Clovelly, I will make arrangements for you to be shown over my island as soon as it is possible."

Clovelly spread his hands helplessly. "Under the circumstances," he acquiesced, "we can do nothing but submit. But you must promise that we meet with no treachery."

The Chinaman inclined his head. "Have no fear of that," he assured us. "And now I shall show you around. You shall see that this is no wild dream of mine. It has taken years to accrue the knowledge and effects, but it is all to the one purpose."

With his quick, silent walk, he crossed over to the crimson curtain and pausing before it, spoke for some moments in the pure liquid Ho Man dialect. From inside there came a rustle of silken garments and suddenly, as we listened, there arose again that evil voiceless murmuring that we had heard on the previous occasion. Ho Ming turned to and waved a hand in the direction of the curtained aperture.

"My illustrious Father—The Great Bald One—The Learned Wong K'tai, who first wrested the priceless formula from the Lama pigs and to whose patience and saintly perseverance, this island owes its existence."

So that was the solution of the peculiar sounds, and I was about to pace forward, when Ho Ming, with a peculiar smile held out restraining arm. He then picked up a slim ivory wand, and with a quick movement stabbed it at the curtain. Immediately there came a *szz* and a bright flash as something shot through the air, but so quick—so unexpected—was the whole action that I did not have time to glimpse the object. The next moment the Chinaman, with a bland smile, moved forward and held aside the curtains.

The room into which we looked could not have been more than six feet square, but screened on all sides as it was by rich hangings, it gave the illusion of depths that was very cleverly carried out. The black velvet hangings were worked with a bewildering array of birds and flowers, in colours both rare and wonderful. Scarlet parrots, blue peacocks were entwined with crimson poppies and roses of every shade and hue. Gaudy though it undoubtedly was, there was nothing in it to offend the eye, for the colours were blended with the skill of an expert.

In the center of the room, in a huge chair that almost enveloped the slight form, sat the oldest Chinaman I have ever set eyes on. He was thin to emaciation and the rich purple robe he wore hung in folds about his skinny frame. His head, bowed slightly with the weight of years, was as bald as an egg and the long beard that hung from his chin was white as the driven snow. The face was seamed with a thousand wrinkles and only the beady eyes, sunk deep in the lined countenance, gave a hint of vitality. He sat motionless, like some grotesque idol, a fit parent to this place of sinister secrets.

Ho Ming entered the room and pausing before the chair, fell upon his knees. For some moments, there was a silence, then slowly, like one in a trance, one claw-like hand, yellow as ivory, was raised in salute. For a second it remained poised, then, as though its owner lacked strength to hold it in place, it fell limply back onto the chair. Ho Ming rose to his feet.

"The great one salutes you, and wishes you well. Gentlemen, you may consider yourselves doubly honoured."

He re-crossed the room and as he made his way through the doorway, the curtain dropped behind him. Synonymous with it came the swish and the flash, and the Oriental with quick movement touched a portion of the woodwork. Immediately the object came to rest and for the first time we saw it. It was a blade, some six inches wide and the width of the doorway, a blade razor-edged and weighted at the top. It ran down between the doorposts on a concealed wire, very much on the principle of the French device, the guillotine, at an almost incredible speed. The Oriental released it, and it disappeared into a slot in the floor.

"Quite Chinese," he purred. "Borrowed from the palaces of the Emperors. By the way," he turned to Follansbee, "It was as well that I arrived when I did, this morning, for had you stepped across the threshold, you would have been cleft in half." He walked to the book- lined wall and moved his hands in the circular manner we had noticed before. With a click of concealed machinery, the section swung back, and we filed into the dimly lit passage. "Now," our guide cautioned us, "keep close to me and offer no resistance, no matter what happens."

## CHAPTER IV
## AWAITING THE STORM

The contrast between the brightly lit room and the semi-darkness of the passage was so great that for some moments I could perceive nothing, far less distinguish any objects. The luminous dial of my watch told me that it was just past the noon hour and I could not but help reflecting that we had certainly spent a crowded hour. It seemed incredible that all our strange adventures had been compassed in such a short space of time; already we seemed to have spent months on the island, and England and Prince Alfred's Hospital seemed very far away.

Gradually, as my eyes became accustomed to the light, I made out the various doors leading from the strange apartment. The Oriental Ho Ming took the lead and we others trailed behind him. At the end of the passage he paused before a door.

"This," our guide explained with a gesture, "is the laboratory. Here it is that the serum is compounded that speeds up our workers and helps them to overcome the laziness that they inherit from the anthropoid side of their nature. Adrenin, obtained as you know, from the adrenals near the kidneys, forms a large percentage of the serum. Adrenin is the greatest and most natural stimulant known to mankind."

He threw open the door and we surveyed a long low room, with wooden benches running the entire length. Upon these were placed a heterogeneous collection of scientific instruments—microscopes, galvanometers and centrifuges. Everything was scrupulously clean and three assistants in spotless overalls hovered silently about the room. Ho Ming gave a sharp order and immediately one of the men crossed to the bench and procured a test tube half-full of some dirty brown liquid. This he placed in his master's hand.

"This is the inoculation serum," explained the Chinaman. "You must understand that the ape-glands are incredibly strong and that if left to themselves, must ultimately reduce their owner to a state of bestial idiocy. To prevent this, an injection of the serum is necessary at least once a week. The result of the adrenin in the blood is at once apparent. It speeds up the sluggish heart beat, drives fatigue from the muscles, and prepares the body for emergency function. A very simple formula," he returned the tube to its place as he spoke, "I discovered it something like two years ago."

He closed the door and we retraced our steps along the passage. "Removal of the thyroids and parathyroids necessitates cutting away certain portions of the larynx," he was explaining to the doctor. "We tried cutting through the windpipe into the cricoid cartilage—" and he rambled away into the realms of surgery with Clovelly listening delighted and entranced.

I took advantage of his immersion to drop back with Follansbee. "What do you think of it all, anyway?" I muttered.

He surveyed me for a moment, his grey eyes lighted humorously. "Two things strike me with perturbing force. One is that our Oriental friend is a loyal fanatic and means every word he says. The other is that we are in the very devil of a hole and I don't mind telling you young fellow, that just at present, I fail to see the tiniest loophole of escape."

"Do you think the man is mad?" I murmured, having digested the somewhat disturbing statement of the other.

Follansbee shrugged his shoulders—"He may be," he assented. "There is no doubt that he is clever—and cleverness and insanity often go hand in hand."

I glanced to where the two men were holding excited converse. "I do believe that Dr. Clovelly is really enjoying himself," I remarked softly. "He's hanging on to the Chinaman's words as though they were pearls of great price."

The other man smiled, a trifle grimly. "I think that the doctor will be quite safe," he returned. "It's little us that's worrying this child. You see, we may be guests of honor for as long as the childish vanity of our hosts continues, but one day, they'll run short of raw material, and then—" he made an expressive gesture.

I was about to reply, when the Chinaman paused with his hand on another door. He regarded us suspiciously as we walked up together and his voice was as sweet as honey as he observed.

"Do not linger behind, my friends," he glanced over his shoulder as he spoke. "There are many strange things in the abode of Ho Ming. Fingers that claw and grasp, hands that tear and break. It is very foolish to stray behind."

WITH that he pushed the door and as it swung open, we glimpsed a well- lighted apartment, with twin rows of beds running along either side. Around two of the nearest, white screens were placed and from behind one of these a faint moaning emanated. The air was charged with the acrid tang of carbolic and as before, everything spoke of scrupulous attention to detail.

"My hospital," it was explained. "My patients come here from the operating tables and from here they emerge to the outbuildings, to do their allotted share among their fellows. There is no intervening period, which we know as convalescence. A week in hospital is long enough for the newly grafted gland to function. Then sunlight, fresh air and hard work do the rest. It is amazingly simple."

"But," I interpolated, "Where do you get your material to work on? It must come rather hard to find men willing to sacrifice themselves to this sort of Roman holiday."

"Convicts from the State Prisons furnish us with much work," was the cold reply. "Murderers, servants, and occasionally a few are pressed into service by my assistants, who form a modern equivalent to your old-time press-gang."

I grinned a trifle rudely. "Bang goes your dream of world revolution," I returned, "if that is how you progress. After weeding your prisons clear of undesirable characters the magnum opus will languish and finally die of insufficient means of support."

Ho Ming turned his unfathomable black eyes upon me. "Presumptous fool," he said, coldly. "China now possesses an army of six thousand men, drilled and perfect in the art of war. As soon as circumstances will allow sufficient serum will be despatched and under the treatment of my assistants, every soldier will become a Gland Man. After that every man who enters the army will be likewise glanded, and in time we shall possess an entire army of these supermen."

I raised no more questions, for if the Oriental was insane, there was assuredly method in his madness. In fact the gigantic scheme was too complete, and for the first time, the true meaning of this man's insane dream chilled me with its appalling possibilities. The doctor's voice broke in on my reflections.

"And are all your operations successful?" he asked. "In such a delicate business as this, one would think the failures outweighed the successes."

Ho Ming looked at the speaker, his eyes alight with a peculiar gleam. "Yes," he said, slowly, "we do have failures, in spite of our precautions. Before you see them, I warn you—they are not pretty to look upon."

He led the way through a side door and we found ourselves once more in the day light. The weather had changed completely since our sojourn inside. The sky, brassy before, was now almost clear, the hard blue sullied by a thick band of black clouds that spread themselves like some ebon canopy across the eastern sky. Little puffs of wind stirred the dust and dried leaves at our feet, whirling them into the blue. The atmosphere was thick and heavy, so heavy indeed, that some difficulty was experienced in breathing, and the sun poured down with a fierce heat that was almost unbearable. The silence was broken intermittently by a low sibilant hum.

Follansbee glanced curiously around him. "It's coming," he said appreciatively, "It's coming, and by Heaven, I pity this place if it strikes it."

We skirted the main building and passed through the high wooden stockade till we reached the outbuildings. Some little way further on, we could perceive a number of the queer inhabitants engaged in erecting a new structure. They swung the huge tree-trunks as though they were light sticks and in an amazingly short time, the central framework was raised.

We passed a long building, constructed of rough-hewn timbers, containing a number of small cubicles. Each separate room had its neatly folded mattress and shining eating utensils. The place contained no comforts whatever—just the bare necessities of living, and was obviously the domestic quarters of the strange beings that Ho Ming called his Gland Men.

## CHAPTER V
## THE REVENGE OF NATURE

A peculiar smell was predominant here increasing in strength as we made our way onward. Everyone is familiar with the loathsome, animal smell that is prevalent wherever beasts are incarcerated. It emanated from a tiny hillock, built over an underground cellar. A gate led us down about a dozen steps cut in the earth and brought us up before a massive iron door, with a barred grating set in the top. The snapping and snarling of animals came clearly to our ears, and the words of the Oriental "they are not good to look upon" took on fresh significance.

The Chinaman, who was in the lead, stepped forward and sliding back the grating motioned me up. I peered in, scarcely knowing what to expect, and hardly had I taken one brief glimpse when I recoiled with a gasp of horror. Even Dante, in his journey through the innermost Hells, could scarcely have viewed such horrible creatures as haunted that underground pit.

There must have been over a dozen of them—loathsome—terrible. Some twisted beyond any semblance of recognition, others with stunted bodies and bloated appendages growing in various parts of their anatomy. They stood silent as I glimpsed them, looking at me mildly with their blood-shot eyes, gesticulating with their crooked, shrunken limbs. But the crowning horror was the undeniable fact that once these things had been men, even as you and I, living—hating—breathing.

As I stumbled up the stairs, sick with horror, I was joined by the Oriental, who stood watching me with a sardonic smile on his lips. I did not speak, but stood there, drinking in the thick air in thirsty gulps. And then suddenly it happened.

It began by the sunlight fading, and glancing up, I saw that the monstrous black cloud had overshadowed almost all the sky, leaving only a portion over the sea, that glowed eerily with an uncanny elfin radiance. The low intermittent humming had risen in cadence and was coming nearer every second. A patter of feet made me swing round, and there, his face white with terror, was one of the overalled assistants. He stepped up to the Chinaman and poured forth a string of incoherent language, that for a moment eluded even his countryman. Then I saw Ho Ming's face turn a sickly green, his eyes protruded, and he barked back a question into the other's face, and I distinctly heard the name K'tai. Then without a word, Ho Ming turned on his heel and, side by side, the two raced for the main building as fast as they could move, leaving me standing wide-eyed with amazement.

A moment later I was joined by my companions, and to them I explained the sudden departure of the Chinaman. As I spoke, several big drops of rain commenced to fall, and Dr. Clovelly glanced anxiously at the sky. "Hullo!" he ejaculated. "Here's that storm that you promised us, Follansbee."

But that gentleman jumped to his feet as though he had been stung. "Storm be damned," he exclaimed, "That 'storm' is a number one size typhoon, and it is heading this way. I give it five seconds to strike the island."

The terrific upheaval of Nature lasted three hours, and to us adventurers, crouched in the groaning swaying forest, it was the final denouement of our astounding adventures on the Island of the Gland Men. Towards evening the hurricane dropped, but the rain poured down with unbridled fury, sweeping and lashing the vegetation before it. Such a deluge it is almost impossible to describe, rather it was as though the skies had opened and the seven seas poured their waters through the gap. Even in the thick of the matted vegetation, we were drenched to the skin, and it was almost dark when we eventually crawled forth from our shelter and took our last look at the Island. The downpour had abated somewhat, but it still swept in our faces with the sting of a whip-lash, and at length, wet, half-blinded and weighed down by the weight of our sodden garments, we gazed at what had once been the realization of a fanatic's dream.

Such a scene of destruction and chaos beggars description. The sturdy buildings had been swept away like match boxes before a summer breeze. The heaps of wood and iron were still faintly smouldering and when I remembered the volatile chemicals that were ranged along the shelves, I perceived that combustion must have wrecked quite as many of the edifices as the howling typhoon.

There was the half-erected framework, now splintered and scattered. There too, the poor dumb beasts that had once been men. The cataclysm had burst upon them before their bestial minds had time to realize its significance. The rain swept mercilessly down on the inanimate hairy bodies, as though gloating in its power over mere mortals.

The high stockade was, by some miracle, still standing in places. In other places it gaped open, showing the destruction within the walls. Here the bodies were piled, corpses torn, scratched and bitten, telling of the panic that must have enveloped the community, as it fought for freedom. I wondered if any of the hideous denizens of the underground pit had escaped, but a glance assured me. The ruins of the main building were piled feet high over the vault of horror.

Of Ho Ming there was no sign. It was impossible that he had lived through the chaos that had enveloped the Island, but it was hardly probable that everyone was dead. We, to be sure, only owed our lives to our sheltered positions, but there might have been others.

The Island must have been situated in the very centre of the catastrophe; otherwise there was no manner of accounting for the terrible amount of damage. It seemed strange—ironical—that the toil and labour of a decade should thus be destroyed in a few hours. The Chinaman's scheme had been a marvel of completeness, but the best-laid plans—.

We retraced our steps in silence, each one a little chastened by the tragedy that we had passed through. We were nearly to the beach when I put the question.

"What made the Chinaman rush away like he did?" I asked Follansbee. "He turned a sickly colour and went for his life."

"Didn't you say that you heard his father's name mentioned?" the big man asked. "Well, it's obvious that the servant told him of the coming storm and he rushed off to comfort and protect his father. The paternal reverence is very strongly developed in the Oriental races, and he evidently cared for nothing as long as his father was safe. Recollect that all he had was made possible by the sacrifice of his parents."

We had reached the electric launch, beached high and dry where we had left it. As we swung it round, I voiced the unspoken question of the trio.

"Will anyone believe us?" I ruminated, "when we tell them where we have been and what we have seen? I very much doubt that I would, were a person to recount to me the—"

I broke off suddenly. The ground beneath our feet was shivering and heaving, and for a moment, I doubted the evidence of my eyes. The next moment it was still again, and I was about to ridicule the idea when Follansbee grasped me by the arm.

"Did you feel that?" he said. "For God's sake, get that launch on the water. There is going to be a lot of funny things happen here before long. Come on."

In less than twenty minutes we were in sight of the ship once more and then it was that Follansbee made the final remark.

"Not a word about our adventures," he warned, "I'll get Sparks to radio Port Moresby for a destroyer to clean up that Island. I suppose that it will be necessary to give them a bare outline."

And I turned to see the foreshore of the Island, still brooding and sinister, disappearing into the tropical night.

There is but one incident worthwhile recording, however, and it took the form of a radiogram that Follansbee received after his detailing the story to the Naval Authorities at Port Moresby.

"Searched water for some time in latitude given. Find no trace of Island. Suspect some elaborate hoax. Am temporarily dropping matter."

What is the explanation of that message. Can it be, as Follansbee informed me, that Ho Ming made his headquarters on one of these roving islands that are never in the same place for any length of time? Were the mysterious tremors we felt forerunners of another upheaval?

And if that is so, I often pause to think of the misguided genius that lies fathoms deep in the ocean and the terrible formula that must remain a secret till the sea gives up its dead.

# THE INNER DOMAIN
## PHIL COLLAS
### (1907-1989)

*Amazing Stories,*
October 1935

## PROLOGUE

The Chief Engineer of the Radio Corporation of Australia leaned back with a puzzled frown. The huge aluminium panels, studded with black dials and switches, seemed to revolve themselves into malignant, grinning faces which mocked his vain attempts to solve the great enigma. Yet the Chief Engineer's coldly scientific mind told him that the large receivers were but the medium of expression and that he would have to look further for a solution.

For five weeks past every station on bands between 1500 and 550 kilocycles had been receiving strong signals from an unknown source. They came in at full strength, over fluctuating wavelengths and blocked ordinary reception to a great degree. All over Australia this interference was causing much annoyance to the commercial newscasting companies and to other users of the ether.

Phonographic records of the apparent messages, taken and then reproduced slowly, were unintelligible and in spite of considerable research on the part of philologists nothing was found to indicate that the broadcasted utterances were in a present-day language, or akin to any tongue known to science. Indeed, the guttural, somewhat animal-like sounds were declared by many scientists to be of purely animal origin and it was suggested that a huge joke was being perpetrated by broadcasting the voice of an ape or other members of simian genus.

A small body of philologists maintained, however, that the messages received were spoken by a rational being, and from the phonographic records kept they proved to their own satisfaction that, because of the similarity of certain sound-groups, the apparent sense of inflection and the general balanced effect of completed sentences, only a human being could be responsible.

The public announcement of this opinion was, appropriately enough, made at a time when news was particularly scarce and both the written and spoken press made the most of the opportunity presented.

The daily papers and newscasters seized upon the problem from all angles. Ridicule and praise were alternately heaped upon the learned scientists who were persuaded to make long statements supporting their views. Much was written of interplanetary communication and budding scientists wrote of the possibilities of life on Venus, Mars and other worlds. All Australia awaited further developments.

The next move came when Professor Henry T. Caldwell, lecturer in ancient and modern languages at the University of Melbourne, after diligent research and study of the phonographic records, definitely stated that the language was human and had its origin on earth and further that it was his considered opinion that it was the tongue of the extinct Arnuna aboriginals, who once roamed over Central Australia.

As the last of this race had died some ninety years previously, on the face of it, the Professor's statement was palpably absurd and the press was not slow in saying so, especially as the Professor was alone in his view and could not, or would not show that any spoken records of this extinct language existed. Professor Caldwell's opinion fell upon an incredulous world and stifled interest in what was becoming a lively question.

The Radio Corporation had not been idle in its attempts to locate the source of the unknown broadcasting station. Direction-finders had indicated that the probable location of the transmitter was in Centralia, in the midst of a desert and careful calculation at last fixed a spot some two hundred miles from Kubana in latitude 26°40' South and longitude 128°56' East. Four fast planes carrying officials of the Corporation, members of the Aerial Control Police and two eminent scientists were immediately despatched to this spot, with instructions to silence the unauthorized station and to obtain an explanation as to the intentions of its controllers.

The planes were fitted with short-wave radiophone sets in duplicate and also with extremely sensitive wave-source detectors and audibility meters, these latter instruments being used to locate, measure and permanently record any wave-form between 15,000 and 50 kilocycles. Constant communication was maintained with headquarters as to progress and audibility-meter readings were sent at intervals.

Within four hours the investigating planes had reached the position indicated on their maps. During the past hour the interfering signals had been increasing in intensity until at last the audibility-meter's trembling pointer rested at "half-deflection." It rose no further but oscillated there while the planes cruised over the roughly refined area which the direction finders had mapped out.

For miles in every direction stretched the hard, sun-baked desert, bare and uninviting. There was no sign of human habitation in any direction and nothing broke the monotony of the flat landscape. It seemed to the occupants of the planes, that they were on a forlorn quest, direction-finders, receivers and audibility-meters notwithstanding. Under the fierce sun, the shimmering heat waves danced with a fierce delight and in spite of the motion of the planes the occupants felt unbearingly hot.

Meanwhile, at headquarters, the Chief Radio Engineer had been summoned to a conference at which various representatives of the bodies who had controlling interests in the Radio Corporation of Australia were present. Scientists, professors and celebrated radio engineers had also been invited and all listened eagerly as the reports came through the loudspeaker with a clear-cut crispness which seemed amazing when the thousand miles air-line of separation was considered.

The planes swept around, and separating, spread out to closely examine the country. For some hours they flew at a low altitude over the desert, even going far beyond the suspected area, but all to no purpose. Nothing relieved the monotony of the landscape and there were no signs that human beings had ever sought to establish themselves on such forbidding, waterless territory. The planes were forced to report their failure to the waiting conference and there presently ensued much discussion on the queer circumstances, both of the transmission and the locality of the unknown station.

Then Dr. Munro, a physicist attached to the Radio and Astronomical Station at Mount Kosciusko, rose to his feet and placed another theory before the gathering. He declared, with conviction, that he was certain that the interference was due to a natural emanation of waves at radio frequency caused by phenomena which, he affirmed, could easily occur in the realms of nature at volcanic centers such as Waikawa, New Zealand, Krakatoa, near Sumatra and Yianyo in Japan.

In other words, subterranean activity, rock grinding against ore, metals coalescing and intermingling with rare elements of the earth had set up an extremely powerful "natural" broadcasting station whose emanations were forced out in every direction. The "ground wave" soon died out but the "sky wave" traveled until it reached the Kennelly-Heavyside layer from which it was reflected at an angle that redirected the accentuated wave to the spot in Centralia singled out by the direction finders. "To put the position plainly," stated Dr. Munro, "the same series of actions, which take place in an oscillating crystal detector, has taken place on an infinitely larger scale in Nature."

Dr. Munro's statement created a profound impression and the controversy was reopened by other distinguished members of the conference who strove to prove that this theory was impossible, and for many days afterwards the scientific world had two minds on the whole question.

The signals continued with unabated strength for a further month and then, as suddenly as they had commenced, they ceased. In a few days the inexplicable occurrences had almost faded from people's memories, and with the fleeting weeks another unsolved mystery passed into the limbo of forgotten things. Nothing remained but a despised collection of phonograph records in the vaults of the Radio Corporation of Australia.

## END OF PROLOGUE

Some three years later, or to be more precise, the twenty-second day of August, 1981, a heavy air plane was droning its way over the southern portion of the Great Sandy Desert, which occupies a large area in Western Australia and extends to the MacDonnell Ranges of the Federal Territory of Centralia. On board the plane were John B. Patterson, president of the Roma United Oil Company, William Langhorn, the Company's Chief Engineer, and Charles Winslow, a nephew of the president and assistant to Langhorn.

The R. U. 0. Company had inaugurated oil-drilling on a profitable basis in Australia and held large concessions in the Roma district of North Queensland, but, unfortunately, the flow of oil was diminishing slowly but surely over the whole area, and it was only a question of time when the fields would be worked out.

The three men were in Perth, West Australia, arranging for an aerial prospecting party to explore the Wiluna district, to sink bores and generally to examine the country with a view to opening up new oil fields. Oil-bearing strata were known to exist far underground and the party was to locate, if possible, the runs of the oil-bearing strata. John Patterson and his associates had intended accompanying the party, for they all felt the need of a change away from the tedious routine of their everyday lives, but an urgent radiophone message from the North had caused an immediate alteration of plans.

An R. U. 0. prospecting party had struck oil in almost unbelievable quantities some miles from the Northern Territorian town of Boolaloola and advice was urgently required in order to prevent wastage, to quickly develop the field and to place the oil upon a hungry market. A plane was immediately chartered and within half an hour the three men were aboard and the huge Austral monoplane was rushing across the continent to its destination.

"Well," said Patterson, when the men had adjusted themselves and were sitting at ease in the comfortable lounge room, many thousand feet above Mother Earth, "Our holiday has evaporated, but we'll make it up later. If the strike at Boolaloola is anything like what Ryan intimated over the phone, the Company will be in an impregnable position and able to compete successfully in the East.

"Australia is near the great markets of China and Japan and yet we have a heavy adverse trade balance. Their oil is at present obtained from Russian wells, but we should be able to land it cheaper than the Russians with their obsolete methods of transportation. We'll build docks on the McArthur River and will only have to run pipe lines three miles or so. The strike was made in a good spot and we'll take full advantage of it?"

"That's right, Chief," remarked Lang-horn. "But have you considered—"

Suddenly the huge airplane swayed violently and lurched sideways, flinging the passengers heavily to the starboard wall. The engines were racing wildly and as the pilot, regaining his feet, leaped towards the controls, they stopped and a dreadful silence, broken only by the wailing of the air sliding past the dropping plane, prevailed. The plane was falling rapidly in a mad spin and the pilot's efforts to open the ship into a glide and to restart the engines were agonizingly futile. Something extraordinary had happened to stop all three engines simultaneously.

The end seemed very near. The pilot wrestled in vain with the controls, while the passengers waited with gritted teeth. Escape was impossible and they awaited the end. The plane spun with tremendous velocity towards the earth. It was only a matter of seconds now. Suddenly it came—the plane seemed to strike the ground with mighty force!

Winslow slowly opened his eyes and gazed around but he could see nothing. Stygian blackness enveloped him like a shroud; indeed so intense was the utter darkness, that it seemed to oppress and weigh him down. He remembered the plane falling, but try as he might, he had no recollection of what had happened—whether the pilot had recovered control or whether they had crashed. What had happened? But he could not think of a possible solution, and he turned to a consideration of his immediate position.

He felt stiff and sore and one arm was paining considerably. He closed his eyes and vainly sought to wrestle with the problem. It was some minutes before he opened them again, and to his surprisethe darkness was now less intense. The blackness, so strangely oppressive, was withdrawing, and in it place was appearing a soft radiance. Slowly the light grew brighter until Winslow could make out the details of his surroundings.

He was in a large square chamber, apparently hewn from solid rock, for no signs of joints of any description were visible. The walls were absolutely smooth and stretched upwards for a dozen or more feet to the ceiling which, in the soft light, Winslow could see was covered with some sort of a geometrically patterned design. The source of the light puzzled him. The whole room was light and there were no shadows.

The engineer turned to a fresh inspection of himself. He was lying on a kind of couch raised but a few inches above the floor. There were no other articles of furniture in the room and he examined the bed with interest. The material covering it was unlike any with which he was acquainted; indeed it appeared to possess a slight radiance of its own and under his fingers felt warm, like a blanket which had been placed before a radiator.

As the light showed no signs of decreasing in strength Winslow considered it high time to investigate his whereabouts. His left arm was still paining and under the light, for the first time, he noticed that it was bandaged and held in position by a curiously wrought strap, soft and pliable, yet obviously made of metal. This gave fresh grounds for wonder. "Whoever it is," he thought, "someone is apparently looking after me."

He struggled up into a sitting position and looking around noticed an opening in the wall behind him, a little to the right. "Here is a chance to find out something," he muttered and, feeling stiff and sore all over, rose from the couch and stood leaning against the wall. A sudden fit of nausea almost overcame him, but presently his head cleared and he commenced making his way towards the opening, steadying himself, as he moved, by the support of the wall.

The engineer had progressed but a few paces when he heard shuffling footsteps approaching him. He paused and anxiously waited. "Who could it be?" he wondered. His last recollections of locality was that the plane was somewhere over the Great Sandy Desert, and it was a well-known fact that, under no circumstances, was it possible to live on the barren, waterless plain.

\* \* \* \*

A figure turned through the doorway and the engineer gasped on beholding the visitor. He saw a large, brown man, clad in a robe draped loosely about his body. Of splendid proportions he was almost seven feet in height and his flashing black eyes seemed to pierce through and sear Winslow's very mind. His head was completely devoid of hair and a closer examination showed that he did not possess eyebrows and but very scant lashes. His legs were bare and shoes made of a glittering metallic substance covered his feet. But he was a magnificent specimen of humanity, beside whom Winslow felt small and insignificant.

The man stopped before the amazed engineer and commenced talking and gesturing. He used a strange guttural tongue which however was soft and not unpleasant to hear, but to Winslow it was utterly strange and totally unlike the languages which he knew or had heard spoken. The stranger pointed aloft and then to the engineer's bound arm and Winslow grasped that the brown man was endeavoring to relate what had befallen. He shook his head incomprehensively and spoke in English. The stranger listened intently, but it was plain that he did not understand. The robed man then changed his tactics and with an unmistakable gesture indicated that Winslow was to accompany him.

The engineer now felt considerably stronger. The sickly nausea had vanished and although his arm was paining somewhat he felt capable of almost anything. The guide led him through the doorless opening and along a wide passage-way which was illuminated by the same invisible lighting as was the room just located.

The queerly assorted pair moved forward at a fair pace. The way was straight and they passed many openings and cross-passages, and the engineer, glancing into the rooms, was surprised to notice that most of them contained machinery, the purpose of which he could not fathom by a casual glance. Many huge machines were working away almost noiselessly and save for a few figures of men who were consulting various dials and regulating a series of wheels set on a panel, there were practically no attendants visible. Some of the rooms were evidently living quarters for a brief glance disclosed inert forms stretched out on couches similar to that which Wilson had not long previously occupied.

"Where was he?" he wondered. Had the plane miraculously recovered and landed somewhere in that part of Northern Australia which had not yet been explored—a territory which, covered with dense jungle and swarming with poisonous insect life, had defied the penetration of exploring parties and which planes never crossed because of the risk attached to a forged landing hundreds of miles from the nearest point of civilization. The pair had now reached the end of the passage-way and a little thrill of excitement shook the engineer as he passed between the massive pillars which flanked the exit. For he was in another civilization—a new world—and a very strange world at that!

Everything was bathed in a soft radiance similar to that which had illuminated the passages, but here the source was apparent. Four thousand or more feet high in the air, a giant crystal ball hung suspended, by what means Winslow could not fathom, and shed a soft, even light in all directions. Further away another shining crystal could be discerned and further distant balls of radiance suggested that these mighty lamps were placed at regular intervals. Remarkably enough, in spite of their close proximity, they shed light only and did not emit heat. This fact Winslow learned later but at the time he did notice that the temperature—a pleasant and moderately warm one—was not appreciably different from that prevailing in the tunnels.

Immense buildings of a unique and peculiar construction rose upwards, to the very suns apparently, whilst along the great roadways which stretched in every direction, sped many strange vehicles, each of which contained one or more persons who presented the same hairless, yet impressive appearance as his companion.

"Where was he?" Strange ideas flitted through his mind, but he could not grasp the magnitude—the wonderful thoughts which they provoked. However, his guide did not allow time for thought or sightseeing, for he was hurried down a slight ramp to the roadway and motioned into a vehicle similar to those which were flashing by.

Winslow glanced at the carriage with interest. About ten feet in length, it was a pure oval in shape, flat like a disc and upon its uppermost surface were arranged two pairs of seats. The carriage was apparently resting on thin air for between the lower side of the oval and the roadway there was absolutely nothing—no signs of wheels or other supports! Yet the machine was poised in the air, motionless, some, eighteen inches from the ground.

The guide left him no time for investigations, for barely had he chosen the rearmost seat on the disc when his companion, manipulating a series of buttons set in a panel along the front of the machine on a kind of dashboard, caused it to move off at a tremendous pace along the great road amongst many similar vehicles, all of which, despite their apparently simple construction, were attaining incredible speeds.

They sped along between high buildings which flanked each side of the street. Built of an almost transparent substance, the like of which was utterly unknown to Winslow, their gleaming walls were colorless, and yet, peculiarly enough, seemed to effuse color of a strange, intangible quality. Many people, replicas of his guide, were hurrying in and out of the vast structures and it was evident that, whatever form their business or occupations might take, they were fully engrossed with their own affairs.

Presently the street widened out until it opened into an immense square which was dominated by a building of truly majestic and imposing appearance. Giant pillars of the translucent material, surmounted by strange and terrifying statues of queerly formed human beings and twined reptiles, supported an immense dome which literally scintillated light and color.

The machine drew up before the huge portico of the domed building and it could be seen that the structure was further supported by an inner wall, upon which great carvings stood out clearly and extended upwards for some twenty feet. Winslow found himself moving up a ramp lined on each side with further giant statues of the same grotesque figures, whilst between these were small images of a strange animal somewhat resembling a mole.

The line of terrifying shapes came to an end and the engineer and his companion stood before an immense golden door, which, unlike most doors, was absolutely spherical in shape, in fact but a ball of metal. It shone with a kind of subdued radiance and Winslow, placing his injured arm upon its surface, felt that same mild degree of warmth that his couch-covering had possessed.

A small golden ball hung by a chain from the wrought bracket affixed to the adjoining wall, and this his companion touched lightly with the tip of one finger. Almost immediately the great door rolled silently upwards, leaving a clear opening through which they passed.

A moment later Winslow found himself standing in the immense hall which he later found was termed the "Hall of the Living Sphere." Tall and stately pillars of the translucent stone, as the engineer concluded it must be, rose on every side to curve gracefully to the rim of the dome which shone with the soft radiance which seemed to be the most familiar feature of this strange domain. But the most amazing feature of the hall was a huge crystal ball, some twelve feet in diameter, which, occupying a spot immediately below the center of the dome, slowly revolved.

This was no ordinary crystal mass, as the engineer immediately perceived, for it partook of the nature of a moving cinematograph screen. Views of many kinds floated in and out of view—tall buildings gave way to busy street scenes, and the crystal occasionally darkened to show vast, underground labyrinths, along which figures were hastening. Another scene depicted men clustered about a large machine from which long tongues of flame were issuing and striking a rock-face which melted beneath the rays.

Winslow was fascinated by the wonderful moving scenes, so lifelike that he seemed to be standing in their midst. Suddenly, he became aware that the guide had left him and that three strangers were before him. He glanced up and saw the inscrutable countenances of three old men who carried staffs, upon the tips of which glowed small balls of crystal.

The men, over six feet in height, were singularly impressive in appearance and their bearing was one of authority. They were, like the other members of this people that Winslow had seen, almost completely devoid of hair and clad in long robes reaching to the ground. The most venerable-looking addressed the engineer, but the language was incomprehensible and Winslow shook his head and gestured that he did not understand.

A second then tried in what appeared to be a different tongue but again the engineer was forced to indicate that he could not comprehend. The three then conferred together in low tones and evidently arrived at a decision for the first speaker beckoned, in an unmistakable manner, for Winslow to follow him. He led the way into a small antechamber and, motioning him to be seated, left the room.

The chamber was some fifteen feet square and the heavily draped wall gave the impression that it was sound-proof. A large machine took up considerable space in the center of the room. Of a design absolutely new to the engineer, he could not even guess its purpose and was about to rise and examine it more closely, when two strangers entered carrying large baskets containing machinery parts, wire, tools and other material. Without taking the slightest notice of Winslow they commenced work on the machine which they partially dismantled and rebuilt in a different form, using the greater part of the apparatus from the baskets. The men worked swiftly and tirelessly and soon completed the task, gathered their tools and spare parts and unobtrusively left the room.

Winslow stood up and was again about to approach the machine in an endeavor to gain an inkling of its purpose, when the three counsellors, as he mentally labeled them, entered. They walked up to and carefully examined the machine, afterwards conferring together to reach an apparently satisfactory conclusion.

From an opening in the rear portion of the apparatus, one of the men procured a large helmet, that in some respects resembled the head-piece worn by deep-sea divers. Constructed of a strange metal, it was fashioned to fit over the top of the head down to the bridge of the nose, thus covering the eyes. Two bulb-like projections were placed in close proximity to the ears and from these a series of wires led to different portions of the machine. Winslow was motioned to a seat near this elaborate piece of apparatus and by signs was shown that the helmet was to be placed over his head.

He did not object. In the first place, with his damaged arm, he could have offered little resistance, whilst in the second he considered himself a sufficient judge of character to infer that no harm was intended. The helmet was adjusted over his eyes and he was in complete darkness. A strange throbbing became apparent and he knew that the machine had been set into operation.

Presently a tiny voice was heard, and marvel of marvels, it greeted him in English! "We greet you, O man from afar and welcome you to the land of the Arnuna." "Hullo," said Winslow foolishly, "How are you? Before you speak further could you possibly inform me of my whereabouts?" "Yes, O stranger, it was with the purpose of communicating with you that we adapted this machine so that it might transmit thought and will. You are in the land of the people of Arnuna and you entered our domain by a strange method.

"Know you that Koona-la, the greatest scientist of Arnuna, recently perfected a machine which he claimed could transpose matter at a distance—that is to say—something which is in one place could be transposed elsewhere, and that which occupied the second position would take up the first position.

"And that is what happened to you. After many delicate experiments, Koona-la successfully proved that he could, by careful and elaborate calculation, so arrange matters that the transfer was almost instantaneous for short distances and furthermore adjoining objects, not coining under the transposition-influence, were not affected.

"Some interesting experiments along these lines were being conducted by Koona-la, but on the last occasion he was called away on other business, leaving the machine in the care of his assistant with strict injunctions to leave the controls alone. The assistant, however, possessed an inquiring nature and desired to experiment himself. He phoned the force upwards, thinking that in this procedure there could be no danger, and set the controls so that a transfer would occur between the Outer and Inner Worlds."

"Outer and Inner Worlds," interrupted Winslow, "But what is the difference?" "Merely my friend, that you of the Outer World are now amongst the Arnuna who dwell within." "What! I am underground, then?" "Yes." "Well, that explains many things."

The voice continued. "But let us proceed in due order. Your questions will be answered later. Koona-la's assistant duly manipulated the controls and arranged for the transference of Inner and Outer World atmosphere. But, unfortunately, his knowledge of the machine was not complete and it so happened that a very extraordinary transfer occurred. One of our large workshops, happily at the time vacant, was transposed to the Outer World and the vessel which carried yourself and others, happening to pass over the field of disturbance, was carried to the Inner World, more or less intact. All your companions were killed and it was fortunate that you, yourself, escaped the same fate."

Winslow felt as one stunned. Now he knew what had happened, and the knowledge was all the more terrible because of the extraordinary circumstances surrounding it. He could not bear to hear more and begged of his informant to relieve him of the helmet.

"Yes," was the response. "We are aware of the shock you have experienced. It is our desire that you now rest and after a short period we shall, by means of a variation of this instrument, which is merely a means of impressing thought messages, instruct you in our language and customs."

Winslow felt sick and fainting for the bad news had hit him hard and he was barely conscious of the helmet being removed from his head. He had a dim remembrance of being carried from the room and then all became blank.

When he again recovered consciousness he was lying on a couch in a great room, the walls of which were decorated with elaborately designed, geometrical patterns that wound in and out in a truly amazing manner, yet all the time preserving one definite symmetrical de- sign. The room was almost bare of furnishings, which consisted only of an ornate hexagon-shaped table with six legs, a stool of the same shape and the couch upon which he was resting. He felt considerably better and his arm seemed almost normal albeit slightly stiff.

One of the counsellors now entered the room and proceeded to examine

Winslow carefully all over with the practiced skill that indicated considerable medical experience. An exclamation of satisfaction escaped him on the conclusion of the examination and the engineer gathered that the physicist was well satisfied with his progress. He next touched a button set in the wall near the head of the couch and an instant later two assistants appeared in the doorway wheeling in the thought-transmission apparatus. The helmet was again placed over his head and the counsellor spoke.

"You have now almost completely recovered your health and your mental powers are normal. It is the desire of the High Council of Arnuna that you be instructed in such history of the people as will lead you to obtain a clear understanding of our civilization and your position. When the history has been imparted to you by means of this machine, the apparatus will be altered and adapted so that you may be instructed in the Arnunan language. At a later period you will have to appear before the High Council, or its officers, to answer questions concerning the Outer World.

"I now commence the story of the people of Arnuna.

Ages ago, when the world was young, the people of Arnuna dwelt upon the surface of the earth in a land which was rich in all things necessary for a happy and contented existance. The Arnuna were at peace with all neighboring peoples and tilled the soil and killed the beasts of the jungle without hindrance from any.

Then disaster came. A mighty force of fair-skinned metal-clad warriors, worshippers of the Sun-God whom they termed Rah, and who carried metal weapons far superior to our spears of wood, came down like a scourge from the northern land of Mu. They took possession of the country wherein dwelt the Arnuna and other tribes and slew, without mercy, all who opposed their passage or desires.

The Arnuna became slaves and lived but to carry out the commands of the conquerors who arrogantly called themselves 'Children of the Sun.' Our forefathers toiled in deep quarries and mined huge blocks of stone used to build mighty edifices that reached far up into the sky. These were the temples dedicated to Rah, the Sun, the god of the oppressors, whilst the poor Arnunan slaves died in multitudes so that the prestige of the Children of the Sun would be sufficiently established in the eyes of Rah, the Mighty.

The people of Arnuna were brave and many times did they arise and slay numbers of the fair-skinned conquerors, but each time they were overpowered and their lot became even worse. It was during one of these risings that a large number of Arnuna, both men and women, managed to seize several sea-going canoes and escaped into the open sea to travel they knew not whither. The canoes had been well-provisioned for a long voyage to Mu and the Arnuna were fortunate in having the wherewithal to keep themselves alive. They had no plans, no definite desire to go anywhere unless to a place where they would be free from molestation.

After sailing before a strong breeze for some twelve days, land was sighted ahead and they disembarked upon the deserted shores of a great country. Palms of many descriptions grew along the beach line, and beyond the palms the voyagers could perceive a dense jungle stretching inland. The elders of the expedition held a conference to decide upon a line of action and it was unanimously resolved that the Arnuna should penetrate inland as far as possible, there to make their home, far from the possibilities of pursuit. It was from one, Dak-la, that the best suggestion arose.

"Oh elders of the Arnuna," he cried. "It is well that we travel inland and keep away from the shores of this land, because _the Children of the Sun may follow us. But consider what we have to face, forcing a passage through thick jungle. I, myself, have inspected this jungle and it is well-nigh impassable. Here is my suggestion. Allow the men of the tribe to scatter far and wide along the coastline in search of a large river that flows from the in-lands. This we can follow to its limits and thus overcome the obstruction of the jungle."

Dak-la's plan was immediately adopted and the Arnuna were not long in discovering several watercourses, both large and small, coming from the in-lands, but the crowning discovery was made by a tribesman who had ventured much further than any of his companions. "'Na,' he cried, as he entered the camp, 'I have to tell of a strange river—a stream which does not flow from the in-lands to the sea but one which courses strongly from the sea through the jungle into the hinterland—a mighty stream which must travel an immense distance.

It will carry us far from the coast!"

\* \* \* \*

The Arnuna embarked again and for many days traveled down the stream. They passed through the jungle and wound by towering cliffs that stretched almost to the sky; by burning deserts and flat treeless plains, but the mighty stream never lessened in volume for it was fed from the inexhaustable ocean. Many fresh-water creeks and streamlets entered the salt river which was fittingly termed 'Lohaloma,' the 'Stream of Life,' by the voyagers. Game of all descriptions was easily obtained from the surrounding country and the Arnuna waxed fat and were well contented. As each favorable spot was reached, many of the tribe wished to end their wanderings and settle but the council of elders ruled otherwise. "The Arnuna must go on until the goal was reached and that goal is at the end of the Lohaloma," they declared, and the journey proceeded.

At length the pilgrimage ended; the promised land had been reached! The small fleet of canoes swept around a turn and at once an exclamation of delight escaped all. For before their eyes—the stream merged into an immense body of water. As far as one could see there seemed to be nothing but water. Near at hand the shores were visible, where the water entered, but they rapidly faded beyond the horizon.

Gaily plumaged water-fowl swam in every direction and signs of animal life were not wanting amongst the thick forests which came down almost to the water's edge. Everything necessary for their simple lives seem to be in abundance and after a little searching a natural clearing, through which flowed a small creek, was selected as the site for the camp. The Arnuna disembarked and set about preparing for a new existence, far from their old associations.

We will now skip through history until the time of the "Great Discovery." During the rainy season the huge lake, as it was later discovered to be, fed both from the sea and by numerous streams, was very full. Over a certain, level, however, the waters never rose and it had not taken enterprising tribes of men long to discover that the overflow passed down an enormous hole situated at the lower end of the lake. In the dry season water did not flow and curious canoemen, passing near the opening, saw a great cavern seemingly reaching into the bowels of the earth. Land parties had, at various times, timorously sought to explore the huge tunnel which, ever descending, appeared to be without end, but they had never ventured very far and learned nothing except that it was of enormous extent and occupied by strange winged creatures which were of little use for food.

One day, when the rainy season was at its height, a canoe-load of young men, sailing perilously close to the hole, was caught in the fierce current, and in spite of strenuous efforts could not force their craft into safer waters. The last that occupants of distant vessels saw was the canoe disappearing from sight down the 'Hole to the Bottom of the World.' This was the end, thought the watchers, and they sped shorewards to convey the sad tidings and the people rendered the usual ceremonies in honor of the dead.

Two wet seasons had come and gone and it was again the time when the water ceased to flow down the hole. Some little time after the cessation a solitary hunter was alarmed and surprised when an apparent stranger, clad in quaint garments, hailed him and requested to be directed by the shortest way to Dak-la, the then ruler of the Arnuna and lineal descendant of the ancient Dak-la who had long ago suggested how they should leave the coast by means of a river. The laws of Arnuna, then as now, allow people, whatever their station, to claim an audience at certain specified times with their ruler and Dak-la, in granting an audience to one who had merely announced his name as Yagi, a not uncommon cognomen, had not thought that by so doing the destiny of his people was to change.

The man entered and greeted Dak-la in the customary manner "I am

Yagi," he said, "one of the six men who were carried down the 'Hole to the Bottom of the World,' at the time of the second wet season past."

Dak-la gasped and felt as if an icy hand had reached out and clutched his throat. A spirit from the Kingdom of the Dead was before him and he knew not what it portended. But Yagi broke the suspense. "I am not a ghost," he said. "I am as alive and as well as you are. If you would but summon my relatives they will, I am sure, vouch that I am indeed Yagi, and I shall then tell of our wonderous adventures."

We shall pass over the joy of Yagi's friends and relations and tell the amazing story of the man who returned from the 'Hole to the Bottom of the World.' Yagi spoke with a clear and convincing voice.

"When the canoe was caught in the torrent we fought desperately to get beyond its influence, but to no avail and before we actually realized what had happened had been drawn on and into the great black opening. As can be imagined, we were terribly afraid and for a long time crouched down below the level of the bulwarks, expecting at any moment to be dashed to pieces. But nothing happened. The canoe was borne along by the flowing waters swiftly and silently. Utter darkness prevailed and even though we extended the paddles as far as possible we could not touch either the sides or roof of the tunnel.

Confidence was returning slowly and we eagerly debated the chances of escaping from our dreadful predicament. If the tunnel suddenly narrowed or rocks protruded above the surface, we might be wrecked; if we continued as we were going we might be forever lost in the bowels of the earth.

The time passed; there was no change in the situation, except that we were being carried further and further along the underground stream. We had been, according to our reckoning, a day in the canoe, when disaster overtook us. The canoe took a sudden lurch and darted forward at a greatly increased speed. We huddled down, scarcely breathing, whilst our craft sped down the sharply inclined slope. We were conscious of falling rapidly and a deafening roar of water smote our ears. Then suddenly the canoe sloped sideways and in the pitch darkness we were precipitated into the howling waters. "It is the end," I thought.

But by a miracle we were not to die. Our six forms, shooting from the canoe, fell into the water far below. We were in a familiar element for since childhood we had been as fishes in the water. Everything was in absolute darkness and we were carried some distance along the stream. By dint of much shouting, which seemed but a whisper above the roar of the water, we somehow managed to keep together and miraculously found shelter on a ledge, which jutted out from what we imagined was the shore.

We huddled together—the six of us—and discussed our situation with voices filled with fear. Were we doomed to die in the blackness of the underworld? For better safety we had worked further along the ledge which evidently extended a considerable distance. The thundering torrent made speech somewhat difficult and we soon lapsed into silence. Our minds and bodies were alike weary and I sank into a troubled slumber, in which great demon creatures with huge circular eyes pursued a canoe that contained six grinning skeletons.

I awoke with a start to hear Yaska, the youngest member of our group, whispering in my ear. "I think I can see light," he said, "but my mind may be going and I want to be sure," he continued plaintively. "Place your head on the ground and look to the right."

Sure enough a very faint illumination was visible, as if light of some description was being reflected from a 'great distance. I cried aloud in my excitement, awakening the remainder of the group and we imported this cheering information—a ray of hope in more senses than one. Eagerly springing to our feet we felt our way along the ledge until we arrived at a rock-wall, and in this we felt the outlines of an opening of some sort and it was from this opening the faint luminescence was coming.

We progressed along the tunnel, as it was found to be, and the illumination became brighter and we were able to see, without difficulty, the details of our surroundings. The passage was wide enough for two abreast and about double a man's height. The walls were of stone and the general appearance suggested that the tunnel had been worn out by the action of the water. We rounded a turn and the source of the illumination became visible. Situated in the passage, which here widened considerably, was a structure about half the height of a man and upon this rested a glittering ball of light that was so powerful as to dazzle our weakened eyes. We stopped in amazement. Who could have erected it, for it was obviously the work of men?

We fell to discussing the problem but our conjectures led nowhere. "Well," said Yeska cheerfully, "There is only one thing to do. We must go on. Somewhere in this underground region there must be beings such as we. Only such as they could have placed the light. We must go on until we find them." So we passed around the light and continued the journey. We had not gone a great distance when another light came into view, affixed as was the first, upon the top of a pillar and set in the middle of the way. As we advanced, these pillars became more numerous until we finally entered a huge hall which literally scintillated light from every portion of its large area.

All was silent in the hall of light. Not a sign of moving creature did we see. The room was, with the exception of a few large blocks of stone arranged around in a circle, completely empty. Again we stopped to confer. We had light but our bodies needed food. Surely there must be an organized intelligence who had placed these lights? Thus we reasoned, and being desperate, were not afraid of what might happen. We crossed the hall and upon the other side saw another entrance to a tunnel similar to the one we had recently left.

To make the story short I shall not discuss our journey through endless passages. It is sufficient to state that we at last emerged from a tunnel into a great open space.

Imagine, if you can, coming from a hole in a mountainside out to a large plain which stretched to the horizon in ever direction except immediately behind us. Imagine further that this plain was situated far below the surface of the earth and even then you could have little conception of what was actually our experience, it was amazing, almost beyond belief, yet this is what occurred.

We emerged from an underground mountainside or wall of rock into an enormous open space, so large that its boundaries were not visible under the light which was almost as brilliant as our sun of the outside world. We were on a roadway that skirted a large river. Trees and plants of strange and weird form grew abundantly on every hand and small animals, the like of which were entirely unfamiliar, scurried in and out of the thick, impenetrable underbrush.

But the most uncanny feature of this subterranean world was the remarkable stillness. No birds twittered; wind did not stir the branches of the trees, and save for the rustlings of the small animals, no sound broke the quietness. We were hungry and thirsty, so, casting discretion aside, we plucked and ate greedily of small blue berries which grew in profusion on surrounding bushes and drank the sweet cool waters of the stream that, strangely enough, was not salty.

With renewed vigor and hope we continued our explorations and followed the great road which bore no signs of having been used for a long time as large trees were growing on it in many places. To the right appeared land which had at one time been cultivated, for the regular lay of the ground suggested fallow. We were in a peculiar position, far underground, yet our present surroundings, in some remarkable way, reminded us of the great land beyond the lake, where we had spent so many happy days.

Presently a cluster of buildings came in sight and we- eagerly moved towards them. Built of stone, they were astoundingly strong in appearance. Each building was circular in shape and the whole group was set in a circle, each building joined by a massive stone wall which was found to be hollow, thus allowing persons to pass from one to the other.

On arriving at an entrance we had let forth a cry, but there was no answer and the sound echoed from building to building, finally dying away, to be replaced by the dreadful stillness that seemed a feature of this place. A round opening beckoned us and with a feeling of dread, and keeping close together, we passed into one of the circular structures.

Dust, dust, everywhere! It rose in clouds as we stumbled about in the semi-gloom and descending covered us with a thin film. Pieces of metal, made into queer and wonderful forms, occupied much space but these objects were likewise covered with dust and had not been used for many moons. We searched everywhere for traces of food but could discover nothing of an edible nature. It was very evident that a long time must have elapsed since the towers had been inhabited and we were glad to make an exit. The journey continued along the road and we entered a number of other buildings, but everywhere was the same deserted appearance and no signs of human life.

We spent many days travelling slowly and subsisting on the blue berries fortunately growing- in plenty near the roadway, and on the ninth day we found ourselves in the heart of a wonderful city—a dead city—deserted by its once thriving population.

It was a city such as you could not imagine without beholding. Buildings of immense size and of marvelous beauty flanked huge streets, along which multitudes must have once trodden. Strange metal vehicles, as we guessed them to be, were very much in evidence, lying haphazardly where their owners had left them. And in all the great city there was no form of human life. We alone were the visible representatives of the human race.

\* \* \* \*

Perhaps the most marvelous feature of this underground world was the fact that it was light and the light compared favorably with that given by our sun. Far, far up in the sky we perceived many huge glowing balls of light, evidently similar in construction to the other types of small crystal lights we had seen, and these lit the city and the whole of the surrounding country. In addition, light-balls were set in buildings and in streets which might not obtain the full benefit of the sky-lights from above.

We made marvelous and stupendous discoveries which would have to be seen to be believed, but from our point of view, the best discovery was that of food. Our curiosity had been aroused by a group of low squat buildings each closed by a heavy circular door. After many attempts we found out how these doors were operated and judge of our surprise, on entering one of the buildings, to see that the first one was literally crammed with food—enough to keep the Arnuna in luxury for a very long period.

Large bins and metal boxes were filled with different kinds of grains, berries and fruits, all in a perfect state of preservation, shelves were stacked high with enormous slabs of a substance, similar in appearance to our taro-root bread, but infinitely better in flavor; piles of sealed caskets, made of a shining metal, contained other varieties of food and large metal casks were found, on investigation, to hold different kinds of sweet liquors. Several other storerooms were also discovered to be packed with food, and another contained clothing, some of which I now wear.

This opportune discovery raised our hopes considerably and with renewed vigor we set out to explore further this wonderful city. We spent many moons in the astounding underground domain, and at every turn were confronted with new and marvelous things—with elaborately wrought metal appliances, wonderful structures, ingenious lighting effects which apparently, once fixed by the original inhabitants, remained functioning perpetually, and other objects whose purpose we could not guess. But nowhere did we find a living human being nor could any human remains be discovered. It was truely a mystery how and where a whole people could have vanished to.

By this time we had become sorely wearied of the great loneliness and longed to see again the cheery faces of our people but the idea of return seemed very remote. We still had vivid memories of the dreadful journey down the black tunnel, and it was clearly impossible, even if we were to reach the underground stream, to make our way back again.

It was in this extremity that inspiration came to me. I remembered that, for a considerable period of the dry season, water ceased to flow and that consequently the tunnel would be dry. Here was an opportunity to return and eagerly we debated the pros and cons of the project. A plan of action was decided upon and we commenced preparations.

Depots of food were established all along the route through the tunnels right to the waterfall, not now flowing, and at this point an especially large food-supply was accumulated. The work meant many weary journeys from the storerooms, but we accomplished them by dint of hard labor and the assistance of some small wheeled carriages which we found. These proved ideal for transportation purposes and considerably lightened the work.

AS YOU may remember, the tunnel in the vicinity of the waterfall was not lighted and we provided illumination by breaking off a number of ' the light-crystals from the large hall and affixing them at intervals along the tunnel and on the shelf of rock upon which we had landed and which led right to the foot of the waterfall.

With the food problem solved we made the ledge our temporary headquarters and set to work at the difficult problem of scaling the great height to the opening far above, down from which we had plunged that fatal day. With the aid of a number of metal tubes we had brought from the city, we built a series of ladders, and after endless failures, managed, by working from ledge to ledge, to reach the top of the cliff and the entrance to the upper tunnel that led back to our home. We now felt that victory was within our grasp. The ladders were so affixed that the full pressure of the water would not strike them and we were confident that they would easily withstand several wet seasons and the consequent floods down the upper tunnel.

This enormous task occupied a very long time and we had just finished placing the last ladder in position when a faint trickle of water warned us that the great stream would soon commence flowing again so we retreated back to the city, there to wait for the next dry season when a serious attempt would be made to reach the upper world again.

During the sojourn in the city we were not idle. We explored it thoroughly and discovered some more food storerooms. We made many journeys to the waterfall and watched the great torrent from which we were lucky to escape with our lives. At last the stream showed signs of abating and we cast lots to see who would make the dash up the tunnel into the world again. It was considered that only one should make the attempt, as it would be a strenuous journey and there was no guarantee that it would be free from danger.

I was fortunately chosen as the messenger and even before the upper tunnel was completely dry I had everything in readiness. I chose food that was light in weight, yet very sustaining, suspended in a cloth bag across my shoulders. For drink I depended on a metal casket filled with a dark-colored liquid, few drops of which quenched one's thirst. In my hand I carried a crystal of light and by my side hung a sharp metal bar. Thus equipped, I bid farewell to my companions who proposed to remain by the waterfall until my return, and I dared the steep upward climb.

I shall not enter into details concerning the difficulties and dangers encountered during the long wearisome journey. It is sufficient that I am here before you now.

Oh, people of Arnuna, a wonderful future lies ahead if you can but take advantage of the knowledge the underground domain holds. There are many wise men amongst us. They can surely solve the mysteries that the city contains.

"And that is the story of the first discovery of the Inner World, told in the actual words of Yagi, as inscribed on ancient manuscript," continued the soft voice of the counsellor.

I shall pass over the immediately succeeding period during which the Arnuna thoroughly explored the Underground Domain and the wise men were gaining some little understanding of its many marvels.

Through the ages geological changes were occurring in the Outer World. The great Lohalorna from the sea had ceased to flow and nearly all other streams which had once entered the lake dried up or lost themselves in the sands.

Our lake shrank year by year; animal life became very scarce and it was difficult to live upon the surface. A great council of the people was held and it was proposed that the Arnuna should leave their home and travel down to the great inner world city, there to take up permanent residence.

Most of the tribe supported this proposal but a section, led by Beelim, refused to do this, and a breakaway occurred. With their goods and chattels the followers of Beelim departed and crossed the desert, going we knew not whither, whilst the balance of the tribe passed down the huge shaft to our underground shelter.

Shortly after the migration had been completed great rumblings were heard in the earth and we were afraid that the roof of our subterranean home was about to collapse upon us. This did not happen but it was found that great masses of rock had fallen and blocked the passage to the Upper World, which we were nevermore to see again.

The migration occurred many ages ago and since that time the Arnuna have progressed far along the path of knowledge. Gradually we learned all that was known to our predecessors—the secrets and powers of the spheres of light; the method of extracting metal ore from rock by fusion and attraction; how to create the translucent metal from which our buildings and many other things are made—in short, everything the original inhabitants knew. We have gone further and invented machines which can read men's thoughts and transmit them for long distance and our learned men are even now working on a machine that will eliminate time. By it we shall be able to see far into the future and away back into the past.

I shall leave you now and you shall sleep. When you again awake the apparatus to educate you into our language and customs will be ready and you shall learn much in a short time. For the present, sleep!"

Winslow was barely conscious of the helmet being removed. He felt terribly tired and weary and almost instantly dropped into a sound slumber from which he did not awake for many hours.

\* \* \* \*

The engineer awoke. An attendant stood by his couch and indicated by signs that he was to partake of food that was set out on the wrought metal table by his side. The food possessed a strange yet delightful flavor, and when he had eaten and drunk of the wonderful liquor which seemed to be the elixir of life itself, he felt prepared for anything and eagerly awaited the coming of the machine which was to induct him further into the mysteries of this strange people, living far below the surface of the earth.

The machine presently arrived, in outward appearance being similar to the thought-machine with which he had had experience. The helmet was adjusted over his head—his education was about to commence. For a few moments nothing happened and then, in an instant, an indescribable confusion became impressed on his brain. Presently his mind cleared and there seemed to float before his eyes graphic word-pictures which definitely showed the structure and use of the Arnunan language.

Rapidly the pictures changed and he was led through all the phases of the tongue until he was seeing elaborately formed scientific words, as pictures, before him. He was reading a treatise on the purpose of the thought-machine and then was answering a question in the Arnunan language. Everything seemed to be occurring with bewildering rapidity, yet he was quite conscious of and understood everything. A voice broke in, speaking Arnunan, and he found that he could understand it perfectly. The voice spoke swiftly and clearly and Winslow listened with close attention to the remarkably concise and clear description of the social conditions and government of the people and felt as if he was listening to an ordinary conversation in English, so clear and impressive was the voice.

The discourse ended and his helmet was removed. Winslow, to test his newly acquired knowledge, immediately questioned the surrounding Arnuna in their own language, and somewhat to his surprise, for he had not altogether trusted the power of the machine, found himself understanding every reply with perfect ease. There was still much that he wanted to know and his listeners were often hard put to satisfy his somewhat strange questions.

Two of the counsellors whom he had first met in the Hall of the Living Sphere presently entered and joined the third who had been in charge of the memory-machine. The three conferred for a moment and then walked slowly towards the man from the Outer World. The tallest of the trio introduced himself. "My name is Alakla-la," he said, "This is Wandra-Uli," pointing to his companion, "Whilst our associate who so kindly conducted the education course is Nooni-Am."

The engineer greeted each in turn and then said, "My name is Charles Winslow and by occupation I am a mining engineer." He did not actually use the latter phrase but the Arnunan words which meant "one who studies the rocks." The three men started somewhat at the last remark and regarded him with fresh interest.

The conversation was maintained easily. All had much to say and Winslow was astounded at the great knowledge, spread over many different fields, possessed by the Arnunan scientists. They had 'progressed far in many subjects, some of which were very much neglected on earth, yet, on the other hand, there were certain elementary facts relating to kindred sciences and to petrology of which they knew nothing. But until he had reason to consider this amazing progress in one direction and neglect in another, Winslow forebore to mention the matter which might be well explained, when he had time to see the vast Arnunan domain, its resources and geological formation.

He addressed himself to Alakla-la and asked this personage what was to be his fate. The scientist thought for a moment, and then said, "As you have been told, every Arnunan, unless he be prevented by sickness or infirmity, must work, and from my analysis of your character I am sure that you will be prepared to follow a suitable occupation. If you will now accompany me we shall endeavour to provide a task commensurable with your abilities. You will also have every opportunity to see all parts of the Domain as you will have much leisure time."

The pair walked from the room, through the hall of the Living Sphere and down to the roadway, where one of the queer dics-cars was waiting. Winslow had learned that these vehicles were propelled by utilizing the repulsion-property of the metal from which the cars were made and the attraction-property of another metal that was used to surface all roadways throughout the Domain, but actually how this was accomplished he did not yet know.

* * * *

They entered the disc-car which started off at the usual paralyzing speed and whirled along the broad thoroughfare. Between the tall buildings which flanked the road the car sped at increasing speed. Overhead the huge glowing spheres shed their even and never-changing light. The inhabitants of the city thronged the sidewalks and filled the roadway with their cars but his guide did not stop to point out these things.

Presently they left the city area and sped by large, squat buildings from which faintly rose the hum of machinery. Then came a large stretch of barren ground and passing this the car swerved to the right and entered a huge tunnel, lit by means of small crystals. Many other tunnels branched into this and Alakla-la directed the machine into one of these, along which it flew at a somewhat lessened pace. Presently it slowed down and stopped and the pair alighted.

Alakla-la led Winslow through,a doorway and into a vast room which was fitted up in a truly lavish manner as a laboratory. Test tubes, queerly constructed retorts and pieces of machinery and apparatus were everywhere in evidence. Large diagrams covered a portion of the walls and a huge furnace took up considerable space in the center of the room. An old man, busily engaged in drawing strange hieroglyphics on a circular chart, looked up as they approached and greeted them with a courteous smile.

Alakla-la responded and added, "Allow me to introduce Sharl-Winsloo, a man of the Outer World. You already know of his arrival and allocation." The man nodded and addressed Winslow. "My name is Coul-Vani and I have asked that you be sent to me so that if possible you may be of assistance. You are aware, of course, how you entered the Inner World. I can only say that at present there is no hope of your returning for such an experiment will not be conducted until the possibility of failure is eliminated. As the Arnuna insist that all must work for their needs, you were allocated to my laboratory. I heard that you have a knowledge of geology and rock-formations. As a scientist, these constitute my special study and probably you will be able to assist me to a considerable extent."

Coul-Vani's wards both alarmed and pleased Winslow. Gone was his every hope of returning to the Upper World and he had now to consider that his destiny was bound up with the Arnuna. He was pleased, however, that his work was to assist a scientist who specialized in a subject of which he claimed to have a fair knowledge. He briefly thanked the two scientists for their consideration and Coul-Vani instructed an attendant to direct him to his quarters which were not far distant.

For some months Winslow worked in the laboratory. The whole system was at first completely strange to him, but as he grasped the methods of Coul-Vani he was frequently able to suggest improvements and to supplement deductions from his own experience. He learned much from the aged scientist, whose knowledge was most profound, especially in regard to the treatment of rocks—their dissolution into the component elements and their reassembling into different forms.

Most of the metals and many synthetic materials were obtained by the disintegration of rock structures and Winslow's work in the main consisted of experimentation towards achieving better or improved results. With more than adequate equipment at his disposal he found the work intensely interesting and he made a number of small discoveries of some value, for which he was commended by his chief.

* * * *

Winslow had been in the Inner World for almost five months when an event of paramount importance occurred. A great summons went forth to all scientists to assemble and behold the tests of the machine which would eliminate the effects of time. The proceedings were to be held in the Hall of the Living Sphere and the crystal itself was to be the screen upon which past and future events were to be portrayed.

Coul-Vani asked Winslow to accompany him and soon they were in a disc- car speeding towards the rendezvous. Here was assembled a large concourse of learned Arnunans, all eagerly discussing the possibilities of a machine which could resolve the past and future into terms of the present. Winslow was introduced to many of the scientists, all of whom were interested in the method by which he had entered the Inner World. They asked numerous questions concerning the world outside and he answered them to the best of his ability. He received invitations to visit each of them in their laboratories and he registered a mental vow to do so. Who knew but that it might be possible, with the whole of the science of the Arnuna at his disposal, to find a means of communicating with the Outer World and Home?

Suddenly all was hushed and the lights of the hall dimmed and faded out. The great test was about to commence. The dim outlines of the machine could be seen and a faint hum became apparent. The huge crystal alone illuminated the room slightly, as if it were lit by an inner fire. Presently it glowed with more vigor, then a haze crept over its mirror surface. The scientist operating the machine twisted several dials and then gently pulled a long lever. Immediately the haze vanished, to be replaced by a picture, clear and distinct, of the central portion of the city. Everything seemed to be normal, then a gasp arose.

A number of scientists had recognized certain features which were not now in existence and they realized that they were gazing on a scene which depicted the city as it actually was some time previously. The picture changed and time had flown back for a very long period. The city had shrunk to smaller proportions and Winslow realized that many ages had elapsed since it was as portrayed. Strange wheeled vehicles, quite unlike the flying discs of the present age, moved along the streets.

Rapidly the scenes changed, each one taking the amazed audience further and further into the past. At length there came a scene depicting the first arrival of the people of Arnuna into the Inner World. Winslow gazed at the ancestors of the persons now grouped around him with peculiar interest. He noticed their remarkable resemblance to aborigines such as he knew them; the typical walk, body markings, weapons and dress could be reproduced by scattered tribes of Australian natives to-day. Gins carried squalling babies and the young lubras crowded together, giggling foolishly. It was a perfect exposition of a typical aboriginal tribe on the move.

The assembled scientists viewed each scene with profound interest. Many were taking copious notes in their queer hieroglyphic script, the medical men in particular devoting much space to opinions of their ancestors. The mirrored screen became blank; then a new picture flashed into being. The spectators saw the arrival of the first Arnunans, the six who had, long ages before, vanished down the "Hole to the Bottom of the World." The audience watched them move from place to place, seeking for human beings and finding none. They saw them discover the granaries of the vanished people and they saw them making preparations for a return to their tribe.

The scene vanished and the spectators looked upon a deserted city. Nowhere was there any signs of life. The buildings alone stood, mute evidence of a civilization that had ceased to be. The grouped scientists stirred and whispered amongst themselves. Were they to now solve the riddle of the ages—the mystery of the vanished race, their immediate predecessors who had disappeared leaving no reason therefore; leaving not a paper, a book or a carving which might throw some light on a truly astounding event.

The machine purred softly and the operator twisted the dials strongly.

The scientists looked out upon a new world. The buildings stood as before, but the whole city was different. Now it was full of activity and life. Human forms moved in every direction, in and out of buildings and along the streets in long queer vehicles. Everyone seemed fully engrossed with his own affairs or the business of the community. Strange people were these predecessors of the Arnuna. About five feet in height, they were clad in gorgeous rainment. Their heads were large, much out of proportion to the thin, almost stalklike bodies beneath them. Long slender arms almost reached the ground whilst huge ears protruded from hairless heads. Yet, for all their oddities, these people were humans and Winslow and the assembled scientists studied them with particular interest. Was the great mystery to be revealed, the mystery of their absolute disappearance? The scientists were busy writing in their queer script and discussing the matter in hushed tones.

PRESENTLY the picture changed and the watchers realized that they were being taken into the future—the future of these strange human beings who had built up a vast subterranean civilization. Like a motion picture the scenes changed, always moving forward, and Winslow followed with keen interest, the efforts and advances of the people.

Then suddenly a mist arose and blotted out the scene. It presently disappeared and an amazing sight was revealed. Strange creatures were moving along the city streets. Huge, shapeless masses of a jelly-like appearance they were. From a more or less round body eight waving tentacles protruded and with the aid of these the creatures were bounding over the ground with quick undulating movements. That they were a dangerous menace to the inhabitants was very apparent, for weapons of all kinds were being used in a desperate attempt to prevent their advance.

Large machines directed a stabbing ray towards the invaders and holes were literally burnt through and through many of the monsters. Still they came on, apparently little the worse for a few holes. Then great bombs were cast amongst them and these burst with destructive effect, blowing many of the creatures into small pieces. But the supply of bombs was evidently very limited, for it was only at long intervals that they were projected.

The monsters were now in the heart of the city. Every now and then one of them would suddenly dart to one side and, extending a tentacle, grasp an unfortunate inhabitant. The creature would then convey its squirming victim into a great maw of a mouth and so clear was the picture and so transparent the bodies of the jelly-creatures that the horrified scientists could distinctly see the process of digestion being performed. It was an awful sight and one that would linger long in memory.

The grim invaders rapidly advanced, entering building after building, and devouring all whom they encountered. The puny weapons of the people had long ceased to function, for their crews had fallen victims to the quivering monsters. The scenes changed slowly and at last it was seen that the invaders alone existed in the city. They had spread in every direction seeking food, and so great were their numbers that all food not stored away in impregnable chambers must soon be devoured.

A new picture appeared on the giant crystal. The jellylike monsters were now skulking in and behind buildings. Every now and then two would meet, a mortal combat would ensue and the victor would finish the struggle very decisively by devouring the body of the vanquished.

Thus had the time-machine revealed the past and the great mystery that had long baffled investigation was solved. The city alone had remained, a mute testimony to a vanished people and an inspiration to a race that was to come.

THE purring of the time-machine ceased and an unnatural silence ensued, to be broken by the calm voice of the scientist who had manipulated the controls. "The past had been revealed, as you all have seen, and I trust that you have learned much. Later, I propose to delve into the future—the future of our people, but before this can be done I must make certain alterations to the machine. What has existed is still in existence and may be revealed by certain processes, but to the future this does not apply, and different methods must be used. For the present I leave you," and with a word of farewell he vanished into an anteroom.

The assembled scientists crowded together and eagerly and excitingly discussed the possibilities and potentialities that had been revealed by the pictures of the past and, somewhat to his surprise, Winslow found himself joining eagerly in the discussions. He had wandered away from Coul-Vani, and was debating the standard of civilization of the first inhabitants of the city with an earnest young man about his own age. A few chance words dropped by his *vis-à-vis*, who had said his name was Iala-Vam, however, had directed the conversation into another channel, and Winslow became suddenly anxious to continue the discussion along the new lines.

Iala-Vam had just said, "I wonder if their system of distant communication worked as satisfactorily as ours." Winslow started suddenly. "The Arnuna have a system of distant communication, then," he thought. "But how is it that I have heard nothing of it?" He then remembered that when he was receiving the education course a slight reference had been made to this subject, but at the time he had not given a thought as to what the statement implied.

He questioned Iala-Vam concerning the operation of the system and the young scientist endeavoured to explain. The technical description was, however, somewhat involved and difficult to follow, so, in order that Winslow might understand the theory and operation of the communication set thoroughly, Iala-Vain invited him to call at his laboratories and see the machine in operation.

Several days later, Winslow climbed into a disc-car, which he could now operate successfully, and whirled through the long tunnels. He stopped the vehicle opposite Iala-Vam's experimenting chamber and entered. Iala-Vam greeted him cordially and without any preliminaries at once entered into a discussion of his special work—distance communication. "As you know," he said, "sound and light travel at certain definite speeds. Both can be diverted and reflected from a straight course and, by the use of certain mechanical devices, sound and light may be controlled and amplified and made use of for many different purposes.

"For many ages the Arnuna have been able to communicate by the use of certain instruments to all parts of the Inner World and our apparatus has now reached such perfection that one can both see and hear all that is going on elsewhere, although strangely enough, the people take but little advantage of these facilities. You have seen the great crystal sphere. It can be so controlled that any part of the Domain can be seen, but it has not the attachment which allows one to both hear and see. Our instruments had reached a standard upon which it was impossible to improve, and, with little to do, the idea came to me that we might be able to communicate with the Outer World which we knew must be still- populated.

"Occasionally faint signals which we could not understand came in on the receivers and by a mere amplification we were enabled to listen to them clearly. The language used was strange and not understandable, but we were able to appreciate the music which, although different from our form, was yet delightful. These indications showed that the residents of the Outer 'World knew of distant communication and we resolved to let them hear a voice from the Inner World.

"By means of a neutralizer we eliminated the resistance of the great thickness of rock which lies between the Inner and Outer Worlds and, at regular intervals for a lengthy period, I and my confreres spoke of the Domain. We scarcely hoped that we should be at first understood but we considered that the intelligence of the Outer World would be such that there would be slight difficulty in recording and interpreting our speeches and then replying. But we obtained no response to the powerful messages and could only conclude that the beings of the Outer World could or would not understand them. Thus ended our attempts to communicate with another people and disheartened we dismantled the apparatus and commenced working on another theory.

"We have known for many ages that the Outer World was inhabited and we believed that we were the only dwellers beneath the surface. But our domain is not of exceptional size, and it is quite possible that other peoples also live below the crust. Several of our scientists believe that this is the case, and we now seek to communicate with these by means of instruments which will transmit impulses through the rock."

Winslow listened with startled wonder. At last there was a chance of establishing a connection with the world he had unwillingly left! He explained rapidly to Iala-Vam the great strides that radio had made in the Outer World during the last few years. He spoke of television and distant control of aircraft and machinery; of the experiments which were being made in connection with the transmission of power through the air.

"Oh, Iala-Vam," he said, "allow me the opportunity of getting in touch with the Outer World. It means everything to me. I shall never leave your country and my people may never penetrate the vast thickness of rock which lies between us, but our two peoples may learn much from each other. No race can hope to progress without knowledge and from the Outer World you would learn much. The Arnuna are skilled in many things, of which we possess little knowledge, and a mutual interchange of thought should prove very beneficial.

"In the days that seem so long ago I knew something of the principles and practice of radio transmission. Allow me now to profit by this knowledge and by your experience and experimentation. Let us together construct another machine such as you have previously built and let us be the pioneers of an intellectual link which will connect the Inner and Outer Worlds—a bond between your people and mine."

Iala-Vam smiled at his friend's infectious enthusiasm. "Yes," he said, "I shall immediately obtain permission to again construct such a machine and together we shall have success. I agree that both your and my peoples will benefit. Indeed, I had this idea in mind when I first endeavored to get in touch with the world outside. The construction of the machine will present no difficulties, as these were overcome in the previous attempt. You, Sharl-Winsloo, will be the spokesman."

The desired permission was readily obtained from Iala-Vam's superior, who manifested a keen interest in the project, and in the time which could be spared from their ordinary vocations the pair labored incessantly at their self-appointed task. Winslow found his slight knowledge of little use in this big task, and he was quite content to be instructed by Iala-Vam whose grasp of the whole subject was remarkably thorough and complete. The keen bond of self-interest further cemented their friendship, and Winslow spoke much of his boyhood and home-life and hopes, and told of the many little things that affect the lives of his people.

Iala-Vam, having built a previous machine, experienced no difficulty in following the same design from the prints that had been kept, and it was not long before it took a definite and reassuring shape. At last it was almost completed and the only thing needed was to connect up the elaborate wiring system which, because of its intricacy, Iala-Vam preferred to undertake alone.

However, before this could be done, an interruption occurred. The great summons rolled forth again from the "Hall of the Living Sphere." The tests of the time machine in regard to its ability to see into the future had been completed and now the scientists were to behold the future reduced into terms of the present, Winslow and Iala-Vam had no thought but to obey the call and with their respective superiors were soon speeding in disc-cars towards the great hall.

The great gathering was eagerly discussing the marvelous power of the time machine and the advantages to be derived by a knowledge of the future. All had seen the unfolding of the wondrous past and no doubt was expressed but that the machine would reveal the future, but upon this precise subject the scientists were divided.

An argument was in force concerning the inflexibility or otherwise of the future and Luin-Ko, an eminent physicist, maintained that the future was an inalterable, inexorable factor, which could not be influenced by man. "The future is unassailable and impregnable," he said. "We may see what the future holds but alter it we cannot." A number of the younger men were opposing this theory. "We shall certainly see what the future holds in relation to our normal evolutionary progress," they exclaimed. "But having thus seen the future it is in our power to alter our present mode of life, to invent new processes and generally to depart from the groove in which we are set. By so doing we shall mould a new destiny and a new future which the machine cannot at present reveal."

\* \* \* \*

The argument would have continued indefinitely but the lights gave a warning flicker and slowly dimmed. The soft throbbing of the huge machine could now be heard, and the audience settled itself to watch the unveiling of the destiny of the race. The crystal began to glow softly and a picture appeared on its mirrorlike surface. The assembled scientists saw the city set out fully, seemingly as it was at present, but a closer examination revealed that many new structures had been erected.

They had certainly taken one step forward into the future.

Like a cinematograph film the moving pictures changed and each time one could note improvement and progress. The disc-cars were now larger, swifter and of an improved design. Televisor stations, like newsstands, were now set at every street corner and pedestrians no longer walked the sideways for there was no need. The footpaths were moving bands and the populace were carried along with extreme rapidity.

The film unrolled and fresh wonders were revealed. The people now seemed infused with haste and bustle and Winslow was strongly reminded of the cities of the Outer World. He reflected that by now they must be closely in touch with the Outside World for men-made transmitters should now be easily able to send television pictures through the rock which separated the two peoples. The buildings presented more of a skyscraper effect, indeed their tops were not visible, for they went far above the levels of the huge glowing crystals which provided the light for the Inner World. The population had increased and the city had spread out in all directions.

It was only a question of time when it would prove difficult to comfortably house the people. Food would never be a trouble for Arnunan science had proved that inexhaustable supplies could be obtained from the very rock itself.

By some inexplicable means the time-machine actually focussed into the screen of a televisor and Winslow gasped at what he saw for he was gazing into the Outer World. The great glowing sun beat down upon a mighty city peopled with men and women of his own race, or so it seemed. A large crowd had gathered around a huge shaft, some two hundred feet in diameter, and apparently going down to an enormous depth. A man walked over to a large board, pressed a switch and an enormous inscription, "20—M," appeared. Winslow could see the people cheering and abruptly they seemed to melt and disappear. Just a glimpse it was and the machine was back again in the Inner World.

Winslow's brain reeled with the immensity of the thought. "20—M," 20 miles? Could it be possible? They were driving a shaft down to the Inner World and soon the way would be opened! He almost laughed aloud as he thought. The way would be open but he was looking into the far distant future. His body would have dissolved into its component elements and be reassembled into other forms long before the shaft was more than thought of.

The operator twirled the control dials and the screen became blurred as the future rolled swiftly backwards. Presently the scenes steadied and slowed down. A great change was now apparent. The focus of the machine altered until the scientists could see, against the wall of rock which formed the west boundary of the Arnunan domain, a wide shaft reaching upwards through the virgin rock. At the bottom of the shaft rested a vast cylindrical machine and through doors in the lower end of this people were passing out. Others were waiting to enter and the whole scene was, to 'Winslow, reminiscent of an elevator in a busy department store on earth.

\* \* \* \*

Presently the machine was full, the heavy doors shut and the vehicle moved upwards at a terrific rate to vanish into the gloom beyond the influence of the crystal suns. The people who had disembarked were moving in the direction of a large building and Winslow's eyes bulged as he perceived an illuminated sign above the entrance bearing the word "Hotel" in English. And, most amazing of all, the people who entered were white. The whole assembly gasped as they realised the significance. Communication had been physically established between the two peoples—the impossible had come to pass!

As the pictures changed it could be seen that many more of the great shafts had been constructed—the roof was literally being lifted from the Inner World, but apparently the Arnunans cared little, for everywhere the whites were treated as equals and they responded in kind. Suddenly there was an interruption; the time machine ceased to function and the lights came on.

The operator's voice clave the silence. "Oh, people of Arnuna," he said, "you have gazed far into the future as you gazed ages into the past, and you have learned in part the destiny of our race. That future is inalterable and though you have seen you are powerless to influence the course which the Arnuna must and will take. Your puny knowledge is as yet nothing. Generations must come and go before you can hope to learn and apply the slowly-gathering knowledge. I have revealed to you the future and towards that future, whether you like it or no, you will work. The time machine has fulfilled its intention. I cannot show you your ultimate destiny for I alone have seen and wondered much. One must leave to the generations to some their future and having thus shown you as much as I dared, I destroy forever the machine."

And to the astonishment of the startled scientists the operator directed a brilliant blinding ray from an instrument, which he suddenly produced, upon the machine, causing it to dissolve into a little pile of brown dust. The great crystal alone remained, glowing softly and unharmed. He turned to his guests. "The performance is now over, gentlemen," he said sorrowfully, and turning, walked slowly from the room.

Immediately a babble of conversation arose in the hall. Everybody wished to talk and but few wanted to listen. Winslow and Iala-Vam had much to say to each other and they withdrew to a corner where they could talk undisturbed. "Your prediction will be fulfilled," remarked Iala-Varn. "We have seen that the people of the Outer World at last penetrated the rock and that even before this occurred we and they were in communication with one another. We shall be the pioneers, the ones who will first establish the connection. After the next work-session I shall complete my machine and the Outer World lies before us. Call upon me after the second session and together we shall make the tests."

Winslow could scarcely contain himself during the time which was to elapse before he could see Iala-Vam. Several times old Coul-Vani spoke to him and so abstracted were his thoughts that he did not hear. He could scarcely sleep and at the earliest possible moment was in his disc-car speeding at a dangerous rate through the passages to Iala-Vam's laboratories. His friend greeted him with a smile. "I have everything ready," he remarked.

* * * *

It was an unbelieving, incredulous world that listened to the first messages from far under the earth's surface. The tremendous power of the Inner World had been projected through thirty miles of solid rock and on a 1000 kilocycle band had blocked every other transmission. The engineers of the Radio Corporation recognized the same force which had interrupted commercial radio some years previously, but in this instance the unknown announcer was using English and speaking of seemingly impossible things.

The voice gave itself a name. "I am Winslow," it said, "and I am speaking from the laboratories of Iala-Vam in the country of the Arnuna situated thirty miles below the Great Sandy Desert of Centralia." The engineers and other listeners gasped as they heard the words and hastily the direction finders were brought into operation from every quarter and, to the amazement of all, each pointed towards the interior of the Australia continent, to that great sandy waste which supported neither man nor beast.

Then the previous attempts of years ago to locate a transmitter in this territory was remembered and the data concerning this was brought to light. The world was beginning to believe, as it listened to the powerful voice of Charles Winslow telling his story and the story of the Arnuna people. The complete disappearance of the R.U.O. Co.'s plane was still fresh in the memories of the present officials of the company and gradually, as the story was unfolded, a sceptical world believed, and having believed, urged the Government to release from his underground prison the unfortunate engineer. But this was easier said than done and in spite of the vast knowledge at their disposal, experts were aghast at even the thought of penetrating through so many miles of the earth's crust.

The years rolled on and communication between the Arnuna and the peoples of the Outer World continued. With Winslow's assistance, learned men of the Outside World now spoke to Arnunan fellow-scientists through the intervening rock. Already attempts had been made to pierce the thickness but there were many difficulties to be overcome and the deepest shaft was only eight miles down with but scant possibility of being deepened.

Time passed and at last the melancholy news of Winslow's death was received from the Inner World and the peoples of all nations mourned him as a personal friend.

The period had not yet come when the two peoples would meet face to face but science was making tremendous progress. The whole world looked forward to the time when the Arnunan Domain would be accessible to their friends of the Outer World.

# THE BLUFF OF THE HAWK

## DESMOND HALL AND HARRY BATES
### (1911-1992)        (1900-1981)

*Astounding Stories,*
May 1932

Had not old John Sewell, the historian, recognized Hawk Carse for what he was—as creator of new space—frontiers, pioneer of vast territories for commerce, molder of history through his long feud with the powerful Eurasian scientist, Ku Sui—the adventurer would doubtless have passed into like other long-forgotten spacemen. We have Sewell's industry to thank for our basic knowledge of Carse. His "Space-Frontiers of the Last Century" is a thorough work and the accepted standard, but even it had of necessity to be compressed, and many meaty episodes of the Hawk's life go almost unmentioned. For instance, Sewell gives a rough synopsis of "The Affair of the Brains,"* but dismisses its aftermath entirely, in the following fashion (Vol. II, pp. 250-251):

"…there was only one way out: to smash the great dome covering one end of the asteroid and so release the life-sustaining air inside. Captain Carse achieved this by sending the space-ship Scorpion crashing through the dome unmanned, and he, Friday and Eliot Leith-gow were caught up in the out-rushing flood of air and catapulted into space, free of the dome and Dr. Ku Sui. Clad as they were in the latter's self-propulsive space-suits, they were quite capable of reaching Jupiter's Satellite III, only some thirty thousand miles away.

"Then, speeding through space, Captain Carse discovered why he had never been able to find the asteroid-stronghold. He could not see it! Dr. Ku Sui had protected his lair by making it invisible! But Carse was at least confident that by breaking the dome he had destroyed all life within, including the coordinated brains.

"So ended 'The Affair of the Brains.'

"The three comrades reached Satellite safely, where, after a few minor adventures, Captain Carse…"

Sewell's ruthless surgery is most evident in that last paragraph. Of course his telescoping of the events was due to limited space; but he did wish to draw a full-length, character-revealing portrait of Hawk Carse, and with "reached Satellite III safely, where, after a few minor adventures, Captain Carse…" learned old-John Sewell slid over one of his greatest opportunities.

The resourcefulness of Hawk Carse! In these "few minor adventures" he had but one weapon with which to joust against overwhelming odds on an apparently hopeless quest. This weapon was a space-suit—nothing more—yet so brilliantly and daringly did he wield its unique advantages that he penetrated seemingly impregnable barriers and achieved alone what another man would have required the raybatteries of a space-fleet to do.

But here is the story, heard first from Friday's lips and told and re-told down through the years on the lonely ranches of the outlying planets, of that one dark, savage night on Satellite II and of the indomitable man who winged his lone way through it. Hawk Carse! Old adventurer! Rise from your unknown star-girdled grave and live again!

Thirty thousand miles was the gap between Dr. Ku Sui's asteroid and Satellite III, the nearest haven. Thirty thousand miles in a space-ship is about the time of a peaceful cigarro. Thirty thousand miles in a cramped awkward space-suit grow into a nightmare journey, an eternity of suffering, and they will kill a good number of those who traverse them so.

For, take away the metal bulkheads and walls, soft lights and warmth of a space-liner, get out in a small cramped space-suit, and space loses its mask of harmlessness and stands revealed as the bleak, unfeeling torturer it is. There is the loneliness, the sense of timelessness, the sensation of falling, and above all there is the "weightless" feeling from pressure-changes in man's blood-stream—changes sickening in effect and soon resulting in delirium. Nothing definite; no gravity; no "bottom," no "top"; merely a vacuum, comprehended by the human mind through an all-enveloping nausea, and seen in confused spectral labyrinths as the whole cold panorama of icy stars staggers and swirls and the universe goes mad. Such a trip was enough to churn the resistance of the hardiest traveler, but for Hawk Carse, Friday and Eliot Leithgow there was more. On Ku Sui's asteroid they had gone through hours of mental and physical tension without break or relaxation, and they were sleep-starved and food-starved and their brains fagged and dull. What would have been a strong reaction on land hit them, in space, with tripled force.

So Friday—our ultimate authority—remembered little of the transit. He had but short periods of wakefulness, when the recurring agony of his body woke and racked him afresh, and only during these did he see the other two grotesque figures, sometimes widely separated, sometimes close, dazzlingly half-lit by Jupiter's light. But he was conscious that one of the three was keeping them more or less together, though only later did he know that this one was Carse—Carse, who hardly slept, who drove off unconsciousness and fought through nausea to keep at his task of shepherding, failing which they would have drifted miles apart and become hopelessly separated. He was able to maintain them in a fairly compact group by his discovery of a short metal direction rod on the breast of the suit, which gave horizontal movement in the direction it was pointed when its button was pressed.

But though it seemed endless, the journey was not; Satellite III grew and grew. Its pale circle spread outward; dark blurs took definition; a spot of blue winked forth—the Great Briney Lake. The globe at last became concave, then, after they entered its atmosphere, convex. This last stretch was the most gruelling.

Friday remembered it in vivid flashes. Time after time he dropped into confused sleep, each time to be awakened by Carse jarring into him, shouting at him through the suits' small radio sets, keeping him—and Leithgow—attentive to the job of decelerating. The man's efforts must have been terrific, taxing all his enormous driving power, for he at that time was without doubt more exhausted than they. But he succeeded, and he was a haggard-faced, feverish shell of himself when at last he had them in a dangling drunken halt in the air a hundred feet from the surface.

Primal savagery lay stretched out below, and there seemed to be no safe spot whereon to land. The foul, deep swamp that reached for miles on every side, the towering trees that sprouted their spiny trunks and limbs from it, the interlaced razor-edged vines and creeper-growths—all was a stirring welter of tropic life, life varied and voracious and untamed. From the tiny poisonous banal insects layers deep on the nearest tree to the monster gantor that crouched in a clump of weeds, gently sawing his fangs back and forth, all the creatures of this world were against man.

Carse scanned the scene wearily. They had to land; had to sleep under normal conditions, and eat and drink, before they could go further. But where? Where was haven? He snapped out the direction rod, moved away a short distance, and then glimpsed, below and to the left, a small peninsula of firm soil which seemed safe and uninhabited. And there was a pool of fairly clear water before it, containing nothing but an old uprooted stump. He came back to the others, shook them, and led them down to the place he had discovered.

They landed with a thump which seemed to shake all life from two of them. Friday and Eliot Leithgow collapsed into inert heaps, asleep immediately. Carse extracted a ray-gun from the belt of Leithgow's suit and prepared to stand watch. But that was too much. He overestimated his capacity. He had come through thirty hours of hellish sleep-denied delirium, and he could not stave sleep off any longer. He staggered and went down, and his eyelids were glued in sleep when his body hit the ground.

But mechanically, with, an instinct that sleep could not deny, his left hand kept clasped around the butt of the ray-gun…

\* \* \* \*

Satellite III's day has an average of seven hours' duration, her night of six. It was perhaps the last hour of daylight when the three metal- and fabric-clad figures lying outsprawled on the little thumb-shaped piece of soil had landed. Now quickly the huge sweeping rim of Jupiter plunged down, and night fell over the land.

Fierce darkness. Jungle and swamp awoke with their scale of savage life. Swift swooping shapes winged out from the trees, prey-hungry eyes gleaming green. And from the swamps came bellowings and stirrings from monster mud-encrusted bodies, awakening to their nocturnal quest for food. The night re-echoed with the harsh cacophony of their cries.

With lumbering caution, its smooth knob head waving on a long reptilian neck, its heavy armored tail dragging behind its body's 'folds of flesh, a giant night-thing came stumping out of a copse of jungle growth—a buru. Its eyes were watchful, but centered mainly on the pool of water to one side of the peninsula of firm soil. Its drinking water was there. With several pauses, it went right out on the spit, and a flat-bottomed foot twice the size of an elephant's missed one of the sleeping forms by inches. But the buru cared not for them. It was not a flesh-eater. Its undulating neck stretched far out; its head dipped; water was lapped up—until it caught sight of the up-rooted giant stump lying pitched in the pool. The beast drank but little after that, and retreated as cautiously as it had come.

Five or six of its fellows of the swamps followed at intervals to the water, grotesque hulking shapes, odorous and slimy with mud. All drank from the same spot; all ignored, save for a tentative rooting snuffle, the unconscious figures lying puny beneath them. But all noticed the twisted roots of the stump, sticking out in a score of directions, and avoided them.

And then there came smaller, more cautious animals who did not drink from the favored spot, who surveyed it, sniffed, hesitated, and finally retreated. There was a good reason for this caution.

For with the falling of night the stump had been at least thirty feet out in the water; now it was not ten feet from the side of the spit, and not twelve feet from the nearest sleeping figure. The suits that clad the three figures were sealed, the face-plates closed, so there was probably—after their trip through the void—no man smell to attract the giants of swamp and trees. But those three figures had moved. That was lure enough for one monster.

When the first ruddy arrows of Jupiter's light laced through the jungle's highest foliage, the twisted, gnarled stump was settled on the peninsula's rim, half out of the water. And when day burst, when Jupiter's flaming arch pushed over into view, the long seeming-roots eeled forward in sinuous, reptilian life.

IN one second Hawk Carse was snatched from sleep into the turmoil of a fight for life.

Something hard and enormously powerful was wrapping his waist with a vise-like grip that threatened to cut him in two. He felt a leg go up and crumple back, almost breaking under the force of a lashing blow. He was squeezed in, caged, compressed, by a score of tough, encircling tentacles, and his whole body was drawn toward a wide, flexible, black-lipped mouth yawning in the center of the monster he had thought a stump. Moving with loathsome life, its sinewy root-tentacles sucking him whole into the maw, the thing hunched itself back to the water.

The water frothed around Carse. He had been too dazed to resist; he had not known what had gripped him in his unconsciousness and weakness. But he remembered his ray-gun.

The lips of the hideous mouth were pressing close. Both were now under the surface. Carse's suit was still tight and he could breathe even while totally submerged in the water. He strained his left arm against the tentacle that looped it, worked the ray-gun still clasped in his hand in line with the thing's monstrous carcass, and at once, gasping and sick, pulled the trigger clear back.

The orange stream sizzled as it cleared a path through the water and bit true into the gaping mouth. There sounded a curious, subterranean sob; beady eyes on each side of the mouth bulged; the woodish body quivered in agony. Its tentacles slackened, and, half fainting, the Hawk wrenched free. He staggered up onto the land, streams of water running off the suit, and toppled over; and from there he saw the thing drag its writhing shuddering shape farther out from the shore. When perhaps sixty feet away it again subsided into a "harmless" uprooted old stump...

CARSE lay resting and collecting himself for a quarter of an hour, while Leithgow and Friday slept on, unconscious of what had happened; then he got to his feet, opened their face-plates and bathed Leithgow's pale brow with water. The scientist awoke with the quickness of old men, but Friday stirred and stretched and blinked and sat up at last, yawning.

The Hawk answered their questions about his wet suit with a brief explanation of the fight, then got down to business.

"There's water here, but we must have food," he said. "Friday, you go back and find fruit; some isuan weed, too, if it's growing nearby. A chew of it will stimulate us. Keep your ray-gun ready. I wouldn't be here if I'd not had mine."

The isuan was a big help. In its prepared form it is degrading, mind-destroying, but in natural state it gives a powerful and comparatively harmless stimulation. Chewing on the leaves that the Negro brought back, they made strength and renewed vitality for their bodies, and came, for the first time since they had started their flight through space, to a near-normal state. Meaty, yellow globules of pear-like fruit, followed by prudent drafts of water, aided also. Friday's long-absent grin returned as he bit into the juicy fruit, and he announced through a mouthful:

"Well, things're lookin' sunny again! We've got food and water inside us; we can reach Master Leithgow's laboratory in these here suits; an' to top it all we've finished high an' mighty Ku Sui. He's dead at last! Boy, it sure feels good to know it!"

Eliot Leithgow was lying back, breathing deeply of the fresh morning air. His lined, worn face and body were relaxed. "Yes," he murmured, "it is good to know that Dr. Ku is now just a thing of the past. He and his coordinated brains." He glanced aside at the Hawk, sitting silent and still, and stroking, as always when in meditation, the bangs of flaxen hair which obscured his forehead. "Why so serious, Carse?" he asked.

THE adventurer's gray eyes were cold and sober. No relaxation showed in them. His hand paused in its slow smoothing movement and he spoke.

"Why I overlooked it before," he said quietly, almost as if to himself, "I don't know. Probably because I was too tired, and too busy, and too sick to think. But now I see."

"What?" Leithgow sat up straight.

"Eliot," said the Hawk clearly, "doesn't it seem strange to you that Ku Sui's asteroid continued to be invisible after we had smashed through its dome?"

"What do you mean?"

"We've assumed that our smashing the dome and opening it to space killed Ku Sui and everyone inside, and destroyed all the mechanisms, including the coordinated brains. But the mechanism controlling the asteroid's invisibility was not destroyed. The place remained invisible."

The old scientist's face grew tense. Carse paused for a moment.

"That means," he went on, "that Ku Sui provided the invisibility machine with special protection for just such an emergency. And do you think he would give it such protection and not his coordinated brains? Wouldn't he first protect the brains, his most cherished possession?"

Eliot Leithgow knew what this meant. The Hawk had promised the brains in that machine—brains of five renowned scientists, kept cruelly, unnaturally alive by Dr. Ku—that he would destroy them. And his promises were always kept. There was no evading the logic of this reasoning. The Master Scientist nodded. "Yes," he answered. "He certainly would."

"I couldn't damage the case they were in," Carse continued. "The whole device seemed self-contained. It means just one thing: special protection. Since the mechanism for invisibility survived the crashing of the dome, we may be sure that the brain machine did too. And more than that: we may assume that there was special protection for the most precious thing of all to Dr. Ku Sui—his own life."

Friday's mouth gaped open. The old scientist cried out:

"My God! Ku Sui—still alive?"

"It would seem so," said Hawk Carse.

He amplified his evidence. "Look at these space-suits we're wearing. We got them and escaped by them, but they're Dr. Ku's. Couldn't he have protected himself with one too? He had plenty of time. And then the construction of the asteroid's buildings—all metal, with tight, sealed doors! Oh, stupid, stupid! Why didn't I see it all before? Here, in my weakness and sickness, I thought we'd killed Ku Sui and destroyed the coordinated brains!"

Leithgow looked suddenly very old and tired. The calamity did not end there. There were other angles, and an immediate one of high danger. In a lifeless voice he said:

"Carse, our whole situation's changed by this. We intended to go straight to my laboratory, but we may not be able to. The laboratory may already be closed to us. And even if not, there'd be a big risk in going there."

"Closed to us by what?" the Hawk demanded sharply. "A risk from what?"

Old Leithgow pressed his hands over his face. "Let me think a moment," he said.

\* \* \* \*

There were very good reasons why Eliot Leithgow maintained his chief laboratory on the dangerous Satellite III. Other planets might have offered more friendly locations, but III possessed stores of accessible minerals valuable to the scientist's varied work, and its position in the solar system was most convenient, being roughly halfway between Earth and the outermost frontiers. Leithgow had counterbalanced the inherent peril of the laboratory's location by ingenious camouflage, intricate defenses and hidden underground entrances; had, indeed, hidden it so well that none of the scavengers and brigands and more personal enemies who infested Port o' Porno remotely suspected that his headquarters was on the satellite at all. Ships, men, could pass over it a score of times with never an inkling that it lay below.

After a short silence, Eliot Leithgow began his explanation.

"You'll remember," he told the intent Hawk, "that Ku Sui's men kidnaped me from our friend Kurgo's house in Porno. There were five of them; robot-coolies. They took us entirely by surprise, and killed Kurgo and bore me to Ku Sui's asteroid.

"Well, I had come to Kurgo's house in the first place to arrange for supplies for building an addition to my laboratory, and I had with me a sheaf of papers containing plans for this addition. The plans are not important; they tell nothing—but there was a figure on one of the papers that might reveal everything! The figure 5,576.34. Do you know what that stands for?"

The adventurer thought for a moment, then shook his head. Leithgow nodded. He went on:

"Few would. *But among the few would be Ku Sui!*

"You'll remember that on building my laboratory we considered it extremely important to have it on the other side of the globe from Port o' Porno—diametrically opposite—so that the movements of our ships to and from it would be hidden from that pirate port. Diametrically opposite—remember? Well, the diameter of Satellite III is 3,550 miles. This diameter multiplied by 3.1416 gives 11,152.68 miles as the circumference, and one half the circumference is 5,576.34 miles—the exact distance of my laboratory from Port o' Porno!"

"I see," Carse murmured. "I see."

"That figure meant nothing to you, nor would it to the average person; but to a mathematician and astronomer—to Dr. Ku Sui—it would be a challenge! He would be studying the paper on which it is written down. One of Eliot Leithgow's papers. Plans for an addition to a laboratory. Therefore, Eliot Leithgow's laboratory. And then the figure: half the circumference of Satellite III. Why, he would at once deduce that it gave the precise location of my laboratory!"

The Hawk rose quickly. "If those papers fell into Dr. Ku's hands—"

"He would know exactly where the laboratory is," Leithgow finished. "He would search. Its camouflage would not hold him long. And that would be the end of my laboratory—and us too, if we were caught inside."

"Yes," snapped the Hawk. "You imply that the papers were left in Kurgo's house?"

"I had them in the bottom drawer of the clothes-chest in the room I always use; The coolies did not take them. At that time they wanted nothing but me."

Friday, rubbing his woolly crown, interjected: "But, even if Ku Sui's still alive, he wouldn't know about them papers. Far's *I* can see, they're safe."

"No!" Leithgow cried. "That's it!—They're not! Follow it logically, point by point. Assuming that Dr. Ku's alive, he has one point of contact with us—Kurgo's house, in Porno, where I was kidnaped. He wants us badly. He will anticipate that one of us will go back to that house to care for Kurgo's body, to get my belongings—for several reasons. So he will radio down—he probably can't come himself—for henchmen to station themselves at the house and to ransack it thoroughly for anything pertaining to me. The papers would fall into their hands!"

"All right," said Carse levelly. "We must get those papers. They will either be still in the house or in the possession of Dr. Ku's men at Porno. But whichever it is—we must get them before Ku Sul does." He paused.

"Well," he said, "that means me." He turned and looked down at the old man and smiled. "There's no use risking the three of us. I'll go to Kurgo's house myself."

"If the papers are gone, suh?" asked Friday.

"I don't know. What I do will depend on what I discover there."

"But," said Leithgow, "there may be guards! There may be an ambush!"

"I have a powerful weapon, M. S. Unknown, so far; new to Satellite III. Ku Sui himself supplied it. This space-suit."

The Hawk scanned the "western" sky and began giving brisk orders.

"Eliot, you've got to go to some place of safety until this is all over. You too, Eclipse, to take care of him. Let me see… There's Cairnes, and Wilson… Wilson's the one. He should be at his ranch now. You remember it: Ban Wilson's ranch, on the Great Briney Lake? Right. Both of you will go there and wait. I'll meet you there when I'm finished. And at that time I'll either have the papers or know that Ku Sui has found the laboratory."

Again on his feet, the old Master Scientist regarded anxiously this slender, coldly calculating man who was his closest friend. He was afraid. "Carse," he said, "you're going back alone into probable danger. The papers—the laboratory—they're important—but not so important as your life."

There was visible now in the Hawk's face that hard, unflinching will-to-do that had made him the spectacular adventurer that he was. "Did you ever know me to run from danger" he asked softly. "Did you ever know me to run from Ku Sui?…" And Eliot Leithgow knew that the course was set, no matter what it might hold.

Carse again glanced at Jupiter, hanging massive in the blue overhead. "About three hours of daylight left," he observed. "Now, close face-plates. We must go up—far up—to get our bearings."

Altitude swept back the horizon as they arrowed up through the warm, glowing air. From far in the heavens, perhaps twenty miles, Carse saw what he looked for—a bright gleam of silver in the monochrome of the terrain, where Jupiter's light struck on the smooth metal hides of a group of space-ships resting in the satellite's lone port, Porno. Eighty, a hundred miles away—some such distance. Into the helmet's tiny microphone he said:

"That's Porno, over to the 'north,' and there to one side is the Great Briney. It's not far: you won't have to hurry, Eliot. Head straight for the lake and follow the near shoreline toward Porno, and you'll come to Ban Wilson's ranch. Now we part."

The three clinging, giant forms separated. The direction-rods for horizontal movement were out-hinged. A last touch of mitten-gloves on the bloated suits' fabric; a nod and a smile through the face-plates; and a few parting words:

"Good luck, old comrade!"—in Leithgow's soft voice; and the Negro's deep, emphatic bass: "Don't know how far these little sets work, suh, but if you need me, call. I'll keep listenin'!"

And then white man and black were speeding away in the ruddy flood of Jupiter-light, and Hawk Carse faced the danger trail alone, as was his wont.

Caution rather than speed had to mark his journey, Carse knew. Several ranches lay scattered in the jungle smother between him and the port—stations where the weed isuan was collected and refined into the deadly finished product. They were worked for the most part by Venusians allied with Ku Sui; the Eurasian practically controlled the drug trade; and therefore, if any alarm had been broadcast, many men would already be on the lookout for him.

So the Hawk dropped low, and chose a course through the screening walls of the jungle. It did not take him long to attain full mastery of the suit's controls, and soon he was gliding cleanly through the hollows created by the mammoth outthrusting treetops in a course crazy and twisted, but one which kept him pointing always towards Porno. Presently he found an easier highway and a faster—a sluggish, dirty yellow stream, quite broad, which ended, he was sure, in a swamp within a mile of his destination.

Flanked by the jungle growth which sprouted thickly from each bank, a gray, ghostly shape in the shadows lying over the water, he sped through the dying afternoon. He kept at least ten feet above the surface, well out of reach of such water beasts as from time to time reared up through the placid surface to scan him. Once a huge gantor, gulping a drink from the bank, snorted and went trumpeting away at the grotesque sight of him—flying without wings!—and once too, on rising cautiously above the treetops to reconnoitre Carse saw life far more perilous to him: a small party of men, stooping over a swamp-brink and plucking the ripe isuan weed. At this he dived steeply and fled on; and he knew he had gone unobserved, for there came no outcry of discovery from behind.

\* \* \* \*

Jupiter lowered its murky disk as the miles streamed past, breeding a legion of shadows welcome to the fabric-clad monster skimming through them and to the creatures who blinked and stirred as night approached. The stream broadened into shallow pockets; patches of swamp appeared and absorbed the stream; and Carse knew he was close to his destination.

He cut his speed and glanced around. Ahead, the dark spire of a giant sakari tree climbed into the gloom. It would be a good place. The man rose slowly; like a wraith on the wind he lifted into its topmost branches; and there, in the broad, cuplike leaves, he warily ensconced himself. For man-sounds came into his opened helmet, and through a fringe of leaves, across a mile of tumbled swamp and marsh, he could see the guarding fences of the cosmetropolis of Porno.

A last slice of blotched, flaming red, the rim of setting Jupiter, still silhouetted Porno, sprawled inside its high, electric-wired fences, and the flood of fading light brushed the town with beauty. The rows of tin shacks which housed its dives, the clustered, nondescript hovels, the merchants' grim strongholds of steel—all merged into a glowing mirage, a scene far alien to the brooding swamp and savage jungle in whose breast it lay. Here and there several space-ships reared their sunset-gilded flanks, glittering high-lights in the final glorious burst of Jupiter-light...

The planet's rim vanished abruptly, and Porno returned to true character.

For a moment it appeared what it was: a blotched, disordered huddle, ugly, raw, fit companion of the swamp and jungle. Then beads of light appeared, some still, some winking, one crooked line of flaring illumination marking the Street of the Sailors, along which the notorious kantrans flourished, now ready for their nightly brood of men who sought forgetfulness in revelry. Soon, Carse knew, the faint man-noises he heard would grow into a broad fabric of sound, stitched across by shrieks and roars as the isuan and alkite flowed free. And all around the lone watcher in the sakari tree the night-monsters were crawling out in jungle and swamp on the dark routine of their lives as, in the town, two-legged creatures even lower in their degradation went abroad after the dope and liquor which gave them their vicious recreation.

The night flowed thicker around him.

FROM somewhere behind, the Hawk heard a suck of half-fluid mud as a giant body stretched in its sleeping place. A tree close to his suddenly fluttered with the unseen life it harbored. A hungry gantor raised its long deep bellow to the night, and another answered, and another.

It grew pitch black. Only a sprinkling of pin-points of light marked Porno to the eye. The sky beyond the town matched the sky to the rear. Jupiter's light now had fled the higher air levels. The time had come.

Cautiously Carse brushed the branches aside, rose upright and pressed the mitten switch over to repulsion. In instant response his giant's bulk lifted lightly. He sped upward, straight and fast; and at two thousand feet, still untouched by the sinking planet's rays, he brought himself to an approximate halt and peered below.

Port o' Porno lay spread out beneath, one thin line of light-pricks off which angled fainter lines, extending only a short distance and then dying widely off. There were perhaps two thousand men in the town—men from all the countries of the three planets inhabited by creatures that could be called human—and of these at least three quarters knew Hawk Carse as an enemy, because of his intolerance for their dope-trade. His approach to the house Number 574 had to be swift, direct, unseen, unheard.

He was able to make it so. Pointing the direction rod, he winged forward until directly above an estimated spot, then dropped a thousand feet. A pause while he searched; another drop. He knew Kurgo's house well, but the scene was confusing from above, and the street the house was on was always dark at night.

He made it out at last. The squat two-storied structure, similar to other merchants' strongholds, seemed unlit and unwatched. Carse swung back the hinged mittens of the suit and slid his hands out ready for action. In his left he took his ray-gun; then, pressing the mitten-switch, he dropped straight, silent, swift, like the Hawk he now truly was.

A single window-port, high up, broke the smooth rear of Kurgo's house. It faced a silent alleyway. The steel shutters were closed, but a pull swung them noiselessly outward. For a brief moment Carse's bulging giant's figure of metal and fabric hung black against the shadowed window-port. The room he peered into was solid black. He heard no sound. Clumsily he thrust out and stepped in.

Silence. Inky nothingness—but the air was weighted with many things, and among them one which brought the short hairs on the Hawk's neck prickling erect. A smell! It was not to be mistaken—a faint, but rank and fetid and altogether identifying smell—the body-smell of a Venusian!

For a moment Hawk Carse's breathing stopped. Metal clanked on metal for an instant as he moved from the window-port and became one with the darkness inside; then silence again, as his eyes trained into the vault and his hand held ready on the ray-gun. He waited.

Was it a trap? He had seen no guards watching the house; had sensed it deserted. But the steep shutters, unlocked, readily permitting entrance—and the smell! Even if not still there, a Venusian had been in the room, and a Venusian of Port o' Porno was an enemy. A Venusian... There were only some sixty on the whole satellite, and, of these, fifty were the men of Lar Tantril. Lar Tantril, powerful henchman of Dr. Ku Sui, director of the Eurasian's drug trade on Satellite III. But that line of thought had to wait.

"I see you!" he whispered suddenly and sharply. "My gun's on you. Come forward!"

No answer; not the slightest sign or stir in the darkness. He breathed again.

Carse knew the arrangement of Kurgo's house. He was in his second-story sleeping-room. There was a door in the wall ahead, leading into the room Leithgow was accustomed to use on his visits, and there the papers should be. But first he would have to have light.

His ears pitched for any betraying sound, Carse moved heavily to his left until a wall arrested him. He felt along it, located the desk he sought for and scoured through it. His fingers found the flash he knew was there.

The darkness then was slit by a hard straight line of white. It shot over the room picking out overturned chairs, a bowl that had toppled to the floor, scattering its contents of ripe akalot fruit, a sleeping couch, its sheets and pillows awry, and—something human.

A half-clothed body lay sprawled beside the couch, its hands thrust clutching forward and its unseeing eyes still staring at the door whence had come the shots that had burnt out the left side of its chest. Dead. Three days dead. The murdered master of the house, Kurgo, lying where Ku Sui's robot-coolies had shot him down.

The Venusian-smell swept more strongly into his nostrils as the adventurer opened the door into Leithgow's room. No Venusian had ever been in those room *before* the abduction.

Carse's light danced over the room's confusion: a laboratory table overturned; apparatus spilled; several chairs flung around, one splintered: mute signs of the struggle Eliot Leithgow had offered his kidnapers.

In a corner stood a metal chest. In the bottom drawer was the all-significant answer. Hawk Carse crossed the room and slid it open.

The papers were gone!

Methodically Carse hunted through every drawer and corner of the room, but he found no trace of them. Every article that would be of value to an ordinary thief was left; the one thing important to Dr. Ku Sui, the sheaf of papers, was missing.

The presence of the Venusian body-smell started an important train of thought in the Hawk's mind. It signified that the papers had been taken by henchmen of Ku Sui, which in turn signified that Ku Sui had survived the crashing of the dome and was alive and again aggressively dangerous. But was the Eurasian already on Satellite III? Was he already in personal possession of the papers?—perhaps conducting a search for Leithgow's laboratory?

Or did it mean that Dr. Ku had merely radioed instructions for his Venusian henchmen to ransack the house, take whatever pertained to Leithgow, and wait for him?

Venusians... There was only one logical man; and as Hawk Carse thought of him in that dark and silent house of tragedy, his right hand slowly rose to the bangs of hair over his forehead and began to stroke them...

His bangs were an unusual style for the period; they stamped him and attracted unwanted attention; but he would wear his hair in that fashion until he went down in death. For he had once been trapped—trapped neatly by five men, and maltreated: one, Judd the Kite, whose life had paid already for his part in the ugly business; two others whom he was not now concerned with; the fourth, Dr. Ku Sui; and the fifth—a Venusian...

That fifth, the Venusian, was Lar Tantril, now one of Ku Sui's most powerful henchmen, and director of his interplanetary drug traffic—Lar Tantril, who possessed an impregnable isuan ranch only twenty-five miles from Port o' Porno—*Lar Tantril, who probably had directed the stealing of the papers from this room! The papers, if not already in Ku Sui's hands, should be at Tantril's ranch.*

Carse's deduction was followed by a swift decision. He had to raid Lar Tantril's ranch.

He knew the place fairly well. Once, even, he had attacked it, in his *Star Devil*, seeking to wipe out his debt against Tantril; but he had been driven off by the ranch's mighty offensive rays.

It was impregnable, Tantril was fond of boasting. Situated on the brink of the Great Briney, its other three sides were flanked by thick, swampy jungle, in which the isuan grew and was gathered by Tantril's Venusian workers. Ranch? More a fort than a ranch, with its electrified, steel-spiked fence; its three watch-towers, lookouts always posted there again the threat of hijackers or enemies; its powerful ray-batteries and miscellany of smaller weapons. A less vulnerable place for the keeping of Eliot Leithgow's papers could hardly have been found in all the frontiers of the solar system.

He, Carse, had raided it in a modern fighting space-ship, and failed. Now, with nothing but a space-suit and a ray-gun, he had to raid it again—and succeed!

* * * *

The adventurer did not leave immediately. He thought it wise to make what preparations he could. His important weapon was the space-suit; therefore, he took it off and studied and inspected its several intricate mechanisms as well as he could in the carefully guarded light of his flash.

It was motivated, he saw, by dual sets of gravity-plates, in separate space-tight compartments. One set was located in the extremely thick soles of the heavy boots; the other rested on the top of the helmet. He saw why this was. The gravity-plates for repulsion were those in the helmet; for attraction, those in the boot-soles. This kept the wearer of the suit always in an upright, head-up position.

The logical plan of attack had grown in Carse's mind: down and up! Down to the papers, then up and away before the men on the ranch knew what was happening; he could suppose that they, like all others on the satellite, had no knowledge of a self-propulsive space-suit. The success of his raid depended entirely on keeping the two gravity mechanisms intact. If they were destroyed, or failed to function, he would be locked to the ground in a prison of metal and fabric; clamped down, literally, by a terrific dead weight! The suit was extremely heavy, particularly the boots, and Carse learned that the wearer was able to walk in it only because a portion of the helmet's repulsive force was continually working to approximate a normal body gravity.

A chance to succeed—if the two vital points were kept intact! If they failed, he would have to slip out of the imprisoning suit and use his quick wits and deadly ray-gun in clearing a path to Ban Wilson, his nearest friend, whose ranch, fourteen miles from Tantril's stronghold, was where Eliot Leithgow and Friday would be awaiting him.

It was characteristic of Hawk Carse that he never even considered calling on Wilson's resources of men and weapons to help him. A Hawk he was: wiry, fierce-clawed, bold against odds and danger, most capable and deadly when striking alone...

After scanning the whole project, Carse attended to other needs. He ate some of the akalot fruit spilled over the floor of the adjoining room; opened a can of water and drank deeply; limbered his muscles well; even rested for five minutes. Then he was ready to leave.

He soon was again in the cold space-suit, fastening on the helmet.

He left the face-plate open. The left mitten he hinged back, so as to be able to grip the ray-gun in his bare hand. Then, a looming giant shadow in the darkness, he shuffled to the rear window-port.

Carse steadied himself on the sill. The night-bedlam from the Street of the Sailors, punctuated by far, hungry bellows from swamp monsters, sounded in his ears. Enemies, human and animal, ringed him in Kurgo's house; but up above lay a clean, cold highway, an open highway, stretching straight to the heart of the danger which was his destination. He turned the mitten-switch over to quick repulsion and leaped up to the waiting heavens.

On the ground was a world of night; a mile up showed a great circle of black, one edge of which was marked by a faint, eerie glow from further-setting Jupiter.

Save for that far-off spectral hint of the giant occulted planet, Hawk Carse sped in darkness. Through the open face-plate the night wind buffeted his emotionless, stone-set face; his suit whistled a song of speed as the gusts laced by it. Down and ahead his direction rod pointed, and with ever-gathering momentum he followed its leading finger. The lights of Porno dwindled to points, grew yet finer, then were gone. Several times a sparse cluster of other lights, lonely in the black tide of III's surface, ran beneath him, signaling a ranch. The last of these melted into the ink behind, and there was a period unrelieved by sign of man's presence below.

And then at last one bright solitary spot of light appeared, far ahead. It was a danger signal to the Hawk. He had to descend at once. From then on, speed had to be forsaken for caution. Watchful eyes were beneath that light, lying keen on the heavens; a whole intricate offense and defense system surrounded It. It was the central watch-beacon of Lar Tantril's ranch.

Carse swooped low.

He came into the night-world of the surface. No faint-lit horizon showed; there was only the darkness, and darker shadows peopling it. At the height of a mile there had been no signs of the satellite's native life, but at an elevation scarcely above the treetops the flying man was brought all too close to the reality of the denizens of the gloomy jungle below. Out of the black smother came clues to the life within it: sounds of monstrous bodies moving through the undergrowth and mud, recurring death-screams, howls and angry chatterings...

\* \* \* \*

This below: there was more above. He was not the only living thing that soared in the night. Swift fleeting batlike shapes would appear from nowhere for one sharp second, would beset him one after another in an almost constant stream, thinking his comparatively clumsy, bloated bulk easy prey, and then be gone. He snapped shut his face-plate under their assault. Sometimes there came different, more powerful wings, and he would duck in mechanical reaction, sensing the wings sweep past, often feeling them as, with sharp pecks and quick thudding blows, they sought to stun him. But the suit was stout; the repulsed attackers could only follow a little, glaring at him with fire-green malevolent eyes, then leave to seek smaller prey.

The watch-beacon began to wink more often through the ranks of intervening trees as he neared the ranch. Carse was gliding so low that often branches raked and twisted him in his course. His low transit allowed one tree to loose great peril upon him.

The tree loomed a black giant in his path. Fifty feet away, he was swerving to wind around it when he noticed its dark upper branches a-tremble. He had only this for warning when, with chilling surprise, what appeared to be the entire top of the tree rose, severed itself completely from the rest and soared right out to meet him.

A shape from a nightmare, it slid over the adventurer. He saw two green-glowing saucer-sized eyes; heard the wings rattling bonily as they spread to full thirty feet; heard the monster's life-thirsty scream as it plunged. The stars were blotted out. It was upon him.

But even in the sudden confusion of the attack, Carse knew the creature for what it was: a full-grown specimen of the giant carnivorous lemak, a seldom-seen, dying species, too clumsy, too slow, too huge to survive. His ray-gun came around, but he was caught in a feathered maelstrom and knocked too violently around to use it. Without pause the lemak's claws raked his suit. Unable to rend the tough fabric, it resorted to another method. With a strength so enormous that it could overcome the force of the gravity-plates and his forward momentum, the creature tossed him free. Dizzy, he hurtled upward. But he knew that the bird's purpose was to impale him on the long steely spike of its beak as he came twisting down.

The lemak poised below, snout and spear-like beak raised. But it waited in vain, for Carse did not come dropping down. A touch of the control switch and he stayed at the new level, collecting himself. The lemak, puzzled and angry, wheeled up to see what had become of the victim that did not descend, and found instead a searing needle of heat which burnt through its broad right wing. Then, screaming with pain and in a frenzy to escape, it went with a rush into the far darkness.

The Hawk dropped low again, hoping that his gun's quick flash had not been observed. He had not wished to wound the lemak mortally, for no matter how accurate his shot the monster would take long to die, and scream and thrash as it did so. One short spit of orange was preferable to a prolonged hullabaloo. But even that might have betrayed him…

With elaborate caution, he reconnoitered Lar Tantril's ranch.

FROM above, the ranch clearing was a pool of faint light contained in black leagues of jungle and the edge of the Great Briney. Slanting shadows and the dark bulks of buildings that were unlit rendered the details vague, but under prolonged scrutiny the appointments of the ranch became visible.

The clearing was a circle some two hundred yards in diameter. Just inside the jungle wall was the first line of protection, a steel-barbed, twenty-foot-high fence, its strong corded links interwoven with electrified wires. Well within this fence stood five buildings, low, squat and one-storied, four of them forming a broken square around the central fifth. Two buildings were pierced by low rows of lighted windows, evidence that they were the barracks of the workers; two others, devoted to the processing of the isuan weed, were now dark and silent. The central building was smaller, with window-ports that were glowing eyes in the smooth metal walls. It was the dwelling of the master, Lar Tantril.

Close to the central building rose a hundred-foot tower, topped by the watch-beacon. At three equi-distant points around the encompassing fence, small, square platforms were held sixty feet aloft by mast-like triangular towers, up which foot-rungs led. And on each platform could be made out the figure of a Venusian guard.

Ceaselessly these guards turned and scanned the jungle, the heavens, the unbroken dark prairie of the lake, alert for anything of suspicion. Lar Tantril had good reasons for maintaining a constant watch over his stronghold, and his guards' eyes were sharpened by knowledge of the severe payment laxness would bring. Close at hand in the platforms were knobs which, pressed, would ring a clanging alarm through all the buildings below; and each guard wore two ray-gun holsters.

Despite the guards and the ugly spikes of the fence, however, the ranch from above appeared peaceful, calm and harmless. No men were visible on its shadow-dappled clearing. Even the surrounding jungle, in the watch-beacon's shaded underside, might have been nothing but a stage set, were it not for the occasional signs of the life that crept unseen through it—a long, far-distant howl, a quickly receding crashing in the under growth, a thumping from some small animal.

The guards were used to this pattern of nocturnal sounds. It was only when, from a tree not thirty feet from one of the platforms, there came a sudden sharp shaking in the upper branches, that the Venusian on that platform deigned to grip his ray-gun and peer suspiciously. All he saw was a large bird that flapped out and winged across the clearing, mewing angrily.

The guard released his grip on the gun. A snake, probably, had disturbed the bird. Or some of those devilish little crimson bansis, half insect, half crab....

* * * *

Hawk Carse breathed again. He had been sure his position would be revealed when, drifting with almost imperceptible motion into the tree, the bird had pecked at him, then flapped away in alarm. A long, painfully cautious approach from tree to tree to the selected one had been necessary to the daring scheme of attack he had evolved.

He seemed to be safe. Through a fringe of leaves he saw the guard on the platform glancing elsewhere. Carse steadied himself, rose slightly and again scanned the ranch.

Yes, it looked harmless, but he knew that nothing could be further from the reality. Spaced around the inside edge of that spiky fence were small metal nozzles protruding a few inches from the ground; and on the turning of a control wheel, they would hurl forth a deadly orange swathe, fanning hundreds of feet into the sky. He had tasted their hot breath once when attacking the ranch in his Star Devil. Then there were the long-range projectors whose muzzles studded the central building. And the ray-guns of the tower guards.

These were dangers that he knew, for he had experienced them. What others the ranch held, he could not well surmise. But he saw one significant thing that gave him pain, and brought lines to his brow.

The ranch was expecting trouble. Over to one side of the clearing rested a great rounded object, on whose smooth hull gleamed coldly the light from the beacon—Lar Tantril's own personal space-ship—and alongside it a smaller, somewhat similar shape, the ranch's air-car! The space-ship signified that the Venusian chief was present; the air-car, that all his men were gathered in the barracks, and not, as was their custom, in Port o' Porno for a night of revelry!

All waiting—all gathered here—all ready! All grouped for a strong defense! Did it mean what it would appear to—that he, the Hawk, was expected?

He could not know. He could not know if a trap was lying prepared there against his coming. He could but go ahead, and find out.

The only plan of attack he could think of had grown in his mind. Down and up: that was the essence of it: but the details were difficult. He had worked them out as far as he could with typical thoroughness. He had to reach the heart of the fort lying before him: had to reach the central house, Lar Tantril's own. The precious papers would be there, if anywhere.

The Hawk was ready.

He gathered his muscles. His face was cold and hard, his eyes mists of gray. There was no least sign in the man that, in the next few all-deciding minutes, death would lick close to him.

He poised where he was precariously balanced. His ray-gun was in his bare left hand; his face-plate was locked partly open. He raised his fingers to the direction rod on the suit's breast, gazed straight at the guard on the nearest watch-platform and snapped the direction rod out, pointing it at that guard.

What happened then struck so fast, so unexpectedly, that it took only thirty seconds to plunge the quiet ranch into chaos.

The Hawk came like a thunderbolt, using to its full power his only weapon, the space-suit. The sight of him might alone have been enough to strike terror. From the dark arms of the tree he hurtled, his bloated monstrous shape of metal and fabric dull in the glow of the watch-beacon, and crashed with a clang of metal into the platform he aimed at. Nothing there could withstand him. One second the guard on it was calmly gazing off into the sky; the next, like a nine-pin he was bowled over, to topple heels and head whirling to the ground sixty feet beneath. He lived, he kept consciousness, but he was sorely injured; and he never saw the outlandish projectile that struck him, nor saw it streak to the second watch-platform, bowling its guard out and to the ground likewise, and then repeating at the third and last!

A crash; a pause; a crash; a pause; then a third crash, and the thing of metal had completed the circuit, and all three watch-platforms were scooted empty!

Then came confusion.

There had been screams, but now a crazed voice began crying out mechanically, over and over:

"Space-suit! Space-suit! Space-suit! Space-suit!"

It came from the second guard, who lay twisting on the ground.

His tongue, by some trick of nervous disorganization, beat out those words like a voice-disk whose needle keeps skipping its groove—and the effect was macabre.

The central buildings disgorged a crowd of men. Short, wiry, thin-faced Venusians, each with skewer-blade strapped to his side and some with ray-guns out, they came scrambling into the open, swearing and wondering. The second guard's insane repetitions directed most of them in his direction; and they piled in a crowd around him. They had no attention for what was happening behind, within the buildings they had emptied. That was what Hawk Carse had planned.

A voice of authority roared up over the general hubbub.

"Rantol! Guard! Rantol, you fool! What happened? What attacked you? Cut that crazy yelling! Answer me!—you, Rantol!"

"Space-suit! Space-suit! Space-suit! Space—"

"Lar Tantril!" A man with suspicious eyes caught the attention of the one who had spoken first. "Space-suit, he says! A flying space-suit! Only Ku Sui has space-suits that fly; or only Ku Sui *had* them, rather. You know what that must mean!"

He paused, peering at his lord. The coarse yellowy skin of Tantril's brow wrinkled with the thought, then his tusk-like Venusian teeth showed as his lips drew apart in speech.

"Yes!" Lar Tantril said. "It's *Carse!*"

And he ordered the now silent men around him:

"Circle my house, all of you, your guns ready. You, Esret"—to his second in command—"out gun and come with me."

Even as Lar Tantril spoke, a giant shape was passing clumsily through the kitchen of his house. Carse had entered from the rear, unseen. With gun in hand and eyes sharp he crossed the deserted kitchen with its foul odors of Venusian cookery. Quickly, his metal-shod feet creating an unavoidable racket, he was through a connecting door and into the well-furnished dining room. All was brightly lit; he could easily have been seen through the window-ports rimming each wall; but he counted on the confusion outside to keep the Venusians engaged for several minutes more.

Then he went shuffling into the front room of the house, and saw at once the most likely place.

It was in one corner—a large flat desk, and by it the broad panel of a radio. Scattered over the desk were a number of papers. In seconds Carse was bending over them, scanning and discarding with eyes and hands.

Reports of various quantities of isuan...orders for stores...a list that seemed an inventory of weapons—and then the top page of a sheaf covered with familiar, neat, small writing. Yes!

Plans and calculations dealing with a laboratory! And, down in the, margin of the first page, the revealing, all-important figure—5,576.34!

He had them—and before Ku Sui! Now, only to get away: out the front door and up—up from this trap he was in—up into clean and empty space, and then to Leithgow and Friday at Ban Wilson's!

But, as the Hawk turned to go, his eye took in a little slip on the desk, a radio memo, with the name of Ku Sui at its top. Almost without volition he glanced over it, hoping to discover useful information about Ku Sui's asteroid—and with the passing of those few extra seconds his chance for escaping out the door passed too.

Carse's back was partly toward the front door when a voice, hard and deadly, spoke from it:

"Your hands up!"

The adventurer's nerves twanged; he wheeled; and even as he did so another voice bit out from the rear door:

"Yes, up! One move and you're dead!"

And Hawk Carse found himself caught between ray-guns held unswervingly on his body by a man at each door. He was not fool enough to try to shoot, even though his own gun was in his hand: his best speed would be slow-motion in the hampering space-suit. He was fairly caught—because for a few precious seconds he had let his mind slip from the all-important matter of escaping.

At a shout from someone, both doors filled with men, and thin faces appeared at the window-ports. Their ray-guns made an impregnable fence around the netted Hawk.

And then a well-remembered voice, harsh as the man from whom it came, cut through the room.

"Apparently you're caught, Captain Carse!"

The cold gray eyes narrowed, scanned the room, the blocked doors, the barricade of guns held by the grim men at doorways and window-ports.

"Yes," Hawk Carse murmured. "Apparently I am."

Lar Tantril, the Venusian chief, smiled. He was tall for one of his race, even taller than the prisoner he faced. Clad in tightfitting, iron-gray mesh, he had the characteristic wiry body, thin legs and arms of his kind. Spiky short-cropped hair grew like steel slivers from the narrow dome of his long hatchet head, and the taut-stretched skin of his face was burned a deep hard brown. He looked what he was: a bold and unscrupulous leader of his men.

"The gun in your belt," he said, "—drop it. Right on the floor. There—

better. I like you not with a gun near your hand, Carse."

The Hawk regarded him frigidly. "And now what?" he asked.

Lar Tantril continued smiling. His ray-gun did not move for an instant from the line it held on the metal and fabric giant. He said at a tangent, quite pleasantly:

"Think fast, Captain Carse—think fast! Isn't that one of Dr. Ku's new suits?—a little space-ship all your own? Why not plan a sudden sweep for that door in an attempt to crash through my men and get free up in the air—eh?"

"Why not?" said the Hawk.

"It might be possible," Tantril continued, "with your luck. *Unless something went wrong with your helmet gravity-plates.*"

At this the Venusian's gun moved. Deliberately it came up and aimed at the crown of the adventurer's helmet. Tantril squeezed the trigger.

*Spang!*

A pencil-thin streak of orange stabbed between Venusian and Earthling; sparks hissed out where it struck the tip of the helmet; and for an instant life and strength seemed to leave the grotesquely clad figure. Carse slumped down under a quick crushing weight. Weight! It bent him low, and it was only with a great effort that he was able to straighten again. For the suit's full load of metal and fabric was upon him now, its enormous boots binding him to the ground since their weight was unrelieved by the partial lift of the helmet plates. An inch-wide, black-rimmed hole in the mechanism above the helmet told what had happened.

Lar Tantril chortled, and his men, most of them only half comprehending what he had done, echoed him.

"But even yet you've got a chance," the Venusian went on.

"There's another set of plates in the boot-soles, for attraction. If you got a chance to stand on your head outside, you'd be gone! So—"

This time he lowered the gun, and carefully, accurately, he sent two spitting streams of orange through the soles of the great boots.

The danger Carse had feared had come to pass. His one weapon had been destroyed. He was worse than helpless: he was in a cumbersome prison, all power of quick movement gone. He was a paralyzed giant, tied to the soil, the ways of the air hopelessly closed. The slightest step would cost great effort.

"You have protected yourself well, Lar Tantril," he said slowly.

Now Tantril laughed deeply and unrestrainedly. "Yes, and by Mother Venus," he cried, "it's good to see you this way, Carse, unarmed and in my power!" He turned to his circle of men and said: "Poor Hawk! Can't fly any more! I've put him in a cage! So thoughtful of him to bring his cage along with him so I could trap him inside it! His own cage!" He guffawed, shaking, and the others laughed loud.

Through it all Hawk Carse stood motionless, his face cold and graven, his slender body bent under the burden of the dead suit. He still held in his right hand, limp by his side, the sheaf of papers and their all-important figure—and the thumb and forefinger of his hand were moving, so slowly as to be hardly noticeable, in what seemed to be a lone sign of nervous tension.

"You know, Carse," Tantril observed after his laugh, "I've been half expecting you, though I don't see how you knew I was the one who took those papers you're holding. Dr. Ku radioed me, you see. I think you were reading his message at the time I entered. Did you finish it?"

"No," said the Hawk.

"You'll find it interesting. Let me read it to you." And Tantril took up the memo.

"'From Ku Sui to Lar Tantril: Search House No. 574 in Port o' Porno closely for anything pertinent to Master Scientist Eliot Leithgow or giving clue to his whereabouts. Keep what you obtain for me; I will come to your ranch in five days. Watch for Hawk Carse, Eliot Leithgow and a Negro, arriving from space at Satellite in in self-propulsive space-suits.'"

There followed some details concerning the suits' mechanism; then: "'Carse caused me certain trouble and came near hurting my major inventions. I want him badly."

AT this the adventurer's face tightened; his gray eyes went frosty. All he and Leithgow had deduced, then, was true. Dr. Ku had survived the crashing of the asteroid's dome. The mechanisms had also survived—and certainly the coordinated brains—the brains he, Hawk Carse, had promised to destroy! Now trapped, it seemed that promise could never be fulfilled...

Yet even through this torturing thought of a promise unkept, the Hawk's thumb and forefinger moved in their slight grinding motion on the first sheet of the sheaf of papers...

Lar Tantril reached out his hand for the sheaf. "So, obeying Dr. Ku's orders, I had the house searched and got these papers. They must be valuable, Carse, since you wanted them so badly. Ku Sui will be pleased. Hand them over."

With but the barest flick of gray eyes downward, Hawk Carse gave the sheaf to Tantril.

But his brief glance at the topmost sheet told him all he wanted to know. Gradually, methodically, the motion of thumb and forefinger had totally effaced the revealing figure 5,576.34, the one clue to the location of Leithgow's laboratory. Enough! What he had set out to do was finished. The chief task was achieved!

"And now, perhaps," Lar Tantril chuckled, "a little entertainment."

His men pricked up their ears. This language was more understandable.

Entertainment meant playing with the prisoner—torture. And alkite, probably, and isuan. A night of revelry!

But Hawk Carse smiled thinly at this.

"Entertainment, Tantril?" his cold voice said. He paused, and then added slowly: "What a fool you are!"

Lar Tantril was not annoyed by the words. He only laughed and slapped his thigh.

"Yes?" he mocked. "Truly, Captain Carse, you must be frightened, to try and anger me, so I'll shoot! Do you fear a skewer-blade so much? We would leave most of you for Ku Sui!"

Carse shook his head. "No, Lar Tantril, I don't want you to shoot me. I'm telling you you're a fool—because you think me one."

With a wave of his hands the Venusian protested: "No, no, not at all. You're infernally clever, Carse. I'll always be the first to admit it."

"Then do you think I'd attack your ranch alone?"

"You'd like me to believe you have friends hidden somewhere?" Tantril asked, smiling tolerantly.

Carse's voice came back curtly. "Believe what you like, but learn this: It's your boast that your ranch is impregnable, guarded on every side and from every angle. I'm telling you it's not. It's vulnerable. It's wide open to one way of attack—and my friends and I know it well."

For a second the Venusian's assurance wavered.

"Vulnerable?" he said. "Open to attack? You're just stalling!"

Whip-like words cut through.

"Wait and see. Wait till the ranch is stormed and wiped out. Wait twenty minutes! Only twenty!"

Hawk Carse was always listened to when he spoke in such manner. Lar Tantril stared at the hard gray eyes boring into his.

"Why do you tell me this?" he asked. Then, with a smile: "Why not wait until my ranch is wiped out, as you say?" His smile broadened. "Until these hidden friends attack?"

"Simply because I must insure my living. Nothing my friends could do would prevent your having plenty of time to kill me before you yourselves were destroyed. I think, under the circumstances, you *would* kill me. And I must go free. I have made a promise. A very important promise. I must be free to carry it out."

"Just what are you aiming at?"

"I'm offering," said the Hawk, "to show you where your fort is vulnerable—in time for you to protect it. I'll do this if you'll let me go free. *You need not release me till afterwards.*"

Lar Tantril's mouth fell half open at this surprising turn. He was unquestionably taken aback. But he snapped his lips shut and considered the offer. A trick? Carse was famed for them. A trap? But how? He scanned his men. Fifty to one; fifty ray-guns on an unarmed man helpless in a hampering prison of metal and fabric. If a trap, Carse could not possibly escape death. But yet…

Tantril walked over to his man Esret, and, stepping apart, they conferred in whispers.

"Is he trying to trick us?" the chief asked.

"I don't see how he can hope to. He can hardly move in that suit. It ties him down. We could keep tight guard upon him. He couldn't possibly get away. And at the slightest sign of something shady—"

"Yes; but you know him."

"What he says is sensible. Naturally he wants to live. He knows we'll shoot him if he tries to trick us, and he knows we'll do it if we're attacked! We'll of course leave men at all defensive stations. If there is a weakness here, if the ranch is vulnerable—we should learn what it is. It'll cost us nothing. We can't lose, and we might be saving everything. Of course we won't let him go afterwards."

Tantril considered a moment longer, then said:

"Yes. I think you are right." He turned back to the waiting Carse.

"Agreed," he said. "Show this vulnerable point to us and you'll be released. But no false moves! One sign of treachery and you're dead!"

The Hawk's strong-cut face showed no change. It was only inwardly that he smiled.

Their very manner of accompanying him showed their respect for the slender adventurer.

He had no gun; he was stooped by the unrelieved weight of the massive helmet, the suit itself and the chunky blocks of metal which were the boots; his every dragging step was that of a man shackled by chains—but he was Hawk Carse! And so, as he shuffled out through the front door of the house and lumbered with painful effort across the clearing, he was surrounded by a glitter of ray-guns held by the close-pressing circle of men. Tantril's own gun kept steady on his broad fabric-clad back, and of its proximity he kept reminding Carse.

New guards were already on watch on each of the three watch-platforms, their eyes sweeping around the clearing and the jungle and the dark stretch of the lake, and often returning to the crowd which marked the stumbling giant's progress below. Each point of defense was manned. In the ranch's central control room, a steel-sheathed cubby in the basement of Tantril's house, men stood watchful, their hands ready at the wheels and levers which commanded the ranch's ray-batteries, their eyes on the vision-screen which gave to this unseen heart of the place a panoramic view of what was transpiring above. And all waited on what the grotesque, bloated figure they watched might reveal.

Watch—watch—watch. A hundred eyes, below, above, beside the Hawk, were centered and alert on each move of his clumsy progress. The barrels of two-score ray-guns transfixed him. Under such guard he arrived at the ranch's fence where it approached the Great Briney.

"Open the gate," said the Hawk curtly. "It's down there."

He pointed to where the lake's pebbled beach shelved downward to the tiny murmurous waves, a ten-foot stretch of ghostly white between the guarding fence and the water.

"Down there?" repeated Tantril slowly. "Down to the lake?"

"Yes!" Carse snapped irritably. "Well, will you open the gate? I'm very tired: I can't bear this suit much longer."

Lar Tantril conferred uneasily with Esret, while his men cast shivering glances out over the dark wind-rippled plain of the lake. But no enemy showed there. The beach was clear for fifty yards on each side.

"By Iapetus!" the adventurer complained harshly, "are you children, to be afraid of the dark? Tantril, put your gun into me, and shoot if I try anything suspicious! Open the gate!"

Finally the lock was unfastened and the gate swung out. Tantril stationed a man there, ready to close and lock it in case of need, and then, Hawk Carse, still surrounded by the alert Venusians, shuffled down to the edge of the water.

Over the Great Briney was silence. No shape broke its calm. The air held only the nervous whispers of the crowd and the scrape and crunch of the lone Earthling's dragging boots as they made wide furrows in the hard pebbly soil of the beach.

The men had fallen back a little, and now were a half circle around him down to the water's brink. The watch-beacon's light caught them full there, and threw great blots of shadows lakeward from them. Their ray-guns were gripped tighter as their shifty eyes darted from his huge bulk to the water ahead, and back. Doubt and fear swayed them all.

The Hawk wasted no time, but stepped out to knee-high level on the sharply shelving bottom. At this Tantril objected.

"Hold, Carse!" he roared. "You play for time, I think! Where is this point of attack?"

The bloated figure did not answer him, but bent over as if searching for something under the tiny waves which now were slapping his thigh. He reached one hand down and probed around with it, apparently feeling. The eyes watching him were wide and fear-fascinated.

"Here—or no," the Hawk muttered to himself, though a dozen could hear him. "A little farther, I think... Here—but no, I forgot: the tide has come in. A little farther..." He stopped suddenly and straightened, turned to the Venusian chief. "Don't forget, Lar Tantril, you have promised I can go free!"

Then he resumed his search of the bottom, the black surface of water up to his waist. Again the fearful Venusian leader roared an objection:

"You're tricking us, little devil—"

"Oh, don't be an ass!" Carse snapped back. "As if I could get away— your ray-guns on me!"

Another half minute passed; a few more short steps were taken. A muttered oath came from one of the wet, uncomfortable men in the grip of fear. Several there were on the brink of turning in a panicky dash for the safety of the enclosure behind, the warm buildings, guarded by ray-batteries—and yet an awful fascination held them. What metallic horror of the deeps was being exposed?

"Just a, second, now," the Hawk was murmuring. "You'll all see... Somewhere...right...here ... somewhere..."

He held them taut, expectant. The water licked around the waist of his suit. One more slow step; one more yet.

*"Here!"* he cried triumphantly, and clicked his face-plate closed. And the men who stared, faces pale, hearts pounding, ray-guns at the ready, saw him no longer. The water had closed over that shiny metal helmet. Only a mocking ripple was left.

Hawk Carse was gone!

* * * *

Gone!—and laughing to himself. The space-suit, his heavy prison of metal and fabric, would protect him from water as well as from space! It offered his golden—his only—opportunity. It had been pierced by Tantril's shots, back in the house, but only the gravity-plate compartments, which were sealed and separate. It was still—after he had closed the mittens—airtight, an effective little submarine in the dark waters of the Great Briney!

So Carse followed his black course over the lake-bottom laughing and laughing. In his mind he could see what he had left behind: the men, shivering there in the water for an instant, completely befogged, and perhaps firing one or two shots at where he had disappeared; then turning and breaking back in a grand rush for the fence and safety. And the ray-batteries, all manned and centered on the lake; Tantril, in a very fury of rage, but fearful, preparing for a siege; preparing for anything that might loom suddenly from the water! And all of them wondering what lay beneath its calm surface; what he, Hawk Carse, had gone to join!

For days they would stare fearfully at the lake, while the tides rolled steadily in and out; for days the ray-batteries would be held ready, and none would venture outside the fence. It might take hours for the realization of his trick to sink in—but they still would not be sure of anything, and would have to keep vigilant against the still-possible attack.

Fourteen miles up the coast was Ban Wilson's ranch, and Eliot Leithgow and Friday waiting there. He would rest for a while, and then the three of them would go home to the laboratory—whose location was now still secret. And then, later, there was his promise to the coordinated brains to be kept...

But that was in the future. For the present, he went his dark, watery way laughing. Laughing and laughing again...

Yes, John Sewell, first of all Hawk Carse's traits was his resourcefulness!

*See the March, 1932 issue of Amazing Stories.

# THE REIGN OF THE REPTILES

## ALAN CONNELL
## (1915-?)

*Wonder Stories,*
August 1935

## CHAPTER 1
## HUMAN GUINEA-PIG

Kane stood up and stared at me heatedly. "There are a hundred different things," he said, "that go to prove the theory of man's evolution from lower forms of life. I don't see why you shut your eyes to them and insist that our ancestors were created instaneously out of nothing."

"I'm satisfied," I said. "I'll stick to religion—you can have science."

"Religion?" said Kane. "In twenty years-"

"Why can't we have them both?" I interrupted him and quoted:

> *"'A Fire Mist and a planet*
> *A crystal and a shell*
> *A jelly fish and a saurian*
> *And caves where the cave men dwell;*
> *Then a sense of law and beauty,*
> *And a face turned from the clod—*
> *Some call it evolution,*
> *And others call it God.'"[3]*

"Oh, shut up!" said Kane, with customary disrespect for poetry—especially when called upon to support arguments. He got up, went from the room. I heard him tramp down the stairs, slam the front door after him. I smiled.

Kane Sanders is related to me in some indistinct way, and I first met him

---

3     William Herbert Carruth.

when he wrote asking me whether I could give him work. I invited him to come and see me. I liked him then—and have grown to like him even more.

He stayed to look after the business side of life—which is far from complicated, involving as it does a mere disinterested correspondence with the fed-up publishers of my short stories. Fed-up because, through other interests forcing themselves on me, my material has deteriorated from common poorness to something unmentionable.

During my two-year association with Sanders I discovered only one flaw—and *it* was of little consequence—in a very pleasant personality. He was too fond of arguments. Since I am a victim of the same fault, and it became habit and tradition to oppose him, things might have been disagreeable if one of us hadn't always been able to see the humor of the thing before it went very far.

On this night I paid little attention to Sanders' departure. He would, I thought, be now walking morosely down the road to the beach. And he would return in his usual high spirits before very long.

I was right on the first score but wrong on the second.

* * * *

Some time in the early morning I awoke and remembered that I had not heard Sanders come in. I got up and went along the passage to his room. Just as I opened the door I heard the click of another door downstairs. I waited and presently a man came up the stairs. At first. I did not recognize him. The clothes were tight on his broad frame, the shoes were laceless. Then I saw it was Sanders.

A stubble of crudely-removed hair grew on his chin and cheeks. I think it was this that struck me as most fantastic at the time—Sanders had left me not many hours before, perfectly shaved. Now his face was covered with traces of recently removed black bristle!

There were other incredible things. He was browner than I had ever seen him before. Always big-limbed, he was now superhumanly developed. His hair, I saw when he came closer, was longer than it had ever been before.

He greeted me with a faint smile, took my arm and drew me into his room. When he switched on the light the half-seen details of his transformation stood out starkly. I had an experience I never hope to have again. I felt the blood running out of my cheeks, felt my face go dead white.

Sanders looked at me with strange eyes. "You remember our arguments about evolution and God?"

I nodded.

"I have an awful kind of suspicion that we were BOTH wrong," he said. "Did you know," he went on abruptly, "that there was a time millions of years ago when reptiles ruled land, sea and air?"

Without waiting for me to answer he took something from his pocket and unrolled brown paper from it.

Stark in the white light was a black-scaled five-fingered thing, loathsomely suggestive of the reptilian. It had been severed smoothly at the wrist and in the bent clutch of the wrinkled fingers was the dim reminiscence of some nameless threat.

Fantastically too, about each of those members was a blue-jeweled ring!

"Fulu, emissary of Luada," said Sanders, half to himself. "I wonder what he thinks now!"

"*Kane!*" I said. "What—"

He thrust away the black claw. "Sorry," he said. "Listen and I'll tell you." He hesitated and added fretfully, "These clothes are choking me." Then he took off coat and shirt and sat on the bed with knees drawn up in an odd squatting position. And while I stared dumbly at the leathery brown of his chest, he told me what follows.

\* \* \* \*

When he left the house wandered down the track to the road with the idea of walking to Salabec. But dusk fell and he stood hesitating on the concrete. He heard the sound of a car and saw its headlights come around the bend. He stepped aside to let it pass but it halted, crept slowly forward, then stopped again like a man in doubt.

Presently someone got out and came around to stand between the headlamps. Sanders felt a man's keen eyes staring at him and he turned away, flushed and ill at ease. But a voice stopped him. "Just a moment—do you mind?"

Sanders said, "Well?" and faced the man. He was short, fragile-framed and loosely dressed. His gray hair was untidy above a white face.

His bright eyes studied Sanders from head to foot and, sensing the young man's discomfort, he said, "Your pardon. I was looking for a man,"

"Why?" asked Sanders. "Is something wrong with your car?"

"Why—yes! My car—"

"Then I'm sorry," Sanders said, "I can't—"

"I'm sure it's something insignificant," the other interrupted. "I'd like you to look."

In the face of this point-blank request Sanders went to the man's side as the latter lifted the cover from the engine.

"There—I think the trouble's there," said the man, indicating the ignition. "I'll hold this torch while you look."

Later Sanders was able to see humor in his acting as this man's mechanic—this man who probably knew more about machinery, from the simplest system of pulleys to the most complex electrical apparatus, than anyone else in the world.

For several minutes he fumbled in the yellow light, then straightened. "I can't see anything," he began stopped. There was a peculiar tenseness about the stranger's face and involuntarily Sanders' eyes went to the back of the car, where there were two dim faces. He was conscious of dwelling in a strange atmosphere and his lips formed a question. Then something whipped up from the darkness and smothered his face. He choked and began to fall.

\* \* \* \*

For a time that he could not estimate a heavy grayness lay about him. Then suddenly it fell away. For a while he stayed quiet, then opened his eyes. He was lying on the bed of a plainly furrnnished room. Three men stood over him. One was the man from the car—the second he judged to be a Japanese—the third was a thin fair youth whose eyes held something greater than mere genius.

During an unembarrassed silence the three stared down at him. Then the first man said to the other two, "All right. Go and get everything ready. I'll talk to him."

As the two left the room Sanders made an effort to get up—a vain one, for he was handcuffed to the bed. "Let me up!" he demanded. "What—"

The man held up a hand. "There's not much time to waste. Listen—my companions and I are what you might call experimental scientists. Tonight we were driving to Salabec in search of a man for one of our experiments. I saw you. I knew you were the type I wanted, so I took you. Do this thing willingly and I'll pay you well. Otherwise—"

"You can go to the devil!" said Sanders, heaving on the bed.

"I thought you wouldn't. But we'll use you just the same. Now listen even more carefully.

"Juan, the young fellow, is an abnormal. You've heard, I suppose, of mathematical geniuses and people with fantastic memory powers. Juan is frankly a freak intelligence. His brain really belongs hundreds of years in the future. I don't think he has ever read technical work on higher mathematics, but by sheer power of reasoning he knows more than all the mathematical giants of the world put together.

"Takashai and I discovered him. We attached ourselves to him because we realized his possibilities and because—to be frank—we want a share in the fame that must inevitably come to him. Juan as yet doesn't worry about making money.

"When we began to develop- his talents he insisted that our first work of importance be the contriving of an apparatus for transporting objects along time-lines so that he can confirm certain monstrous theories he has formed from studying palaeontological data. Under Juan's supervision Takashai and I have built that apparatus.

"Already we've tested it on bricks and guinea-pigs—transported them along artificial time-lines to both past and future. Now Juan is impatient to settle his horrible ideas on the origin of Man. He'd go himself, I believe, if his presence were not needed at the apparatus."

Handcuffed to the bed, reflecting on the oddities of fate that had thrown him among these madmen, Kane Sanders looked straight at the man and said, "You're mad."

His captor bent over him. "I am not mad," he said distinctly. "I ask you, what would a man of the year one hundred A.D. think of our present-day science? Wouldn't it be plain magic? And you and I are just the same when confronted with Juan's plans and ideas—for I'm as much a child as you are when Juan speaks. His thought-processes are almost unimaginable."

The Japanese came into the room. "Everything is ready, Carlyle," he said. "Juan is impatient."

Carlyle produced a heavily-scented pad and pressed it to Sanders' nostrils, leaving him in an unresisting half-stupor.

"I'm sorry to do this," Carlyle said, "but it's necessary, since I can't convince you that we are only overzealous scientists."

Sanders was carried into a brilliantly lighted chamber and placed on a metal table. Half-dazed he looked about him. He felt a shock of doubt. Across the ceiling a giant power cable was slung in drooping loops. In far corners crouched green polished machines, oddly vital. Near at hand, circling him, were bright complexities of copper wire and giant silver tubes. If the men were mad, Sanders thought, then their madness had followed strange paths.

He felt hands at his waist. A belt was fastened about him. "Water, food, an automatic and ammunition," Carlyle explained, then went to help Takashai with the machines in the corner. As Juan, silent and aloof, took his place before a keyboard that seemed the vital part of the whole mechanism, Carlyle returned.

"When you next open your eyes," he said, "you will be somewhere about the close of the Mesozoic, the age of reptiles, some millions of years in the past. But. I warn you, don't be afraid. Remember you are armed—and there is Juan, who will draw you back when he thinks you have had time to examine the conditions. Juan turned, hesitated, said doubtfully, "I would like you to notice what life there is."

"Yes," said Carlyle and he pressed Sanders' hand. "I think I'm insane to force this on you," he went on, "but I can't help myself." He drew back.

## CHAPTER II
## THE ROOM OF HORROR

Sanders fell jarringly on one shoulder. His eyes went swiftly around a vast gloomy room. Through the half-ovals of windows far to his left white moonlight poured.

He did not know where he was. It did not occur to him that Carlyle's fantastic predictions might be fulfilled and he wondered where his three captors had gone.

He went to one of the windows, which were glassless, and as he gazed out, the first terrifying doubt came. Below him was a dim expanse of sloping roof, then a belt of darkness, then a wall of impregnable thickness that rose sharply, shutting out jungle growth of such unbridled magnificence and gigantic size as he had never imagined could exist.

Somehow allied with ferns but incredibly bigger they reached their plumes hundreds of feet into the night sky, looming high above the building in which he stood until they seemed to touch the moon. It was a strange moon, big and tinted with green—but its peculiarities were negligible before the chilling terror of the gargantuan forest—chilling despite the warm tropical breeze that blew in his face.

As he turned from the window Sanders heard an unnatural screaming emanating from the dark forest, a roaring and bellowing. He hurried back across the room, blundered into something that rocked unsteadily and, with eyes rapidly becoming accustomed to the half-light, he stared at it.

He saw that it was a glass globe supported on flimsy legs—and in it was a great wet thing, soft and shapeless, that stirred stupidly. From it came a nightmarish sucking and squeezing as it heaved itself up and down.

With a terror that was silent but none the less real, Sanders went back and forth across the horrid chamber. Each step brought a new ghastly sight imprisoned in a transparent vessel—luminous eyes sunk in white membranous bags of skin—eyes that followed with insensate intentness his every move. There were things that swam like butterflies in amber liquid—jelly-like, pulsing things—mutilated forms floating lifeless in the fluids of their containers. And there were tables loaded with instruments and shapes he dared not look at. There was death unspeakable and life madder than the weirdest dream.

Sunk into one of the walls was a shelf of vessels filled with strange-smelling chemicals and as he felt his way along this he thought he heard a shuffling sound in other regions of the building. He groped forward with new speed until he touched what resembled the bars of a cage. He looked between the bars at the sight of the thing that leered at him from within—a swaying apelike creature with pouting lips, sightless eyes and mutilated limbs—he involuntarily voiced a hoarse cry.

Almost simultaneously, it seemed to him that the far-away shuffling took on a quicker and more definite rhythm. With an overwhelming instinct to hide he sank beneath the shadow of a bench.

For minutes he crouched there, listening to the shuffle and scrape of the nameless feet as they hastened to their hiding place. Instinctively he knew that whatever inhuman thing owned this room of horror was coming to investigate the sounds he had made. And again, in spite of the tropical warmth of the night, he felt cold.

Now the wall farthest from him grew faintly luminous and soon he made out outlines of a high oval-topped doorway, between which, deep in the darkness beyond, a spot of light bobbed up down. Nearer it came, reached the portal, hovered there a moment.

It entered the room, shedding a glow of flat white light about it. And now it revealed itself as a transparent sphere, with some phosphorescent substance. On two sides of its surface were black blurs.

It came closer to Sanders. He felt the beat of blood at his temples.

The globe was held by a creature like a mythical devil incarnate! Its oily green needle-fanged head hovered just above the luminous sphere, the hellish red eyes darting from side to side in search of the intruder.

Where the shoulders should have been were hunched lumps that made the man think of folded wings. The body and shuffling feet were invisible. The claws appeared in silhouette on the surface of the globe that the monstrosity held before it.

Back and forth like an embodied demon it roamed, thrusting its long, hideous snout suspiciously into corners, pausing to hold its strange lantern beneath benches, even stopping to peer from the windows as though it expected someone of having made a hasty exit.

But incredibly good fortune was with Sanders for the devil-thing, though it hesitated near him, eventually passed him by. Satisfied that nothing was amiss it betook itself and its luminary from the chamber and shuffled along the corridor.

Many minutes later Sanders stirred, rose to his feet and groped to the doorway. In the corridors beyond he soon found himself lost and in the unrelieved darkness he fumbled and felt as though through a maze, all sense of direction gone. At odd times sounds from other quarters of the building stopped him like an animal at bay—but mostly all was still.

At length, with dying hope and in utter dejection, he sat down with his back to the wall and stared at the dark until his eyes grew heavy.

* * * *

HE awakened suddenly to daylight and got stiffly to his feet. Before and behind him a corridor stretched. It was colored vividly and grotesquely and in merging hues which changed so subtly that he could not detect the exact spot of transition.

Sleep had been a stimulant and clarifier to Kane Sanders. He knew now that all this was neither dream nor imagination. There was no more doubt—Juan's almost magical apparatus had thrown him back across the ages of time to a prehistoric past.

Recognition of this, without the horror of the night, gave him immeasurable relief and a kind of growing courage to win his way through this new existence. He had brains and strength and at his hip was a weapon. Behind all that was the everlasting promise that Juan would again bridge the time gulf and draw him back to reality.

He drank some water and ate a little of the concentrated food at his belt. But before he had finished, he heard a hissing and soughing like the beat of wings. Far along the corridor he saw an approaching shape. Caution uppermost he ran in the opposite direction until he reached an oblong of curtain cleverly set in the wall.

He pushed through it nor was he too soon, for a moment later a creature soared past him. It resembled slightly a gigantic lizard and the fanged snout, if not the same one, was at least practically identical with that Sanders had seen in the room of horror.

In daylight it had lost its supernatural and diabolical aspect, appearing still hideous but only in a reptilian way. It propelled itself on hissing leathery wings and its sinuous body was clad in a blue silken robe. About its ugly brow was a jeweled diadem. Its claws were alight with jewels.

Alive now to the dangers of the main corridors Sanders made his way along the side passage which the curtain had hidden. He came to another curtained doorway, hesitated, then tentatively parted it.

The room beyond the draping was as fantastically hued as the corridors. From the ceiling, suspended on golden chains, hung a number of canoe-shaped couches and in each of these sprawled a hideous monster like the flying lizard of the corridor—but these were smaller and evidently females.

Their faces were repulsive, with flat tooth-rimmed snouts and little red eyes, but in their claws they held polished metal plates in which they constantly admired their frightful images. They were garbed in cloths swathed tightly about them and on their smooth skulls were set turbans or head-dresses.

Grouped about these monstrosities were smaller abject creatures of another reptilian species—but these were unclothed and evidently slaves. They held urns from which they sprayed their mistresses with jets of perfume.

Presently one of the monsters in the swinging couches elevated herself and began what seemed like a song—though its compound of garbled hissing and screaming bore no likeness to any music Sanders had ever heard.

At the song's conclusion the slaves flapped their atrophied wings in ap-plause and another monster took up the tune. Sanders turned away. As he did so his foot caught in the curtain, strained it taut and released it fluttering.

He stood frozen. The singing had stopped! He parted the curtain and saw that each of the lizard-creatures was staring at him.

As he ran he heard a shrill shrieking and the flutter of ungainly wings. Intent on escape he passed back to the main corridor and fled along it. Be-fore long he knew that he was being pursued and ran even faster amid the clatter of his heavy-soled boots.

This last proved his undoing for one of the flying lizards, attracted by the noise, soared from a side passage and threw itself upon him before he could reach the revolver at his belt. Boney claws dug into his arms and held him until three more monsters arrived.

One, who wore a jeweled circlet about his brow, muttered some shrill words. Sanders stood quiescent, aloof, lips firm. The monster repeated the words, then fastened its crimson eyes on him and gave him his first glimpse of the uncanny power of thought transference possessed by these creatures.

Two questions built gradually up in his mind. "How did you escape? Why did you disobey?"

Sanders did not attempt to answer.

By what seemed like endless mental repetition, another question was on him. "To whom do you belong?"

Again Sanders was silent. He watched his questioner dismiss his fel-lows. Then, with both arms tightly held, he was beneath the clacking wings of his captor, carried through great lengths of corridor, until they alighted in a room.

It was the room of his ghastly experience of the night before—the room that he was to know as the creative laboratory of the reptile scientists of Luada.

## CHAPTER III
## THE MYSTERY OF THE PIT

In the yellow light of day the room had lost much of its horror but still there was a breath of unholy mystery in its lizard-like inhabitants as they bent with shining knives over bizarre distortions of human bodies that were etched on tables before them. Blood trickled from those tables and down into the little gutters that carried it to the brownstained drains in the floor.

On the walls hung parchments inscribed with anatomical cross-sections, some of which suggested oddities of inner structures to Sanders.

At the entry of captor and captive the monsters looked up from their work and stared at Sanders. Again he was aware of the mental questions,

"Why did you disobey?" and then, "To whom do you belong?"

When there was no answer one of the creatures gave an order. The one who held Sanders gave a garbled reply, then thrust its claws into his clothing and ripped every thread from him, even bending to tear off his shoes. The thing was done so quickly that Sanders' fingers could not reach the revolver before it was torn away with his belt.

As the man's clothing vanished, the reptiles pressed forward with hissing cries. Screeching with fanatical glee they laid possessive claws on him. He caught a jumble of mental communication which they abruptly resorted to.

"A first-class specimen. He must be from my pit."

"No," interposed a second. "You have none as good as this. I am certain he escaped from my pit."

"He belongs to neither of you," interrupted a third. "I was working on a particularly good specimen. I feel sure that this is the one."

Now a monster larger than the rest came forward and took hold of Sanders. "None of you seems to know whom he belongs to. Therefore he shall go in my pit, where in any case he probably belongs."

Sanders was taken down the aisles of tables past the loathsome things in the glass vessels to a table near the end of the room, where the lizard scientist opened a metal trap-door in the floor and dropped him through the opening.

Sanders felt himself fall one or two feet, then struck a slide and rushed diagonally through the darkness. A spot of light appeared ahead, swelled and he was spilled into hot sunlight. His prison was a roofless pit, walled to a height of twenty feet on four sides.

Behind him, above a slope of lower roof, were the windows of the laboratory. The far wall held back the gigantic fern forest that towered green above it to the vivid sky in which burned the brilliant sun.

Standing back a little, his face turned from the jungle, Sanders could see the mingling of marble domes and granite turrets that made up the great city-palace of the reptiles. This pit was one of many walled squares projecting from the main body of the palace.

Sanders was not the only prisoner. In scattered groups about him were creatures of both sexes and some that were doubtful. Almost without exception they were covered with apelike hair and all who were not entirely naked wore only meager strips of cloth.

All were human in a disconcerting way, and a few—these were practically hairless and more sanely built—looked comparatively intelligent. Many of the creatures showed the marks of recent wounds and Sanders could not avoid thinking of the shapes on the tables in the laboratory.

One of the men shouted some words at Sanders. They were oddly like the speech of the reptiles. Sanders did not attempt to answer but leaned against the wall in a kind of detached wonder.

He thought of Juan who was to draw him back across the unguessable centuries, of Juan's quest. There was surely much material about this reptile city if he could only plumb its significance—this strangely distorted condition where lizard monstrosities dominated a grotesque humanity.

Sanders smiled bitterly. Was it likely that he would ever have an opportunity to present such material to Juan? Wasn't it more logical to suppose these four walls and the patch of tropic sky would be all he would ever see for the rest of his life?

The day faded into twilight. A number of the smaller reptilian slaves flew over-head erratically and dropped strips of flesh into the pit. Sanders chewed a little, reflecting that he might as well accustom himself to the fare.

That night he slept uneasily on the cold ground, dreaming repeatedly that all was normal again, only to awaken to the hopeless reality.

Sitting in the shade of a wall in the sultry heat of the next morning to pass the time, he began to fashion a crude loin-cloth from the furry strips of skin left from the previous night's meal.

While he was thus occupied the man who had addressed him on his advent in the pit squatted before him and again spoke to him, this time at sufficient length to convince Sanders that the tongue was identical with that of the reptiles though with a minimum of the hissing inflections.

Sanders looked at the heavy-browed fellow with a sense of superiority. Then he smiled—he himself was more ignorant than a baby in this new world. He made himself open to friendship to Nu-Az, as the man named himself, by a gift of the meat that was dropped in the pit that morning. A companionship was established which, through the days that followed, gave him an insight into the new language.

* * * *

When the first glimmerings of coherency were built up Sanders was subjected to puzzling questions.

"Who are you?" Nu-Az, wanted to know. "You don't belong in this pit."

"I don't understand," Sanders answered. "I don't belong in any pit." Nu-Az drew back suspiciously and Sanders realized that he was setting about things in the wrong way. He went on, stumbling over the new tongue taught him, and now he employed subterfuge.

"I can't remember anything. I had a fall and hurt my head. Perhaps if you told me a little, everything would come back."

Nu-Az hesitated, accepted the story. "You are in the pit of Lo-Lo, greatest of the evolutionary scientists. You and all of us are the subjects of his experiments. Each of the scientists has a pit like this. And there are many scientists in Luada."

"What is Luada?" Sanders asked.

"Your injury was bad," said Nu-Az. "Luada is the palace and domain of Luad, emperor of the ruling reptiles. I have been told that there are other palaces and other emperors across the great seas and forests but of these things I am not certain."

"Where do your people live?" This question puzzled Nu-Az. "These are my people," he said, indicating the beast-creatures about him. "These and those in the other pits."

"But where do the others of your race live?" Sanders pressed, "the people from whom you were captured?"

"There are no others. I was never captured."

"You mean that the reptiles killed them all?"

"There are no others," Nu-Az repeated patiently. "The reptiles reign everywhere. We of the pits are the only ones of the new race. There are none outside. You and I and the others of the new pits were made by the scientists."

Cold seemed to creep up Sanders' spine. There were vague stirrings of unholy theories in his mind and he thought of the puzzling, vacant factors in the evolutionary tree built up by men of the twentieth century.

A great fear of this ghastly mystery of the past came over him and he dared not question any further. He looked across the pit at the colossal fern forest, at the shadowy green aisles of its inner depths.

"The jungle would be kinder to us than the reptiles," he said. "You and I could easily escape once we had scaled the wall."

Nu-Az was disturbed. "It is wrong to think of leaving the pits. The scientists have forbidden it. You know that we are to be their new slaves in place of the Zori, who cannot be had in sufficient numbers."

The Zori, thought Sanders, must be the smaller reptiles who waited on the female Luadans. Evidently there were not enough of them to do all the cloth-spinning and food-gathering that the Luadans required, so there was to be a new race of slaves.

Sanders said, "Yes, it may be wrong to leave the pits—but that's what I'm going to do. Will you come?"

A longing look crept into Nu-Az's eyes. "I will come," he said. "But there is a young girl in the next pit I want. She must come with us."

They waited until nightfall, then Nu-Az climbed the wall. Sanders came more slowly, feeling precariously for the little crevices and protuberances. When he was within reaching distance, Nu-Az leaned down and drew him to the top. The dark warmth of the forest stole about them and they heard the stir of invisible bodies in its far reaches.

Nu-Az was uneasy and hesitant but Sanders urged him on. They went along the wall a little way, then Nu-Az descended into the darkness of the next pit. Sanders watched. He heard movement, whispering voices, and on the jungle side of the wall there was a vast slithering sound that he could not define.

Nu-Az came back up the wall. At his side was a long-haired black-browed female, who clung to his arm in terror. She wore a strip of stiffening hide, which gave her a certain unconscious superiority over Nu-Az, who wore nothing.

The three crept farther along the wall to a tangle of thick vines. "Here we can climb," said Nu-Az. "We can climb to the tops of the trees and be safe."

He thrust the girl and she grasped the creepers and began to climb agilely. Nu-Az followed, then Sanders.

## CHAPTER IV
## THE PRIMEVAL JUNGLE

They clambered higher and higher on the rubbery tendrils and soon Sanders was envying the muscular energy of Nu-Az and the girl, who both climbed tirelessly and without effort. A hundred feet from the ground he had to loop his foot through a creeper and rest. Thereafter he repeated this at every fifty feet.

It was during these rests that he became aware to the full of the creeping rustling life that seemed to fill this jungle. He saw nothing but in the sliding and climbing of those invisible entities he began to sense a greater peril than he had dreamed of. His ascent became faster.

The vines ended in a mat of parasitic upper growth that covered the tree-tops and here he found Nu-Az and the girl lying on the vegetation with great leaves wrapped around them. He followed their example with the leaves, lay down in a yielding bed of creeper and slept.

The next day and the ones that followed did not have much significance for Kane Sanders. He was aware that, accompanied by Nu-Az and the girl Yzul, he wandered through the upper reaches of that gigantic semi-fern forest, eating peculiar nuts and fruits, drinking from little tree cavities where water gathered. But all this was an exotic nightmare—it was too far removed from reality to impress itself seriously upon him.

There were, of course, some things that left a terrific impression. Once he swung down from the upper foliage, among the huge leaves and vines, and there below him he saw the ground and on it rolled two horned and armored beasts in a shrieking death struggle. There was blood and a hideous roaring and an earthshaking thunder as the monsters fell over and over each other, crushing the lesser vegetation in a welter of flying green.

Sanders watched, dry-mouthed, until one of the brutes broke away, shook itself and lumbered out of sight. Then he began to climb slowly back to the safety of the upper foliage. He realized now that much of the story of the dawn ages was lost irretrievably to palaeontologists of the twentieth century. He had seen many restorations of the prehistoric giants of this era but none even approached in size the battling creatures he had just witnessed.

When he regained the tangled garden of the tree-tops he found Yzul in a state of panic and Nu-Az clumsily trying to comfort her. "She says something"—he waved his hands in inadequate descriptive gestures—"chased her."

"Don't worry," said Sanders. "All the monsters are on the ground. This is the only safe part of the jungle."

But he was wrong. That night, as he lay in a natural hammock of leaves and creepers, he awakened suddenly to hear a rustling and sliding. And as he lay there staring at the darkness, an unimaginably huge cylindrical body swayed and heaved across his vision and two green slant-eyes turned briefly to look at him. Then it was gone.

* * * *

The next morning Sanders made himself a rough spear—a tough six-foot barb that he tore from one of the thorny ferns. He saw too that Yzul and Nu-Az were similarly armed. He no longer felt that the treetops were safe.

Toward midday he set off to hunt for a yellow berry that was his favorite food. His search took him down to the middle terraces, where the berries grew—one of many parasites in this jungle—from crevices in the giant trunks of the ferns.

He swung downward with the easy grace of a trapeze artist, slipping down the vines like a spider on a web. Where the foliage was less tangled he walked fearlessly across great natural bridges from tree to tree, careless of the green depths below.

On one of these bridges he went down on hand and knee to reach down for the yellow berries. As he crouched there he felt the great bough vibrate. Looking up he saw the thing writhing along the aerial path toward him.

It was a snake. But it was two hundred feet in length, and its vast heaving body was six feet thick.

For one instant Sanders stared at the polished coils driving toward him—then he turned and ran. A few dozen paces, a glance back at the sliding monster and he saw the futility of trying to outpace it. He swerved to the side of the bough, leaped into a bunch of creepers and slid down with feverish speed. He looked up. The head of the incredible serpent peered down from the branch above. For a moment the slanted green eyes watched the escaping prey, then the great spade-shaped head drove downward with the speed of an arrow.

Sanders' feet had touched another bough but there was a mossy growth on it that gave underfoot and threw him on his face. When he regained his feet the head was almost upon him and further flight was useless.

He had no fear of poisonous venom for such a monster as this had no need of subsidiary weapons, but one snap of those gigantic jaws would cut his body into two distinct pieces. He snatched his spear from his belt, and as the head rushed upon him, he drove the point into one of the emerald eyes. Then in the brief instant that the monster recoiled he threw himself from the branch.

For thirty feet he fell, then a matted mass of leaves and creeper caught and held him. He lay still while a crashing turmoil raged overhead, moving not a muscle until that king of snakes ceased its frenzied lashing and raged away to another region of the forest.

There was quiet again. Sweating from heat and excitement Sanders resumed his search for food. When he had eaten he hurried back to Nu-Az and Yzul and told them that all three must look for a new home.

They moved across the forest-top all the rest of that day and the whole of the next, putting as much distance they could between them and the haunts of the giant serpent, though Sanders began to think that flight was useless and had an uneasy conviction that they were surviving in this jungle more by luck than anything else.

Once during their long travels they passed the fringe of the prehistoric wilderness and saw the white breakers and far-reaching blue of an ocean or great lake. For almost an hour, Sanders stood on the limb of a giant tree, staring out over the glittering waters as though at any moment he expected some weird craft of this forgotten age to heave into the shore.

But none came and soon something of the loneliness of those uncharted waters began to seep into him and he turned back to the companionship of Nu-Az and Yzul. The old bitterness against Juan returned and hope was dying. He felt now that he was doomed to spend the rest of his days in this immemorial world of the past, naked and forever flying from perils whose extent he could only guess at.

He said to Nu-Az, "In the morning we'll move on again."

Nu-Az agreed but this wandering was not what he wanted. With Yzul always at his side, an idea of a place of permanency and stability was developing in him—the desire for a fixed shelter in a fixed locality.

Back across the forest leagues they ranged, dawn after dawn, night after night. Now Yzul began to complain about the restless, aimless roaming.

"Stay with me one more day," said Sanders, who hated to part with his companions and found no less abhorrent the thought of settling down to watch their home-making. So they went on through the morning.

In the cool of the afternoon he swung down to the lower terraces of the trees and there he found something that froze him into keen-eyed stillness.

Plodding along a newly beaten trail was a string of about twenty naked human beings, each bearing a woven basket filled with freshly picked fruit. For an instant Sanders was in doubt, then he guessed that these hairy creatures were from the pits of Luada.

This was soon confirmed for behind the basket-bearers came two of the ruling reptiles, wings folded, walking on ungainly feet. Each carried a long club but it was evident that they relied less on force than on the ingrained obedience of their slaves to keep things in order.

From the party's heavily laden state, Sanders deduced that it was on its way back to Luada, so he swung on ahead of them. Presently he glimpsed a patch of granite through the dense green ahead and his fears were realized. He had wandered right back to the city of the reptiles!

He climbed to the utmost height of the forest, crawled on to a projecting limb of ferns and looked down on the domed roofs of Luada. Even as he watched a number of reptile slaves appeared on a high balcony with a great quantity of meat. With pieces of this in their claws they flew over the pits of the scientists, dropping their burdens with piercing cries. It was feeding time.

One of the slaves flew close to Sanders and stared directly at him, so he drew back and climbed away in search of Nu-Az. He found him sprawling on a great leaf, basking in the sun, and swung lightly to his side.

"Luada is nearby," he said.

Nu-Az sprang to his feet. Yzul crept to her lord's side.

"We'd better move on," Sanders counselled. "It wouldn't be safe to stay so close."

"Yes," agreed Nu-Az. Then Yzul shrieked and pointed up.

Hovering above and a little behind them were three Luadans!

In a flash Sanders knew that the flying slave had seen him and informed its masters. "*Down!*" he cried. "Down to the lower terraces!"

But it was too late. The reptiles alighted on the huge fern frond. One, robed with grotesque richness and heavily jeweled, stood forward.

"We have found you. But Luad is merciful and though the penalty for disobedience has always been death I, Fulu, am charged to tell you that you will not be punished if you return to Luada with me without resistance."

Sanders followed the garbled words with difficulty. "We're not going back."

"You will come," said Fulu, "and for your resistance you will warrant death." He signed to his companions. They darted forward with true reptile swiftness, seized Nu-Az and Yzul and bore them struggling away in the direction of Luada.

Fulu advanced on Sanders. "Back," said the latter and he began to retreat.

"Do not try to escape," Fulu commanded. "You are a strange specimen. You exhibit new traits of disobedience for which I cannot find an explanation and I intend to have you thoroughly examined when I have you back in Luada. Come willingly. I do not want you killed. Look, the other two have been taken and are even now entering Luada. It is foolish for you to resist."

"I'm never going back," said Sanders.

"You shall!" Fulu cried and sprang with wings and claws extended.

Two things were confusingly synchronized. Sanders saw the crimson-eyed lizard leap toward him. At the same instant he felt a dizziness and the air about him was tinted with blue crackling sparks. He felt the claw of Fulu fasten about his wrist, then he lost consciousness.

He was lying on a cold table.

In his ears was the dying hum of great machinery, the fading of immense power. Bending over him were three faces--and suddenly he remembered and understood. The faces were those of Carlyle, Juan and Takashai.

And the most concrete reminder of all that had happened—clutched about his arm was the severed claw of Fulu!

"You are back," said Takashai, "and the experiment is a success."

"Yes," Sanders said with a ghost of ar smile. "A success."

# CHAPTER V
## MAN FROM REPTILE

When Sanders finished his story he thrust his hands into the pockets of his borrowed trousers and slipped his legs back to the floor. "You don't believe me?" he said.

I had been staring wide-eyed at him.

"Of course," I protested. "Yes, of course. But there's so much—"

"Yes," he interrupted; "there's a lot unexplained. You want to ask questions? Well, go ahead."

I thought over the many things that were puzzling me then decided to start at the beginning. "You traveled in time?"

"Yes. Or better, time-rates were altered for me. Juan told me something about it and I'll try to give you what I can remember.

"Time is not a constant. Juan told me about a practical experiment performed some fifteen years ago, which definitely proves this. You may not know it but the plain sodium atom is a better clock than you can buy in any shop. For when its electrons are excited it emits electro-magnetic waves at a frequency of something like five hundred nine and one half millions of vibrations per second—and this is the same for any sodium atom, no matter what peculiarities of condition and surrounding it is subjected to.

"Now there's lots of vaporized sodium in the chromosphere of the sun and spectroscopic analysis of this shows that its atoms vibrate *at a slower rate* than the earth atom. In other words time—as a measure of physical change—passes more slowly on the sun.

"That then was Juan's basic principle. Time is not a constant. Then he went further to discover what time really is a product of and the ready solution was that the variation in solar and earth time can be accounted for by difference in mass. In other words, in the presence of a gravitational field greater than the earth's, time passes more slowly. Similarly you can conceive of time traveling faster on a midget world."

I said, "I still don't understand how Juan picked you out of a whole vast world of sea and jungle."

"Juan didn't pick me out—that part was practically automatic. You see, I and my clothes were the only foreign elements, the only things that didn't *belong* at that particular world-point."

"How—" I began.

"Wait. Imagine Juan's laboratory. It is fifteen minutes after my departure into the Mesozoic. Juan is ready to bring about my return. He has calculated—from time and gravitational-potential relationships between earth and sun and from the power of the gravity field he could create without collapsing space—that my journey to the past would occupy some three hours.

"But once having dispatched me he is no longer concerned with that part of my life. He chooses a point in the world-line—which is the path of a body through both space and time—a point a month in advance of the one he sent me to. Then he creates two more gravitational fields and projects the inner one to that point.

"There it made contact with me and within its deadening influence time passed slowly, while outside as it were whole centuries of earth-time rolled by, ultimately reaching nineteen hundred and fifty and Juan's laboratory. If I had been conscious and watching a clock it would have been only a four hours' journey to me."

"Four?" I asked. "Why not three, the same as before?"

"That had Juan puzzled a little. He did suggest that part of the gravitational field must have fastened itself on my clothes somewhere in Luada— thus lessening the power of my field and stretching the trip to four hours.

"I wonder where those clothes are now? The miniature field may yet land them in the laboratory in a day or two. Or, since Juan has relinquished control, they probably finished up in the Ice Age!"

I said, "And to think that the last remnant of that almost unimaginable reptile civilization must have long ago vanished from the earth!"

"Not everything," Sanders reminded me. "Remember the claw of Fulu, who must consider himself lucky that he didn't have his head taken off by the field. Anyhow that's the wrong way to look at it. It's a queer thing—past, present and future—all seeming to exist at once like—like a reel of movie film unrolled along a road.

"Only by moving along the film do you get the illusion of movement in it and the idea of time. Yet past, present and future are all there at once, though the people in the film have to follow the path set out for them. If only those people could free themselves from the film—though of course they're only images—they'd have the whole panorama of time open for their inspection. I think it was something like that with me."

"There's something else," I said. "Those reptiles were intelligent—like human beings."

"Like human beings," Sanders repeated as though the words held some secret meaning. "Yes—Juan thinks that the civilization of Luada was Nature's last try at giving the reptiles the scepter of world supremacy.

"One of the prime essentials of survival is tribe-making, and that's why the ants may one day rule this planet. But when the Luadans started to play about in their laboratories they undid all Nature's plans and unconsciously brought about their own downfall."

"By the way," I asked, "did you discover where Nu-Az and Yzul and those others *did* come from?"

Sanders sprang up angrily. "Have you missed the whole meaning—the whole truth of the thing? Remember Nu-Az's words, 'and we were made by the Luadans.' Now do you understand? *The human race was created in the Luadan laboratories!*"

"That's pure madness," I said, controlling myself with difficulty at the grotesque statement. "They couldn't create life."

"Why not? Life is only a chemical curiosity. And that isn't the solution as Juan sees it. The scientists of Luada experimented *with germ-cells from their own bodies*—a warped and planned ectogenesis—and man and his evolution were started. So you see Juan isn't so far from the common theory of Man's descent from the reptiles. He's just filled in the main link."

"I refuse to believe," I said. "It's too fantastic, revolting. You were misled."

"I hope to heaven I was—though it all fits in with what Juan anticipated before the experiment."

"That reminds me," I said suddenly. "Those men—you must know where they are. I'll call police headquarters and have them taken for—"

"No," Sanders said, smiling wanly at my excitement, "you won't do anything like that. You see, I've made arrangements. Tomorrow I'm going back to the fern jungle and Luada—to learn the truth once and for all."

\* \* \* \*

And even as he promised so he went.

And as I write the conclusion to this my mind toys with Sanders' incredible theories. Reptiles—man—next the insects.

And who knows what non-protoplasmic cycles of malevolent monstrosities shambled in the primal ooze and vapor of a coalescing Earth aeons before Nature even thought of the reptiles? Who can even guess at what anthropomorphic shapes will straddle the deathless night of this planet when our sun is an ember and reptile, man and insect are all a forgotten dream?

Sometimes, in moments of doubt, I envy Sanders, for it is in his power to know these things.

# DREAM'S END

## ALAN CONNELL
### (1915-?)

*Wonder Stories,*
December 1935

When David Lane finished his daily work in the giant Carmen wheat-fields, there was husk-dust in his hair and grease on his hands. He was tired and depressed.

Bella was changing.

In just what way she was changing he could not think. But there was an oddness about her at times that alternately amazed and frightened him.

Why, he wondered, had she lost her power of speech last night? Why had she glided suddenly from his side with an impossibly levitated grace as though in the grip of some fathomless inconstancy? Why had the bewildering impression come to him—that in the dark her eyes were beginning to assume the glow of feline phosphorescence?

His path took him past Bella's house. He stopped and called to her, "Bella! Bella!"

She opened a window and looked out at him. "Yes?"

"Bella, do you want to walk in the park tonight?"

"Why not? We always do." She seemed puzzled.

Lane went on down the road. Bella had been normal, he reflected. Did her apparent strangeness exist then only in his own imagination? He did not drink. Drugs were unknown to him. He could not reason why he felt the touch of some vast insanity incalculably far beyond mortal conception.

For the walk in the park Bella had clothed her narrow body in a long white gown that gave her a swanlike aspect. She seemed to glide rather than to walk and Lane had trouble in keeping pace with her. "You're walking fast," he protested as they neared the Angels' Gateway. "Why?"

"Am I?" she said. "I hadn't noticed. I'm sorry."

But she did not change her pace. "How was the work today?" she asked.

"The same," he said, brightening at the everyday nature of her query.

"We're reaping the southern field. We'll be able to finish the western by Tuesday if the rain keeps off. The other sections are nearly done too."

"That's good," she said. "I like to hear that."

He supposed that that was natural, for the Carmen wheat areas were owned by Scott, her cousin, who had financed her college education and the small tutoring establishment she had set up.

They reached the bench at the Angels' Gateway where they usually rested. But Bella would have passed it by if Lane had not caught her arm.

As they crossed the grass to the seat Lane glanced down and a mind-shattering realization came to him—in fully fifty percent of her strides Bella's exquisitely clad feet did not so much as touch the ground!

He sat beside her, a sweat of horror on his brow. She looked at him and indicated no astonishment at his fear. Before God, what was she?

He began to think of her as something unholy for he could have sworn that there had been no mistake—she had as much floated as walked through the park. And here she sat at his side, no longer the girl he loved but a monstrosity who could defy normal laws with the magic of her unholy necromancy! What was she?

She leaned back in the seat and spread her arms.

"It's a lovely night," she said, admiring the dark interlacing weave of foliage over her head. "So still, so quiet—"

He fought against his old love for her and lost. He caught her in his arms and kissed her. She responded automatically.

She was real!

It was he then who was not normal. His own insanity was ascribing to her fantastic abilities. But could a madman comprehend his own madness? Doubts assailed him; he could not think what was right and what was wrong.

Bella stood erect. He looked at her and again the sweat started to his brow.

Before his eyes her body was waxing exotically beautiful—was writhing, twisting, undulating, throbbing—was elevating itself through consecutive moulds of splendor toward some unguessable zenith!

"Heaven help me!" Lane prayed aloud. For this was real! This was no fever of mind, no imagery of night!

From Bella's lips issued murmurings and moanings, hints of song, grating whispers, querulous mutterings. Coincidentally she began to voice a thousand scale notes and to speak in a hundred tongues—yet Lane heard all of this at one and the same time.

He sprang to her side and fastened his arms about her as though his strength might restore her. She seemed to shiver in his grasp—to grow impalpable and dim like some extra-dimensional unsubstantiality—and horror mounted in him. "*Bella!*" he screamed. "What are you?"

Her eyes glowed purple and gold and other more alien hues and on and on went the vile soaring mutations that carried her ever upward and farther from Lane's understanding. She was like a shell in his grasp—a shell filled with struggling abnormal entities, each striving frantically to look through her eyes, to speak through her mouth and mould her body to the apexes of their own bizarre desires.

Then there was a moment of quiet and she spoke in her own voice. "What am I? What am I? I don't know. David hold me!"

She shivered, blurred to the consistency of a wraith. She vanished from his hands like a shred of mist in the sun—fading miraculously as a shadow, before an onmarching dusk.

Lane stood trembling. He was alone. Athwart the stars he thought he could perceive a ghostlike vision of Bella, immeasurably expanded. It hovered there, mocking the ruin of his life, then receded with instantaneous velocity into galactic distance.

The moon swayed in the sky. Bands of color stole across its surface and began to glow and alternate.

Yet, incredibly, the moonlight in the park remained flat and white.

The trees whipped suddenly to the thrust of an undetectable wind. The ground shivered and lifted. Grass sprouted in fevered bursts. The very cosmos seemed poised on the brink of impossible catastrophe.

Then with an abruptness that was unreal all was normal again and Lane walked away, groping through the dusk of the night and the twilight of his own mind.

\* \* \* \*

Massey Dune, controller of the giant Westmore Observatory and its new 200-inch mirror, flung himself from his wire-straddled chair, swore fierce oaths, and thrust his first assistant into the place he had vacated.

"Do you see what I see?" he shouted. "Do you see it? Do you see Forty-two Aries moving?"

The assistant spun a wheel, then turned a white face on Dune.

"I saw it. Yes—moving. I couldn't keep pace with it."

Dune roared curses and fled up to the roof. He stood at the low parapet and flung a finger through the icy night air.

"*Look!* Forty-two Aries! It *moves!*"

The sparkling point of the remote triple star, to all purposes rendered motionless by the colossal distances separating it from Earth, now drove down the sky like a skyrocket and vanished below the horizon.

"Madness!" Dune shouted. "Impossible! Madness! For us to see a movement in Forty-two Aries the star must travel unaccountable billions of times the velocity of light! Look, it's gone."

A coldness crept into his heart. His first assistant had followed him to the roof—had stood at his side—and now the man had disappeared like the hellish vapour of a phantom!

The landscape rocked. Portions of it and portions of the building on which Dune stood faded into obscurity. Stars that were familiar to him as the fingers of his own hands were obliterated from the constellations. Others sprang across the heavens with unnatural velocities, pursuing each other in demoniacal races to the last fringes of the horizon.

"I am mad," Dune said. "Insane."

A host of fluttering birds flew about his head, and he could not think whence they had come…

The Atlantic giant, Queen Elizabeth, was one day at sea with a heavy passenger list, when a report reached its commander that the ship was losing buoyancy. No diagrammed measurements were needed. By looking over a rail the commander could see with his own eyes the calm sea creeping up the Queen's mammoth sides toward the first open deck. He hesitated, puzzled, on the verge of a drastic order.

And in that instant, as though the liner had gained inestimable weight or age-old laws had been disrupted, the Queen Elizabeth slipped down through the ocean into the Atlantic's awful chasms—so swiftly that no wireless message could go out from her, no single scream break from the throats of its drowned thousands…

Mizala Ecava, the soprano with range and technique indescribably superb, advanced onto the platform on the night of her third New York concert. She stood for a moment, delighted by the size of her audience, then signalled her accompanist for the opening notes of *Wind Trill*, an aria far beyond the powers of any other singer.

She opened her red mouth and began to sing. A shock of awe ran across the faces of the audience, travelling from the de luxe lounges to the hazy reaches of the gallery. The voice of Ecava was a hoarse, vile croaking!

There she stood, gowned in white, booming like a human frog! More ghastly—it was evident that she was entirely unconscious of the horror of her transformed voice. She boomed and croaked on, throwing her arms in absurd gestures and smiling indulgently at her listeners. She stopped. The blood drained from her cheeks.

Her audience had seemed to waver—had collapsed into a maelstrom. Then it was gone, just as a splotch of dust might go in the passing of a swift wind!

A band of mad formless light fell through a vanished ceiling, lashing itself from wall to wall in a titanic chromatic tempest. It stormed, drew back in mindless eddies and with it into a nameless limbo went Mizala Ecava and her incomparable voice…

Mary Tallon had planted some poppy seed in her little garden. She watered them and covered them carefully. Then she turned to ponder the disposition of some new ferns the florist had sent her.

She heard no faintest sound and her back was to the poppy bed for not more than thirty seconds, yet when she turned, she saw four crimson flowers sprouting from her garden. She stared at them with no understanding.

For from the undisturbed earth to the tips of their scarlet petals they towered higher than a skyscraper.

\* \* \* \*

Herbert Dexter was small and quiet, and he lived inconspicuously, but his brain was attuned to heights unreached by many men better known than he, for he had a priceless gift of imagination denied to most of the foremost scientists of the world.

Dexter had watched the newspapers closely in the last few days, noting the almost numberless disappearances of men and women recounted there and poring over the records of the bizarre events that clutched the world.

Phenomena had come to him personally as well and it was only when he had learned to appreciate the utterly fantastic nature of the majority of them that he had begun to build the hundred pieces into the catastrophic solution of a vaguely comprehensible whole. He sat in his study and began to write in a note-book. He wrote:

> Today is the sixteenth of April. The truth comes gradually to me, and it is almost too much for me mentally to shape, let alone write here. Last night, with the naked eye, I watched three constellations recede into infinity.
>
> A star which I have identified as Alpha Centauri acted in a fashion that makes me deduce that it drove in out of interstellar space, passed through our Solar System and fled on, its double suns leaving no detectable heat or light in their passing.
>
> There have been too many disappearances in the daily papers for me to attempt to record here and there have been even stranger things that are only barely hinted at. I am a little afraid lest I too should be snatched away.

\* \* \* \*

> Today is the seventeenth. I am right. Heaven help me but I am right.
>
> The sun has vanished and in its place there is a cluster of coloured spheres that alternately hang in suspension and flee in

night-destroying races across the sky. They shed changing light but little heat and are subject to no knowable laws.

How long before the end, I wonder. How long?

* * * *

The eighteenth. The swiftness of change almost eludes me. Sometimes I feel the very pen in my hand grows unsubstantial and the paper of my book flows like water, indeterminate as to whether it shall assume the consistency of vapour, liquid or solid.

The sun has returned—but it dawned in a smothering host of nameless colors and it has a heat that bites through insulated walls and sears the body with a force unlinked to ordinary heat.

I am afraid, so pitifully afraid.

I shall try to write down what I have deduced but it will be difficult.

There is, or was, a scientist—my mind waxes foggy and I cannot recall his name—and it was from words of his that I gathered my inspiration.

He said in essence that our Cosmos might be but a dream in the mind of a sleeping Entity—an Entity that exists where It is and conjures in its drowsing brain the phantom images of our galaxies, of our planet, of ourselves.

It can be said that this cannot be—that we have wills of our own—that we are not imagined puppets. But I think—"Can I be rich tomorrow if I am poor today? Can I walk through a solid wall, stride through the upper air, multiply myself as I choose? How far does this free will of mine really extend?"

And I know then that we are all bound in little grooves. Each action we make is but a preconceived idea in the million-channeled intelligence of an incomprehensible Entity.

It has grown dark now, even though it was but recently dawn, and my electric system does not function. A candle burns purple as I write this and I cannot tell when it may choose to obey other laws, or expanding to crushing size or vanishing utterly. I feel heat and cold coincidentally and the sensation is beyond description.

* * * *

The nineteenth. The end must be very close. How long now? How long?

The Entity is stirring to wakefulness and this, our universe, which is the dream in Its sleeping brain, is disintegrating and its form runs into riotous shapelessness before the onslaught of the Entity's waking lucidity.

Disintegration, obliteration—yet who can deny it? Has it not been a scientific concept that all that we considered to be matter is reducible to electron and proton, which are but electricity, and which in turn is nothing? We are nothing! We are a dream!

What a brain must be the brain of this Entity that it can govern a dream of so vast and intricate a universe.

The sky is alight with flickering fires and I see only by red light, so that the bizarre landscape that confronts me through the window, is bathed in a blood flame. Emotions battle in me and sensations roar through my body with a force never before experienced. I cannot rise or sit down or turn my head—but I am aware that the walls of my little house are long gone and that the desk is impalpable beneath my elbows. Yet I do not fall, for forces such as gravity have ceased to claim existence in the Dream…

Later. It is near now, so very near. I see things impossible and I look from one end of the galaxy to the other and even beyond and all is chaos.

I see monstrosities feathered with fire stride across my red landscape and they bow and sway to the thunder of gigantic symphonies of sound. They do not recognize me and pass on.

I see oceans flood across me and in them triumphant things disport without reason in liquid paradises and I am conscious that I no longer breathe. I see my world transmuted into an empire of crystal that glitters like ruby in the red light and whose million outcroppings flower hellishly sentient with the waxing and waning of the crimson that feeds their evil.

I see limitless forests, the march of galactic hordes of shapes too bewildering to trace. I feel heartbreak and joy, fury and greed and other emotions that I have neither will nor desire to control.

So near now—so near. Farewell to life—farewell forever. For us at least it was real and true…

# ABOUT THE AUTHORS

## ERNEST FAVENC

Ernest Favenc was born on 21 October 1845 at 5 Saville Row, Walworth, Surrey, the son of Abraham George Favenc, and his wife, Emma, née Jones. His father was a merchant by trade and his occupation appears to have sent him to different locations as Favenc was educated at Temple College, Cowley, in Oxfordshire, and in Berlin.

With his two sisters, Edith and Ella, and his brother, Jack, Favenc came to Australia while still a teenager in 1863. After a few months working in Sydney, Favenc moved to a cattle station owned by his uncle in north Queensland where he worked as a drover. He spent the next sixteen years in north and central Queensland working on stations, usually as a superintendent. His experiences as a drover in the outback provided the backdrop several of his stories. By 1871 he was writing fiction and poetry for the *Queenslander*, and in 1878, Gresley Lukin, the proprietor and literary editor of the *Queenslander* placed Favenc in charge of an expedition to survey a route for a railway line from Brisbane to Port Darwin. After travelling from Brisbane to Blackall in central-western Queensland, the small party set off northwest into the Northern Territory, discovering and naming natural features like creeks, lagoons and lakes as they went. Near disaster occurred in November 1878 when they were stranded on Creswell Creek due to water shortage, and they were forced to wait until rain replenished the water supplies. Their supplies almost exhausted, they reached the Overland Telegraph Line north of Powell's Creek station in mid-January 1879.

Although the proposed railway line was never built, the expedition had a profound influence on Favenc's prose and verse, and he also wrote several accounts of the expedition that appeared in newspapers and periodicals. Favenc's journalism and his successful land speculations in the Northern Territory in the early 1880s allowed him to marry and settle down in Sydney. On 15 November 1880, Ernest Favenc married Bessie Mathews, whom he had first met in Brisbane in the mid-1870s, at St John's Baptist Church, Ashfield, Sydney.

Bessie was born in Whimple, Devon, on 22 November 1860 and had come to Queensland in 1871-72 with her parents and eight siblings; her father, Benjamin, worked as a teacher for the Education Department. Ernest and Bessie had a daughter, Amy Eleanor, born on 24 September 1881, while another child was stillborn in late 1882 or early 1883.

At this time he was working as a journalist in Sydney, contributing substantial serial essays to the *Sydney Mail* on topics like "The Queensland Transcontinental Railway," "White Versus Black," "The Far Far North," and "The Thirsty Land." "The Far Far North," which appeared in August and September 1882, described an expedition Favenc took from Normanton in far north Queensland to Powell's Creek station in order to establish cattle stations. "The Thirsty Land," serialised in November and December 1883, describes a journey to the same region made during March to May 1883. On this occasion Favenc was accompanied by Harry Creaghe, a business associate of Favenc's, and his wife, Caroline, who left a detailed diary of the expedition. Leaving the Creaghes at Powell's Creek station, Favenc continued north-east with two companions, exploring the headwaters of the Macarthur River, which they followed to the coast. They then travelled west, arriving at Daly Waters on 15 July. Soon afterwards, Favenc led a survey ship, the *Palmerston*, commissioned by the South Australian government to chart the mouth of the Macarthur and the Sir Edward Pellew group of islands in the south-west corner of the Gulf of Carpentaria.

The years following this flurry of activity were relatively barren, in terms of both writing and exploration. Favenc appears to have returned to Sydney where he experienced ill health, which according to Favenc's biographer, Cheryl Taylor, could be a euphemism for the drinking problem that affected him intermittently for the rest of his life. It was not until the end of the decade that he began to write regularly again. The monograph *Western Australia, Its Past History, Its Present Trade and Resources, Its Future Position* was published in 1887, and resulted in a commission to explore the Gascoyne region northeast of Geraldton, which he undertook between March and June 1888. In the same year he published the magisterial *The History of Australian Exploration*, which has remained a classic of its kind and is still regarded as a useful source. Dedicated to the Premier of New South Wales, Sir Henry Parkes, the book reveals Favenc's passion for exploration and adventure; he wrote in the preface that a complete history of the exploration of Australia can never be written as "[t]he story of the settlement of our continent is necessarily so intermixed with the results of private travels and adventures." To some extent Favenc filled out his history in his fictional accounts of explorations into the outback.

The 1890s were Favenc's most productive period as a writer. He had abandoned the discursive, over-complicated plots of his early short fiction in *The Queenslander* in favour of tightly controlled shorter pieces that dealt with the hard life of the Outback.

The 1890s also saw the separate publication of two novels and a novella. *The Secret of the Australian Desert* was serialised in the Queenslander in 1890 before being published by the London publisher, Blackie & Son, in 1895. Like the best of Favenc's fiction, the novel weaves fact, fiction and speculation. *The Secret of the Australian Desert* traces the fortunes of an expedition that sets out northward from Central Australia in search of fate of Ludwig Leichhardt's famous expedition, which disappeared without trace. The novel crosses over into fantasy in its portrayal of a lost tribe of aborigines "wholly unlike any tribes known ever to have existed" which draws heavily on contemporary interest in the lost land of Lemuria.

Similarly, *Marooned on Australia* (1897) is based on fact. As indicated by its subtitle, *Being the Narrative of Diedrich Buys of His Discoveries and Exploits "In Terra Australia Incognita" About the Year 1630*, the story speculates about the consequences of the wreck of the Dutch ship Batavia and the depredations committed by the mutineers. The first person narrator, Diedrich Buys, is one of the two mutineers who escaped execution and were instead marooned in North West Australia. As he battles to survive in a hostile land he comes across the Quadrucos, a race distinct from the Aborigines because its technology is too advanced and culture too sophisticated.

A novella, *The Moccasins of Silence,* was published by the Australian publisher, George Robertson, in 1896, and featured strange native shoes that were worn to attack enemies by stealth at night. The same shoes appear again in the late story, "The Kaditcha: A Tale of the Northern Territory" (1907). During the 1890s Favenc worked mainly for *The Bulletin*, which was edited by J. F. Archibald whose preference for the unadorned bush yarn may have influenced Favenc's style. Known as 'the bushman's bible,' *The Bulletin* was an important newspaper that helped shape Australia's national literature and published important work by Henry Lawson, 'Banjo' Patterson, Barbara Baynton, Miles Franklin and the cartoonist Phil May, to whose *Summer* and *Winter Annuals* Favenc would contribute.

A selection of seventeen stories published in *The Bulletin* between 1890 and 1893 was published in *The Last of Six: Tales of the Austral Tropics* (1893), the third volume of *The Bulletin's* short story and verse anthologies. In 1894 the London publisher, Osgood, McIlvaine published *Tales of the Austral Tropics*, which dropped six stories from the earlier collection and added two others. A third collection of stories from *The Bulletin, My Only Murder and Other Stories*, was published by the Melbourne publisher George Robertson in 1899; this collected twenty four stories published between 1890 and 1895. A collection of verse, *Voices of the Desert*, was published in 1905.

Favenc was a part of the acclaimed group of *Bulletin* writers living in Sydney during the 1890s, and was a good friend of Louis Becke who was also a master of the short form, compared in his day with Robert Louis

Stevenson. In 1898 Favenc joined the Dawn and Dusk Club, a group of Bohemian writers and artists and it was around this time that his alcoholism began to take a toll on his health again. Certainly, by the end of the 1890s he was less productive and there was a marked decline in the quality of his work, although between 1899 and 1903 he did write six stories for Phil May's *Summer* and *Winter Annuals*, including "What the Rats Brought" and "The Land of the Unseen." At that time, the annuals were edited by Harry Thompson, who preferred tales of horror and the supernatural.

By May 1905 Favenc was seriously ill in Royal Prince Albert Hospital, and later in year a bad fall that broke his thigh confined him to St Vincent's Hospital. He died on 14 November 1908 in Lister Hospital in western Sydney.

## H.B. MARRIOTT WATSON

Although H.B. Marriott Watson (1863–1921) is now all but forgotten, in his day he was a prolific author and journalist, partner of the beautiful and talented decadent poet Rosamund Marriott Watson, and a member of the celebrated 'Henley regatta'. He wrote more than forty books in a career spanning thirty years, including seventeen short story collections and a collection of essays, but he never quite achieved the success and recognition that he deserved. His staples were swashbuckling adventures and historical romances, but he also wrote confidently in other genres such as mystery, fantasy, supernatural fiction, and the SF horror story published here.

Henry Brereton Marriott Watson was born in Caulfield, Melbourne, on 20 December 1863. Of Anglo-Irish descent, his grandfather migrated to Australia in 1821 and settled in Tasmania. He was the first child of the Reverend Henry Crocker Marriott Watson (1835–1901), an Anglican priest and an interesting figure in his own right. Born and schooled in Tasmania, he studied for the priesthood at Moore College in Liverpool, New South Wales, graduating in 1860. In that year he became curate at Christ Church, Ballarat, in Melbourne, and three years later, on 2 January 1863, he was made minister at Caulfield. He appears to have felt a strong connection with Hobart and he returned there in March 1863 to marry Annie McDonald Wright.3 He was also a writer and during his lifetime he published two dystopian futuristic fantasies, *Erchomenon, or, The Republic of Materialism* (1879), and *The Decline and Fall of the British Empire, or, The Witch's Cavern* (1890), while a third novel, *Ahmet and Neida,* remains unpublished.

For the first nine years of his life Marriott Watson moved around Victoria as his father took up ministries in picturesque country towns such as Taradale, Inglewood, and Kilmore. Early in 1873 Watson left Australia for good when his father was made incumbent of St John's, Christ Church, in New Zealand. He was never to see Australia again. It is interesting that Watson always referred to Australia as his 'native country' or 'native land' although the country itself does not appear to have made a lasting imaginative impression on him, and he only wrote a few stories with an Australian setting.

Watson went to Christ's College, a distinguished private school modelled on the great public schools of England such as Eton and Westminster. He was a bright student and graduated in 1879, winning a New Zealand University Junior Scholarship to Canterbury College, worth £90 a year. He entered Canterbury College in 1880 and studied for a BA, taking Latin, Greek, English, Mathematics, and Biology, and distinguished himself as a classical scholar by winning the Latin Exhibition in 1882. He graduated from the university in 1883, evidently with a view of entering the church, but his lack of belief prevented preferment.

He moved to England in 1885 and took up journalism, initially living in the inevitable garret off Tottenham Court Road and made a precarious living making occasional contributions to London and colonial papers. He worked for the St James Gazette where he met and befriended J.M. Barrie. The two collaborated on an unsuccessful play, *Richard Savage*, which appeared in 1891.

Watson's first novel, *Marahuna*, a fantasy adventure, was clearly influenced by H. Rider Haggard's *She*, was written rapidly in a few months, accepted by Longman in December 1887, and published in 1888. A watershed in Watson's professional and personal life occurred when he joined the famous poet, critic, and editor, William Ernest Henley, at the *Scots Observer* (renamed the *National Observer* in November 1890 when Henley moved the editorial offices from Edinburgh to London). Most of the tales from his first volume of short stories, *Diogenes of London and Other Fantasies and Sketches* (Methuen, 1893), first appeared in the pages of the *National Observer*, one of an astonishing twenty-eight books that first saw print in the periodical between 1889 and 1894, and which included Thomas Hardy's *Tess of the D'Urbervilles*, J. M. Barrie's *A Window in Thrume*, Rudyard Kipling's *Barrack-Room Ballads*, H. G. Wells's *The Time Machine*, and several volumes of verse by W. B. Yeats. More importantly, however, Watson became a member of the brilliant circle of Henley intimates that Max Beerbohm famously dubbed the 'Henley Regatta'.

In 1893 he began an affair with the gifted poet, Rosamund Ball, the wife of the artist Arthur Graham Tomson. Rosamund moved in with Watson in July 1894, and, although they never married, from 1895 she adopted the name Rosamund Marriott Watson. In that year, on her own birthday, Rosamund gave birth to Richard Marriott Watson, the couple's only child.

Watson continued to publish short stories and novels. In 1895, he published his second collection of short stories, *At the First Corner and Other Stories* (John Lane, 1895), the eleventh volume in John Lane's acclaimed Keynotes series, and the following year saw the publication of *Galloping Dick* (John Lane, 1896), Watson's first collection of stories about the eighteenth century highwayman 'Richard Ryder, otherwise Galloping Dick, sometime gentleman of the road'. Dick Ryder was Watson's most popular and enduring character, and stories about his adventures appeared in many magazines of the time. These were collected in two later volumes, *The High Toby* (Methuen, 1906), which includes a warm dedication to J. M. Barrie, and *The King's Highway* (Mills and Boon, 1910).

Tragedy beset Watson in the last decade of his life. At the end of 1911 Rosamund died of cancer; Watson was too distraught to attend the funeral. Worse was to follow when their son, Richard, was killed in the final months of the Great War. Watson never recovered from this loss, and published nothing after 1919. He died after a long illness on 30 October 1921 and was buried with his wife and son at Shere.

Watson was a tall, handsome young man with an engaging personality, who made friends easily. According to an anonymous appreciation of Watson published in *The Times* after his death, '[h]is plentiful crop of rebellious and curly hair seemed to announce a freedom and independence which were truly his'. 'The Instrument' published in book form in *Chapman's Wares* (1915), may well have been influenced by H.G. Wells' *The Time Machine*; Watson is said to have 'discovered' Wells, who recommended *The Time Machine* to Henley.

## BEATRICE GRIMSHAW

Grimshaw, Beatrice Ethel (1870-1953) achieved considerable fame in the first decades of the twentieth century as a writer of stories, novels, and travelogues about the South Pacific, where she lived and travelled extensively. Although she mainly wrote stories of adventure and romance, she did write in other genres including crime and the supernatural.

Born in Cloona, County Antrim, Ireland, Grimshaw was educated at Caen, Normandy; Victoria College, Belfast; and Bedford College, London. Her writing career started in 1891 as a journalist for a Dublin sporting paper, "The Irish Cyclist", and and from 1895 to 1899 she edited another journal, the "Social Review". Her first novel, *Broken Away*, was published by John Lane in 1897 and is a "New Woman" novel, a literary type with which Grimshaw clearly identified. She was an outdoors enthusiast, enjoyed cycling and maintained that she had broken a 24 hour cycling record, though there is no evidence of this.

The travel bug caught her at an early age and she took a succession of jobs that enabled her to see the world. She worked for various shipping companies including the Cunard Line as a publicist, but resigned in 1903 to take up a position with the *Daily Graphic* to report on the Pacific, which was still largely unexplored and little known part of the world. She continued to work for shipping companies to promote tours and writing travelogues, for example the Union Steamship Company of New Zealand, which enabled her to travel throughout the Pacific Islands. She wrote a travelogue for the company called "Three Wonderful Nations" (Tonga, Somoa and Fiji), which was used as a promotional booklet. In 1907 Grimshaw published two non-fiction accounts of her experiences, *From Fiji to the Cannibal Islands* (Eveleigh Nash, 1907) and *In the Strange South Seas* (Hutchinson, 1907).

1907 was a busy year and she also traveled to Papua, which had been placed under Australian administration in 1905, having been commissioned by *The Times*, London, and the *Sydney Morning Herald* to report on the teritory. It was there that she met and became close friends with the then acting Administrator, Sir Hubert Murray, brother of the famous classicist, Gilbert Murray. Although she only intended to stay in Papua for a few months, she ended up living in Port Moresby for most of the next twenty seven years. Grimshaw was an ardent supporter of and publicist for Murray, who was appointed lieutenant-governor of Papua in 1908, and she wrote about the need for white settlers and investment in Papua in pamphlets and a book, *The New New Guinea* (1910). She also accompanied him on some of his expeditions into the Papuan jungle.

Established in Papua she began publishing a succession of novels and short story collections, starting with *Vaiti of the Islands* (Newnes, 1907), which traces the adventures of the eponymous heroine, the daughter of an English gentleman named Saxon and a South Pacific princess. The stories that comprise the book were first serialised in the *Sydney Morning Herald* and in *Pearson's Magazine* in 1906-7. Grimshaw continued to write stories about Vaiti, and these were collected into *Queen Vaiti*, published by the N.S.W. Bookstall company in 1920. The stories are typical of Grimshaw's later writing, combining adventure and romance with detailed descriptions of the South Pacific islands.

Her first novel of the South Pacific was *When the Red Gods Call* (Mills & Boon, 1911), about the trials and adventures of Irishman Hugh Lynch in New Guinea. The book was a considerable success and Grimshaw later said it was her best book. In the following year she published another adventure novel, *Guinea Gold* (Mills & Boon, 1912).

*The Sorcerer's Stone* (Hodder & Stoughton, 1914) marks Grimshaw's growing interest in the beliefs of the New Guinea natives, particularly the power and influence of the New Guinea witch doctors. In a contemporary interview, she said "I am not a theosophist, but I am inclined to think there must be something in the doctrine, for a theosophist who came to New Guinea declared that the place is full of elemental spirits. Whether it is or not, I do not know, but it certainly is a haunted land. The people have a knowledge that no white people possess, and, like the Ju-Ju in Africa, it is evil." *The Sorcerer's Stone* is an adventure novel about the efforts of two Europeans to secure a massive diamond, believed to have supernatural properties, from a New Guinea witch doctor. Other novels touch on native beliefs and practices, but none are overtly supernatural. Although her novels are mainly adventure and romance fiction, she did write in other genres, including crime, for example *Murder in Paradise* (New Century Press, 1940) and *The Missing Blondes* (Invincible Press, 1945)

The supernatural and fantastic surface more frequently in her short stories, though she was never a prolific writer of fantasy. She published short fiction extensively in the major fiction outlets of the day, such as *The Saturday Evening Post*, *The Blue Book Magazine*, the Harmsworth stable of magazines, *Collier's*, *Liberty*, *Cassell's* and many others. Her best known supernatural tales are "The Cave" and "The Forest of Lost Men" both of which where first published in the popular pulp *The Blue Book Magazine*, in 1932 and 1934 respectively, and reprinted in issues 13 (1950) and 16 (1951) of the *Avon Fantasy Reader*. "The Cave" is about the ghosts of dinosaurs haunting a small South Pacific island, while "The Forest of Lost Men" is about a stretch of forest that native sorcerers have cursed so that people who stumble into it cannot escape.

Other weird tales and ghost stories of note include "The Blanket Fiend" a prehistoric monster tale in *The Beach of Terror and Other Stories* (Cassell, 1931) and "The Ship that Ran Herself", a flying Dutchman tale, in *Pieces of Gold and Other South Sea Stories* (Cassell, 1935). "Lost Wings", reprinted here from *The Valley of Never-Come-Back* (Hurst & Blackett, 1923) is a science fiction story about the discovery of a new metal. It is likely there are other supernatural stories yet to be rediscovered.

Grimshaw was a popular writer in her day, and she could command high sales. In a 1939 interview with *The Sydney Morning Herald*, she said she earned $1,000 a story in America. She continued to travel and explore the region, and typically tried her hand at other ventures, for example in 1933 she set up tobacco plantations near Port Moresby with her brother. In about 1934 Grimshaw left Papua after suffering an illness and in 1936 settled in Kelso, near Bathurst, where she bought and renovated a property that was originally the Bathurst military barracks. She continued to write until she retired in 1940. She died on 30 June 1953 and was buried in Bathurst cemetery.

# ERLE COX

Erle Cox's (1873-1950) Out of the Silence is by far the best known early Australian science fiction novel. It was serialised in The Argus between April and October 1919, and was first published in book form by the Melbourne publisher Vidler. In the following years it was published in London and New York and has been reprinted many times since.

Cox was born on 15 August 1873 at Emerald Hill, Melbourne, and educated at grammar schools in Melbourne. He took up wine-growing at Rutherglen in north eastern Victoria, and later lived in Launceston, Tasmania, where he worked for a tobacco company. In 1901 he married Mary Ellen Kilborn, the daughter of a wine maker from Wahgunyah, not far from Rutherglen, and the couple later settled in Melbourne.

His first short stories appeared in the *Lone Hand*, a popular Australian literary journal, in 1908 and 1909. "The Social Code" appeared there in January 1909. Following the serialisation of *Out of the Silence* he published several stories in the Australiasian, where his father, a teacher and inspector of schools, had published in the 1870s, and contributed columns to the Melbourne *Argus*, which led in 1921 to a post on the editorial staff. Using the non de plume, "The Chiel" he wrote articles, book reviews and film reviews, the latter proving particularly popular with readers. He remained with the Argus until 1946 when he joined the Age and continued to write reviews. Cox wrote two more novels, *Fools' Harvest*, serialised in the *Argus* in November in 1938 and published in book form in 1939, and *The Missing Angel* in 1947. He retired because of ill health in August 1950 and died on 20 November at his home in Elsternwick.

## ROBERT COUTTS ARMOUR (COUTTS BRISBANE)

Robert Coutts Armour (1874-1945) was a prolific writer of science fiction and boys' fiction from the second decade of the twentieth century into the early 1950s. He wrote for British pulp magazines of the day such as the *Red Magazine* and the *Yellow Magazine* and for the Amalgamated Press, which published the Sexton Blake Library and Robin Hood Library for a juvenile readership. He should be better known today as a pioneer science fiction writer and an early Australian writer of pulp fiction.

Armour was born on 14 September 1874 in Brisbane. His parents were Robert Armour and Maria Coutts of Toolburra, near Warwick in Queensland. Robert and Maria married on 15 January 1870 and Robert was their only child. His father ran his own merchant and import business, Robert Armour & Co., which went bankrupt in 1878. Two years earlier, in 1876, he was in the Supreme Court in Brisbane facing a charge of falsely claiming he was owed money by an insolvent company. Maria died on 20 October 1879, when Robert was four, and his father died on 4 June 1895 shortly after leaving Brisbane for England. The following year, Robert Armour successfully sued for the wrongful detention of the title of his father's property in Queen-Street Brisbane, claiming the property and £1000 damages. By 1899 Armour had sold the Queen-Street property and moved permanently to England.

The 1911 census indicates that he and his wife, Edith, were living in a three room house at 6 St Luke's Road, Clapham, in London. Armour's occupation is given as lithographic artist and he was working as a book illustrator; in 1909 he provided colour illustrations for three children's books published by A. Treherne. He may have worked as an illustrator for the Amalgamated Press, for by 1912 he was writing short stories for Harmsworth's *Red Magazine* (he illustrated one of his own stories in the August 1914 issue). His first story for the magazine may have been "A Fragmentary Affair", a fantasy about the head of Medusa which turns people to stone, which appeared on the issue of 1 March 1912. Another story appeared in the next issue (15 March 1912), a science fiction story about a disintegration machine. In all he published about 100 stories for Harmsworth's *Red Magazine*, *Yellow Magazine* and *Green Magazine* under the pseudonyms Coutts Brisbane and Reid Whitly, many of them science fiction and fantasy stories. According to Locke, Armour "made something of a specialty of tongue in cheek stories set on other planets and peopled with the weirdest nonhumans imaginable." Graham Stone adds, "other themes were remarkable inventions, vignettes of future ages, natural catastrophes, monsters, social trends extrapolated to absurdity. He had a light touch but a lot of original thinking." Like Locke and Stone, Mike Ashley argues that Armour has been unfairly neglected and agrees that he did not take his work seriously enough: "His work was often humorous, sometime rather too light-weight to have much impact, but his imagination was fertile and he utilised all of the then prevalent science-fiction concepts."[4] George Locke collected twelve Armour stories in *Denizens of Other Worlds* published by Murqui Press in 1984 in a very limited edition of six copies.

From 1921 Armour became a prolific author for the Amalgamated Press's Sexton Blake Library. Sexton Blake was a detective character, famously described as "the poor man's Sherlock Holmes," who appeared in a wide variety of publications from 1893 to 1978, amounting to over 4,000 stories by about 200 different authors. The copyright to Sexton Blake stories was owned by the Amalgamated Press which brought out dozens of Blake stories every year in various publications. Armour's first Blake story was "The Episode of the Stolen Voice" which appeared in the Sexton Blake

4    Mike Ashley, *The History of the Science Fiction Magazine*, (Liverpool, 2000), pp11-12

Library for May 1921, and his last was "The Mystery of the Red Tower" which appeared in 1940. Armour died in 1945.

In a 1983 issue of *Collector's Digest*, W.O.G. Blake published letters from H. W. Twyman, former Editor of *Union Jack* (1921-33) and *Detective Weekly* which included valuable information about Sexton Blake authors. Twyman had this to say about Armour:

"Coutts Armour was an Australian, big chap with a beard, who walked around like a swagman with a sack on his shoulder—usually filled up with books he had bought down the Farringdon Street market. "Coutts Brisbane" and "Reid Whitley" were two of his pen-names. I first met him when I was editing Detective Library in 1919 in the same office as The Robin Hood and Praire Libraries run by Len Pratt—who afterwards ran the Sexton Blake Library for 35 years. Armour claimed to have originated from a famous English family steeped in history—hence his great interest in historical matters, in which he was a specialist, and really had good knowledge of this subject generally. Only trouble was that his A.P. Robin Hood stories were marred here and there by a kind of heavy-handed whimsicality he couldn't somehow bear to forgo. Armour's character was Dr. Ferraro—certainly not all that popular, like so many of the others. I don't know the circumstances of how he took over Gunga Dass from H. Gregory Hill (probably when Hill died in 1932). At that time I had far more important things on my mind—the change of Union Jack to Detective Weekly."

Apart from the Sexton Blake stories, Armour wrote many boys' adventure stories for Amalgamated Press publications and wrote a series of boxing stories for Aldine, which also specialised in boys' fiction. He also wrote a couple of adventure novels for mainstream publishers including *Here Come the Swords!* (John Lane, 1926), *Madam Madcap* (John Lane, 1927), and *The Secret of the Desert* (Thomas Nelson, 1941). He also published a few stories in the U.S. pulp magazine, *Oriental Stories*.

In the late 1930s and early 1940s, the legendary British science fiction editor, Walter Gillings, used four of Armour's stories from the Red and Yellow magazines for his *Tales of Wonder* magazine. At Gillings' request Armour wrote about his work in a short column which appeared in the Winter 1939 issue:

"To use the formula of the stud book, I might give the origin of the sundry fantastic tales I have written as being by Jules Verne out of a desultory study of the queer fauna of my native Australia. The platypus, *ornithorhynchus anatinus*, that duckbilled, egg-laying mammal, if only on account of his name. Why, I wanted to know, should a creature with webbed feet to able to burrow long tunnels through hard soil? Why was the male provided with sharp spurs on its hind legs?

"Why should the young kangaroo come into the world in such very incomplete trim? Why should the Tasmanian Devil, like the jubjub bird, live in a state of perpetual passion? Why should wombats walk across the bottom of a creek when their partly webbed feet were obviously fitted for swimming? To some of these questions, one may find an answer; others remain unsatisfied. But, having attempted analysis, I naturally went on to attempt synthesis; and created a managerie highly logical, perhaps, yet recalling a zoologist's nightmare. They were possible, but so very improbable on our well-regulated Earth that I must needs plant them in alien worlds.

"So the canals of Mars were proved necessary because the ruling race of that interesting planet retained many of the characteristics of their crustacean ancestry, and especially the constant need of a copious water supply. Because the dominant inhabitants of Venus retained racial memories of that nasty habit of their faroff spider ancestress (you may remember that the female spider invariably devours her smaller and weaker spouse) therefore, the young bachelors of the Planet of Love had to be coerced into matrimony by drastic means. And Saturn was the scene of the last stand of mobile trees against the intrusion of better equipped mammals upon their ancestral peace.

"Anyhow, my yarns have had a basis of logical and biological facts, despite their lighthearted disregard of Earthly limitations. Yet, perhaps because of that very logic which natural man so rightly detests, they have stirred the bile of some of their readers. But I remain unrepentant. A speculative story should be a stimulant, an irritant, a positive incitement to the more violent forms of controversy; for he is a benefactor of the human race who causes two ideas to sprout where but one struggled for being before."

A neglected pioneer of science fiction, Armour is represented here with two stories, both from the Red Magazine, "Beyond the Orbit" and "Take it as Red."

## JAMES MORGAN WALSH

James Morgan Walsh (1897-1952) was a prolific, successful Australian writer of popular fiction, mainly in the mystery, thriller and spy genres, but also in adventure and science fiction. He was born on 23 February 1897 at Geelong, Victoria, son of Thomas Patrick Walsh, a stock agent who was principal in the firm Toyne Bros. and Walsh, and his wife Kate, née Morgan. His family where well-known catholics and James was educated at catholic schools including Xavier College in Melbourne, which he left in 1912 to work in his father's business.

He made the decision to become a writer early in life and by his early twenties had published a number of serials and short stories in newspapers such as *The Leader* and *The Advocate*, and in 1921 he won second prize in the De Garis novel competition.

Walsh's first novel, *Tap-Tap Island*, an adventure story about buried treasure, was issued by the NSW Bookstall Co. in 1921, and was quickly followed in the same year by *The Lost Valley*, issued by the Melbourne publisher C.J. DeGaris. *Overdue, a Romance of Unknown New Guinea*, published in 1925 by the Sydney publisher, The States Publishing Company, sounds like a lost race novel, but is in fact a standard adventure tale beginning with a search for a missing yacht. The copyright registrations for these books in the National Archives of Australia reveal that Walsh sold the rights to the books for £30.

In 1925, soon after his marriage to Louisa Mary Murphy in January 1925, Walsh moved to London to further his literary career. Through the Australian publishing firm, Robertson & Mullens, Walsh placed his early books with the small London publishers, John Hamilton, on condition that Robertson & Muller purchase a thousand copies at a reduced rate for Australian distribution. Hamilton published *The White Mask* in 1925, which Walsh revised from an Australian to and English setting to appeal to a wider readership. Walsh published two or three crime and mystery novels a year with Hamilton until the early 1930s when he moved to Collins. One of his series characters was Colonel Ormiston of the British Secret Service, which one contemporary reviewer said "must be one of the best-known characters in present-day fiction, and must be building up a little fortune for his creator."

Walsh was a prolific writer and published over 100 books. He was a popular and critically successfully author and was described as 'the Australian Oppenheim' and 'the Australian Edgar Wallace', which indicates something of the breadth of his writing.

Under the psuedonym, H. Haverstock Hill, a name evidently taken from the London district name where he lived for a time, he produced five crime adventures of the Pacific islands, similar to the type of adventure and romance tales produced by Louis Becke and Beatrice Grimshaw. He also published boys adventures under the name Jack Carew for Aldine Press and Sheldon Press.

From 1938 Walsh lived at Weston-super-Mare in Somerset. He died there on 29 August 1952 and was survived by his wife, son and daughter.

Walsh published several science fiction novels and series, and about half a dozen stories in science fiction pulps during the 1930s. He developed an early interest in science fiction: in a column in the magazine *Tales of*

*Wonder* in 1938 he wrote that in the early part of the twentieth century, before he turned to writing, "by luck or accident I stumbled upon a complete set of that pioneer of science fiction, George Griffith. How I devoured them! They were new, wonderful, unique. *A Honeymoon in Space* [Pearson, 1901] is the one that lingers in my mind."

His best known science fiction novel is *Vandals of the Void* published in *Wonder Stories Quarterly* in 1931, and in book form by Hamilton in 1931. Its importance as a pioneering science fiction novel was confirmed by its reprinting in 1976 by Hyperion Press in the United States and in 2010 by Chimaera Publications with an introduction by Australian science fiction historian and critic, Sean McMullen. In the twenty-first century interplanetary shipping has become a reality thanks to the discovery of a lunar mineral used to fuel space propulsion engines. Ships are coming under attack by unknown space pirates, and on a trip to Mars, Space Captain Sanders of the Interplanetary Guard is asked to keep an eye out for unusual incidents. *Vanguard to Neptune* (published in *Wonder Stories Quarterly* in Spring 1932) uses the same Earth-Mars-Venus background of the first expedition to Neptune.

According to George Lock's *Spectrum of Fantasy*, *The Secret of the Crater* (Hurst & Blackett, 1930), written under the H. Haverstock Hill psuedonym, is a lost race fantasy: "The race encountered combines the traditional elements of priests etc with some advanced technology such as a form of radio-telepathy and electric weaponry." Some characters in this book previously figured in *Tap-Tap Island* (1921) and *The Golden Isle* (Hodder 1928) giving these associational interest.

Graeme Stone, in his Notes on Australian Science Fiction, lists a couple of borderline science fiction novels, *Secret Weapons* (1940) and *Spies' Vendetta* (1936), but they are essentially spy novels. Stone lists six science fiction tales published in pulp magazines in the U.S. and and England mostly in the 1930s. "Terror out of Space" (published in four parts in *Amazing Stories* in 1934) is about the early interactions of people between Mars and Earth and hostile aliens on an unknown second satellite of earth. "When the Earth Tilted" (*Wonder Stories*, May 1932) is an amalgam of climate change disaster and the lost civilisation of Mu. "The Stick Men" (*Fantasy* #3, 1939) is an alien invasion story and "The Belt" (Science Fantasy #1, Summer 1950) is an interplanetary tale. The story published here, "After 1,000,000," appeared in *Wonder Stories* in October 1931.

## MALCOLM (MAX) AFFORD

Max Afford's (1906-1954) only science fiction story was "The Gland Men of the Island," published early in his writing career, in the January 1931 issue of *Wonder Stories*. It had initially been submitted to *Amazing Stories*, but receiving no reply Afford submitted it to *Wonder*. It was eventually published in *Amazing Stories* in February 1933 under the name "The Ho-Ming Gland."

Born on 8 April 1906 at Parkside, Adelaide, he was known as Max, although "Gland Men of the Island" was published under his birth name, Malcolm. He began his writing career in 1926 as a journalist for the *Adelaide News* and the *Mail*, first as a freelancer, and then on staff at the *Adelaide News* from 1929 to 1932. His first short story was published in *Smith's Weekly*, a popular Sydney broadhseet newspaper, in 1928, and it was probably around that time that "The Gland Men of the Island" was written.

Afford's main interest was writing plays. He was involved in Adelaide theatre groups, but he quickly became interested in writing for the new medium of radio, and in about 1930 he had two plays broadcast for 5CL in Adelaide, *Cats Creep at Night* and *The Flail of God*, both mystery stories. In 1934 he was appointed Production Manager for a commercial radio station, 5DN. 1936 was a big year for Afford—he had two detective novels accepted for publication by John Long in London, won the Advertiser's centenary play competition with *William Light—The Founder*, and an operetta, *Pas de Six*, and a radio play, *Merry-Go-Round*, each won first prize in ABC competitions.

As a result of this success, Charles Moses, General Manager of the Australian Broadcasting Commission put him on contract as a playwright and producer, and he moved to Sydney in 1936.

While working in the theatre in Adeaide he had worked with a young costume and set designer named Thelma Thomas. The year after Afford moved to Sydney, she followed him to work on the New South Wales sesqui-centenary celebrations, and in 1938 she and Afford were married.

These days Afford is best known as a writer of detective and crime thrillers, dosed with humour and wit. He created the charming and witty husband and wife detective team of Jeffery and Elizabeth Blackburn. There were several blackburn radio serials, a number with Peter Finch and Neva Carr Glyn playing the Blackburns. Most of his novels also feature Jeffery Blackburn.

Not surprisingly, Afford was a keen student of the crime story, and expressed his enthusiasm for the ingenious plot devices invented by the great crime writers of the day. His 1938 radio play, The Fantastic Case of the Four Specialists, featured Sherlock Holmes, Philo Vance, Hercule poirot and Father Brown solving a case in the distinctive idioms invented by their creators.

Afford left the ABC in 1943 and became a prolific and celebrated writer of radion serials. He wrote 624 quarter-hour episodes of First Light Fraser, about a British agent and his female companion in war-torn Europe. Amongst other serials he wrote 624 episodes of a Blackburn radio show, *Danger Unlimited*. He continued to write plays, one of which, *Lady in Danger*, was unsuccessfully produced in Broadway, but others were produced successfully in Australia, particularly *Dark Enchantment*, which toured the English provinces in 1950. In 1944 he also worked on the film treatment for the Kingsford-Smith feature film, *Smithy*.

In 1950 Afford was Sydney President of PEN international, and in that capacity attended a conference in London, where he also oversaw the fortunes of Dark Enchantment, which opened at the New Royal Theatre in Bournemoth.

He returned to Australia with a changed perception of his work—his subsequent work was more serious and focused on Australia and important Australian themes like immigration and bush life. He died of liver cancer at the age of forty-eight in 1954.

## PHIL COLLAS

Felix Albert Edward Collas (1907-1989), a leading Australian philatelist and compiler of the *Australian and New Zealand Philatelic Directory* (1936), published a single notable piece of science fiction, "The Inner Domain", in *Amazing Stories* in October 1935. He was born in South Australia on 15 March 1907 to British parents and moved to Sandringham, Melbourne, where he completed an intermediate certificate at the University of Melbourne, and subsequently completed the public service examination.

He joined the Victorian State Emergency Service where he wrote various A.R.P. publications and was responsible for publicity material relating to lighting restrictions during the war, as well as organising black out tests. He edited a confidential weekly bulletin, circulated to members of the State Emergency Committeees and was editor of a monthly publication, *A.R.P. Review*. He also coordinated the activities of the seven State Emergency Committees. He was a member of the Citizen Forces from about 1938 and attained the rank of sergeant. Between March-December 1941, he attended Officers' Training School at the A.A.O.C. Drill Hall in East Melbourne, but was unable to take up a commission in the A.M.F. owing to an inability to obtain a release from the State Emergency Council. He applied for a commission in the administrative branch of the Royal Australian Air Force in April 1942 and was discharged in February 1946, achieving the rank of Flight Lieutenant. He was maried to Athol Elizabeth Collas and had a daughter, Patricia Mary, born in May 1935. He died 14 March 1989 (*The Age* 20 March 1989).

# DESMOND HALL

Desmond Winter Hall (1911-1992) was born on 15 March 1911 in Sydney, the son of two New Zealanders, Winter Hall, an actor, and Katherine Young, a concert pianist. In 1918 the family moved to Hollywood and Desmond Hall was educated at the University of California. According to Sam Moskowitz he started writing for Clayton Magazines in 1927, and he worked as assistant editor of Clayton's *Astounding Stories of Super Science* under Harry Bates, who was editor from 1930-33. Hall also worked as a journalist, and wrote reviews of Holywood films, for example in the Melbourne newspaper, *Table Talk*. While working at *Astounding* Hall and Bates collaborated on several stories for the magazine, the best known of which are the Hawk Carse adventure stories, which where eventuually published in book form as *Space Hawk* in 1952. It was popular enough to be translated into German and Italian. He published fourteen stories in *Astounding* between 1931 and 1933, the stories mostly in collaboration with Bates under the pseudonyms Anthony Gilmore and H.G. Winter.

For most of his life he worked as an editor, mostly for Street & Smith publications, including *Mademoiselle* at its inception in 1935. Hall served in the U.S. Air force in World War II, and worked for a time as a literary agent. He continued and write, and contributed articles and fiction to *The Atlantic*, *Esquire*, *The Saturday Evening Post* as well as pulps like the *Blue Book* magazine. His novels include *I Give You Oscar Wilde* New American Library, 1965) and *A Woman of Forty* (Dial Press, 1948), reprinted in paperback by Popular Library in 1952.

During the 1970s he acquired *16 Magazine*, a monthly fan magazine for teenagers published in New York. He had two daughters, Katherine Hall Ryan, who published *16 Magazine*, and Suzanne Cooper. He died of pneumonia on 28 October 1992 at the Methodist Hospital in Brooklyn.

# ALAN CONNELL

Alan Herbert Connell (1915-?) was a talented writer who published in many of the best literary magazines of the 1930s and 1940s but is all but forgotten today. He was born in Mosman, Sydney, on 1 May 1915 to British parents and showed an early interest both in writing and in science fiction, having a poem, "In 3028", published in *The Sun* newspaper in 1928:

> *"Any more? Any more for the moon?*
> *The moon-bus is leaving, soon.*
> *Buy your tickets here! Only half-a-crown!*
> *As you may know, it's the best price in town."*

*"This way for the Mars shell!*
  *No other goes just as well.*
  *Ten years they've run this line*
  *And of a breakdown there has been no sign."*

*"Taxi, sir? to any place you care,*
  *To Venus. Saturn, Uranus—or anywhere?*
  *Ours is the quick service line of cars,*
  *It takes twenty seconds to fly to Mars,*

*"Look out! man; the Venus rocket lands there,*
  *No pushing, people, and make sure you have your fare.*
  *Make way now! for the Martian non-stop freight*
  *—Perhaps in three thousand and twenty-eight."*

He was particularly prolific between 1935 and 1937, publishing a succession of short stories in *The Bulletin*, *Flame* and *The Australian Journal*. He also published four science fiction stories in the American pulp managazine, *Wonder Stories*—"The Reign of the Reptiles" in August 1935, "Dream's End" in December 1935, "The Duplicate" in April 1936, and "Fate" also in the April 1936 issue. In *Notes on Australian Science Fiction*, Graeme Stone quotes *Wonder Stories'* editor, Charles Honig as particularly impressed by the first two stories.

According to his militarty service record, between 1941 and 1944 he worked as an aircraft assembler, before which his occupation was given as 'journalist.' In 1944 he applied to enlist as a trainee medical orderly and received six weeks training between September-October 1944. In 1946 he applied for and received a discharge as a result of his homosexuality, which he said made him a subject of ridicule at the RAAF hospital where he worked.

An earlier, unpublished novel was published in three thin digests by the Australian pulp publisher, Currawong, in 1945, *Prisoners in Serpent Land*, *Warriors of Serpent Land*, and *Lord of Serpent Land*. His later life, and the date of his death, are unknown.